Raja Rao's Shorter Fiction

Raja Rao's Shorter Fiction

The Enlightenment Theme

Roshan Lal Sharma

RAWAT PUBLICATIONS

Jaipur • New Delhi • Bangalore • Mumbai • Hyderabad • Guwahati

ISBN 81-316-0263-X

Published by
Prem Rawat for **Rawat Publications**
Satyam Apts., Sector 3, Jawahar Nagar, Jaipur 302 004 (India)
Phone: 0141 265 1748 / 7006 Fax: 0141 265 1748
E-mail: info@rawatbooks.com
Website: www.rawatbooks.com

New Delhi Office
4858/24, Ansari Road, Daryaganj, New Delhi 110 002
Phone: 011 2326 3290

Also at Bangalore, Mumbai, Hyderabad and Guwahati

Typeset by Rawat Computers, Jaipur
Printed at Chaman Enterprises, New Delhi

To

Amma

in whom love and compassion
ever remain luminescent

Contents

Contents

Preface

> When knowledge as Ganga, as jnana-ganga flows, death is dissolved into truth.
>
> Raja Rao in *On the Ganga Ghat*

A friend of mine told me that Raja Rao had died, as she knew I had worked on his stories for my PhD and had done enough of soul-making with him through his writings. That was a couple of days after July 8, 2006. I felt sad. Not because Rao had left his *sthoola sharira* (body), but the subtle chord that bound us right since 1989 received a shock. Of course it didn't snap; it never can. Frantically, I rushed to my study and picked the copy of *On the Ganga Ghat* from the shelf and started flipping through the heavily underlined text. The last four pages in particular looked rather appalling as I had besmeared the entire text so clumsily by overwriting that the original became more or less invisible. However, upon a closer look, the essence shone through. I could see Rao, the *Siddha* in regal splendour squatting on Ganga *ghat* in 'river of reflection mode' and according a warm reception to the profundity flowing into him gently, in a *sahaj* manner:

> Death has no meaning. Man's approbation is for the true. Sit with me and let us listen. The river has depth, and, see, the birds have flight. The boat has eyes, and the bridge its leap.

And a little later:

> Son, has death meaning? No, death is an empty event. It's like the yawl of a crow [...]. Can life die, that is the question? The Ganga answers: Man, you think you die. Burn yourself on my banks and know that what flows cannot but unflow. Death is a superstition, like the flies that sit on the baby's rags, and find nothing there. (*On the Ganga Ghat*: 125–27)

For Rao, *atma-bodh* (consciousness of the Self) was all. He knew his Self as he understood about the essence of the Ganga. That 'something,' which Whitman saw 'in the float of the sight of things,' which Lawrence experienced in the 'quick of quicks' and which Hesse must have perceived through Siddhartha's 'smile of unity over the flowing forms,' remained available to Rao through the 'depth' of the river, 'flight' of the birds, the 'movement' of the boat and the 'leap' of the bridge. Since he was one with the 'flow' of the perennial Ganga, he was established in Truth-consciousness, the Self beyond causation, and hence, beyond death. The 'grandest fib' for him was man's mortality.

Rao was an enlightened literary artist. He had realized the sacredness of the word. Because he could hear the *anahata* (the subtlest sound) and perceive the resonance inherent in the sound-vibrations (*shruti-andolan*), the word had sanctity for him. For him the words emerged from silence:

> I am a man of silence. And words emerge from silence with light, of light, and light is sacred. [...] The writer or the poet is he who seeks back the common word to the origin of silence, in order that the manifested word become light. (From Rao's, 1988, Neustadt Prize acceptance speech)

Thus, the most meaningful word/sound for Rao was the one that could illumine rather than merely tell. Like great sages and seers in Indian tradition, he knew that the word comes from 'silence' and leads you to its source that is 'light.' His access to the 'true sound'/'heart-sound' (*anahata*) that is perceptible only through the subtlest ear, stood him in good stead to imbibe the idiom of a *Shabda-Siddha* who could connect the reader with the nameless, invisible essence of being. He wove tales, sang fiction and composed prose like a recollected and dispassionate *drashta* (seer) *à la* the poised and watchful *Upnishadic* bird.

The present text is based on my PhD thesis on "Enlightenment Theme and Its Motifs in *On the Ganga Ghat* and Other Stories of Raja Rao" submitted to Himachal Pradesh University in 1992. This study is based on the three collections of short stories namely *The Cow of the Barricades and Other Stories* (1947), *The Policeman and the Rose* (1978) and *On the Ganga Ghat* (1989). There are 'stacks' of creative and 'insightful' short stories that are yet to be published as mentioned by Rao's student, David Iglehart in a note on the Raja Rao Publication project (visit <www.rajarao. com/project.html>). Nevertheless, whatever is available in the form of Rao's shorter fiction is ample. He had realized the essence of creativity and expressed it remarkably through three volumes of his stories.

The first chapter "Guru-Disciple Dynamics in Enlightenment Praxis" deals with guru-disciple relationship. In Indian spiritual tradition, this relationship is considered pivotal in enlightenment praxis. The motif of guru-disciple relationship is recurrent in Rao's stories. As such, an overview of guru-disciple dynamics is taken in terms of its evolution from Vedic times. Section II of the chapter deals in detail with connotations of the term 'guru' followed by an analysis of guru-disciple relationship in the light of depth psychology in general, and Jungian precepts in particular. Jungian archetype of the wise old man is discussed at length, as the guru figure in India is a cultural expression of the said archetype. Section III focuses on the importance of guru in the life of Raja Rao. It primarily highlights his guru, Sri Atmananda's role in transforming Raja Rao from a scholar to a creative writer. Section IV forms the core of the chapter, as it were. It undertakes the delineation and characterization of the dynamics of the pervasive guru-disciple relationship as it obtains in the world of Rao's stories. The abstract characteristics of the guru and his role in the transformation of his disciples as well as humanity at large are discussed in Section V. It is followed by a brief discussion of the *Sthithaprajna* sensibility, which is viewed as the highest state of evolution of a guru. The section is rounded off by a discussion of the reflection of this sensibility in Rao's stories. The last section institutes a comparison between the delineation of guru archetype by Rao and by some other Indo-Anglian novelists such as Mulk Raj Anand, R.K. Narayan and Kamala Markandaya.

The guru-disciple relationship is germane to any meaningful search for self-realization/enlightenment in the Indian tradition. The second chapter "The Endless Quest: Multiple Dimensions," therefore, states the meaning of the term 'quest.' It throws light on the Campbellian quest cycle and, in the process, clarifies the meaning of the term 'monomyth.' It is followed by a brief examination of different types of quest (e.g., Vedantic, Sufic and Tantric) as embodied in Rao's stories. An attempt has been made to achieve a synthesis of the different types of quest. In Section II, certain points of divergence and convergence between Jungian and Campbellian thought are analysed. This brief analysis is followed by a detailed description of Jung's individuation process in terms of such stages as catharsis, elucidation, education and transformation. The quest motif is examined in the light of modern western civilization, briefly touching upon the western man's 'quest for identity.' Section III seeks to examine different stages (separation, initiation and return) in the quest journey of the hero as enunciated by Joseph Campbell in *The Hero with a Thousand Faces*. For the most part, however, the analyses are psychological (especially Jungian). The difference between the wise old man and the quester is also clarified. Section IV presents Rao as a myth-maker. Moreover, in order to underline the universality of the quest motif, three quest-adventures have been briefly outlined. The last section illustrates the quest stages of the representative questers—Vision Rangappa, Moti Khan, Sudha, and Rachoddoss Sunderdoss—in Raja Rao's stories in the light of Campbell's schema of quest.

The third chapter "Quester-Characters in Rao's Stories," analyses different quester-characters in Rao's stories. After a brief recapitulation of Campbellian quest-cycle and its Jungian implications, Rao's literary mould of quest has been highlighted. A detailed account of the famous quester-characters in the world of Rao's stories via critically analyzing their progress in their spiritual growth or quest journey is undertaken. Section II sheds light on the similarities and dissimilarities of the above quester-characters specifically keeping in mind the nature of their accomplishments in the quest process. Raja Rao's stories abound with chil'd questers. Section III, therefore, presents a critical analysis of the child questers like Akkayya, Kittu, Pierrot and Narsa. Finally the chapter examines Rao as a *sadhaka*. It is suggested that the intensity of feeling and authenticity of tone, which Rao brings to bear on his questers, derive from the fact of his being a quester himself. His writing is the medium through which Rao seeks to discover himself.

It is evident from Rao's fictional world that he is steeped in Indian mythology, culture and thought. Frequent references to various Hindu spiritual archetypes such as Shiva, Durga, Cow, etc. occur in his stories. As such, Chapter 4 is entitled "Other Archetypes in the Quest Process," besides highlighting the abstract and mythological implications of the archetypes, also focuses on their role in the quest process. The practical utility of the archetypes is underlined primarily to demonstrate the way in which they facilitate the praxis part of enlightenment. Thus the archetype of Shiva is treated as an embodiment of the Self. He represents the archetype of the wise old man in Jungian psychology. He signifies transcendence and the totality of being. Similarly the study of all other archetypes is done keeping in mind their functional role in Rao's stories. Section II discusses the Naga archetype in the context of Rao's two famous snake stories "Companions" and "The True Story of Kanakapala." Section III seeks to evaluate the archetype of the Mother. In Indian mythology, the Mother archetype is represented by 'Devi' whose various manifestations are Durga, Parvati, Kali, etc. After having an overview of Devi or the Mother archetype along with its duality and non-duality signifying the totality of existence, Som P. Ranchan's version of Aurobindo's exposition regarding Mahakali, Mahalakshmi and Mahasaraswati are delineated in detail. The tendencies of Rao's female characters such as Javni, Akkayya, Nimka, Beti Bai, Padma and Nanna have been considered in the light of Ranchan's classification of the Mother archetype. A concomitant of Devi archetype, the archetype of Mother Ganga, is examined in Section IV. Its mythological and symbolic connotations are also touched upon. This is followed by a detailed description of the archetype of the cow. Firstly, the evolution of the cow archetype since its deification is related. In order to explain the significance of the cow archetype the Hindu mythological *Kamdhenu* motif is also discussed. The theme of enlightenment in two of Rao's stories—"The Cow of the Barricades" and the story of Bhedia in *On the Ganga Ghat*—has been examined in the light of the cow archetype. The last section consists of a brief analysis of the archetypes of Hanuman, Rama and Krishna. Finally, the chapter highlights the significance of the above archetypes in the quest process, which constitutes the praxis part of enlightenment.

I owe a profound sense of gratitude to Professor Som P. Ranchan who initiated me into the world of Raja Rao's shorter fiction. He also introduced me to disciplines like mythology and Jungian psychology. The clarifying insights arising out of his *chitti* (the individualized essence of consciousness) would propel me ever to think clearer and deeper. I was immensely benefited by Dr Ranchan's experience of having met Raja Rao personally during his Professorship in the United States.

My indebtedness to Professor V.P. Sharma, my academic guide, goes beyond words as his scholarly depth, sagacity and *Sahaj-sahridayata* can hardly ever fully acknowledged. I was privileged to be his first PhD scholar and get most of his attention as well as affection. He epitomizes simplicity and meticulousness. I am especially thankful to Professor Pabitra Kumar Roy, Fellow, Indian Institute of Advanced Study, Shimla who came into my life as an *Acharya* during my Associateship at the Institute. An eminent philosopher by profession, Professor Roy has a rare literary sensibility of which I have been a beneficiary through and through.

I wish to record a deep sense of gratefulness to my parents for their blessings along with other family members for their wishes. I am equally indebted to Mr. Sant Ram Sharma, my uncle, who made me pursue English literature as a discipline. Mr. Ashok Sharma, PRO, IIAS, Shimla, especially deserves to be thanked for encouraging me in my scholarly pursuits. Mr. Nand Lal Verma's personal concern, care and his meticulous typing are unforgettable. My friend, Mr. Hem Raj Sharma's endurance with my crazy ways of working, his ever readiness to help in typing parts of the manuscripts and the keen interest that he showed in the writing of this book fill my heart with thankfulness. Mr. Ramesh Sharma also deserves a special word of thanks. Acknowledgements are also due to the libraries of the Indian Institute of Advanced Study and Himachal Pradesh University located at Shimla along with Moti Lal Nehru Central State library and Government Postgraduate College library at Solan (H.P.).

Roshan

Introduction

I

The *genre* of short story is "too often relegated to an inferior position,"[1] and it is worth noting that it saw its "rise to the highest level of popularity and just as rapidly decline in its influence as a literary form"[2] during the twentieth century. Short story is a kind of prose fiction characterized by compression of content and intensity of effect. The condensing of the subject matter brings it close to a parable, or a fable, which is a "short narrative in prose or verse" pointing a moral.[3] However, the contemporary short story as it has evolved over a period, exhibits "subtlety of treatment seeking to distinguish between nuances of feeling and sentiment calculated to reveal the complexity of human emotion and motives and the problems that arise from it."[4] This, in fact, throws light on the complexity of the narrative in every *genre* of fiction (viz., novel, novella or short story) owing to great experimentation done with regard to its writing. The Indo-Anglian literature was inaugurated by poetry, the well-known names in this realm being Henry Derozio, Toru Dutt, Sri Aurobindo and Sarojini Naidu. The movement of poetry was followed by fiction both longer and shorter. Like poetry and novel, Indo-Anglian short story was considerably influenced by such Western masters as Chekhov, Tolstoy,

Maupassant, O'Henry and Kipling.[5] It originated during the last decade of the nineteenth century with the publication of Kamala Satthianadan's *Stories from Indian Christian Life* in 1898. After that, a sporadic growth was observed in the writing of short fiction and the prominent writers were K.S. Venkatramani, K. Nagarajan, Rabindranath Tagore (through translations from his Bengali stories), A. Madhaviah, and A.S.P. Ayer.

It was in the 1930s that the real potential of this art form was realized with the magnificent entry of the famous trio—Mulk Raj Anand, R.K. Narayan and Raja Rao—into the domain of Indian writing in English. Essentially known for their novels, they also contributed considerably in the field of short story. Mulk Raj Anand has himself acknowledged the influence of Maupassant and Frank O'Connor on his writing of short fiction. R.K. Narayan's proximity to Chekhov and the impact of French masters on Raja Rao can be seen in their short stories. Nevertheless, appreciating the "innate genius" of these writers, Shiv K. Kumar aptly observes:

> But one must hasten to add that although this distinguished triumvirate—Anand, Narayan and Rao—had used a foreign medium for creative expression, and often displayed Western technical virtuosity in their craft, their innate genius never felt smothered. If Tagore wrote as a folk story-teller, never refracting the psychology of his characters to suit a Western audience, Mulk Raj Anand remained firmly committed to social reality, investing his *coolies* and untouchables with a vibrant humanity that he found lacking in the upper classes. As for Raja Rao, he shaped the English language to suit the Indian sensibility, investing it with a fluidity and suppleness that was foreign to it.[6]

Other important names in this realm are Bhabani Bhattacharya, Anita Desai, Manohar Malgonkar and Khushwant Singh, Ruth Prawer Jhabvala, K.A. Abbas, Chaman Nahal, Kamala Markandaya, Ruskin Bond, etc. Among all the contemporary writers, however, Rao holds a unique place because of the choice of themes, treatment and his specific *Vedantin* stance.

India may proudly boast of having 'invented' the *genre* of short story. Its source can be traced back to the *Vedic* and *Upnishadic* ages. In ancient Sanskrit literature, there is a substantial output in the field of story telling. It not only influenced Indian literature in later times, but also the literature of the world at large. For the propagation of all the religions of ancient India (such as Vedic, Buddhist and Jainist), story/tale telling served as a pivot. For instance, in the Vedic age, the purpose of this art form was not only to explain the religious ideas, but also to impart practical lessons. However, the most ancient clues concerning the *genre* of short story may be found in *Rigveda Samhita*. Later these clues were expanded in the form of *katha* (story) in *the Brahmanas* and *Upnishadas*. Whereas in Jain literature, *Katha Kosha* is a famous collection of short stories, in Buddhist literature, we come across *Jatak Tales* numbering 550 and dealing with Gotama's attainment of Buddhahood (enlightenment) having undergone innumerable births in various forms.

Briihat Katha by Gunadhaya, however, is the oldest collection of folk-tales followed by *Panchtantra*. The latter is the greatest collection of short stories, more aptly fables didactic in nature, by Vishnu Sharma. It served as a source for several collections of short stories that were composed afterwards. For instance, *Hitopadesh* by Narayan Pandit is a collection of forty-three short stories that include twenty-five from *Panchtantra* and eighteen new ones. Similarly, *Brihat Katha* has also been further summarized into three different versions—*Brihat Katha Shloka Sangraha* by Buddhaswami, *Brihat Katha Manjari* by Kshemendra, and *Kathasaritasagar* by Somdev. Not only this, Jambhal Datta's *Vetaalpanchavimshati* is an excellent collection of twenty-five interesting folk tales based on *Brihat Katha*. In addition to it, *Singhasan Dwitrinshika* contains thirty-two stories related to the legendary throne of Vikramaditya.

In view of the above-mentioned details, one may unequivocally postulate that the art of story telling has been an inalienable part of the Indian psyche. In fact, it has its roots in oral literature.[7] The moment Indians think of/talk about a tale, a story, or a fable (all encapsulated into *katha*), they are transported into their childhood in which grandmother, or the grandfather, usually embodies the archetype of the storyteller (*katha-vachaka*). Quite often, these stories are derived from the *Ramayana*, the *Mahabharata* or the *Puranas*. Thus, as the Indian child grows up, he naturally imbibes the art of story telling.

In Hindi literature too, this art form has been extremely successful in the sense that within a very short span of time, a considerable number of short stories were published, its chief exponents being Munshi Prem Chand, Jaya Shankar Prasad, Acharya Chatursen, Janendra Kumar, Yash Pal, Nirmal Verma, Rajendra Yadav, Mannu Bhandari, Kamleshwar, Gyan Ranjan, and others. In regional languages as well, many writers have touched heights in this field. For instance, Rabindranath Tagore wrote in both Bangla and English. Sarat Chandra Chatterjee, a famous Bengali novelist and short story writer, has also been translated into all the major Indian languages.

Short story writing in the West, especially in England, began somewhat late, roughly with Geoffrey Chaucer in the fourteenth century. His *Canterbury Tales*, is in a sense, a collection of stories in verse told by the pilgrims on their way to Canterbury. However, with Stevenson, this art form became more popular and subsequently attained perfection in the hands of writers such as Rudyard Kipling, H.G. Wells, Oscar Wilde and Sir Arthur Conon Doyle. Furthermore, in the twentieth century, writers like John Galsworthy, D.H. Lawrence and James Joyce did new experiments in this *genre*. In other countries too, this art form developed gradually but gained momentum during the nineteenth century with writers such as Edgar Allan Poe and Hawthorne in United States, Maupassant and Balzac in France, and Pushkin, Gorky, Dostoevsky and Tolstoy in Russia.

II

If we evaluate the present scenario of Indian writing in English, we find a rapid development in the art of story writing. Among the major exponents who have contributed to the development of this genre, Rao holds a unique position. Compared to other writers, Raja Rao may not have a large output to his credit in this field, yet soaked as he is in Indian culture, thought, and mythology, he has a unique Indian stance in the delineation of the themes and his characters. A.N. Dwivedi clearly suggests this point of Rao being a writer with a difference as he writes:

> Raja Rao is definitely of a different make up both in his novels and short stories. He is soberer and more serious in evoking a proper atmosphere for the flowering of Indian thought and tradition. He writes mostly on social and political scenes around him with a natural ease and philosophical resignation [...]. Raja Rao goes to the folk-tales and the epic legends to evolve a form of his own with 'all the simplicity and credulity' of a mythmaker.[8]

Indeed, Rao is an innovator who uses myths, legends and folk-tales in his stories to achieve *Pauranic* effects. He has infused a new life into the *genre* by creating his own modern 'monomyths.' M.K. Naik rightly observes:

> Raja Rao seems soon to have realized that to resurrect an old art-form only to make it do the old things in the traditional manner is a far less significant endeavour than to adapt it to the needs of the living present, thus tapping the innate vitality that is always latent in such forms. It is in this sense that *The Cow of the Barricades and Other Stories* is an important landmark in Raja Rao's artistic career.[9]

In Rao's narrative art the fact of his being a *Vedantin* needs to be highlighted. His stance being that of an *advaita vedantin,* distinction between the creator and the creation does not exist for him. So he moves with ease and fluency from the mundane to the metaphysical. In other words, writing for Raja Rao is an exercise in Truth, or a kind of *sadhana,* as he explained to Shiv Niranjan in an interview.[10] It is an attempt to come in contact, howsoever ephemeral, with the ultimate reality. Rao himself clarifies the implication of his remark when he states: "*Sadhana* means to try to be in contact with the ultimate reality. It has been my endeavour all my life to be face to face with the ultimate."[11] Rao's writings reveal his assimilation of the thought and content of the *Upnishads,* the *Ramayana,* and Indian philosophy (especially Vedanta) along with the various philosophical systems of the West. Furthermore, the *Vedantic* concept of *Advaitam,* of the presence of One in all, and the world being the manifestation of the Absolute *Brahman*, often finds an eloquent, epiphanic expression in his writings. Like his short stories, in novels too, he journeys through light and shade, encountering the holy and the unholy, the sacred and the profane, the virtuous and the wicked, to realize the quintessence of enlightenment.

Essentially a novelist of world repute, Raja Rao began his literary career with short stories. His first collection *The Cow of the Barricades and Other Stories* (1947) included most of the stories that were written in 1930s, that is, prior to the publication of his first novel *Kanthapura* in 1938. For instance, Rao's first masterly sketch of an untouchable widow, Javni, appeared in 1933 in the story of the same title. "Akkayya," another heart-rending story, was written in French the same year. In addition to these, "A Client" (originally written in Kannada) and "In Khandesh" were published in 1934; "The True Story of Kanakapala" and the title story, "The Cow of the Barricades," appeared in 1938.[12]

The Policeman and the Rose (1978) included several stories from the earlier collection. It is, in fact, a collection of ten stories with the addition of three new stories ("The Policeman and the Rose," "India: A Fable," and "Nimka") in place of "Narsiga" and "A Client." The gap of more than three decades between the publication of Rao's first and second collection of stories is not surprising because, for Rao, the gestation period is usually long. Moreover, as he explained to Shiv Niranjan, he went through a phase of extreme despair after the publication of *Kanthapura* in 1938. This was so because the basic question that assailed him around this time was whether to continue as a writer, or become a *sanyasi*. Just when he had decided to bid farewell to the Muse of fiction he met his guru, Sri Atmananda,[13] who bade him otherwise. The outcome was his magnum opus *The Serpent and the Rope* in 1960.

Rao's latest collection of short stories *On the Ganga Ghat* appeared in 1989. This collection, as desired by Rao, is "meant to be read as a novel."[14] This draws attention to the fact that all the stories have the same backdrop and that is Benares. The stories seem to have a sense of unity derived from their background as Makarand Paranjape comments, "Once again, we see how he pushes the form of the novel in a new direction. Indeed the question arises, how do these seemingly different stories make one novel?"[15] He further observes that each story is complete by itself without any common protagonist in either of them: "To me the real protagonist of these stories appears to be their setting, Benares."[16] The stories are not titled; nor do they follow a conventionally formal mode. They flow like the Ganga which serves as setting along with Benares. The stories or "vignettes"[17] are episodic and *Pauranic* in tone, method, and narration. Thus, viewed as a whole, Rao's world of short stories has a completeness as it presents a holistic view of life in the sense of the infinite in the infinitesimal, though not in the traditional Indian epical sense of the *Ramayana* or the *Mahabharata*.

III

Rao's greatness as a novelist has been widely acknowledged. However, as a short story writer, "different" and "prominent" though he is, the critical attention due to him is not yet there. This perhaps is so because in comparison to his three substantial novels namely *Kanthapura* (1938), *The Serpent and the Rope* (1960) and *The Chessmaster and His Moves* (1988), and two novellas, *The Cat and Shakespeare: A Tale of Modern India* (1965) and *Comrade Kirillov* (1976), his output in the *genre* of short story is rather slim. A number of commentators on Raja Rao have either merely pointed out or briefly discussed various themes that underlie his short stories. The first piece of criticism on Rao's stories by K.R. Srinivasa Iyenger[18] examines the domestic theme highlighting "the strangeness, the sadness, the horror and the glory of the Indian home." Moreover, Iyenger has also touched upon, though in passing "the silent heroism and selfless sacrifice of Indian womanhood"[19] represented by Javni and Akkayya. He has also taken into account the theme of Gandhian influence on Indian masses in "Narsiga" and "The Cow of the Barricades." P.P. Mehta made a similar assessment in his book *Indo-Anglian Fiction: An Assessment*, in a separate section devoted to Raja Rao. Regarding his choice of characters, Mehta writes: "Raja Rao typically selects the lower and middle class characters from village or small town life and tries to show the nobility that exists even in the midst of squalor, dirt, poverty, superstition and misfortune."[20] Other critics who have commented on Rao's stories are C.D. Narasimhaiah, M.K. Naik, P.C. Bhattacharya, K.R. Rao, Narsingh Srivastava, Shyamala A. Narayan and others.

Another important aspect that has received critical attention is the exploration of "human consciousness" in Rao's stories. These forays into the human psyche at certain intense moments in the life of Rao's protagonists reveal the truth about them. In this context, as K.R. Rao points out, Raja Rao has a tremendous capacity to suffuse a common or ordinary situation in the life of his characters with an authentic, metaphysical import:

> Raja Rao's short stories seek to trace human experience, whether individual or collective, to truth, which is the source of reality. The characters experience the epiphanies of truth in those moments of consciousness when the real world stands bare and void revealing the generic loneliness of man and the creative matrix of being. After the mystic shock of recognition, they are once again reverted to the complex order of apparent reality, but now with a sense of renewed personal equilibrium. The short stories of Raja Rao thus project, in their lyric focus, the writer's quest for identity and order in a world of change and transformation.[21]

C.D. Narasimhaiah, however, has drawn attention to Raja Rao's "mythic imagination" with which he vitalizes his expression:

> While Raja Rao recaptures the magnificent mythical imagination of Indian antiquity successively in the three novels and short stories he has written to date he has at the same time, to use T.S. Eliot's words, 'altered' the 'expression' to accommodate a distinct, profoundly Indian sensibility.[22]

Narsingh Srivastava, another critic of Raja Rao, throws light on the theme of India with which Rao remained occupied in *The Cow of the Barricades and Other Stories* and *The Policeman and the Rose*. He also points to the 'fantastic,' metaphysical and spiritual strains found in the mythological framework of his stories. He observes:

> Some of the short stories of Raja Rao, having a contemporary social and political relevance, are quite representative of Indian life at the material plane even as the others, unfolding a metaphysical truth or embodying a symbolic reality, contribute to the image of India at the metaphysical and the spiritual planes and evokes India's cultural past with its continuing impact upon the present customs, conventions and attitudes. Besides the mythological framework in some and the folk-lore technique in others also contribute to the obvious Indianness of the stories.[23]

Vis-à-vis Rao's identity as a myth-maker and its expression thereof, Narsingh Srivastava further observes:

> He invents a popular form of narration, essentially Indian in tempo, tone and texture, even as he creates new similes and native turns of expression in order to add an Indian colour to his technique. Besides, he creates new myths out of the old ones and lends a legendary structure to his themes for the same purpose.[24]

In the same vein, Meenakshi Mukherjee also points out that Rao's method in his stories "is that of mythologizing contemporary reality. His gifts as a myth-maker can be seen even in his early short stories [...]."[25] Another major strain that finds expression in Rao's stories (including *On the Ganga Ghat*) is his *Vedantic* vision, which makes him see God in the creation with a *samdrashta* sensibility and enables him to plumb the depths of the "Indian collective unconscious." K.S. Ramamurti writes:

> One of the dominant traits of the average Indian character is a belief in destiny, a Vedantic detachment resulting in passive acceptance and patient endurance. This is invariably reflected in Raja Rao's writings and what is more, in Raja Rao's Advaitic vision the entire universe is but the manifestation of the supreme spirit, the Brahman.[26]

Almost all the critics have seen the very first collection of Rao's stories as an important stage in the evolution of a major Indo-Anglian novelist. Thus, C.D. Narasimhaiah observes that in writing *The Cow of the Barricades and Other Stories*, Raja Rao was trying to attain perfection in the art of fiction:

> It shouldn't sound unfair to remark—and Raja Rao can now afford the luxury of adverse, even hostile, criticism—that they [stories] are best seen as products of an inevitable stage in the growth of a mind, in the evolution of a major novelist who was cultivating his craft with the utmost care, a craft which in his very first novel shows all the rigour the mind has gone through.[27]

M.K. Naik contends the same point, though from a slightly different angle. He points out that "'the narrow plot of ground' of the short story imposed irksome restrictions upon him that is probably the reason why he has preferred the limitless freedom of the novel in his maturer work."[28] It becomes obvious that Rao's stories have been denied their real importance and consigned to a sub-altern position. S.P. Chaturvedi rightly comments that Raja Rao's short stories "are yet to receive a comprehensive and dispassionate critical examination."[29]

Like M.K. Naik, K.R. Rao also stands in the same line as he observes that the stories published in *The Cow of the Barricades* "[...] assume considerable relevance in the sense that many themes sketched out in them are later elaborated in the novels."[30] Similarly, P.C. Bhattacharya believes that "[...] the stories are interesting in themselves, and also indicative of the formative years of a major Indo-Anglian writer."[31] There is no denying the fact that these stories did provide inspiration for his novels like *Kanthapura*. However, it is worth mentioning that for Rao short story was indubitably a complete *genre* in the *Pauranic* sense. As such, to place, or to analyse his stories in linear developmental mode, as be the wont with critics, is to limit their scope and to undermine his achievements as a short story writer. Rao's accomplishments as a story-writer have to be evaluated independently, without confusing them with his status as a novelist though one can always establish linkages of these stories with his later novels. In fact, Rao's stories present a complete and conspicuous world of their own. Thus, the contention of Narasimhaiah, Naik, and other critics that Rao's stories are merely a preparation for his novels, in no way seems tenable. As Shyamala A. Narayan affirms: "The range of Raja Rao's stories is amazing. Every facet of India is present in them [...]. Even if he had not written any novel, his stories by themselves would have assured him a permanent place in Indo-English fiction."[32] I.D. Sharma also refuses to view the semantic universe of Raja Rao's stories in a developmental mode and suggests that Rao's stories should not be reduced to a stage in the "diachrony" of his evolution as a novelist.[33] M.K. Naik attaches great importance to three new stories introduced in *The Policeman and the Rose* (1978). For instance, regarding "India: A Fable" and "The Policeman and the Rose" he states that with these stories "Raja Rao has successfully made shorter fiction the vehicle of metaphysical statement." He further states:

> 'India: A Fable' and 'The Policeman and the Rose' have thus added a new dimension to the Indo-English short story. *The Serpent and the Rope* and *The Cat and Shakespeare* are to the Indo-English novel what these stories essentially are to Indian shorter fiction in English, though they make us wish their author had handled this form oftener in this vein.[34]

The critical opinions regarding "Nimka" vary. Whereas C.D. Narasimhaiah calls this story "the greatest of its kind by an Indian writer, at least in English [...]."[35] M.K. Naik treats it as a story which is hardly interesting.

> [...] 'Nimka' is easily the least interesting from this point of view, offering as it does, merely a rather superficial character-sketch [...]. 'Nimka' naturally invites comparison with stories like 'Akkayya' and 'Javni,' and it is clear that the rich inwardness which Raja Rao's studies of the two Indian widows palpably reveal cannot be said to be present to the same degree in this sketch of their Russian counterpart.[36]

Nevertheless, comparisons apart, "Nimka" is a great story in which Rao has remarkably focused on Nimka's sad and tragic plight against the backdrop of her mute heroism marked by endurance and fortitude.

There is not much critical material available except a few articles, write-ups and reviews on Rao's latest collection of short stories *On the Ganga Ghat* (1989). Most reviewers, however, have reflected on certain elements such as the dense texture, whimsical manner, and the light-hearted narrative tone of Rao's stories in *On the Ganga Ghat*. Vijay Shankar observes: "All through the book there is a virtual cavalcade of well-focussed characters whom you almost touch as you walk the lanes, the funeral ghats and the temples of Benares."[37] In another review, "Vignettes of Varanasi," K.S. Duggal calls *On the Ganga Ghat* is "a sheaf of perceptive sketches of the social scene and the spiritual milieu in the city of Varanasi, done with consummate skill by a master artist."[38] In addition to the realistic strain, Rao's "[...] serious preoccupation with the world of superpersonal agencies, either gods and spirits or animals and birds which speak and interact with human beings [...]"[39] is evident not only in Rao's earlier collections but also in *On the Ganga Ghat*. Rao's stories in *On the Ganga Ghat* are different from the earlier ones in which the social, domestic, metaphysical and mystical strains are predominant. In this collection, Rao has blended the fabular, occult and supernatural elements, thereby achieving a synthesis of all the above strains.

Raja Rao unfolds various facets of Benares in *On the Ganga Ghat* in the form of "musings," as observed by Rajesh Mehta:

> Raja Rao's third short story collection *On the Ganga Ghat* (1989) includes eleven stories. It marks his return to the form of short story after a long gap. Of eleven short stories, the first is purely about the author's arrival at Benares, and the last is entirely reflective of his personal offerings, it does a series of musings on Benares, the Ganga and the life in general. The remaining nine stories are separate narratives of different characters, who participate in the action at Benares.[40]

Ragini Ramachandra is not surprised about Rao's choice of locale in *On the Ganga Ghat* apropos of Rao's constant spiritual "engagement." Moreover, she appreciates his "consummate" skill as an artist:

> To those conversant with Raja Rao's works, notably *The Serpent and the Rope* and his profound engagement with the spiritual past of India, it does not of course come as a surprise that he should make Benares the backdrop of his latest work, *On the Ganga Ghat*. Nor is it surprising that he, the consummate artist

> that he is, should succeed in depicting life's "multiple riches" in less than a hundred odd pages. But the book demonstrates how a truly distinguished writer can spring delightful surprises on the reader in the very *handling* of his material.[41]

For Esha Dey, Rao's latest work "marks a brilliant achievement as a classic of fabulation."[42] She perceives it as "the new narratology of non-happenings," which signifies the "final stage" in Rao's evolution as a literary artist:

> In this final stage of evolution, the new form emerges as a fusion of the short story and the novel as he himself tells the readers [...]. A meeting of the artist and the pilgrim brings to life India as a timeless existence ruled by orthodoxy, peopled by men and women content to live in an age-old hierarchy of structure. For the lifelong exile in the modern west, India is all that the contemporary age is not—a mythical entity in wish-space and wish-time built with deliberate simplicity and apparent innocence that mark the height of Rao's success as India's greatest anti-modern modern writer in English.[43]

As a whole, Rao's stories in all the three volumes published till date emerge as "the representative of the Indian life and attitudes, both at the social and metaphysical planes [...]."[44] Makarand Paranjape insightfully writes about the metaphysical implications of Rao's portrayal of Benares in *On the Ganga Ghat*:

> It is Benares, as a sort of miniaturized India, that stands for the Truth of this world. It can unveil the mystery of human life and misery by showing the way to transcendence through the dissolution of the ego.
>
> Each of these stories in this delightful book touches on this theme. Together they portray an entire society with all its strata and castes and how each of these, in its own unique way, seeks the same thing—liberation, salvation, transcendence.[45]

Moreover, Rao's language, expression and style are all soaked in Indian thought, and cultural heritage. As Rao himself has stated, that he uses "Sanscritic" or Indian English[46] in order to impart a typical Indian flavour to his stories. Rao's contribution to the Indian English short story, indeed, is great. He has enlarged the scope of the short story both with respect to content and form. The variety of themes and the "levels of consciousness" that Rao has explored in his stories are exceptional and justify Rao's evaluation by critics as an "innovator" in Indo-Anglian shorter fiction. The publication of *On the Ganga Ghat* in 1989 has demonstrated with finality that the short story, far from being a stage in the process of Raja Rao's evolution as a novelist, is a unique, independent and complete entity in the existing body of Indo-Anglian literature.

IV

In all the three volumes of short stories, Raja Rao has dealt with a wide range of themes—domestic, social, political, psychological, metaphysical and spiritual. However, the theme of enlightenment arches over all these and involves, on Rao's part, an intensity of feeling and depth of thought, which are redolent of the epiphanic and the numinous.

The term 'enlightenment'[47] has deep philosophical and spiritual connotations. It denotes wisdom as well as comprehension of all knowledge. Enlightenment, in one sense, is associated with a person who realizes the Absolute Truth by following a strict and rigorous code of moral discipline. In brief, great sages, saints, *siddhas,* spiritual teachers, *gurus* and poets are revered as enlightened ones. It is, however, pertinent to note that Raja Rao has enlarged the spectrum of the term by presenting a 'demythified' view of enlightenment in the sense that he presents ordinary human beings as character-questers who consciously/unconsciously, volitionally/reluctantly, conventionally/non-conventionally pursue (and at times are even forced to pursue) the path to realize the essence of being. In addition to bringing the abstruse concept of enlightenment to the level of an average commoner, Rao's conventional schema of quest offers a enormous scope to be viewed and examined in the light of Jungian concept of individuation and Campbellian "monomyth" of the hero as delineated in *The Hero with a Thousand Faces.*

Most of the characters in Rao's stories seem to belong to the theistic schools of Indian religious thought for they have faith in God, the *Vedas* and rebirth. In other words, the psyche of Rao's characters is steeped in Hindu mystique and lore. Two of the most significant aspects of Indian thought have been summed up by M. Hiriyanna thus:

> These are two elements common to all Indian thought—the pursuit of Moksha as their final ideal and the ascetic spirit of discipline recommended for its attainment. They signify that philosophy as understood in India is neither mere intellectualism nor mere moralism, but includes and transcends them both [...]. They have represented as the two wings that help the soul in its spiritual flight. The goal that is reached through their aid is characterized on the one hand by *jnana* or illumination which is intellectual conviction that has ripened into an immediate experience and, on the other, by *vairagya* or self-renunciation which is secured by reason of the discovery of the metaphysical ground for it.[48]

Most of Raja Rao's characters have a religious disposition as exemplified in their repeated intoning of mantras, frequent prayers and recurring references to the holy scriptures like the *Vedas*, the *Puranas*, and the *Ramayana*. The quintessential aspects of Indian thought have contoured their consciousness. Many characters are in pursuit of *moksha* and follow a tough code of moral discipline for its attainment.

Raja Rao's preoccupation with the theme of enlightenment is reflected in his choice of epigraphs not only for his collections of stories but also, in certain cases, for individual stories. The epigraphs are not in any sense decorative or pedantic. On the contrary, they are summations, germane to stories capturing their gist. For instance, *The Cow of the Barricades* has for its epigraph four lines from Kabir. The epigraph throws light on the ubiquity of suffering.

> 'On all roads I go, they suffer,
>
> The hermit and the householder,
>
> When I tell them the truth, they are angry,
>
> And I cannot lie.'[49]

Similarly, at the start of "Javni," Raja Rao introduces a highly suggestive couplet by a famous Kannada poet, Kanakadas, who exercised a deep influence on him (Rao).[50] The couplet suggests the futility of casteism and poses a highly relevant question.

> Caste and Caste and Caste you say,
>
> What Caste has he who knoweth God? (*CBS*: 1)

Likewise, "Companions," another story by Rao, is preceded by Hafiz's dictum that reads thus:

> Alas till now I did not know
>
> My guide and Fate's guide are one. (*CBS*: 164)

This profound pronouncement by Hafiz is indicative of his realization of the basic oneness of his inner guide (*antaratma*) and the Absolute Brahman (*Paramatma*).

Raja Rao's guru, Sri Atmananda's words in the epigraph to *The Policeman and the Rose* are worth studying from the standpoint of the enlightenment theme as they are an apt description of the *Vedantic* process of enlightenment:

> If one looks through the gross organ eye, gross forms alone appear. The same relation exists between other gross organs and their objects.
>
> Leaving the physical organs if one looks through the subtle organ called mind, subtle forms appear. Looking through the attributeless pure Consciousness, one sees Consciousness only and nothing else. (*P&R*: ix)

Furthermore, in the epigraph to *On the Ganga Ghat*, Rao quotes yet another maxim of his guru—"Water does not flow"[51] —which is highly symbolic. In the concluding part of the book, Rao discloses the secret of 'unflowing' water which connotes *jnana ganga* or the stream of 'inner knowledge' and as Rao perceives it is 'unflowing.' Hence his final request to the 'unflowing' water (i.e., *jnana ganga*) is to "flow" (*OGG*: 127) .

V

Although a number of books on Raja Rao's novels have been written, no study has so far been done on all his short stories that are twenty three in number, barring *The Semantic Universe of Raja Rao* by I.D. Sharma who confined himself only to the twelve stories in the first two collections and did not include *On the Ganga Ghat* within the ambit of his critical analysis. As noted, the remarkable thematic variety, poetic richness and inherent appeal of these stories are in no way secondary in importance to Rao's novels. Narasimhaiah also realizes this fact and suggests: "Even so his [Rao's] short stories have yet to receive critical attention [...]."[52] Casting Narasimahiah in a fallacious "developmental" mode and accusing him of having "[...] queered the pitch and veered the attention away from the short stories,"[53] would, perhaps, be stretching the point too far. Undoubtedly, the world of Rao's short fiction is complete and offers a large enough scope to be examined separately; but would it really be justified to forcibly wean his longer fiction away from shorter? The fact of the matter, however, is that both the *genres* grew simultaneously within Rao's creative being, and therefore, viewing them separately may prove rather fallacious, thereby hampering clear, holistic understanding of either of the two. The present writer proposes to analyse each of Rao's collections of stories in terms of Campbellian quest cycle of " separation-initiation-return," which has been dealt with in details in Chapters 2 and 3.

Critics like M.K. Naik, C.D. Narasimhaiah, K.R. Rao, P.C. Bhattacharya, and Narsingh Srivastava have examined Rao's stories in their books on Rao as a fiction writer, and have unfolded various aspects of his short stories. The study of thematics, semiotics and of different sociological, political and philosophical aspects including religious, spiritual, *Vedantic* and mythological strains has been variously done by these exegetes. However, the theme of enlightenment, which forms the core of the *Weltanschauung* of Rao's shorter fiction, has strangely escaped critical attention. Hence, the thrust of this present study is to unfold Rao's scroll of enlightenment and the motifs germane to its praxis.

Notes

1. H.M. Williams, "The Short Story: Some Observations," in A.N. Dwivedi, ed., *Studies in Contemporary Indian English Short Story*, Delhi: B.R. Publishing Corporation, 1992, p. 3. Williams observes that compared to the "restricted" range and "sketchy" character of short story, the novel has always arched over the former due to its "enormous" and "ample" scope to develop the narrative and present a fuller picture of life.
2. R.S. Gwynn, ed., *Fiction: A Pocket Anthology*, New York: Penguin Academics, 2002, p. 5.
3. J.A. Cuddon, *The Penguin Dictionary of Literary Terms and Literary Theory*, London: Penguin Books, 1991, p. 322.
4. Krishna Chattopadhyay, *Modern English Short Story: A Critical Appreciation*, Calcutta: Minerva, 1991, p. vii.
5. As Shiv K. Kumar observes, that short story in India "whether written in English or any Indian language [such as Hindi, Urdu, Bengali and Tamil], grew under Western tutelage." See Shiv K. Kumar, *Contemporary Indian Short Stories in English*, New Delhi: Sahitya Akademi, 1991, p. 2.
6. Ibid., p. 2.
7. The moment one refers to oral narratives, their "primal mythic source" comes to mind. Regarding the "mythic origins" of the short story, Charles E. May observes that "the wellsprings of the form are as old as the primitive realm of myth." Studies in anthropology suggest that brief episodic narratives, which constitute the basis of the short story, are primary, preceding later epic forms, which constitute the basis of the novel." See Charles E. May, *The Short Story: The Reality of Artifice*, New York: Routledge, 2002, p. 1.
8. A.N. Dwivedi, *Indian Writing in English*, Delhi: Amar Prakashan, 1991, p. 131.
9. M.K. Naik, *Raja Rao*, 1972; Bombay: Blackie & Son, 1982, p. 45.
10. "An Interview with Raja Rao," in Krishna Nandan Sinha, ed., *Indian Writing in English*, New Delhi: Heritage, 1979, pp. 19–28. Raja Rao says: "I just enjoy writing. I have written several sentences several times that for me, writing is a *sadhana*. It is a mode of prayer. Writing is a prayer for me. I get pleasure. I want others to get what I have. I write just because I wish to write. It is a *sadhana* for me."
11. Ibid., p. 20.
12. Shyamala A. Narayan, *Raja Rao: Man and His Works*, New Delhi: Sterling, 1988, p. 5.
13. Sinha, ed., p. 22.

14. Raja Rao, *On the Ganga Ghat*, New Delhi: Vision, 1989, p. 5. All subsequent references to this edition are cited as *OGG*.
15. See "Introduction," in Makarand Paranjape, ed., *The Best of Raja Rao*, 1998; rpt. New Delhi: Katha, 2000, p. xxii.
16. Ibid., p. xxii.
17. K.S. Duggal, "Vignettes of Varanasi," a book review in *Indian Express*, December 17, 1989, p. 4.
18. K.R. Srinivasa Iyenger, *Indian Writing in English*, Bombay: Asia, 1973, pp. 386–89.
19. Ibid., p. 387.
20. P.P. Mehta, *Indo-Anglian Fiction: An Assessment*, Bareilly: Prakash, 1979, p. 200.
21. K.R. Rao, *The Fiction of Raja Rao*, Aurangabad: Parimal, 1980, pp. 46–47.
22. C.D. Narasimhaiah, *Raja Rao*, New Delhi: Arnold-Heinemann, n.d., p. xii.
23. Narsingh Srivastava, *The Mind and Art of Raja Rao*, Bareilly: Prakash, 1980, p. 120.
24. Ibid., p. 121.
25. Meenakshi Mukherjee, *Twice Born Fiction*, New Delhi: Arnold-Heinemann, 1971, p. 139.
26. K.S. Ramamurti, "Gods and Men in the Commonwealth Short Story," in R.K. Dhawan, ed., *Commonwealth Fiction*, New Delhi: Classical, 1988, p. 129.
27. Narasimhaiah, p. 3.
28. M.K. Naik, *Raja Rao*, New York: Twayne, 1972, p. 59.
29. S.P. Chaturvedi, "Raja Rao as a Short Story Writer," in K.K. Sharma, *Perspectives on Raja Rao*, Ghaziabad: Vimal Prakashan, 1980, p. 109.
30. K.R. Rao, p. 32.
31. P.C. Bhattacharya, *Indo-Anglian Literature and the Works of Raja Rao*, Delhi: Atma Ram & Sons, 1983, p. 237.
32. Narayan, pp. 22–23.
33. I.D. Sharma, *The Semantic Universe of Raja Rao: Mind and Art of Raja Rao as a Story Teller*, Delhi: Indian Publishers and Distributers, 2006, p. xv. Sharma has critiqued only twelve stories of Raja Rao (published in the first two collections in 1947 and 1978 respectively) in terms of thematics, stylistics and hieroglyphics. He has not included *On the Ganga Ghat*, which was published in 1989, in his analysis. Since Rao's latest collection explicitly marks the culmination of his journey as a weaver of tales, or, more precisely, a maker

modern 'monomyths,' this book seeks to offer a complete and holistic analysis of all his short stories numbering twenty three.

34. M.K. Naik, *Raja Rao*, 1972; Bombay: Blackie & Son, 1982, p. 56.
35. Narsimhaiah, p. 12.
36. Naik, p. 46.
37. Vijay Shankar, "On the Ganga Ghat," a book review in *Sunday Herald*, October 29, 1989, p. 5.
38. Duggal, "Vignittes of Varanasi," p. 4.
39. Dhawan, ed., p. 124.
40. Rajesh Mehta, "Raja Rao's *On the Ganga Ghat*: Benares Redefined" in Kamal Mehta, ed., *The Twentieth Century Indian Short Story in English*, New Delhi: Creative Books, 2004, p. 98.
41. Ragini Ramachandra, "*On the Ganga Ghat*: An Assessment" in Ragini Ramachandra, ed., *Raja Rao: An Anthology of Recent Criticism*, Delhi: Pencraft International, 2000, p. 186.
42. Esha Dey, *The Novels of Raja Rao: The Theme of Quest*, New Delhi: Prestige, 1992, p. 248. See Postscript II entitled "*On the Ganga Ghat* and Other Stories" in particular, pp. 246–55.
43. Ibid., p. 249.
44. Srivastava, p. 120.
45. Paranjape, pp. xxii–xxiii.
46. Raja Rao, "Preface" to *The Policeman and the Rose*, Delhi: Oxford UP, 1978, p. xv. All subsequent references are to this edition referred to as P & R and indicated with page numbers in parentheses. Regarding the choice of appropriate idiom, Rao states: "If I wanted to write, the problem was, what should be the appropriate language of expression, and what my structural models—Sanskrit contained the vastest riches of any, both in terms of style and word-wealth, and the most natural to my needs [...]. Thus to stretch the English idiom to my needs seemed heroic enough for my urgentmost demands. The Irish, remember, had done it, not only with Yeats, but again with Frank O'Connor and Sean O'Faolain [...]. So why not Sanskritic (or if you will, Indian) English?"
47. Usually the term 'enlightenment' is equated with "realisation," "self-realisation," "awakening," etc. According to Nitin Trasi, enlightenment signifies a "[...] clear and intuitive perception ('apperception') or intuitive understanding (not just belief or intellectual comprehension) of the entire situation, that is, of the Unity of Consciousness and of the absence of the 'me' or 'I' as a separate autonomous entity." See Chapter 4 "Enlightenment" in Nitin Trasi, *The Science of Enlightenment: A Scientific Explanation*, New Delhi: D.K.

Printworld, 1999, pp. 53–70. In this sense, enlightenment signifies illumination or the dawning of wisdom regarding the fundamental riddle of existence. In fact, enlightenment in the context of the present book is not even remotely concerned with the Age of Enlightenment in Europe. Its oriental implication, not in the specialised, Buddhist sense, but in the sense of *moksha* (a Sanskrit term signifying liberation from the cycle of birth-death-rebirth) as enunciated in Hinduism, is what forms the very core of the present analysis. Trasi considers *mukti* (salvation) and Buddhist concept of *nirvana* (enlightenment) synonymous with *moksha*. Nevertheless, he makes it emphatically clear that these terms are in no way suggestive of some "entity" that attains enlightenment/liberation: "They refer rather to a body-mind complex in which the phenomenon of Enlightenment or Liberation has occurred, and in which therefore the illusion of its being a separate entity has disappeared." See Chapter 5 "Liberation" in Trasi, pp. 53–70. *Moksha* in Hinduism is attained after the individual soul (*atman*) perceives its relationship with the Oversoul (*Parambrahaman*). However, in Advaita Vedanta, it is believed that the Oversoul/Super-soul remains beyond all tangible perception. As such, *moksha* is viewed as ultimate release from one's worldly understanding of self, thereby shedding the illusion of duality of the visible and the invisible, phenomenal and the transcendental and connect with one's quintessential self. Dvaitins (dualists), on the contrary, view the soul and the Oversoul in terms of duality. Here, it is worth mentioning that Rao was himself an Advaita Vedantin and therefore, his perception of the concept of *moksha/enlightenment* presupposed the dissolution of duality of any kind. He equated the illusion of duality with the traditional Advaitic *rajju-sarpa* (rope-snake) delusion.

48. M. Hariyanna, *Outlines of Indian Philosophy*, London: Allen, 1956, p. 24.
49. Raja Rao, *The Cow of the Barricades and Other Stories*, Madras: Oxford UP, 1947, p. iii. All subsequent references to this edition have been cited as *CBS*.
50. Srivastava, p. 8.
51. Raja Rao, *OGG*, p. 7.
52. Narsimhaiah, p. 2.
53. Sharma, p. xv.

CHAPTER **1**

The Guru-Disciple Dynamics in Enlightenment Praxis

I

Origin and Evolution

The guru-disciple relationship has its roots in Hindu religious practice and mythology and the philosophy of the Hindu way of life. Today the true spirit of this relationship is nowhere evident except perhaps in the fields of Indian classical music and dance. However, a deeper analysis reveals that this guru-disciple relationship is still alive, vibrant and active, and forms a considerable part of the psyche of an average Indian. Regarding the origin of the guru-disciple tradition, Akhileshwara Jha makes a pertinent observation:

> The origin of the *guru-shishya* tradition lies both in the dependence of Hinduism on the performance of certain rituals and in the nature of the knowledge enshrined in the ancient scriptures which through several centuries have governed and conditioned the Hindu mind.[1]

Rituals, whether religious or social, derive their origin from the *Vedas*. In *Vedic* times, *samskaras* played a pivotal role in the life of a Hindu. These *samskaras* have been explicated variously in the *Vedas, Brahmanas, Grahyasutras, Dharmasutras* and *Smritis*.

Samskaras, as we understand them, are certain religious performances or ceremonies meant for the purification of body, mind and soul in general and the environment of an individual in particular. Classified in five broad categories, these *samskaras* include prenatal *samskaras* performed before the birth of a child, the *samskaras* of childhood and youth, education, marriage, and the funeral *samskaras*. This shows that the stages of Vedic life were sustained by these religious ceremonies (*samskaras*) performed under the direction of the *acharyas* (*Vedic* teachers or gurus). The disciples' (*brahamacharis'*) initiation, performed by the *acharyas*, engenders a rebirth of the *shishya*, technically a second birth.

The disciples resided with their *acharyas* till the conclusion of their education (worldly, in the sense of functionality, i.e., duties and the importance and delineation of role; and religious and spiritual) for which in return they used to render their services to the guru in the form of begging alms, tending his cattle or collecting fire-wood from the forest, cooking and serving other material needs. During this period the *acharya* was responsible for his disciples' physical, spiritual, moral, psychological and aesthetic development. The *acharya*, though a guru of highly formal and ritualized mode, was also a facilitator of the flowering of the *shishya's* personality.

For the dissemination of knowledge of any kind, the technique of oral tradition was in vogue in the *Vedic* times. This esoteric knowledge could only be imparted to the disciples by an exceptional human being, a father figure, or to be more traditional and precise, by the guru. The guru, the repository of all *Vedic* knowledge, primarily used the oral mode of transmission possibly because he was convinced that this method was the most effective. It was osmotically traditional from the viewpoint of both the teacher as well as the disciple and their role in society as it was then conceived and perceived.[2] With the passage of time as the values eroded (history and its ramifications), the oral tradition was marginalized and lost its primary character. Though practically extinct, it still obtains in the form of *katha-vachakas* and *Purana-vachakas*.

In Indian mythology, the guru is associated not merely with the famous Hindu Trinity—Brahama, Vishnu and Mahesh (the Creator, the Preserver and the Destroyer)—but also with the Absolute Brahman (*Parambrahma*). For example:

Gururbrahma Guruvishnu Gururdevo Maheshwara
Gurursakshat Parambrahma Tasmaishri Guruve Namah.

Each member of the Trinity is regarded as supreme and of highest importance; none is greater than the other and each may act as the Guru. For instance, in the Bhasmasura myth Vishnu becomes the Guru of Shiva by assuming the form of a beautiful, fascinating woman, Mohini, who subsequently kills the demon. Thus, the guru is capable of alchemical transformation, performing miracles for the rescue of the disciple, both literally and figuratively. To further illustrate, after churning the ocean for nectar (*amrita*), the poison fell to the lot of gods (*devas*). Shiva became the guru by scooping the poison, drinking it, and holding it in his throat (which is why he is called '*Neelakantha*' or the One with a Blue Throat), and thus rescuing the gods from mortality. Shiva can therefore be said to altruistically work for the welfare of his devotees and disciples—a necessary aspect of 'guruship.' Brahma emerges as a Guru to Vishnu and Mahesh in the sense that he is revered as the repository of all knowledge and wisdom. He is also believed to be the Creator of the Vedas, the divine scriptures of Hinduism.

India's greatest spiritual teacher and the famous expounder of *Advaitism*, Sri Sankaracharya (8th century AD) considers the guru as one who is established in *Brahma-vidya*, literally the knowledge of the Absolute. However, if we explore this at a deeper level, we stand face to face with the light of wisdom and its concomitant comprehension of the ultimate reality. Observe:

> A true seeker of the self (*atman*) should learn to enquire and to meditate, AFTER duly approaching a guru who is himself-well-established in Brahmavidya (i.e., wise and peace-giving knowledge of the realness of things), and is an ocean of kindness. (Sankara, *Vivekachudamani*: 15)[3]

Sankaracharya also emphasized *jnana* (right perception), control of the senses and the mind, and liberation from worldly bondage, as indispensable essentials for the realization of the Absolute Truth. Ramanuja, the great exponent of Vishishtadvaita, differed from Sankara's point of view and preferred *bhakti* (intense love for God), to *jnana*, as the most efficacious method of liberation of the self (as meant in Hinduism) or being. As a result of the introduction of the *bhakti* strain, the guru became the focal centre in Hinduism. This resulted in the idealization and elevation of the guru to the status a veritable God. According to Akhileshwara Jha:

> He has naturally enjoyed, and still continues to do a very exclusive status in the society. It is not merely the status of an intermediary between man and the knowledge he seeks but also between him and his soul's salvation. The *guru* is often revered as the divine soul directly in communication with god. Not unoften he is worshipped as god himself.[4]

After Ramanuja, other philosophers and medieval saints like Madhava, Vallabha, Chaitanya, Kabir and Nanak speculated along the same lines. Kabir, an enlightened saint, brought about a change in the perception of the guru in the sense that he imparted greater importance to the guru because of his accessibility as well as role as a medium to relate the disciple with God:

> Guru and God are both standing, whose
> Feet shall I touch first?
> I shall touch yours O guru, for
> You revealed God to me.[5]

Ramakrishna Paramhansa, in our own times, also inclines towards the same view. The technically non-literate mystic-saint, who may be called an 'enlightened rustic,' states that the divinity within the guru must be glimpsed before the disciple can graduate further, i.e., towards God. The guru is the leader who holds the disciple's hand on the pathway to God. God is manifested to the disciple through the guru:

> We should not consider our Guru to be mere man. Before the disciple sees the Deity, he sees, the Guru in the first vision of Divine illumination. And it is the Guru who afterwards shows

> the Deity, being himself mysteriously transformed into the form of the Deity. Then the disciple sees the Guru and the Deity as one and the same.[6]

The same idea is explicated somewhat differently by Sri Aurobindo. He states that surrender to the guru is surrender to the Divine in him.

> In surrendering to the Guru it is to the Divine in him that one surrenders—if it were only to a human entity it would be ineffective. But it is the consciousness of the Divine Presence that makes the Guru a real Guru, so that even if the disciple surrenders to him thinking of the human being to whom he surrenders that presence will still make it effective.[7]

Moreover, he regards the guru as a source of all knowledge, consciousness and spiritual salvation. Peter Brent also observes in the like vein—"He [guru] is known as human, but understood as divine."[8] Karishna spoke to Arjuna in the guru-God mode in the *Gita,* and said that to misperceive him as humanly embodied being would be a mistake.

In Indian spiritual thought it is believed that the human soul is always in search of salvation, incessantly striving for liberation from the relentless cycle of birth, death and rebirth, the eternally revolving wheel to which man is inexorably chained. The attainment of salvation (*moksha,* or freedom from this bondage) without the help of a spiritually enlightened person thus seems next to impossible. To be more exact, not all seekers of spirituality do necessarily have the capability to tread this "razor-edged path."[9] Therefore, they have to depend on human teachers known as gurus who show them the way to enlightenment. The followers or the initiates to whom this knowledge is disseminated are called *shishyas* (disciples).

Nirad C. Chaudhuri calls a guru "the religious protector" and "the spiritual guide" whose religious support is needed to tread the right path in religion. He observes:

> Religiously-minded Hindus have always sought a guru of this type, because it is a Hindu conviction that no right path in religion can be found without instruction, through initiation,

> by a qualified guide. Therefore, when a man and a woman has chosen a Guru he or she also follows his directions without question, surrendering all his or her spiritual and moral freedom and judgement.[10]

Nirad C. Chaudhuri further contends that after completely surrendering themselves to the guru, the disciples immensely increase their spiritual strength, thereby enabling themselves to confidently confront the problems of life. Swami Prabhvananda also stresses the need of the guru in order to gain spirituality and to attain the knowledge of God:

> All Hindu schools of thought, in fact, maintain that submission to the direction of a competent teacher is essential if one is to attain the knowledge of God, for religion is a practical science to which neither books nor scriptures can be a complete guide. The aspirant must therefore associate himself with one who is competent and holy, who has demonstrated the truths of religion in his own life, and who can therefore initiate the disciple into the secrets of spiritual enfoldment.[11]

Prabhvananda lays great emphasis on the capability of the guru as well as the state of his spiritual advancement, i.e., his holiness. According to Debabrata Sen Sharma, the guru is a mediator who transmits the Divine Grace to the disciples. He is the means to an end, the end being the realization of the Absolute Truth. Sharma comments:

> This medium is normally an embodied being [...]. This medium not only functions as relay centre for transmitting Grace from the Spiritual Lord to the individual being but also as the agent of the Divine will of the Supreme Lord on a lower level of imparting Divine knowledge to the uninitiated seekers. Such persons are technically called Acharyas or Gurus.[12]

It is time now to note what the term 'guru' means. As already stated, traditionally this term is applied to a teacher who imparts spiritual and religious instruction. In this sense, a guru is an instructor who performs the most important function of instructing and pointing to the right path in life. Several terms such as *Acharya* (a spiritual teacher), *Swami* (one who has taken the vows of renunciation), *Mahatma* (a great soul), etc., have been applied to signify the term 'guru.' If we observe the entity called guru as a whole, he emerges before us as a wise and enlightened teacher having realized the essence of being. The extent, scope and depth of his knowledge, transcendent in form and content, replete with wisdom and concomitant truth, make him the spiritual beacon to the struggling disciples. Endowed with these accomplishments as he is, he enables disciples to see and follow the path to enlightenment.

As a matter of fact, the guru-force operates at three levels. Firstly, the guru teaches by instruction; secondly, he teaches by example in the sense that his life is an example of what he instructs or teaches; and thirdly, he becomes a subliminal influence which penetrates the disciple's psyche bringing about osmosis with respect to knowledge, living, wisdom, etc. In other words, the disciple learns through an effortless, often unconscious, absorption or assimilation of the ideals and wisdom of the guru force. The method is also one of boundless love and affection for the disciple. Technically, however, the guru is never a 'philosopher;' as the term has the rings of scholarship and argumentative around it. The guru is basically a inspired spiritual instructor and a guide whose influence is not limited spatio-temporally; it is, indeed, transcendent and drenched with compassion. The guru shows the disciples to look inward and outward, connect with being to unravel the fundamental riddle of existence. Regarding the guru's three levels, Peter Coukoulis observes:

> Teaching, example, influence—these are the three instruments of the Guru. But the Teacher will not seek to impose himself or his opinions on the passive acceptance of the receptive mind; he will throw in only what is productive and sure as a seed which will grow under the divine fostering within. He will seek to awaken much more than to instruct; he will aim at natural process and free expansion.[13]

The guru is an eternal companion of the disciple. Gradually with the spiritual growth of the disciple, the guru becomes his *antaratma*. As Sri Aurobindo says, "Guru is the inner guide [...]

secret within us. To activate this secret, the human guru will lead the disciple through the nature of the disciple."[14]

The guru activates the hidden potentialities and talents of the disciple. In other words, he does the job of a psychologist by connecting the disciple with his deep nature. As the hidden facets of his personality unfold, his holistic growth begins. As such, the guru is not just the one who instills things into the mind of the disciple from without; he rather has the capacity to connect the disciple with his inner process. The guru, established as he is in the domain of collective unconscious, has also a transcendental spiritual power to connect the disciple with life, pristine depth and God. Thus the guru is not just a person; he represents a principle and is an epitome of experiential wisdom, perfection, realization and enlightenment. He is committed to the overall growth of his disciples.

Som P. Ranchan's rejection of "infantile dependencies" on the part of the disciple seems to be apt in the sense that self-dependence is necessary for the disciple's psychic-spiritual growth. Over-dependence on the guru, in a sense, implies lack of natural urge and essential will to learn or to progress on the path to enlightenment. Similarly, extra transference on the guru is also an obstacle in the process of spiritual growth of the disciple. That is why a little bit of questioning (resistance) on the part of the disciple is necessary in order to prevent this, for, without it, the disciple's state of being markedly distinct and distinctly unique is lost (in terms of the individuation process). One may mistakenly assume this uniqueness to be an entirely Western concept, but it is, however, necessary insofar as Eastern thought is concerned, because it is the gateway to the release from the chains of worldliness (*samsara*). Regarding such 'infantile dependencies' and 'extra-transference' on the part of the disciple in terms of the process of the relationship in which the guru is the facilitator, Ranchan comments: "Without commitment to the process there is no disciple—The process is the Guru. The human is only facilitator of the process."[15]

As an initiator, the guru primarily dispenses grace to the disciple and then lifts the veil of impure, mayavic cover (*avarna*) from the mind of the disciple to show him his real, i.e., true self.

In this process, the latent energies in a disciple are activated and through *diksha* (initiation) become a pointer towards realization. The real initiation is possible only if there is a complete surrender to the guru on the part of the disciple.

Sometimes a disciple is partially committed to the guru and leads his life in a mundane manner by occasional contact with the latter. However, even partial commitment (constituting surrender) cannot be questioned because such a disciple may gradually widen his spiritual horizons and may finally succeed in attaining enlightenment under the occasional but effective guidance of the guru. At times, we come across disciples who are 'total disciples.' They completely surrender themselves before their guru and renounce the world. With the passage of time, after seeking enlightenment, they become gurus themselves. They serve their guru with complete devotion; the guru is the veritable God in their eyes. The guru, in turn, facilitates the self-knowledge of the disciple by spotlighting initially on his talent and aptitude. A real guru is an epitome of divinity.

Debabrata Sen Sharma maintains that "[...] three classes of Divine Teachers are recognized in the *Agamas*. They are the *Daiva* (celestial teachers), the *Siddha* (superhuman teachers) and the *Purusha* (human teachers)."[16] *Purushas* or *Manava* gurus are human teachers, evolved spiritually, who guide the disciples effectively as they (gurus) have a direct link with divinity or the Divine Being. Superhuman teachers or *Siddhas* are elevated beings due to the element of purity in them and their relationship-cum-connection with God. *Daivas* or celestial teachers are the presiding deities who dispense their grace to those aspirants who have already attained the highest known degree of perfection. In Jungian terms *Daiva* gurus are considered as pure archetypes.

While classifying the *Manava* Gurus (human teachers), Ramakrishna Paramhansa mentions three classes.[17] In the lowest class of religious teachers, he places those who are indifferent to their disciples' actions. They are hardly concerned whether their disciples try to perceive what is being imparted to them, or not. The second type of teachers exerts effort to make their disciples follow the path of righteousness, devotion and truth, and are, therefore, better. Such teachers adopt the methods of gentle persuasion, affection, and caring as a means of inspiration for the disciples to find the right path. The greatest and the most evolved teachers even use force, if necessary, to show the path to enlightenment. They may adopt any/every method for the welfare of their disciples.

II
Guru and the Wise Old Man

Now these traditional formulations will be seen in the light of depth psychology in general, and in terms of Jungian concepts, in particular. The figure of the guru in India finds its parallel in Jungian psychology where it is called the archetype of the wise old man. Jung himself states: "The figure of the wise old man can appear so plastically, not only in dreams but also in visionary meditation (or what we call "active imagination"), that, as is sometimes apparently the case in India, it takes over the role of a guru."[18]

The archetype of the wise old man or guru is representative of the archetype of 'self,' which is a symbol of wholeness. Similarly, some archetypes, such as those of 'meaning' and 'spirit' have much in common with the archetype of the wise old man. Analysing the dream of a young student of theology, in which two magicians dressed in white and black respectively appear. Jung observes that they are "two aspects of the *wise old man,* the superior master and teacher, the archetype of spirit which symbolizes the pre-existent meaning hidden in the chaos of life."[19] In this way, we see that the archetype of spirit represents a superior master who personifies meaningfulness.

The following are the characteristics of the archetype of the wise old man that are analogous to those of the guru figure in India. Like the archetype of the spirit, the wise old man, through liberality and spontaneity, unshackled by time and space, inspires, stimulates, vivifies and spurs the disciple to unlock the hidden potentialities within. He has the power of piercing through "the chaotic darkness" of life and replacing it with the "light of meaning." In this sense, the wise old man is a guru, a teacher, a psychopomp and an enlightener who is the "[...]

carrier and mouthpiece of his own Dionysian enlightenment and ecstasy."[20]

The wise old man has a remarkable faculty of restraint, prohibition and interdiction. Apparently, he gives counsels of wisdom rather effortlessly. He is decisive, firm, authentic and authoritative in his convictions. The wise old man also removes the veil of illusions thereby acting as a revealer of the 'self.' He also has the capacity to persuade authoritatively and cogently with little argument.

The wise old man appears when the disciple is in a desperate condition; he gives him some hope without helping him unnecessarily. He makes him face the problem and thereby inculcates a spirit of self-dependence and generates belief in himself. The method is subtle and precise, yet flexible. It may seem technically rigid in form to a common man. The wise old man helps one emerge from depression, from a "hopeless and desperate situation," and points towards the right path in life's journey.[21] Omniscient, and hence having an excellent sense of anticipation, he warns the disciple of the dangerous obstacles he is likely to encounter on the journey, this search for the self, and teaches him how to overcome them. The guru is very critical by nature and shows the disciple his faults till he achieves perfection and evolves into a higher state of being. Moral strength is a hallmark of the guru, who as the wise old man is always prepared to co-operate with the disciple to pierce through the veil of *maya*. He helps everyone indiscriminately, be they disciples or people whom he happens to come in contact with. Sometimes the objective intervention of the wise old man in life becomes necessary for the attainment of enlightenment by the disciple. To quote C.G. Jung:

> But the intervention of the old man—the spontaneous objectivation of the archetype–would seem to be equally indispensable, since the conscious will by itself is hardly ever capable of uniting the personality to the point where it acquires this extraordinary power to succeed. For that, not only in fairytales but in life generally, the objective intervention of the archetype is needed, which checks the purely affective reactions with a chain of inner confrontations and realization.

> These cause the who? where? how? why? to emerge clearly and in this wise bring knowledge of the immediate situation as well as of the goal. The resultant enlightenment and untying of the fatal tangle often has something positively magical about it—an experience not unknown to the psychotherapist.[22]

This objective "intervention" of the wise old man operates at a very subliminal level. It is purely a subtle, inner process that may take place at a rapid/slow pace depending upon the disciple's faculty of perception. The disciple is not always aware of the process which is effected by the objective "intervention." However, the resultant wisdom makes the disciple more insightful and perceptive. Through this subliminal and invisible alchemical process, a realization of the inner truth dawns upon the disciple and makes him worldly wise.

Finally we may say that the guru helps the disciple in overcoming his negative traits by connecting the disciple with the most active archetype in him. As Coukoulis states: "The objective is not to fixate the disciple's attention and devotion on the personal-ego aspects of the human guru. The main goal is to activate the archetypal forces dealing with the impersonal aspect of the guru."[23] Not only that, the disciple is also exposed to the external reality, i.e., life as a whole. The guru endows the disciple with true perception of reality and makes him experience wholeness of being.

In the *Bhagvadgita,* the concept of guru is represented by the ideal of *sthithaprajna*—the one who is steadfast and unshakeable in knowledge. He accepts everything in a non-discriminatory manner and form, and thereby treats everyone equally irrespective of anything. He is untouched by caste consciousness and devoid of attachment and detachment; he is non-attached. Som P. Ranchan has analysed the concepts such as guru, *sthithaprajna,* etc., in the light of Jungian psychology. In *Revisioning Gita,* he writes:

> The guru obviously if he is worth his name is a sthithaprajna, Brahmajnani, gunatita, a Bhakta [...]. Krishna himself is an example of a guru par excellence [...]. As a guru he has an enormous, frightening amount of knowledge, all experiential;

> he knows his becoming and being. Though established in pure consciousness, essential to a guru, he is so well versed in the contents of the cultural and collective unconscious which enables him to be a great psychotherapist.[24]

As such, the guru is an enlightened being insofar as his spiritual status is concerned. Viewed existentially, he is the embodiment of the essence of all knowledge.

III
The Role of Guru in Rao's Life

Let us focus briefly on Raja Rao's life in this context. Born in a traditional Brahmin family, Raja Rao was considerably influenced by the traditional, religious, spiritual, and intellectual environment of the family. In his family tradition, there had been scholars like Vidyaranya Swami, an eminent propounder of Advaita Vedanta after Shankaracharya, and his own grandfather who was an erudite scholar. Raja Rao has imbibed the traditions of a typical Indian Brahmin family as he admits in the opening lines of his magnum opus *The Serpent and the Rope* (1960), an autobiographical novel: "I was born a Brahmin—that is, devoted to truth and all that. 'Brahmin is he who knows Brahman' [...]."[25] And the life he lived stands as an evidence of the fact that he had always been in pursuit of knowing. As a result of this, he became a naturally learned philosopher having the knowledge and understanding of nearly all the religious and philosophical traditions of the world.

Raja Rao attaches great importance to the guru figure. This guru stance is obvious not only in his novels but also in all the three volumes of short stories, namely, *The Cow of the Barricades and Other Stories* (1947), *The Policeman and the Rose* (1978) and *On the Ganga Ghat* (1989). P.P. Mehta writes:

> Returning to India in 1940, Raja Rao spent the war years in India. Looking for the spiritual traditions of India in Banaras, the spiritual home of India he shut himself up in a room for a number of days, trying to decide whether he should become a sanyasi. This spiritual turmoil in his mind would have ended a great literary career, had he not met Swami Atmanand, the

great Vedantist philosopher. Raja Rao accepted him as his spiritual teacher. Swami Atmanand advised him to continue his writing profession. The echoes of this spiritual conflict of Raja Rao are found in his great novel, *The Serpent and the Rope*. Before Raja Rao résumed his career as an author, he spent three weeks in meditation at the well-known temple of Mahakal in Ujjain.[26]

In the light of the above occurrences in Rao's life, one can see what a crucial role his guru, Atmananda, had played in his transformation from a scholar into a creative and committed writer. Thus it was his spiritual guide who made him discover himself and realize his real aptitude as a creative writer. Moreover, it would be proper to mention hence that unlike other Indo-Anglian writers such as R.K. Narayan, Mulk Raj Anand, Bhabani Bhattacharya and Kamala Markandaya, whose portrayal of guru figures is superficial and inauthentic, Raja Rao's personal experience imparts a sense of authenticity and depth to his delineation of guru characters in his fictional world. Regarding *The Serpent and the Rope*, which essentially is a statement on the realization of 'self,' Raja Rao says that it was an outcome of "[...] spiritual fulfillment, that is to say that it was born after I had met my guru."[27] In the final phase of the novel, Rao has beautifully described the nature of illusion and reality, besides explaining the role and function of the guru. He is the one who shows the path to enlightenment and also bestows upon the disciple the natural truth or the secret of perception which is reasoning (*viveka*), a faculty to discriminate between truth and untruth, real and unreal, ignorance and enlightenment. Ramaswamy, the protagonist of the novel, becomes the spokesman of the novelist when he says:

> The world is either unreal or real—the serpent or the rope [...]. But in true fact, with whatever eyes you see there is no serpent, there never was a serpent [...]. You see the serpent and in fear you feel you are it, the serpent [...]. Once—the Guru—brings you the lantern; the road is seen, the long, white road, going with the statutory stars. It is only the rope. He shows it to you. And you touch your eyes and know there never was a serpent.[28]

Thus, to speak metaphorically, the serpents are illusions and therefore necessarily misapprehensions. The guru, as the facilitator, helps the disciple to recognize them (serpents) as such. Once comprehension dawns, the disciple takes a leap towards truth.

IV
Guru-Disciple Relationship in Rao's Stories

In the pages to follow Raja Rao's characterization and delineation of the dynamics of the guru-disciple relationship pervasive in his stories is proposed.

In the first story (all the stories are untitled) in *On the Ganga Ghat*, the character of Moti Ram has been drawn at great depth and with finesse. Moti Ram, an "elderly, round-faced" person communicates effectively, though in a staccato rhythm, the ultimate Truth in germinal form like a guru. He may be misinterpreted by the reader and initially even by the first-person-narrator, who happens to be a well-educated person. This is mainly due to his (Moti Ram's) humility and his modesty. But once we put social prejudices aside, Moti Ram's purity and experiential wisdom magnificently blaze forth. He is illiterate and poverty-stricken; a "good man," a wonderful drummer, and an ardent devotee of Lord Shiva. This Shiva-*bhakta* is elevated from the common lot to a highly evolved spiritual state, totally oblivious of his station in society which, generally speaking, is one circumscribed by environment. In spite of this spiritually evolved state of the mind and psyche he is quite earthy even to the point of being worldly-wise insofar as the essentials of living are concerned. Thus Moti Ram knows the business of living with respect to his world. In fact, the grassroots wisdom that he has imbibed is extremely profound and it magnifies his stature endowing him with nobility of a high rank. To illustrate:

> 'Moti Ram,' I said, 'how many children have you?'
>
> 'Three, sir,' he answered ever so reverentially.
>
> 'I had four. And one of them died.'
>
> 'Died of what, Moti Ram?'

'He died of death, sir, that is all. One morning we awoke, and found him dead.'

'Was there some black magic behind it, you think?'

'Who would do magic against a grave good boy? He used to carry fuel from the fuel shop to the Ganga banks for cremations. He had seen too many souls die.'

'No, he must have died of something.'

'Well, sir, we must all die of something. Does it matter the manner he was taken away? His time was come, and he was taken away.' (*OGG*: 14)

This simple piece of dialogue (ostensibly too naive to the uninitiated) is actually an enlightening discourse on philosophical issues like the meaning of death and time. That Moti Ram is an enlightened guru, is further corroborated by the following excerpt: "To beat a leather instrument with God-given hands is easy. But to beat drum that Shiva's silence become sound could only be the gift of Mother Parvathi" (*OGG*: 18). Thus we see that Moti Ram firmly believes that the realization of Lord Shiva is possible through the grace and benediction of Mother Parvathi who opens the doors of darkness to allow divine light to touch the devotee.

Keeping in view the spiritual dimensions of Moti Ram's self and his state of being we observe that he enjoys the perfect and supernal bliss of a purely egoless state. This is why he emphasizes the extinction of the ego, a prerequisite of the path to enlightenment: "He alone beats the drum true who knows he is never there" (*OGG*: 18). The beating of the drum is a medium through which Moti Ram "rubs off" a little of his 'heavy karma.' The beating of the drum is also a manifestation of a holistic bonding with Lord Shiva. It symbolizes Moti Ram's spirituality of being, a state that he has reached purely through the *bhakti* mode. In essence, Moti Ram is a guru incarnate, though not in a mythified sense, since he wanders in the maze of divinity brought about due to his earnest simplicity, unpolluted worldliness and its concomitant state of egoless being. In short, this illiterate guru, a juggernaut of spirituality, unconsciously taking the appearance of a primitive canoe leaves the character, Rao in a reflective and somewhat elevated state as he (Moti Ram) has given him (Rao—the protagonist) an iota of other-worldliness, specifically spiritual which Rao (the author) may use as the stepping stone to higher state of psychic evolution through the transcendental mode of pristine *bhakti*.

The tenth story in *On the Ganga Ghat* is an account of Sudha, Ranchoddoss' extraordinarily sensitive daughter, who acquires extraordinary dimensions in the course of the story. Sudha, a student of St. Mary's convent school, hates marriage as she considers it "stupid" and "sinful." Hers is a religious disposition of the *bhakti* mode; she worships Lord Rama.

> Sudha, however, sat for hours on end in the family sanctuary, repeating the Name of the Lord. "Rama, Sri Rama," she said and went on naming His Name a thousand times, and little by little three thousand times a day. She even started on fasts and days of silence, and sometimes took a vow to name the Name-of-Rama a lakh of times in ten days. She grew pale but beautiful. The family did not worry—she was after all only fifteen. (*OGG*: 115)

Another reason for Sudha's aversion to marriage is that upon becoming a widow in her previous life, she discovered that she loved her husband more than "[...] she did God himself" (*OGG*: 116). This painful realization provided an impetus to and effected a change in her viewpoint, indeed, her entire philosophy of life. Thus, she spurns marriage.

Sudha, since her life in the previous births, comes across three gurus—one of them being the inheritor of her husband's guru who initiates her and gives her a 'secret-*mantra*' in the previous *janama* (birth); another, her previous birth's husband who embodies Sadhu Sunderanandji, becomes her guru in the present life and initiates Sudha to "sannyas" (renunciation of the worldly pursuits/pleasures); and the third one her guru's (Sundernanandji's) "Sat-Guru" at Badrinath who later initiates Ranchoddoss also on the path to enlightenment. Through these encounters Sudha grows and develops in keeping with the idea and ideals of spirituality that are a part of her psyche. This is specifically done through *guru-mantras* (powerful psychic-spiritual tools) to enable the *shishya* to find and relate to his inner being. In short, Sudha becomes a *jogin* (one who practices spirituality) herself and guides her father on the path to spirituality. This guru-replete modern day parable best illustrates Rao's cosmic vision which is perspicacious. It is an epitome of "guruhood."

To use the terminology of Jung, the archetype of the wise old man has already performed its function of inspiring, activating and stimulating Sudha's hidden potentiality, in her previous birth. As such, she needs just a paddle push in this birth, since she is already in the process of attaining wholeness of being. In other words, the archetypes of transformation are already in operation. "They are," as Jung says, "not personalities, but are typical situations, places, ways and means, that symbolize the kind of transformation in question."[29] To make this point clear, we may recall the time before Sudha dies in her previous birth—she succeeds in apprehending the shallowness of her devotion to God. In addition to it, it is worth mentioning that she has already been given a secret mantra, traditionally and technically called *guru-mantra*.

Sudha, as we can see, and as she admits herself, is not at all a scholar; it is all due to her guru that she becomes capable of understanding all the abstruseness of Vedanta philosophy. She also understands Shankar's *Mayavada*, and can answer earnest questions regarding the complex states of dream, sleep, wakefulness, and deep sleep as well as about illusion and reality.

The story of Bholanath, a wheelwright's son from Rajgarh, is also a tale representing remarkably the dynamics of the guru-disciple relationship. Bholanath, an expert mechanic, comes in contact with Pandit Vishwanathji, a guru figure, who, though not soaked in formal knowledge, spreads the divine message to those who cross his path. He does this in a simple and direct manner, as he is clear-hearted and despite the fact that his social standing is merely one of a company cook.

Bholanath follows his ancestral profession. While growing up he has a strong and deep bond with his nephew, Bhim. Though a rustic and illiterate, he is, right from the beginning, spiritually inclined and of a religious bent of mind as well. Bholanath's mechanical expertise takes him across the seas from the orient to the occident where he meets Vishwanath, a spiritually evolved being who is steeped in ancient Indian lore, specifically, *Tulsi Ramayana* and *Brihat Stotra Ratnakar*. The meeting evolves into a relationship of guru (Vishwanath) and disciple (Bholanath). Bhola, a dogmatically honest man, also embodies the virtues of persistence and devotion for the Lord. An enthusiastic singer of *bhajans* (devotional songs), the psycho-dynamics of Bhola's simple world is magnified intensely. In fact, his relationship with Vishwanath brings about a quantum leap in his spiritual consciousness, which is not in any sense antithetical to the business of ordinary living.

Vishwanath, an unnoticed and thereby socially 'invisible' guru, is the spark that ignites of the spiritual spark in Bhola, the simpleton. Vishwanath does not suffer from any type of guru-complex, and insofar as Bhola is concerned, is literally an 'accidental' guru. He feels a great moral responsibility in facilitating his disciple's inner growth. On this aspect, Vishwanath comments: "He [Bhola] looks after me out, and I look after him in" (*OGG*: 83). Bholanath, however, living in a purely egoless state (as befits a true disciple, a true seeker of truth) humbly says: "'I'm no one to look after any one. The great Vishwanath high up there looks after every one in the world, and this Vishwanath here looks after me'" (*OGG*: 83).

Soon after returning to India and his family, Bhola has a son whom he names Vishwanath. This shows his devotion to Vishwanath, the guru. Unfortunately, however, his mother, wife and son die in Benares and Bhola decides not to go back to Rajgarh. He stays in Benares and serves his guru Vishwanath. Here Bhola contemplates the Lord on the banks of the Ganga and voices a thought, "Never a home be a home where Mother Ganga floweth by not" (*OGG*: 83). Thus we see that Bhola has a meaningful connection with Indian mythology especially with reference to the importance of *gangajal* (the holy water of the Ganga), a symbol of purifying qualities, possibly even purgative, which is, of course, steeped in the tradition of Hindu belief, *dharma*, an inseparable part of the tradition of India, particularly of Hinduism. Metaphorically, Bhola can be said to live and die each moment for the Ganga and its extension, i.e., Vishwanath. The spiritual-emotional bonding of place, time and guru and disciple on the macro-canvas of the Ganga is evident in the following lines:

> Sometimes when the red dawn breaks on the Ganga, I cannot bear the veiled white silence over the river—it brings tears to my eyes. I do not know why, but never for father or mother have I wept as I do for the Ganga—this Ganga is my father, this Ganga is my mother. (*OGG*: 84)

In this statement, the guru is not absent as he is the receptacle of spiritual consciousness which, as already stated, makes for the growth and development of the disciple (Bhola). Bhola, deeply immersed in an environment in which service to the guru is an integral part, is firmly footed on the path to salvation, to enlightenment. This is a blissful state of spiritual-religious ecstasy (of which the dissolution of the ego is a prerequisite) through which the devotee catches glimpses, howsoever ephemeral, of the Lord who is omniscient, omnipresent and of course sagacious and eternal like the Ganga. Regarding this Bhola states:

> If the Ganga does not say
> Who then will go on naming Ram,
> If I do not say (!)
> You alone will remain, O Ram. (*OGG*: 85)

The story "The Cow of the Barricades" in the book of the same title is somewhat unusual in form as the protagonist is Gauri, the cow. The story, though obviously nourished by and derivative of Hindu tradition (the cow being a sacred animal) is a skillfully woven *mandala*, which can be likened to a modern myth of utmost devotion (to the guru) that finally brings home the message of compassion of the highest order. Regarding the use of the animal motif in the present story, K.R. Rao states: "The symbolic grafting of the 'Kamdhenu' motif to the national theme in 'The Cow of the Barricades,' anticipates Raja Rao's metaphysical use of the animal motif in *The Cat and Shakespeare*."[30]

Gauri, the cow is an enigma to the villagers (many of them, are devotees of the Master), as they cannot comprehend the relationship that the Master (a guru figure) and Gauri (the disciple) share. Every Tuesday[31] evening Gauri comes and nibbles at the Master's hair. This is basically a silent communication, indeed a communion, regarding which the Master tells his human disciples: "Perhaps she is the great Mother's vehicle" (*CBS*: 175).

Gauri seems to be indifferent to everyone, the sole exception being the Master. Since the Master accepts her, she is honoured and worshipped by the simple villagers. However, "Gauri would pass by them all like holy wife among men, and going straight to the Master, would nibble at his hair and disappear among the bushes" (*CBS*: 175).

The Master (of a Gandhian mould) has attained realization through the self. Jung propounds the same belief when he states that one can only know oneself through the self. But East and West diverge, because in Western terms the focus is more on individuality than on abstract and apparently remote. Eastern concepts like enlightenment, which must be initiated by a guru. Nevertheless, the point of interception is not to be disregarded as both the Eastern guru and the Western psychologist are facilitators.

To return to the point, the Master has attained realization through the self. As such, he seems to be a benign spiritual magnet for Gauri, the "compassionate and true" soul who occasionally bathes in the Master's *darshan* (sight) and whose presence harmonises with and purifies even the natural surroundings and the atmosphere of the Ashram. Rao explicitly states: "[…] for when the seeker finds harmony, the jackal and the deer and the rat and the serpent become friends" (*CBS*: 175).

Gauri is a seeker of enlightenment whose rebirth as a *Yogi* is assured because of her honesty and compassion. According to K.R. Rao "Gauri is like the Mahatma an ubiquitous presence, an embodiment of everything that is lovable and compassionate, glorious and powerful in the universe."[32] This can be seen in the light that Gauri is a surreal *avatar* (incarnation), although still living in the womb, who is likely to bring about a regeneration of spirituality. The story is, indeed, one rooted in mythical modernity.

The focus then shifts to Gandhi's Swadeshi Movement, a pacifist war to re-establish the fragile indigenous economy destroyed by the British. Amidst the chaos and turmoil, Gauri's weekly routine is not broken and she visits the Master every evening. The Master with whom she empathizes, dissuades the workmen from violence. But the rage cannot be checked and the Master retires into meditation to prevent bloodshed. Before retreating to this state he declares: "No barricades in the name of the Mahatma, for much blood will be spilt [...]" (*CBS*: 177).

In the absence of the Master (guide), Gauri (his extension) becomes the focal point of the people who perceive her as divine, believing "She will protect us. Now it's sure she will protect us" (*CBS*: 180). Initially the workmen resent her when she approaches the barricades. On her passing, away however, they prostrate themselves and call her "Goddess." Gauri is killed when she reaches the top of the barricades by a British bullet and "[...] she fell a vehicle of God among lowly men" (*CBS*: 181).

Gauri is initially a disciple but at the end, embodies Mother India who sacrifices her life to protect her children. In fact, her sacrifice is in the spirit of the Master's aspirations and objectives in which non-violence (*ahimsa*) is the only just way to accomplish anything. Thus, her devotion to the Master, her guru, is beyond any doubt.

Gauri symbolizes the virtues of love, purity and compassion. This idealism, which is focused entirely on the guru in the beginning, undergoes an alchemical transformation bringing about the quest for truth. Regarding the 'Mother India' image and the other aspects, Vasant A. Shahane observes:

> 'The cow of the Barricades' is a fine example of Raja Rao's art, synthesis of symbol and reality, of truth and fiction. The cow is a symbol of purity and divinity, compassion and unity, and yet she is also real, a creature of flesh and blood, an animal affected by the divine power. The cow—Gauri—dislikes barricades and divisions and while she upholds the principle of unity, she is shot by red-men's bullets. Thus, the cow stands for truth, the

principle of freedom, and yet she is part of a fictive world, an arcade of symbolism.[33]

Gauri's approach to the barricades is a sort of dedication that culminates in '*samadhi*' which Swami Atmananda has translated as 'absorption.' Peter Brent quotes the *Bhagvad Gita* in this regard: "Meditation is approaching the object of worship by visualizing it and continuously on the idea of the object alone in the unbroken current, like a flow of oil."[34] Thus through such worship, Gauri becomes the vehicle successfully realizing the Master's dream of avoiding bloodshed, although at the cost of her life. In effect she is a *Yogi* of the moment, who rises to the occasion as 'greatness' has been 'thrust upon' her. Her act is, however, not totally accidental as she is a pure, virtuous and honest soul, a devotee.

The archetype of Gauri can also be viewed in Grecian and Jungian terms. She stoically accepts Hercules' maxim of putting one's "shoulder to the wheel."[35] In Jungian terms, the Master is a wise old man, psycho-spiritual in dimension and an embodiment of spiritual consciousness. Gauri is his protégé, but as the Western view of life in general and of spiritual consciousness in particular is not guru-fixated, it can be said that the disciple (protégé) may overtake the guru. This viewpoint, technically, is not really in conflict with the Hindu way of life, but unfortunately, in this era, guru-fixation is the norm that Indian society dictates and adheres to. In the positive sense, Gauri, although a Hindu *nari* (woman) gives up the ghost not easily but in a heroic manner accomplishing the Master's task. In a nutshell, Gauri unconsciously seems to believe that struggle is dignity.

The wise old man has been introduced as a Retired Police Commissioner in "The Policeman and the Rose." He does not make a physical entry into the story; his presence is merely suggested by the first person narrator. He is both enlightened and an enlightener. The narrator-quester attains spirituality after meeting him at Travancore:

> In Travancore station I descended and said: 'Take me, please, to the Great-man.' And they took me to the Maharaja. But I returned to the station and said to the taxi: 'Take me please to

> the Retired Police Commissioner,' and they took me to Truth. Truth has Two-Feet and smelt of many roses rose. Truth has steps and once you enter, in the verandah, at the footsteps is the Lotus on which Truth stands. I wash myself of my sins—I peel out skin after skin of my tattered body—I speak to the incarnations of the mind—I float in the magnificence of my dreams, and I tell them, 'Adieu, adieu, my memories, my medals, my police uniforms. (*P&R*: 124)

As such, the Retired Police Commissioner embodies the Jungian archetype of the wise old man. He is an epitome of Truth.

Jung's wise old man and his disciple (the protagonist) form the canvas of the story, which traces the protagonist's growth, for the major part in a kind of 'river of reflection' mode. However, time is respected making this 'stream' largely sequential. The inner being of the 'I' (the narrator) is shown to indulge in the process of life through the 'mindscape' technique without any action on the external plane as such. In a traditional sense, with respect to the story as form, the major part of this story is devoid of plot. It is, however, not in any sense 'absurd.'

The story imperceptibly blooms into the search for truth, meandering gradually through the Sankhya theory. The rich symbology of Hindu thought is introduced via the symbol of a red rose representing *rajas* (vitality) that evolves to a white rose *satva* (serenity and wisdom). The story traces the growth of the protagonist within this paradigm. The Retired Police Commissioner signifying Jungian archetype of the wise old man helps the protagonist in this task. The wise old man here does not actually appear but is an abstract figure, a symbol of truth, the beacon for the quester-protagonist. The quest is revealed through the mind of the protagonist. The red rose evolves to a white rose, which then culminates in transformation to the form of a Lotus, Brahma's seat, an island of purity in this scum-ridden universe. The Samkhaya view of gunas and, of course, the larger Indian philosophical canvas of *karma*, ideally constitute the search for Truth in this eternally changing world. To quote Debiprasad Chattopadhyaya:

> In the Samkhya view, everything in the material world was an unstable composition of three kinds of substances or reals,

> technically called gunas, though in the composition of the different objects of the world, one or the other of the gunas predominated. These three were called (1) Sattva, exhibiting qualities of lightness, illumination and joy, (2) Rajas exhibiting qualities of movement and pain, and (3) Tamas exhibiting qualities of heaviness, obstruction and sloth.[36]

The "fabular and fantastic" stages of transmutation of the red rose are explicitly suggested, rooted as these are in indigenous culture and thought:

> Like the policeman it [Rose] was born of the atom, became earth, air, ether, fire and water, rolled into a pumpkin, grew into a tree, became a deer and frisked and frolicked in the forests of Vrindavan [...] suffered and died—died again and again, was born again and again, married a monk, intellectual, army man, was carried off by the Muslims [...] wandered by the Ganges [...] and was sometimes called a weeping rose, for the spot on the petal often in an evening looked a teardrop. (*P&R*: 122)

The intoxication of the rose is gripping, ideally culminating in bliss and is, indeed, the intoxication of life's journey. The rose is the seed fructifying into a Lotus. Regarding the process of intoxication, the narrator-protagonist confesses (literally with respect to rose-oil): "I also drank of it, and the madder I became, I said, 'Rose, you Rose in my heart you weep in me, and I place you on the hair of the gods and you weep still. And what shall I do now?" (*P&R*: 124).

The protagonist journeys to America, France and Japan, and finally to Travancore carrying his red rose which is symbolic of the spirituality of the quest. *Rajas* is the starting point: he becomes restless, passionate, excited and feels the pain of suffering and existence. Here *sattva* takes hold with the red rose becoming white. This symbolizes that the guru, though still unseen, is near. Liberating knowledge is at his doorstep, once he crosses the threshold of the white rose. Thus, the transformation into the Lotus is foreshadowed. The conditioned self shall be overtaken by transmutation of the psyche characterized by fresh perception and intelligence brought about by the divine grace of the guru though still unseen. This journey is reminiscent of Eklavya in the *Mahabharata* who made a clay-image of Dronacharya after being rejected by him, in order to progress by the grace of the guru, likewise unseen, in the mode of the Jungian objective intervention of the archetype of the wise old man. The wise old man does not make physical appearance at all but an invisible presence seems to stay with the protagonist although he is not aware of it till near the end. In Jungian terms the Retired Police Commissioner is an inspiration of the archetype of spiritually oriented and guiding torchbearer that can be interpreted as the 'bringer of enlightenment.'

The guru is like Lord Yama and the narrator is a striving, highly imperfect, Nechiketian individual. There is also a parallel in Greek mythology in which Sharon (the rose in the present context) ferries the souls of the dead to Hades, the land of the dead. But if one is desirous of going there while still living, then one has to meet the dog *Cerebrus*, the guardian of the gateway, like a Theseus or Nachiketa.

Echoes of the *Gita* are heard in the protagonist's mental process: "I laid my petal of rose at the Lotus of Truth and I never beheld it again" (*P&R*: 125). This is, of course, non-attachment, and as such, the evolution of the protagonist is almost complete at this stage.

The story has a somewhat surreal flavour. This surreal alchemy is reflected in the following line: "[...] so there was no rose but the rose [...] it smelt of the Lotus," evidently describing a state of self-realization in which passion and activity have merged into an all-pervasive enlightenment.

Raja Rao himself admits that the story has an autobiographical strain. Various components of the story—its form, method, philosophy and message—singly and collectively contribute to the praxis of the dynamics of the guru-disciple relationship. Narsingh Srivastava aptly observes:

> In the disguised language of a fictional biography [...] the writer gives a realistic account of his own spiritual progress, finally terminating into his initiation by his Guru (Sri Atmanand Guru) at Travancore where one could see his 'white rose bloom' [...] out of his red-rose of holiness and perfect

> purity which he had attained through penitence and resignation of worldly attachments—"memories, medals and police-uniforms"—and lastly through his total surrender to his Guru.[37]

The narrator-protagonist begins to feel the enlightenment when he is about to meet the guru. Bliss (*sat-chit-ananda*) is induced. This shows Raja Rao's firm conviction that enlightenment is possible only through the grace of the guru.

The term 'river of reflection' used earlier is not to be mistaken for 'stream of consciousness.' Unlike the stream of consciousness where formal rigour is of utmost importance, "The Policeman and the Rose" is conducted in a reflective mode, underlining the nature of its meandering thought. Last but not least, the story is a modern myth rooted in ancient Indian tradition in which the Jungian wise old man is the beacon of spirituality.

V

Guru as *Sthithaprajna*: His Abstract Qualities

Now for a brief recapitulation of the abstract characteristics of the guru in general, with a particular focus on the guru's role vis-à-vis the disciple, the initiates and humanity at large. Although this has already been discussed, it is necessary to take an overview of these characteristics in Jungian terms.

The guru, primarily an instructor (not literally, in the sense of a pedant), reveals the mystery of life as a whole—its complexities, twists, and turns. He initiates his disciples into the labyrinth of the self. This brings about confidence among the *shishyas* due to which their 'will' is strengthened and which is pivotal in life's journey to realize the quintessence, the wholeness of being. The guru's dictums or suggestions encased sometimes apparently in a mundane form may be lost in the domain of ordinary perception as generally they are not so dramatic. However, if one listens carefully, they may leave a tremendous impact on the psyche of the disciple.

The guru also instructs by example. He exemplifies divinity thereby alchemizing the disciple's baser nature to a spiritual one. The guru permeates his psyche irrespective of time and place, i.e., in terms of the sense of historicity. For instance, in the story of Muthradas, Guru Shankarananda guides him to enlightenment through revelation and essential initial spiritual exercises. This results in greater spiritual awareness; after this the disciple is taught inward exploration, i.e., of the *antaratma*, the inner guide. Before initiation, Muthradas cannot understand the intricacies of Vedanta, but with the Guru's grace the light of comprehension begins to shine. His doors of perception are cleansed. Now he can understand the nature of wakefulness, dream, and sleep, and, therefore, unravel the whole riddle of existence.

The preceding paragraph contains points that may be understood in terms of Jungian psychology. Western society is extremely aware of the vital importance of role models in a person's life. This point is greatly emphasized by the behaviourists. The rise of the Western industrial society ravaged nature, archetypes and myths. Consequently, man was rendered incapable of coping with the fast emerging disequilibrium. Dreams lost their significance and were largely disregarded until Jung made ramifications of Frieud's theory. He realized the importance of dream, and came to the conclusion that consciousness, sub-consciousness and unconsciousness cannot be compartmentalized for holistic living. In Jung's words, the wise old man (an analogue of the guru) is more likely to appear in dreams because even if one meets him in the waking state, he may pass by unnoticed and go unrecognized. Dreams are a source of reconnection with the archetypes of the unconscious. This is the goal of Jungian analysis. The problem of transference is usually encountered during psychotherapy in which the patient, at times, falls in love with the therapist. To shed more light on the concept of the wise old man (guru) and its similarity to Vedanta, Jung's own words will best illustrate this:

> The wise old man appears in dreams in the guise of a magician, doctor, priest, teacher, professor, grandfather, or any other person possessing authority. The archetype of spirit in the shape of a man, hobgoblin, or animal always appears in a situation where insight, understanding, good advice,

> determination, planning, etc., are needed but cannot be mustered on one's own resources. The archetype compensates this state of spiritual deficiency by contents designed to fill the gap.[38]

The guru is an influencer. His influence spreads pervasively, limitlessly, irresistibly, and overwhelmingly like a divine halo (*ojasva*). In the story of Bhim, the parrot-protagonist is an embodiment of the wise old man: "a mighty mantra intoning Siddha" (*OGG*: 21). His very presence is beneficent and affects the inhabitants of Bindu House and Dasi Lane, notably Krodha (the vulture) whose continual itching on the neck and constant pain "on the bend of his back" disappear when he is near Bhim, and espescially when he (Bhim) is perched on the neem tree. In addition, Krodha, of a base nature, cannot terrify sparrows and Madhu birds in Bhim's presence. Thus, the guru is also a protector and divine healer lifting the disciple from profane consciousness to sacred consciousness.

In addition to the above, the guru teaches by inspiration. This inspiration is a dynamic motivating force enabling the ones in contact to meet and overcome danger by conquering fear, thereby resulting in right initiative and indomitable will. This may be accomplished directly or indirectly through another. In the ninth story, Shivlal, the pimp, is in possession of a guru-*mantra,* which is accidentally overheard by Nanna, the fat Panjabi prostitute. She is overwhelmed by its beauty and power. She insists on Shiv giving her the *mantra,* but he advises her to take it from his guru. Upon their meeting, the guru at first reprimands Nanna, and then asks her to come after a three-day fast in the month of Ashad. After she fulfills this condition, Nanna is given the *mantra*. This *mantra* is transformative and results in Nanna's becoming a seeker of the Truth, a quester of spirituality. Thus it is evident that Shiv, the facilitator, is an unconscious influencer, the accidental guru.

Nanna's spiritual development does not bring about a change with respect to her livelihood. The power of the *mantra* is such that she can spiritually evolve without getting stuck in the mire of worldliness. She is able to reconcile these two divergent aspects effectively as she has become a quester par excellence. Her profession does not contaminate her soul as it is her "dharma" (*OGG*: 109). Thus the story is one of a modern *devadasi* (literally the one who is devoted to God) who is influenced by the unlikely inspiration of a pimp. To illustrate the power and the magnificence of an inflluencer, Jung states:

> The old man [guru] thus represents knowledge, reflection, insight, wisdom, cleverness [worldly intelligence] and intuition on the one hand, and on the other, moral qualities such as goodwill, and readiness to help, which make his 'spiritual' character sufficiently plain.[39]

The highest state of evolution of a guru is that of the *sthithaprajna*, steadfast and unperturbed in wisdom, literally stable (*sthith*) in knowledge (*prajna*)—the knowledge of the Absolute. The guru and *sthithaprajna* are thus one and the same. Ian Kesarcodi and Watson observe:

> The guru then is—or is ideally—the one who knows how to teach you, what it is to be perfected and fulfilled as a person, signs of which are such as inner peace, or that unflappable 'sameness' in the face of tribulation and exquisite joy alike, characteristic of that superior being the *Gita* refers to as Sthitaprajna, 'the one who is steadfast and unshakeable in wisdom.'[40]

In the *Bhagvadgita*, when Arjuna asks Krishna to state the nature of a *sthithaprajnà*, the Lord explains that the tranquility of mind i.e., *samadhi*, is an inseparable and essential state of being of such an evolved soul:

> When a man puts away all the desires of mind, O Partha (Arjuna), and when his spirit is content in itself then he is called stable in intelligence.[41]

Swami Prabhupada defines a *sthithaprajna* as one above sterile intellect, established in Krishna Consciousness (complete merger with the Absolute). Radhakrishnan, on the other hand views the *sthithaprajna* as a sage established in Truth, personifying wisdom and able to comprehend the true nature of reality or illusion with an inward vision. In an interview with Shiv Niranjan, Raja Rao elucidated:

> The sage is one who is truth. The word sage can mean a Rishi or a Guru or the Guru. The Guru is the sage of sages [...]. The Rishi is one who sees. If you mean by that the Guru, then the disciple of the Guru is a Sadhaka. If you mean sage in the sense that he has found the Truth, that would be correct.[43]

Irrespective of any label, a *sthithaprajna* is free from worldly desire. The external world, howsoever traumatic, leaves him unaffected as he is constantly steady, calm and serene. He neither accepts nor rejects the flux of life. This state is not one of passive watchfulness but is rather one of heightened awareness and wakefulness, perpetual in form.

Here it would be pertinent to examine the difference between a guru and a *sthithaprajna* in a worldly and demythified sense. A guru has grassroots wisdom and perceives life and its essence firsthand, thereby connecting the disciple with life as a whole. He has a marginal worldly role. Yogi Raushan Nath comments: "The guru—guide, friend and philosopher all rolled into one—guides your footsteps and helps you keep up human dignity. He initiates and helps you develop a philosophy of life [...]. He is a human [...]."[44] A *sthithaprajna*, on the contrary, inhabits a higher state of consciousness in which relationships and feelings, attachment and detachment, love and hate, etc., are conspicuously and totally absent. But the existence of the body (the temple of the spirit) cannot be denied and thus he is worldly though free of the quicksand of desire, the pursuit of illusion (*maya*). Som P. Ranchan states:

> Now a Sthithaprajna, in addition to being established in pure consciousness, is one who knows and experiences the depth and contingency of people and things with doors of perception which are not merely Blakean, but heightened, greatened, magnified. The knowing, the ontology and esthesis, earnestness and pathos, the eternity and transience involved, naturally, would be exact, penetrating, swift, particular and generalized, intimate and far-reaching.[45]

We can, therefore, clearly see that a *sthithaprajna's* elevated and evolved purity of being, is symbiotically linked with a divine perspicacity and a rich faculty of feeling. This is not a contradiction in terms that a *sthithaprajna* may have begun the spiritual journey as a *bhakta*.

Ranchan believes that a *sthithaprajna* does not necessarily have to be well-versed and well-grounded in the scriptures, but he is "established in the wisdom resulting from post-samadhic consciousness. As a result of it, there is the quality of impersonality about a Sthithaprajna."[46]

Ranchan's "impersonality" intersects Nirad C. Chaudhuri's "disinterestedness." A parallel may be drawn between the concepts of a *sthithaprajna* and a stoic with the latter's emphasis on self-control and indifference to pleasure or pain. dhury, however, goes too far when he categorically states; "It can be set down briefly that the doctrine of disinterestedness came from Stoicism [...]."[47] This assertion seems to have no historical basis, although the point of convergence or similarity is not denied. Talking about the process of creation in an interview published in the *Prajna,* Raja Rao stresses the point of impersonality:

> All creation is entirely impersonal [...]. The great writer sinks into the depths of impersonality. This comes not by contrivance but insight and perception and vibrant experience at the time of writing.[48]

This is not specifically a reflection of a *sthithaprajna,* but is rather one of the *sthithaprajna* sensibility. It, nevertheless, sheds lights on the ontological metaphor of *sthithaprajnahood* in which a *sthithaprajna* is perceived as a being as close to the Absolute as possible while inhabiting the body.

The *sthithaprajna* sensibility which is evident in Rao's stories with respect to his attitude and orientation imparts them depth and authenticity. This sensibility comes to life in the creation of characters such as Jhaveri Bai, Bhedia, Bhim, Rani Rasomani, Kanakapala and Gauri. In the story of Bhedia, Jhaveri Bai, the cow, forms a deep bond with the complex character Bhedia (the protagonist) who is somewhat abnormal. Bhedia relates to the esoteric world of mythology as well as the mundane world of cockfights. Bhedia, living at many levels is shown to be saintly, bearing good will to all, a man of the *sthithaprajna* mode. In the ninth story in *On the Ganga Ghat*, the protagonist, Rani Rasomani, a "husk-skinned aged woman in white sari, white hair sparse over her forehead with a fixed stare and saying her beads" (*OGG*: 86), remains completely lost in the Lord (Shiva) to the point of even forgetting her name. Though oblivious of the world of desire, she still recognizes Ma Anand Mayee, a great saint. Her devotion to Shiva is marked by frenzied religio-spiritual ecstasy.

The above-mentioned examples show that Raja Rao is a *samadrashta*—one who sees God in all creation. This is not possible without having acquired *samadrishti*—a state in which one perceives everything as equal, i.e., an acceptance of all, everything. *Samadrishti* precedes *samatabhava*—an inner state of pure being or consciousness—causing tranquility. Thus the *samadrashta* is a yogi who is an eternally burning candle, untouched and unaffected by the winds of desire, passion, love, hate, etc. In fact, Rao, steeped as he is in *samatabhava/samadrishti*, gives us a glimpse of the *Virata* (as postulated in the *Bhagvadgita*) through the world of his stories which consists of insects, birds, dogs, cows, monkeys, humans, natural vegetation along with innumerable other aspects of creation. This cosmic vision can be said to encompass the spectrum of *sthithaprajnahood* in particular, and that of Hindu tradition in general.

VI

Representation of Guru by Other Writers

The portrayal of guru or the presentation of the guru archetype by other Indo-Anglian writers like Mulk Raj Anand, R.K. Narayan and Kamala Markandaya is not as real and vibrant as that of Raja Rao. Rao's guru figures seem to exude intrinsic spirituality along the lines of Hindu tradition. Rao's personal life follows a traditional trajectory with all the formalities of the guru-disciple relationship being observed, resulting in a unique perception and assimilation of the guru archetype. Rao confesses that after writing *Kanthapura*, he felt dissatisfied and confused. In fact, he virtually gave up writing until he found his guru. This "brought about" *The Serpent and the Rope*.[49] This is not to suggest that one must follow the traditional guru-disciple relationship at all time to progress. At the same time, however, it cannot be denied that Rao's firsthand experience of connecting with a guru and his immersion in the guru-disciple relationship gave him a unique spiritual vision, which lends greater strength and stature to the guru figures in his short stories.

The other novelists mentioned above have merely touched upon the guru-disciple relationship, largely theoretical, without explicating its deep, experiential and practical implications. The guru's pivotal role in guiding, transforming and reshaping the disciple, has not been as effectively communicated. In *Possession*, for instance, Kamala Markandaya's portrayal of Swami is not intrinsically deep. In the novel Lady Caroline takes Valmiki (the protagonist) to be spiritually undeveloped and incapable of developing. But Swami (the guru) has faith in Valmiki, his disciple, and he states to Caroline that Valmiki "[...] will turn to God, unlikely though it seems to you now." The Swami goes on to state that his disciple will return to him and "it will not be the joyless void [...] it will be a homecoming."[50] The prediction comes true. The guru, however, is not convincingly drawn and the role and influence of the guru seem to be rather marginal as these merely highlight a facet or two of his (the guru's) being. Kamala Markandaya has merely scratched the veneer and has not delved deep into the archetype as such. Similarly, Mulk Raj Anand's Dr Mahindra (a doctor who also assumes the mantle of the guide, rescuer and protector of Gauri, the protagonist, inspiring her to independence) in *Gauri* is not convincingly portrayed and appears to be quite contrived. Though Anand is definitely more humanistic in character delineation than Rao, he lacks a real connection with guru archetype in the wider sense. This is reflected in the empirical nature of his work, which is painted on a societal canvas largely restricted to the world of the mundane. Rao, on the other hand, transcends the ordinary as he deals with different phases of consciousness, spiritual striving, and development, and its concomitant, inner being.

In R.K. Narayan's *The Guide*, Raju, the protagonist, a Jungian trickster archetype, masquerades as a holy man-cum-guru. The great role player plans, manipulates and pulls the proper strings to get by, thus living a richer and fuller life all by his wits.

Towards the end, he is accidentally trapped into a fast to propitiate Lord Indra. The fake guru is carried by circumstances like a river carries a log, to the state of being a nearly real guru. No doubt, Narayan employs drama much more effectively than Rao. One of the reasons for this is that Rao prefers a traditional canvas creating modern monomyths. Thus, Rao is timeless and transcends narrow cultural and geographical boundaries. Rao's gurus exercise a strong influence even when physically absent from the work; the actual presence of a guru is also a technique Rao uses well. Rao, a traditionalist, defines guru as the one who brings the highest knowledge in order to dispel the darkness of ignorance, thereby illuminating the disciple's path to enlightenment. Rao's immersion in and osmosis of mythology are pervasive and inseparable from the guru archetype, represented by Lord Shiva in Indian mythology.

It has already been stated that drama is not Rao's strong point but the 'river of reflection' mode of conveying the message embedded in the scriptures and spiritual practices transcends spatio-temporality, thus penetrating deeper in order to unfold rarely glimpsed dimensions. Narayan, Markandaya and Anand seem to have only a theoretical understanding of guru-disciple dynamics in general and the guru archetype in particular. Though far better employers of drama than Rao, their work does not ring with deep spiritual realization. Unlike them, Rao seems to have internally imbibed, harnessed and spotlighted spirituality. Thus Rao's *Vedanta* is not superimposed; it rather forms the very core of his fictional universe. This is perhaps why he has been a great writer far ahead of his contemporaries.

Notes

1. Akhileshwara Jha, *The Imprisoned Mind*, New Delhi: Ambika, 1980, p. 19.
2. This statement is not to be misconstrued to mean that the guru was a Western style manager or psychologist *à la* Freud. This clarification is essential because modern day analysis is necessarily tinged with a Western flavour due to the pervasive spread of Western influence,

particularly insofar as it is bulldozing the rest of the world, for better or worse.

3. Quoted in Ian Kesarkodi and Watson, *Studies in Hindu Wisdom*, New Delhi: Allied, 1981, p. 32.
4. Jha, p. 1.
5. Vishal Mangalwadi, *The World of Gurus*, New Delhi: Vikas, 1977, p. 10.
6. Quoted from *Sayings of Sri Ramakrishna: An Exhaustive Collection*, Madras: Sri Ramakrishna Math, n.d., p. 209.
7. Sri Aurobindo, *Letters on Yoga*—II, Pondicherry: Sri Aurobindo Ashram, 1979, p. 615.
8. Peter Brent, *Godmen of India*, London: Allen Lane/Penguin, 1972, p. 13.
9. C.G. Jung, *The Archetypes and the Collective Unconscious*, trans. R.F.C. Hull, Princeton: Princeton University Press, 1968, p. 217.
10. Nirad C. Chaudhuri, *Hinduism*, New Delhi: B.I. Publications, 1979, p. 303.
11. Swami Prabhvananda, *The Spiritual Heritage of India*, California: Vedanta, 1963, p. 147.
12. Debabrata Sen Sharma, *The Philosophy of Sadhana*, Karnal: Natraj, 1983, p. 96.
13. Quoted in Som P. Ranchan, *An Anatomy of Indian Psyche*, Delhi: Ajanta, 1987, p. 113.
14. Ibid.
15. Ved Sharma, ed., *A Profile in Creativity: Poet, Professor, Person: A Festschrift on Som P. Ranchan*, Delhi: Konark, 1992, p. 101.
16. Debabrata Sen Sharma, p. 96.
17. *Sayings of Sri Ramakrishna: An Exhaustive Collection*, pp. 210–11.
18. Jung, pp. 215–16.
19. Ibid., p. 35.
20. Ibid., p. 37.
21. Ibid., p. 217.
22. Ibid., p. 220.
23. Quoted in Som P. Ranchan, *An Anatomy*, p. 112.
24. Som P. Ranchan, *Revisioning Gita*, Delhi: Konark, 1991, p. 129.
25. Raja Rao, *The Serpent and the Rope*, Delhi: Orient Paperbacks, 1968, p. 5.
26. P.P. Mehta, *Indo-Anglian Fiction: An Assessment*, Bareilly: Prakash, 1979, p. 197.

27. K.R. Rao, *The Fiction of Raja Rao*, Aurangabad: Parimal, 1980, p. 67.
28. Raja Rao, p. 335.
29. Jung, p. 38.
30. K.R. Rao, p. 37.
31. According to M.K. Naik, "Tuesday is a day sacred to certain goddesses." M.K. Naik, *Raja Rao*, 1972; Bombay: Blackie & Son, 1982, p. 41.
32. K.R. Rao, p. 33.
33. Vasant A. Shahane, "Fiction and Reality in Raja Rao" in M.K. Naik, ed., *Perspectives on Indian Fiction in English*, New Delhi: Abhinav, 1985, p. 69.
34. Peter Brent, pp. 8–9.
35. Quote from *Aesop's Fables*, New York: Magnum, 1968, p. 100.
36. Debiprasad Chattopadhyaya, *Indian Philosophy: A Popular Introduction*, New Delhi: People's Publishing House, 1986, pp. 109–10.
37. Narsingh Srivastava, *The Mind and Art of Raja Rao*, Bareilly: Prakash, 1980, p. 137.
38. Jung, p. 216.
39. Ibid., p. 222.
40. Kesarcodi and Watson, pp. 34–35.
41. S. Radhakrishnan, *The Bhagvadgita*, New Delhi: Blackie & Son, 1976, p. 123.
42. Swami Prabhupada, 1972; rpt. *Bhagvad-Gita As It Is*, Mumbai: The Bhaktivedanta Book Trust, 1986, p. 144–45.
43. Shiv Niranjan, "An Interview with Raja Rao" in Krishna Nandan Sinha, ed., *Indian Writing in English*, New Delhi: Heritage, 1979, pp. 25–26.
44. Yogi Raushan Nath, *Hinduism and Its Dynamism*, New Delhi: Rakesh, 1987, p. 113.
45. Ranchan, *Revisioning Gita*, p. 112.
46. Ibid., p. 121.
47. Chaudhuri, p. 267.
48. Naik, p. 10.
49. Sinha, ed., p. 22.
50. Kamala Markandaya, *Possession*, Bombay: Jaico, 1967, p. 100.

CHAPTER 2

The Endless Quest: Multiple Dimensions

I
Quest as Monomyth

In common parlance the word 'quest' means search. This can be amplified to specifically include the act of seeking, pursuit, adventure, enquiry, investigation, etc. This chapter seeks to examine various kinds of quest in detail and their manifestation in Raja Rao's stories. The analysis of the quest motif has been attempted in the light of Jungian psychology with special reference to myth of the hero as enunciated by Joseph Campbell in *The Hero with a Thousand Faces*.

Raja Rao, well versed and well grounded in Hindu mythology, remoulds the quest motif, which is not only spiritual in nature, but also culture-specific. However, he manages to cross the narrow geographical, historical boundaries to create miniature monomyths that ring with universal truth. Interestingly enough, Raja Rao's life was somewhat akin to Campbellian quest journey of separation (leaving the land of his forefathers), initiation (formally by his guru but also a contact with the West), and return (re-discovery of the power of Hindu myths and their dissemination). In no case is it suggested that Rao was a Prometheus or a Vishwamitra. What is meant by using the terms—separation, initiation and return—is that this was Rao's inner psychic journey to connect with the self or, as Jung calls it, the collective unconscious.

Campbell passionately believes in the universality of myth being common to all cultures. To make the point clear, he uses James Joyce's term "monomyth."[1] Campbell's hero is a quester. Campbell informally uses psychoanalysis as a tool to bring out the meaning of myth and the hero's role in it. Lee T. Lemon defines a "monomyth" as the myth of the hero. Providing a generally accepted outline of the "monomyth," Lemon writes:

> [...] (1) he is born in mystery and/or danger; the son of either a deity or a great man, his parentage cannot be acknowledged and often his very birth must be concealed; (2) as an infant he is saved miraculously from death and raised by foster parents; (3) he shows signs of unusual ability, wisdom, or aristocratic bearing early in life (sometimes he is merely a misfit because of the discrepancy between his station in life and his inherited abilities); (4) he begins to sense vaguely his rightful place in society or nature (as king or god) but must undergo great danger in order to achieve his place; (5) his effort to attain what is rightfully his requires that he separate himself from society in order to demonstrate or acquire some quality (courage, wisdom or knowledge) or some talisman (a fleece, a magical apple, etc.); (6) he is aided and hindered by mysterious forces; (7) he returns triumphantly to society, where he assumes his destined role.[2]

Jung realized that modern man's psychosis was due in large measure to the fact that man had lost contact with the archetypes, the models of the intuitive ancient interpreters of the truth. Jung's collective unconscious can be seen in the light of racial memory and is indeed quite suggestive of the Hindu theory of the eternal wheel of birth, death and rebirth in which all past experience and memory, individual and collective, are stored. This is how and where Jung, Campbell, and Hinduism converge.

Now, it would be worthwhile to elaborate briefly the different types of quest as delineated (consciously or unconsciously) by Raja Rao in his stories. This analysis, however, does not have anything to do with the technical terms as specifically used in Sufism, Vedanta and Tantra; it rather aims at presenting a synthesis of different types of quest (e.g., Vedantic, Tantric and Sufic), thereby underlining their essential oneness.

Quest, as already defined, is a perennial urge in man to know the essence of being. Similarly, Vedantic quest may be understood as embarking on self-realization, i.e., the realization of the Absolute or Brahman. In other words, Vedantic quest may be taken as an entry into the 'self' that culminates in *samadhi* (complete absorption in the Absolute). Not infrequently, even *moksha* (deliverance) from the world of Maya is taken as a goal to be achieved in Vedantic quest. Describing salvation as a major concept in Vedanta, Saroj Kulshreshtha writes:

> In Sanskrit terminology, Mukti, Moksa, Kaivalya, Brahma-Samsaparsha, Nirvana, etc., are synonyms of the English word 'Salvation' or 'Release.' Of course, the connotations of all these terms differ from one another. Literal meaning of all these terms taken in a general sense is 'release from bondage to the sensuous and individual, the narrow and finite.' It also means release from worldly affairs, including man's desires, attachments and sufferings.[3]

In yet another sense, salvation is also understood as freedom from the endless cycle of birth-death-rebirth.

Raja Rao was an erudite philosopher who suitably presents in his fictional world the true Vedantic concept of Advaitam (non-duality), of the presence of One in all, and the world being the manifestation of Brahman. Vedantic quest, as a matter of fact, implies the quest to realize the soul or the self, which ultimately paves the way for the dissolution of illusions, ignorance and the ego-ridden personhood, finally culminating in the emergence of an enlightened self or Pure Consciousness.

The term 'sufism,' from the very beginning of Islam, is understood as a kind of mysticism, though more commonly it implies purity that comes through wisdom or holy spiritual exercises and renunciation of worldly desires and glories. Sufism is marked by intense love (*bhakti*) of and devotion to God. F.A. Klein points out that Vedanta school of thought had been a source of the ideas, ideals, and principles of Sufism.

> Sufism as it has developed in the course of time is, according to learned Orientalists, mainly borrowed from Indian philosophers of the Vedanta School. Its chief doctrines are that the souls of men differ in degree, but not in kind from the Divine spirit, of which they are emanations, and to which they will ultimately return [...].[4]

Sufic quest aims at exposing the quester to the hidden real inner self. This real self is then developed fully. Unlike *Yoga*, which suggests withdrawal from the phenomenal, fullness of living is propagated in Sufic quest: "Sufism is designed as the means to help awaken man [...]. Those who waken are able to return [not literally], to start 'the journey' while also living this present life in all its fullness."[5]

In Sufic quest, for the transformation and purification of the soul, a seeker has to undergo the first stage of *Sharqat* which means the company of a master (*murshid*). *Marfat,* the second stage is marked by, the thinning and refinement of personality of the seeker which is effected by the company of a *murshid*. This stage moreover, is in the service of *Barqat* (Grace) dispensed by the *murshid*. It also signifies the transformation of the seeker. J. Spencer Trimingham in his book *The Sufi Orders in Islam* mentions seven stages of the process of purification. He observes that:

> The aspirant has: (d_1) to purify his nafs, i.e., his personality-self, from its inclination to Shahavat, that is, the thoughts of desires of natural man, and (d_2) substitute these with love (mahabba), then (d_3) he must be cast into the flames of passion (ishq), to emerge (d_4) in the state of union (wusla), with (d_5) transmutation of self (fana), through (d_6) the gifts of dazzlement of wonder (haira), to (d_7) everlastingness (baqa).[6]

In "Companions," Raja Rao synthesizes Hinduism (represented by Pandit Srinath Sastri) and Sufism (represented by Moti Khan) and thereby suggests the essential convergence of the two religions. Moti Khan, the quester-protagonist first experiences anger, lust, carnality and vanity. He then acquires knowledge, patience, essential gentleness, and tranquillity of soul. Finally, he attains the wholeness of being and thus, in effect, completes the quest cycle.

Literally, 'Tantra' means to spread, to get across and also to weave (the roots *tan* and *tra* signify the knowledge or the power that spreads, saves, and gets one across towards transformation). Essentially, to use the terminology of Jung, Tantric quest is a seeking for one's special archetype of anima (*Devi*) or animus (*Deva*), represented by archetypal synergy of *Shiva-Shakti* in Indian mythology. Tantric quest (more specifically *sadhana*) is of three kinds—"physical, verbal and mental."[7] The physical operates at the level of body; the verbal is achieved through senses and the mental through the mind.

Raja Rao's cosmic vision of duality in non-duality is monomythic containing the polarities of the male and the female principles. This is represented by *Shakti-Shakta* in Tantra and it takes the form of awakened *Kundalini* in the process of *sadhak's* transformation.

> The materialistic and psychological spheres are Tantra's starting point and Absolute Reality is its final goal. The quest journey begins from the circumference towards the centre. The thread that binds these two becomes what in spiritual terms is called kundalini. Inert, it lies buried in Mooladhar, for it cannot enter the subtlest void of the Susumna, the central nerve. But when awakened, it assumes the form of Shiva-Shakti. When it is animated, from one thread of this 'creeper' shoot forth many filament which expand in to a mysterious 'tantu' (fabric).[8]

Shiva-Shakti is the operative word with respect to the previous assertion about Rao's cosmic vision of duality in non-duality with its delicately balanced Anima-Animus.

Basically in Tantric *sadhana*, mainly practical techniques are stressed in the quest for enlightenment. In this sense, Tantra is a method, a path to reach a definite and naturally the desired end, i.e., enlightenment, a state of perfect bliss, categorized as the wholeness of being. The importance of ritual practices has been highlighted as well by Agehananda Bharati in his book, *The Philosophical Content of Tantra*. He contends: "What distinguishes Tantric from other Hindu and Buddhist teaching is its systematic emphasis on the identity of the absolute (paramartha) and the phenomenal (vyavahara) world when filtered through the experience of Sadhana. Tantric literature is not of the philosophic genre; the stress is on Sadhana."[9]

As such, the ritual practices involved in Tantric Sandhana cannot be ignored, be they physical or external, psychic or mental. Ajit Mookerji and Madhu Khanna mention four stages[10] through which the highest state of human consciousness (complete merger with the Divine) can be attained. The first stage is purification in which the body and mind are purified on both the physical and mental levels; rituals such as the chanting of *mantras, nyasas* (physical postures) and purification of the *sadhaka's* environment (called *asana shuddhi*). The second stage is that of identification and internalization in which the object of worship is identified with and internalized so much so that it becomes a part of one's being. Rituals, in the form of *mudras* (gestures), concentration through the incessant intonation of *mantras*, and *pranayama* (breath-control) are performed. Thirdly, harmony and equilibrium between opposites (Anima-Animus) are achieved through proper regulation of the gross body via physical postures or sexo-yogic practices (*asanas*). And lastly, as a result of the balance achieved in the third stage, unity with the object sought comes about. In other words, it may be seen as analogous to the realization of the Absolute (*Shiva-Shakti,* the union of the divine male and female principles), the psychological equivalent of *coniunctio* which in Indian mythology is represented by Shiva-Parvati, Radha-Krishna; in Tibet Yab-Yum; in China Yin-Yang and in Jungian psychology Anima-Animus.

The destination of Tantric *sadhana* is almost the same as that of Vedantic quest which aims at the attainment of non-dual Pure Consciousness. Sir Henry John Woodroffe underlines the similarity between the essence of Tantric quest and that of Vedantic in the following lines:

> In what sense can, for example, Self and the Supreme Self be identified with each other? Tvam identified with Tat? It is absolute real (though ordinarily veiled) identity, according to Pure Advaitism (the realization being So'ham or Sa'ham). It is relative and pragmatic identity according to Visistadvaitism and the various forms of Dvaitism. Man is only the image of God; His part; and so on: there is real difference between Self

> and Supreme Reality (or Fact) which persists even when the former is without the veil. The Tantra as a Sadhana Sastra leads to the realization of So'ham or even beyond (i.e., the transcendental, a logical state beyond the polarity of Tat and Tvam), but in the discipline it provides, there is, to begin with, practical recognition of duality.[11]

In other words, the above-delineated quests constitute pure mana (a mysterious power), *mana* in animism, cosmic in scope and form wherein each dwells in the other. It is the microcosm in the macrocosm, vice versa and beyond. Transcendence is distinct, yet indistinct, immanent and all pervasive. To continue with Woodroffe:

> It is not enough in Philosophy to know continuity; by Sadhana we must realize it. As realized it is Amrtatva—Blissful Deathlessness. There are paths leading to Amritatva—through Science, through Art; through Philosophy; and through Sadhana, when we realize So'ham or Sa'ham (He or She am I).[12]

After having analysed different types of quest, it would be worthwhile mentioning that Raja Rao's vision as a short story writer, soaked as it is with an understanding of Vedanta, Tantra, mythology, folklore, various philosophical systems (Eastern as well as Western), and specifically Indian culture and tradition, is philosophical. This aspect has been critically evaluated by various critics such as C.D. Narasimahiah, M.K. Naik, S.C. Harrex, E.J. Kalinnikova and Narsingh Srivastava. P. Dayal of course differs from other critics and suggests that to see Rao as just an erudite Vedantin is to limit the sweep and perspicacity of his vision, the roots of which lie in Tantra. In the Preface to his *Raja Rao: A Study of His Novels*, Dayal points out that Rao "[…] collates and synthesizes Indian metaphysical tradition with corresponding Western motifs to form his Vedantic Tantric *Weltanschauung*." He further observes that:

> There is a little doubt that Raja Rao is susceptible to the influence of Vedanta. But to say that he is only a Vedantist is to limit his copious vision which is stimulated by Tantrism and certain strands of Western cultural tradition. To interpret Raja

Rao's fictional works without reference to Buddhist Tantrism and European influences may be a fruitless endeavour as he not only projects the Vedantic metaphysics but also portrays the Tantric philosophy in his novels.[13]

Many of Rao's stories, such as, "The Policeman and the Rose," "India: A Fable," "Companions," "The True Story of Kanakapala," "The Cow of the Barricades" and almost all the stories in *On the Ganga Ghat*, are lucid and effective, well-delineated parabolic expressions focusing on various dimensions of the aforesaid quests. For example, Moti Khan's quest in "Companions" may be seen in terms of the Sufic quest which culminates in his enlightenment through the help of a Hindu quester, Pandit Srinath Sastri (in his previous birth) who lives with the juggler (Moti Khan) as a snake-companion.

In Tantra, the snake symbolizes the *Kundalini* power, which, if awakened, helps the seeker to realize the Brahman (Pure Consciousness). In Indian mythology, it is symbolized by a serpent "[...] coiled into three and a half circles with its tail in its mouth and spiraled around the central axis or Swayambhu-linga, ready to ascend upwards and unite with the cosmic consciousness."[14] The snake-companion's help of Moti Khan on his path to self-realization is equated by Narsingh Srivastava with the awakening of *Kundalini* that helps Moti Khan find God. He observes:

> The snake also embodies the *Tantric* idea of *Kundalini* which has its head turned downwards till we are given to sensual desires and deeds, and turns upward for its movement through the six plexuses of the spine when we attain to liberation from sex and move forward in the direction of total liberation. The snake in the story becomes a companion of Moti Khan quite like the awakened *Kundalini* which works as a true and helpful companion of the God-seeker.[15]

Thus, to speak symbolically, Moti Khan's *Kundalini* is awakened and it facilitates his spiritual ascent through six *chakras* or psychic centres (*Muladhara, Svadhisthana, Manipura, Anahata, Vishuddha, Ajna*). It finally merges with *Sahasrar* (the seventh *charka* technically known as the thousand petalled lotus) which lies above the head, an equivalent of Vedantic Pure Consciousness. On the other hand, Vedantic quest underlies the total framework of *On the Ganga Ghat*. Rao's famous novel *The Serpent and the Rope* is primarily a statement on Vedanta philosophy in fictional terms.

II
Comparing Jung and Campbell

The quest motif is as old as time. It is common to all cultures—primitive, pre-historic ancient and modern—it may carry the spatio-temporal veneer of the specific environment, but underneath it, after ripping away the wrapped package, one comes face to face with the primordial monomyth bearing the stamp of the essential oneness of the psyche, East or West, Old World or New World. At the surface level, the quest is apparently naive and obvious: winning the hand of a princess, winning a battle, slaying the enemy, becoming a king, or finding the pot of gold at the end of the rainbow, etc. These examples are not meant to be taken lightly as they are deeds of heroism and in no way can they be profaned. The intention is to start from a literal basis to establish the psychological, psychic premise of the quest motif. Joseph Campbell is absolutely right in his assertion that the theme or the message of the monomyth transcends all cultures without being compromised in any way whatsoever. This view is rather too mystical for the common man bound to a culture-specific environment. Jung's thought, which is pragmatic in form and content, can be used to show how to reconnect with myth without totally disregarding empiricism. Campbell seems to have imbibed the spirit, reflection and aura of the ancient teachers he admires so much. In this regard, he can be likened to a modern mystic, a Shaman, the revealer of truths known by the ancients. These truths are *a priori* and thereby self-evident. Jung, however, was able to understand Shamanism. This is perhaps what made him propound the theory of the collective unconscious.

Now to deal with certain points of divergence and convergence between Jungian and Campbellian thought. Campbell, as compared to Jung believes in the superiority of the "ancients."

He categorically states that the "ancients" knew the truth of myth as their spiritual guides, teachers or Shamans (medicine-men) were in touch with what Jung calls the unconscious, individual and collective. As such, he seems to negate the modern empiricism. He also believes that the "moderns" can at the most equal the "ancients." Insofar as the question of the equality of the "ancients" and the "moderns" is concerned, Robert A. Segal makes a pertinent statement:

> 'Moderns' for Campbell have nothing to teach ancients, whom they can at most only equal. Psychoanalysis, then, is either a modern technique that ancients, directly in touch with myths, never needed or, less likely, a universal technique that ancients themselves employed.[16]

Segal further states that "The difference between ancients and moderns is that ancients had teachers, or 'sages,' to interpret myth psychologically. Until psychoanalysis moderns have had either no teachers or ignorant ones, ones who obtusely interpreted myth literally."[17]

The same idea is partially touched by Jung also when he states that "Mankind has never lacked powerful images to lend magical aid against all the uncanny things that live in the depths of the psyche. Always the figures of the unconscious were expressed in protecting and healing images and in this way were expelled from the psyche into cosmic space."[18] The terms such as "powerful images," "magical aid," "figures of the unconscious" and "protecting and healing images" throw light on different facets of the "ancients." However, this does not in any way suggest that Jung and Campbell are merely disguised versions of each other. They differ.

Jung's voice to link with the lost archetypes, the goal of which is holistic living and functioning (in society), was like a breath of fresh air, a lone candle in the empirical darkness of modern man, especially Western industrial man. But Jung, being child of industrialism, did not devalue materialistic, exterior living that heavily impacted on an average psyche. Because, for Jung, as Segal states, "[...] the initial focus of consciousness is the external [...] the goal of the first half of life [...]."[19] Thus we see that Jung is a firm believer in the everyday world of ego-consciousness which cannot be extricated from the self in totality. In other words, what Jung means to say, is that the "external world" (even if it is Advaitic *maya*) cannot be completely negated. He rather prefers "adjustment" (in the manner of total acceptance) to this world, which results in the actualisation of the Collective Unconscious (Pure Consciousness in Advaitic terms) that encompasses conscious, subconscious and personal unconscious.

Here Campbell seems to be in consonance with Jungian precept of ego-consciousness. The Campbellian hero (quester) bestows the boon on mankind to initially sublimate and consequently dissolve ego-consciousness, i.e., the trap of desire and its springs of joy and sorrow. As such, he states that the hero "[...] does not abandon life. Turning his regard from the inner sphere of thought-transcending truth [...] outward again to the phenomenal world, he perceives without the same ocean of being that he found within."[20] Consequently with the resultant perfected vision, separateness disappears and the hero "[...] is ever in the presence of his own essence [...]."[21] This concept of ego dissolution seems to be quite Brahminical and Buddhistic wherein the vital importance of individuality is negated as false. However, it should not be misconstrued that Campbell is negating individuality. It is forcefully contradicted when he reaffirms individuality as a dynamic force. The above-mentioned ego-extinction, emanating from a personalistic vision and the reassertion of individuality after touching the divine, may be taken as a self-enclosed cycle. It is analogous to the Hindu cycle of *Karma*, the ultimate goal of which is to complete the loop and liberate oneself from the cycle of corporeal existence. Thus, we see that for Campbellian hero, individuality is both the starting and the finishing line.

Seen comparatively, Jung's view regarding the reconnection with the archetypes of collective unconscious is an attempt to effectively counterbalance the conscious and the unconscious, and thereby enriching life and creating one's own individual myths in the personal journey of life. Robert A. Segal pertinently traces the difference between Jung and Campbell who essentially reach the same end, i.e., the realization of the self in totality:

> For both Campbell and Jung, myth functions above all to link humans to the unconscious. But they differ over the linkage. Campbell whose knowledge of the unconscious derives from reading myths, has a detached, imperious attitude toward the unconscious. He seeks to *use* myth to enrich human lives. Jung whose knowledge of the unconscious stems from a terrifying encounter with it has a warier and humbler stance. While he, too, seeks enrichment from the unconscious, he also fears the unconscious, which he realizes can overcome those who attempt to control it. Where Campbell can confidently advocate surrender to the unconscious, Jung, trepidatious at the prospect, promotes only a "dialogue" with the unconscious. Where Campbell assumes that the ego will somehow remain in place, Jung does not.[22]

Finally, by way of summing up, we may say that Jung is more of a modern than Campbell as he accepts empiricism and consistently stresses individuality. Jung is a seeker, knower and dispenser who makes arduous journey of life comprehensible for mankind. But the ego as a revelatory source of adjustment and transformation is his major premise around which the archetypes revolve interacting with human consciousness. A healthy ego is an operative principle, the goal being living in the everyday world of failure and success, joy and sorrow on all the three levels—unconscious, subconscious and conscious. The conscious level is the most dominant and relevant as it is the most concrete reality apropos of sense perception. Campbell, on the other hand, is a "primitive ritualist" who faithfully and totally subscribes to the myth. His unswerving belief in the intuitive, *a priori* truths of the ancients, makes him technically more of a wise old man than Jung. In fact, he does not question esoteric knowledge finding it to be self-evident. Jung is more of a hero, although a sceptic, compared to Campbell who evolved into *a* wise old man, but not *the* wise old man. The divergence and convergence of these two great masters can be summed up in one phrase: Jung is a quester; Campbell is a wise old man. In short, Campbell can be likened to a 'Cabirian ancient'[23] and Jung to a 'Cabirian modern.'

Let us now consider Jung's individuation process. In essence, individuation is a striving towards the attainment of the psychological wholeness of an individual. In other words, it stands for the evolution, organization, development and establishment of one's individuality. Individuation, as Robert A. Segal understands it, is an "ideal psychological state"[24] which is indivisible, whole, and complete in itself. Jung states, "I use the term 'individuation' to denote the process by which a person becomes a psychological 'in-dividual,' that is a separate, indivisible unity or whole."[25] In order to attain this state of psychological wholeness, one has to grapple with, and overpower the opposing forces (complexes) of the personal unconscious as well as to counterbalance the power and role of various archetypes of the collective unconscious. To further clarify the point, we may say that on his way to psychological wholeness (individuation or realization of the self), an individual (quester) may encounter various archetypes: of persons (or mask that stands between an individual's reality and society at large, or in other words, a means that makes one acceptable in the outer world); of anima-animus (the male and female principle, technically representing "the divine syzygia, the divine pair,"[26] anima representing feminine component in a male psyche, and animus being representative masculine component in a female psyche); of the wise old man (a personification of intelligence, wisdom, superior knowledge, enlightenment, etc. and the embodiment of the guru in Indian culture); and of the "self" (symbolic of wholeness, totality of being, and also analogous to the archetypes of 'meaning' and 'wholeness').

Thus, the process of individuation primarily aims at unfolding and understanding the personal unconscious and its superficial layers consisting of complexes. As such, after transcending the sphere of the ego, a larger consciousness is encountered which is an inseparable part of the individual psyche. During the individuation process, both the conscious and the unconscious poles of the psyche are freely allowed to have their way because if either is blocked, it may hinder the process of individuation. The racial memory, or the collective spirit of the ages and of time immemorial which constitute the ingredients of the collective unconscious, comes to a person through various archetypes of the collective unconscious.

However, this is not the end, psychological individuation is possible only if the 'uniqueness' of an individual and the collective unconscious are interfused. This element of 'uniqueness' remains absent in the Eastern concept of self-realization, or the Vedantic attainment of pure consciousness in which the individual (*jiva*) merges completely with Brahman. Jung equates individuation with a *process of differentiation,* which, however, aims at the "development of the individual personality."[27] By *differentiation,* Jung means "[...] the development of differences, the separation of parts from a whole."[28]

Thus the individuation process may be understood as a quest or a seeking for 'selfhood' or individual wholeness. This individuation process involves four major stages—catharsis, elucidation, education and transformation. Catharsis is characterized by the complete and total purgation through one's expression, which is an outcome of one's harsh and bitter experiences. It may result after one's liberation from his parental images, his family, so that he may grow freely to explore the world at large in an adventurous manner *à la* Campbellian hero. Elucidation is marked by sorting out various psychological intricacies, conflicts and shadow-complexes via a medium (person), or, following a model (in most cases the model is one's inner potential self). But it must be remembered that elucidation mostly is in the service of the better reconstruction of one's personality. In this very stage, one may also start questioning and examining things on one's own if guidance from parents or guides is not available. The third stage, i.e., education, is that of assimilation (*atmasatkarna*) of what is sorted out in the second leg of the individuation process. After the discovery of the shortcoming in the personality, new attitudes develop. This realization may dawn upon the individual through the encounter with the archetype of the wise old man who may appear in any form—teacher, doctor, or anyone possessing authority. At this stage, which is of course the most crucial one, a definite way is paved for a seeker, or, in other words, he gets the right direction. The last stage is that of transformation, in which the total personality changes; the psychic energy (which can be utilized for constructive purposes) of the quester is released; and one is established in the Self thereby becoming a psychological whole. The following excerpt encapsulates the individuation process in a nutshell:

> Individuation is a psychological "growing up" the process of discovering those aspects of one's self that make one an individual different from other members of his species. It is essentially a process of recognition—that is, as he matures, the individual must consciously recognize the various aspects, unfavourable as well as favourable, of his total self. The self recognition requires extraordinary courage and honesty but is absolutely essential if one is to become a well-balanced individual.[29]

The quester is the hero; the hero is the quester. The quest in its ultimate form is for the inner being. However, the basic quest is that of survival. The quest of the prehistoric man, for instance, was for food, shelter, clothing, and a mate—food being the most important. The cave man literally ate to live and lived to eat. The process of transcending this raw, vulnerable state of nature and her majesty began to shift with the gradual invention of implements. Thus man compensated for physical weakness in comparison to the other members of the animal kingdom. The discovery of fire was a quantum leap in man's evolution and ability to adapt and survive. This is aptly illustrated in the Greek myth of the Titan Prometheus who stole fire from the gods to benefit man. The hero's punishment, was perennial, and also heroic as he was chained to a rock and an eagle would eat his heart without actually providing the relief of death. Quest has been inseparable from man from the time immemorial. It is innate, timeless, and primordial and takes on many undertones such as survival, glory, fame, mating, religion, philosophy, spirituality, and so on. This is common to all cultures.

In order to clearly understand the modern quest (especially Jungian and Campbellian), it is essential to examine quest in terms of modern Western civilization. Western man seems to have lost touch with the roots in a too compressed span of time. The general environment is marked by a frenzied activity which has vitiated the psyche and has desecrated the archetypes. Old values have been destroyed without any suitable replacement. The result is complete anomie which but naturally results in crises—the most important one being the personality crisis or more aptly, identity crisis. As such, the modern man's quest is what Erik Erikson calls the "quest for identity."[30] Despite this pervading gloom, however, Western man has somehow managed to cope remarkably well through the assertion of individuality. The assertion, reassertion, and development of individuality may be taken as the first step towards individuation process. The identity-quest, in fact, culminates in what Karl Jaspers calls "being-in-itself" (a term that signifies the authentic, self-contained and holistically realized Being of a person whose "existence" points towards the indefinable experience of freedom and possibility thereby making him aware of "the encompassing" by facing the trials and tribulations of life. This term was earlier used by Martin Heidegger, Jean-Paul Sartre and Simone de Beauvoir). The identity quest overtly seems to be personalistic, however, it builds the very foundation of the quest for inner being or Jungian wholeness.

III
Campbell's Quest Cycle

In this context let us take a brief overview of Campbell's quest cycle in terms of stages. The first stage is that of *separation*. It is marked by the severing of the bond of family, home, and the known, in response to the primordial, "mythic summons." The second stage, *initiation*, is marked by the hero's contact with novelty, its unfamiliarity and danger which bring about a new *weltanschauung*. The third and final stage, *return* is characterized by the hero's rediscovery of the old truths and values, somewhat different now in the light of uninsulated experience. The hero is thus enabled to make a meaningful contribution to the community, nay, society at large. In addition to these three stages, there are two intermediate phases of the wounded. The first occurs at the time of separation as it is a trauma, an inalienable wounded feeling resulting from the hero's dissociation from his roots. The second phase of the wounded state precedes, and is inseparable from a return. It requires great courage, indomitable will, and a burning desire to return to one's roots and be acknowledged by the old world. It is an immensely difficult task as, at times, the one returning is viewed lightly. Moreover, this return metaphorically signifies the climax of the hero's journey. The term 'wounder' in Jungian sense means a hero, who has successfully crossed the bridge of demons, pain and anguish thereby becoming able to empathize with others and be of help to those undertaking a similar quest. Thus, the 'wounded wounder' is a healer of immense power and grandeur along with being a great facilitator to those who dare to undertake the heroic quest. In Jungian terms, he is the wise old man.

The hero's quest is not devoid of inspiration and guidance. The guide is the wise old man, who may appear in any form—human, animal or divine. The encounter may be physical, in the 'real world' or even manifested in a dream, or in a state of trance, or any other form of consciousness. It may be in the world beyond, or it may be an experience of the paranormal and the occult. Moderns have of late begun to touch upon this aspect in the relatively newer science of parapsychology. But this intuitive truth was known to, worshipped, and disseminated by the ancients. Jung and Campbell are the modern pioneers of rediscovering, recreating and shedding light on the truths of the ancients, long lost and hidden beneath the crusty layers of exteriority and empiricism. This does not mean that they came upon a lost package, simply unwrapped it, and displayed it for all to see. The myth never dies. It is perennial. The monomyth, too, is immortal, timeless and chimes perennially with eternal truth, *a priori* and empirical, though not culturally restrictive. The myth-makers (such as Campbell's sages and Jung's wise old men) are not dead—neither are the ancient teachers, nor the modern ones. The ancients live in the myths. But that is not all. The myth-makers also breathe and eat in the modern age. They live amongst us.

Here, it is important to differentiate between the wise old man and the hero. The wise old man is a spiritual savant and empirically transcendental. He is the torch-bearer for the hero in his quest. The wise old man may be a quester, but his esoteric mystical knowledge may also have been gained through dreamless encounters with self via the practice of Yoga, rumination, reflection or ethereal imagination. The hero, however, has to encounter naked danger and to conquer it by burning ambition for the quest. The hero has the capability to become a wise old man, but the latter may not necessarily be of heroic proportions. Thus it is more likely that the hero transforms himself into the wise old man, but the reverse is not necessarily true. The hero, as an inspiration is necessarily corporeal, whereas the wise old man can be whole phenomenon simultaneously inhabiting the concrete world. In general however, with respect to being an inspiration for the mass of humanity, the wisdom of the hero embedded in courage/adventure is the beacon that most of mankind is also to understand and follow. The hero is part and parcel of popular culture in which the wise old man represents too abstruse a concept for the layman to emulate. The hero is concrete and thus can serve as the first step of the journey to 'wise-old-manhood.' The hero, a pragmatist, may often serve as the spokesman of the wise old man's knowledge. But the hero decides, follows, and makes his own trajectory to spread the spiritual message. The most relevant and dramatic example is that of Ramakrishna's Mahasaraswati (wise old man) and Vivekananda's Mahakali (the hero).

IV
Rao as a Myth-Maker

In the manner of James Joyce, Dostoevsky, and Hemingway, Raja Rao too has been a mythmaker and cartographer, although his stories (modern monomyths) are not so dramatic but turn on equanimity. He in fact, emerges as a fashioner of the ancient Hindu myths. He has been highly derivative[31] and a firm-believer in the physical presence of the wise old man. Moreover, as an important mythmaker his work is an embodiment of the link with the past to show the ancient intuitive truth to mankind today. His stories possess a serene poise (e.g., "The Policeman and the Rose," the story of Bhim and the story of Sudha in *On the Ganga Ghat*) which run like a gently flowing stream of thoughts in the mind, the self, the inner being.

The apparent lack of heroism and the absence of extreme drama is deceptive as the stories unfold subtly and tenderly like a slowly blooming lotus. The lack of heroism and drama in the traditional sense does not mean that they are "anti-myths," rather a recreation-cum-transcreation in form (*roopa*) and message. Despite their tradition, Rao's stories are original creations which can be interpreted as nascent legends which crystallize into myths, modern monomyths. For instance, in "The True Story of Kanakapala" Raja Rao vibrantly images and recreates the myth of the serpent as the protector of gold. The serpent signifies the virtues of truth, sincerity, honesty and righteousness. According to Meenakshi Mukherjee:

> The material Raja Rao works with is [...] quite different [...]. His method is that of mythologizing contemporary reality. His gifts as a myth-maker can be seen even in his early short stories [...]. The two serpent stories in it, "Companions" and "Kanakapala," are most certainly made up of the elements of a folk legend or myth: a dream vision, a curse, a quest, fulfillment and finally something tangible (a tomb, or a temple) as testimony to the truth of the legend.[32]

Now, before we examine the stages of Rao's questers, let us briefly outline some mythological quest-adventures—two from the *Upnishads* and one from famous gypsy folklore—that bring into light variegated facets of the quest process. It is also intended to discuss side by side the universality of the quest motif.

The *Chandogya Upnishad* is the receptacle of the celebrated story of Satyakama Jabal. Acharya Gautam (the great guru), after making some enquiries about his (Satyakama's) caste and family background is impressed by the child's sincerity, honesty and truth-consciousness. Subsequently Gautam initiates the child, and gives him four hundred weak and frail cows and bulls to tend. Satyakama Jabal undertakes a vow of not returning until the number of the cows increases to one thousand. And surprisingly enough, Satyakama returns with a thousand cattle. As a result, the guru, pleased with Satyakama's devotion, dedication and commitment, tells the young boy that his face is shining like

"Brahmajnanis" (knowers of the Absolute Truth/Brahman). In a sense, the *teja* (divine halo/light/visible aura) on Satyakama's *mukhamandala* (face) symbolizes spiritual enlightenment. Finally, Satyakama offers himself on the holy feet of his guru and thus is given the knowledge of the Absolute that makes him perfectly enlightened.

Rao has also recreated exuberantly the same myth through the story of Narsiga who is an orphan and perchance reaches the Master's abode (*ashrama*) where he gains spirituality. The Master's brother (also a guru figure) rescues Narsa from the ruthless clutches of his "angry and effusive" aunt, and helps him become self-dependent by providing him sheep to tend. As such, Narsiga becomes an earning person and starts tending the sheep of Rangayya, uncle Sampanna and carpenter Sidayya on payment basis. Narsiga delights in this job and relates to the cattle freely and independently, and thus confidently progresses on his path to spirituality.

Similarly, other mythic characters like Savitri and Nachiketa can be taken as model questers in Indian mythology. Their ceaseless endeavours and difficult struggle to comprehend the unfathomable mystery of death are remarkable. Nachiketa's story is found in the *Kathopanishad* in which he is a prince who protests against his father's (king Udyalaka's) deceiving the priests and God by offering them sickly and unworthy cows as offerings for a great *Yajna* (an oblation or a religious rite) at the royal palace. Nachiketa observes this all and feels agitated. He asks his father thrice whom would he (Nachiketa) be given to. Udyalaka, the king, becomes infuriated and declares that he has decided to give his son (Nachiketa) to Yama, the Lord of Death. Nachiketa, a dutiful son, obeys his father and takes his leave, goes to Yama, and becomes a quester par excellence, bent upon knowing the secret of self-knowledge (*atma-jnana*). At the beginning, Yama asks him to demand anything else except the secret of self-knowledge. But Nachiketa adamantly and courageously sticks to his demand. After realizing the intensity and firmness of Nachiketa's resolve to seek the knowledge of the self, Yama removes the mayavic veil covering the Absolute, the Ultimate Truth. Thus Nachiketa's quest journey bears fruit, resulting in his enlightenment.

In the story "The Princess from Ice Mountain,"[33] a gypsy folk tale, Fedma, a wealthy man, spurns the affections of the princess of the kingdom, preferring to pursue the cold, beautiful Princess of Ice Mountain. On the way, he rescues the gypsy Rojeo, his identical double, from the hangman's noose. The grateful Rojeo, a celibate (*brahmachari*), a man of great strength, accompanies Fedma and wins the Ice Princess' hand for him in her powerful giant brother, Hormond's presence. Rojeo also simultaneously destroys the source of the Princess' magical powers by a feigned accident. On the way home, Rojeo, through esoteric knowledge, evades death twice. In Fedma's room he (while masquerading as Fedma) saves Fedma's child from the clutches of a giant bird, an agent of evil Hormond. A misunderstanding develops, compounded by Fedma's revelation to the Princess that Rojeo actually won her hand for him (Fedma). Rojeo, no longer welcome, leaves Fedma's house for Ice Mountain. He learns of Hormond's weakness through trickery, gains all of Hormond's strength, kills him and loots the palace.

Now rich, Rojeo returns and marries the princess of the kingdom and soon afterwards becomes king. As king, he tells Fedma unthinkingly of the esoteric knowledge of Ice Mountain. The subsequent curse of revelation begins to turn him to ice and he frantically tells Fedma that only the blood of his (Fedma's) child can save him. Fedma meets the test and Rojeo is saved. Misunderstanding vanishes and the two friends and families live happy and contented from that time onwards.

Thus we see that in the aforementioned quest adventures, the essential oneness, or, the universality of quest is evident. Basically, the quest is the same, though its manifestations vary. Nachiketa and Satyakama may be taken as the models of the Eastern quest whereas Fedma and Rojeo represent the Western quest. Satyakama and Nachiketa's quest is centred on the realization of the inner self, whereas Fedma and Rojeo's quest has materialistic advancement as its focus. The Western quest, in fact, is "quest for identity" in which the focus is more on carving out a niche for oneself in the world of day to day realities. Viewed comparatively, the Eastern quest primarily aims at the attainment of inner knowledge or the realization of Self. Similarly, in Rao's stories, the quest is primarily to attain enlightenment, or to realize the essence of being. It is, in fact, far removed from the Western quest for materialistic advancement and for proper placement in the society. Like Nachiketa's, the Eastern quest transcends mayavic exteriority and aims at the realization of the essence of being.

V
Rao's Questers: Their Stages of Growth

Rao's stories abound with different types and forms of mythic quest. This may be illustrated by analyzing in detail the stages in the quest journey of some of Rao's representative questers in the light of Campbell's elucidation of quest-cycle in *The Hero with a Thousand Faces*. Hosakere Rangappa in "The True Story of Kanakapala" becomes Vision Rangappa after a vision of Kashi Vishweshwara (Lord Shiva) and his divine consort (Goddess Paravathi). Vision Rangappa has completed the quest cycle *à la* Joseph Campbell. Hosakere Rangappa, after joyfully receiving a "mythic summons" leaves his home (representative of roots, a comfortable womb; separation is the first and the most difficult step in the quest journey), undertakes a pilgrimage to Kashi Vishweshwara (symbolic of his quest for spiritual enlightenment) that is cut short by an initiating vision of Lord Shiva and Mother Parvathi. The vision transforms him. He then returns home, enlightened and self-realized. It can be affirmed by what the Divine Couple (Lord Shiva and Parvathi) reveals in Vision Rangappa's dream:

> 'We have been touched by your indestructible devotion, and we show ourselves unto you that you may be protected from the blisters of pilgrim ploddings and the pinches of the weary spirit. You are sanctified by our holy presence. Your pilgrimage is now over. But on the top of the hill before you there raise unto us a temple that we may sprout through the earth and live for ever amidst unfailing worship. Your duty is to look after the temple, and generation after generation of your family will be beloved of us. May our blessings be on you.' (*P&R*: 3–4)

Thus, Vision Rangappa after attaining enlightenment returns to make a meaningful contribution to his community like Joseph Campbell's archetypal hero who serves, enriches and enlightens not just a community but also the society or the whole humanity. The return is not necessarily literal but is a symbol of personality development of which, diffusion and dissemination of the divine power is vital, and inseparable. It embodies myth, its significance and majesty. It cannot be repressed once the cosmic and dynamic divine energy is released. It is innate in existence and just needs a spark from the unconscious to ignite it.

Moti Khan, the protagonist-quester in "Companions," unlike Vision Rangappa, does not have a natural urge to seek God; he is rather forced in this direction by a snake-companion who was Pandit Srinath Sastri in the previous birth. The snake-companion tyrannically goads the reluctant quester (Moti Khan) to actively seek God. Moti Khan has to surrender to this form of despotism and he does as the self-appointed guru commands. Through this imposition and subsequent action (the quest journey), Moti Khan gets in touch with the self, the inner being, which culminates in his enlightenment.

Regarding Moti Khan's submission to coercion, which he eventually realizes, is for his own benefit. K.R. Rao states:

> Moti Khan, the juggler, goes from place to place in search of God, so that he may vanquish the festering demon within himself and find his ultimate peace. Clearly he can achieve this only by stepping out of his own confused self-hood with the grace of a 'Guru' [...]. The experience of vision through the ordeal of the flesh and the creative suspension of the self is vividly focused.[34]

As such, Moti Khan, after finding God returns to society and, as suggested by Sheikh Chisti, marries the beautiful daughter of Maulvi Mohammed Khan, settles down in Fatehpur Sikri and becomes the guardian of Sheikh Chisti's tomb. Thus, Moti Khan completes his adventurous quest cycle.

In "The Policeman and the Rose" the narrator-quester is an intellectual. He realizes the essence of Truth in the kingdom of Travancore, the abode of his guru. But here the stage of return is absent. As such, he may be seen as the one who has been through with the second stage of *initiation* and is yet to accomplish the traumatic return with his hard-acquired insight, wisdom, and essence of human existence.

In *On the Ganga Ghat*, all the protagonists are seekers of salvation having reached the last phase of their quest journey. Muthradas from Vrindavan, for example, has not yet attained enlightenment though he has already been initiated on this path of self-realization by his guru Sankaranandji. Here, Rao remarks: "He [Muthradas] had not yet discovered the true similarity between the waking state and the dream state, but there are still so many life cycles to come [...]" (*OGG*: 46). Thus Muthradas' struggle for seeking salvation has just commenced.

Nanna, the Panjabi prostitute in the ninth story, like Ranchoddoss Sunderdoss in the tenth, has just begun her quest-journey, whereas Sudha, on the contrary, has completed her quest cycle and has now returned to make a meaningful contribution in the community that she hails from. This is evident to the reader when he sees that she reads out the *Vasista Ramayna* to the devotees of the Lord who listen to her devoutly. Sudha herself elucidates her enlightened state: "She was no scholar, she explained, but she understood, because of the Grace of her Guru, the nature of what people say is the most difficult of all things in philosophy—Shankara's theory of Mayavada" (*OGG*: 121–22). She also has the capability of answering the earnest queries regarding "the serpent and the rope, or the dream and waking states" (*OGG*: 123).

Thus we see that there is no refusal to *return* on Sudha's part. She rather accepts it gladly and returns in accordance with the guidelines given by her Guru's Satguru in Badrinath to carry on the readings of *Vasista Ramayana*. Sudha, who is described as a "sincere soul," once enlightened, initiates her father too on the same path. As such, Ranchoddoss has stepped into the second stage of his quest. This stage puts one in touch with certain abstruse and unknown domains of truth, displacing the ego, which is the biggest hurdle on the path of attaining the wholeness of being. The successful quest has a dramatic climax. Ranchoddoss eulogizes the Lord singing the great sage Shankara's words:

> The cessation of all mental activities is the supreme peace—that is the holiest of all holy places of pilgrimage, the Manikarnika (in me); the ever-flowing stream of knowledge is the pure primeval Ganges (in me); (thus) I am the Kashika, of the form of pure Consciousness of Self. (*OGG*: 123)

Another persistent motif in the world of Rao's stories is that of death-rebirth which becomes more relevant if seen in the context of the process of quest. Rao's characters (like himself) believe in the cycle of 'birth-death-rebirth' before accomplishing liberation from this endless cycle. The story of Bhim, in *On the Ganga Ghat*, highlights this motif through the portrayal of Bhim, the Siddha who was Queen Prabhavati in his previous birth: "And of course Bhim was Prabhavathi, and her companion (who soon joined him) was born as Rupvati" (*OGG*: 21).The only reason for Bhim's becoming a Siddha is that he (as Prabhavati), was fully devoted to God. Rupvati, Bhim's wife, on the contrary, is not enlightened because she was too attached to the Queen resulting in the exclusion of God. Even when she bathed herself in the Ganga, she was only concerned with "the pride of her palace surroundings, bells, carpets and elephant—trumpetings [...]" (*OGG*: 21). Like Muthradas from Vrindavan who has not yet fully understood the complexity of waking and dream states, Rupvati is yet to attain enlightenment; she is fated to be reborn: "[...] there are still so many life cycles to come" (*OGG*: 46). In the tenth story, Sudha recalls her previous incarnation as a wife deeply in love with her husband. Upon her husband's death, Sudha found that she loved him more than "[...] she did God Himself" (*OGG*: 116). During his lifetime, her husband was a devoted disciple of a great guru. She is unsuccessful in contacting this guru as he has expired. The disciple, upon whom the guru's mantle falls, gave her a secret mantra as a guru. Despite the esoteric mantra she died without "even having intimation of His Holy Presence" (*OGG*: 116). She is born to Ranchoddoss in this birth and thus resumes the quest in the present birth (*janma*). Marriage is out of the question in this lifetime since she has already lived a married life. Ranchoddoss Sunderdoss' story spans many incarnations. Ranchoddoss Sunderdoss, unlike his materialistic sons, loves to read the *Vishnu Purana* and *Bhagavatham*. His favourite myth described a mythic king, who in the decaying years of his life, loses interest in the splendorous world and gets attached to a deer. He is born a deer in his next birth because "You are reborn as your last thought be" (*OGG*: 117). Even as a deer he is spiritually evolved and clearly recalls his past life. He is born a Brahmin after this and becomes a palanquin bearer of king Suvera. In this life he realizes life's true essence. This is evident in the following statement:

> 'Just as the universally distributed air, going through the holes of a flute, makes for the variegated melodies with sariga, sariga notes and all that, yet all this is but one piece of bamboo. There is no I, there is no you.' (*OGG*: 118)

In this way the Brahmin is freed from the cycle of birth, death and rebirth.

In the story of "The Cow of the Barricades," Gauri, the cow is a seeker on her way to salvation. Truth and compassion foreshadow her rebirth as a holy man, ascetic or monk. This is due to her status as an evolved *karmayogini* (one who believes in deeds). Rao's description is most apt: "And Gauri was no doubt a fervent soul who had sought the paths of this world to be born as a sage in the next, for she is so compassionate and true" (*CBS*: 175). Gauri's altruistic sacrifice for humanity is the climax, but she continues to live in the hearts of the people and the Master assures them: "Gauri is waiting in the middle of heavens to be born. She will be reborn when India sorrows again before she is free" (*CBS*: 182).

The death-rebirth motif with its underlying principle of quest has been beautifully worked out in the story "Companions" in which the snake-companion, Pandit Srinath Sastri of Totepur in its previous birth was a great *bhakta* (devotee) of Goddess Lakshamma. But unfortunately, he becomes a victim of avarice when offered two boons by the Goddess. He begged for "A bagful of gold and liberation from the cycle of birth and death" (*P&R*: 29). He was, anyhow, granted these spiritually contrary boons. This blunder leads to his rebirth as a serpent who is nevertheless devoted to God as well as chastened by his devotion in the previous lifetimes. He facilitates Moti Khan's spiritual growth, is, indeed, its veritable vehicle. Karma is his divine guide.

However, he is born a serpent in the next birth and thereby strives to attain liberation. He also becomes a vehicle, a means for Moti Khan, the juggler's salvation. Not only that, Moti Khan has got to liberate himself from the fetters of carnal desires to resume his quest journey from the point he left it in his previous birth when he was a true and committed seeker of God.

According to M.K. Naik, "Companions" "[...] is another story of vision, curse, miracle, rebirth and expiation."[35] Narsingh Srivastava also hints at the death-rebirth motif by stating that:

> Employing a legendary theme and a narrative of the folk-lore style, "Companions" presents a triumph of the metaphysical symbolism of redemption from the cycle of Karma and this liberation from the bondage of life and death or attainment of God—the supreme reality.[36]

The serpent's and Moti Khan's relationship is reciprocal in nature. Each helps the other to progress spiritually. Similarity and dissimilarity are seen as complementary, and in fact, two sides of the same divine coin. K.R. Rao realizes this and effectively presents it when he points out the "[...] mysterious adjacence and interaction of facts and experiences actually incongruous and incompatible in themselves, but unified at the moment of spiritual realization."[37]

Finally, it is worth mentioning that the stages of Rao's questers on their journey have been examined mainly in the light of Campbellian quest cycle. Jungian individuation process has not been touched upon as its applications will be dealt with in detail in the following chapter.

Notes

1. Joseph Campbell was a renowned scholar of James Joyce. He borrowed the term "monomyth" from Joyce's *Finnegans Wake*, New York: Viking Press, Inc. 1939, p. 581. It usually refers to the journey of the hero, which is cyclical in nature as enunciated by Joseph Campbell in *The Hero with a Thousand Faces* (1949). With the help of various myths based on his exploration and understanding of numerous world mythologies and religions of mankind, and, through clarity of perception and simplicity of delineation,

Campbell brings forth the universality of "monomyth." Tracing the mythological adventure of the hero Campbell evolved a formula which has a ring of universality and which he described as "the nuclear unit of the monomyth." According to him, "A hero ventures forth from the world of common day into a reign of supernatural wonder: fabulous forces are there encountered and a decisive victory is won: the hero comes back from this mysterious adventure with the power to bestow boons on his fellow man." See Joseph Campbell, *The Hero with a Thousand Faces,* Princeton: Princeton UP, 1949, p. 30.

2. Lee T. Lemon, *A Glossary for the Study of English,* Delhi: Oxford UP, 1974, p. 105.
3. Saroj Kulshreshtha, *The Concept of Salvation in Vedanta,* New Delhi: Ashish, 1986, p. 8.
4. F.A. Klein, *The Religion of Islam,* New Delhi: Kitab Bhawan, 1977, pp. 233–34.
5. Idries Shah, *Thinkers of the East,* London: Penguin, 1971, p. 196.
6. J. Spencer Trimingham, *The Sufi Orders in Islam,* London: Oxford University Press, 1971, p. 155.
7. Arthur Avalon, ed., *Principles of Tantra,* Madras: Ganesh, 1960, p. 124.
8. Ramakant Sharma Angiras, *Trilogy of Tantra,* Karnal: Natraj, 1989, p. 114.
9. Agehananda Bharati, *The Tantric Tradition,* London: Rider, 1969, p. 18.
10. Ajit Mookerjee and Madhu Khanna, *The Tantric Way: Art, Science, Ritual,* Delhi: Vikas, 1977, pp. 127–28.
11. John Woodroffe, *The Word as Power,* Madras: Ganesh, 1957, p. 398.
12. Ibid.
13. P. Dayal, *Raja Rao: A Study of His Novels,* New Delhi: Atlantic, 1991, p. 3.
14. Mookerjee and Khanna, *The Tantric Way,* p. 68.
15. Narsingh Srivastava, *The Mind and Art of Raja Rao,* Bareilly: Prakash, 1980, p. 134.
16. Robert A. Segal, *Joseph Campbell: An Introduction,* 1987; rpt. New York: Penguin, 1990, pp. 31–32.
17. Ibid., p. 37.
18. C.G. Jung, *The Archetypes and the Collective Unconscious,* trans. R.F.C. Hull, Princeton University Press, 1968, p. 12.
19. Segal, p. 262.
20. Joseph Campbell, *The Hero with a Thousand Faces,* Princeton: Princeton University Press, 1968, p. 165.

21. Ibid., p. 386.
22. Segal, p. 262.
23. From 'cabiri,' a plural noun [Latinised from Greek Kabeiroi], signifying "a group of gods, probably of Eastern origin, worshiped in mysteries in various parts of ancient Greece, the cult centres being at Samothrace and Thebes." See *Random House Unabridged Dictionary*, Random House, Inc. 2006. These were also known as "ancient mystic divinities," *Chamber's Twentieth Century Dictionary, 1959*. 'Cabirian,' and 'cabiric' are adjectival forms of 'cabiri,'/'cabeiri.'
24. Ibid., p. 261.
25. Jung, *The Archetypes and the Collective Unconscious*, p. 275.
26. C.G. Jung, *Psychology and Religion*, New Heaven: Yale UP, 1964, p. 34.
27. C.G. Jung, *Psychological Types or The Psychology of Individuation*, London: Kegan Paul, Trench, Trubner, 1946, p. 561.
28. Ibid., p. 539. Jung is quite logical in this regard. For him "individual standpoint" may be "differently oriented" but is certainly not "antagonistic to the collective norm." Moreover, this leap into the process of individuation may at best be construed as beginning of the realisation of the Self, which is cosmic as well as collective in character. To quote Jung: "Since the individual is not only a single, separate being but, by his very existence, also presupposes a collective relationship, the process of individuation must clearly lead to a more intensive and universal collective solidarity, and not to mere isolation," pp. 562–63.
29. Wilfred L. Guerin et al., *A Handbook of Critical Approaches to Literature*, New York: Harper & Row, 1966, p. 137.
30. See Segal, p. 34. Also see Erik H. Erikson, *Young Man Luther*, New York: Norton, 1958.
31. The term 'derivative' is not used in a pejorative sense, Cf. Emerson: "The greatest genius is the most indebted man." "Shakespeare or The Poet" in Edmond D. Jones, ed., *English Critical Essays*, 1916; rpt. Delhi: Oxford University Press, 1984, p. 458.
32. Meenakshi Mukherjee, *Twice Born Fiction*, New Delhi: Arnold-Heinemann, 1971, p. 139.
33. M. Voriskova, *Gypsy Folk Tales*, London: Paul Hamlyn, 1967, pp. 147–62.
34. K.R. Rao, *The Fiction of Raja Rao*, Aurangabad: Parimal, 1980, p. 38.
35. M.K. Naik, *Raja Rao* 1972; Bombay: Blackie & Son, 1982, p. 40.
36. Narsingh Srivastava, p. 133.
37. K.R. Rao, p. 38.

CHAPTER 3

Quester-Characters in Rao's Stories

I

Rao's Character-Questers vis-à-vis Jung and Campbell

Raja Rao's portrayal of his character-questers is steeped in the cultural heritage of India. Before examining Rao's characterization, it will be of help to recapitulate the Campbellian quest cycle along with its Jungian application. Moreover, the literary mould of Rao's personal quest as a *sadhak* (for whom writing had been a *sadhana* all his life) will also be taken up followed by a critical discussion regarding his quester-characters' spiritual growth as depicted in the world of his short stories.

Campbell's quest whether conscious or unconscious, whether the hero actively seeks it or is initially drawn into it by chance, is of heroic nature. Separation, the first step of the heroic quest, 'a journey of a thousand miles,' is like leaving the insular womb of family, culture and society that signify his roots to begin the process of recognizing, identifying, and if successful, merging with being eventually. Separation is followed by initiation. Initiation may take the simple form of guidance by an entity usually more sagacious in an *a priori* sense, as well as empirical. Or the quester may, on the other hand, be counselled and shown the path by the unfolding of phenomena itself (i.e., the totality of phenomenal world), which is perceived, consciously or unconsciously, during the search or adventure. If the initiation is successful, then the next stage is that of return. After winning the princess' hand and slaying the dragon, the quester returns and makes a meaningful contribution to society. This usually is in the form of the power to bestow boons on others. It must be reiterated that the return is not necessarily literal. The whole process of the hero's journey is one of unfoldment of the deeper personality. The quest may not be successful in every case. But the attempt is what lends meaning to life. Campbell contends that one is incomplete unless one has enlarged oneself and touched another.

Campbell asserts that the game of the spiritual is the game of the possible. It extends beyond oneself. In an interview with Bill Moyers he states:

> A hero is someone who has found, or achieved, or done something beyond the normal range of achievement, experience. A hero probably is someone who has given his life to something bigger than himself, or other than himself.[1]

Jung a fervent propagator of the vital importance of the conscious state, on the other hand, does not exalt the inner being to as great a height. He knows it is vital to connect, and stay connected with the unconscious. But he seeks a delicate, finely tuned balance between consciousness and unconsciousness. Jung's individuation process is an attempt to connect with the wholeness of being, that is, an intelligent integration of conscious, subconscious and unconscious. Jung's method is generally one of peeling off the layers of consciousness including, of course, the ones that are subterranean. Campbell would accept the fact that they are subterranean. He may, in fact, even advocate plunging into the bowels of the cavern. Jung, however, with functionality as his premise, would not advocate such a traumatic method in most cases. But recognition and partial identification with the archetypes stressed as purgation in the sense of catharsis, is of utmost importance as long as one does not dangerously tilt the see-saw of consciousness. Jung's stages of catharsis, elucidation, education and transformation in the individuation process are definitely the see-saw of consciousness which is necessarily cognitive and in which the senses—visual, auditory, olfactory, tactile and gustatory—are inseparable. Physicality is not denied. Campbell does not deny physicality either, but Jung can be said to give it a greater importance because functionality in this given and imperfect world is what he strives for Campbell being a mystic believes much more in the realm of the beyond which is there, if one just dares to reach out and touch it. Perhaps this gulf, though not a major one, between Jung and Campbell lies in the fact that Jung had a massive and debilitating encounter with the archetypes. Campbell's mystical journey, on the other hand, followed a longer trajectory as it, in a sense, formally began with myths, folklore, and fairytales. This much recapitulation regarding the convergence and divergence of the two thinkers should be enough for the moment as it has already been considered in detail in the previous chapter.

Before we highlight the quest motif with reference to Rao's questers, it is necessary to make an important qualification regarding the literary mould of the questers' journey as presented by Rao. Rao's world of short fiction can be viewed both in Campbellian and Jungian terms. The cartography of Rao's quest-cycle follows a path where designated (in the sense of formal) gurus are essential. The pursuit as well as the method of the quest process is Indian in the cultural and conventional sense. There are certain markers such as gurus and disciples as characters, formal initiation *(diksha), guru-mantras,* holy places, sacred names, chanting of hymns, singing of *bhajans,* etc., that corroborate the formal pattern of the quest process as delineated in Rao's stories. Nevertheless, Rao does not adhere too stringently to the formal mould of quest cycle as he tends to transcend it more often than not. To do it meaningfully and convincingly, he employs the device of demythification, which imparts rare psychological depth to his understanding and portrayal of diverse dynamics of guru-disciple relationship. To cast characters such as Moti Khan, the taxi driver and Shiv, the pimp in the guru-mould, and the like of the cow, the snake and Nanna, the prostitute in the quester-mould emerge as ample evidence to lend support to Rao's stature as an eternal experimenter and innovator in the realm of fiction in general and short fiction in particular. This chapter gives a detailed account of different questers in the world of Rao's stories, analyzing critically their progress and accomplishments thereby attempting to categorize them in terms of the Campbellian quest cycle (separation-initiation-return). This analysis will be interspersed with Jungian formulations regarding the individuation process. However, it is worth mentioning that all of Rao's character-questers are not typically Campbellian in regard to their status and place in society. According to Campbell, "The composite hero of the monomyth is a personage of exceptional gifts. Frequently he is honored by his society [...]. In this sense, Rao's characters seem not to qualify to be Campbellian heroes. But Campbell himself admits that howsoever "ridiculous" or "sublime" the questers may be, their "journey varies little in essential plan."[2]

"Narsiga" is the story of a five year old orphan who comes in contact with the guru via his accidentally adopted parents—Lingayya and his wife, who is an "angry and effusive" woman (*CBS*: 97). The marriage is, in fact, contracted by this so called aunt, mainly to provide Narasiga with a father. Fortunately, through these adopted parents, Narsiga, by chance, comes in contact with the Master (an embodiment of the archetype of the wise old man) and becomes a resident of his Ashram along with his foster parents. The Master's brother, his spiritual extension, becomes fond of Narsa and acts as a pivot for Narsa's physical and spiritual growth. This is evident in the following quote in which the Master's brother cuts off Narsa's hair as an act of affection and personal care:

> 'You little fool,' cried the Master's brother, touched and amused, and going back into his room, brought back a pair of long silvery scissors, and cut away Narsa's swarthy hair. Only a little soft hair remained—such as the city people have—and the Master's brother brought perfumed oils and combed Narsa's head till it shone like black beads, and caressing it, Narsa went into the woods, the sheep before him. (*CBS*: 98)

The Master's brother finds Narsa appealing due to his innocence, simplicity and purity—the seed of divinity *à la* Blake.

The orphan's psycho-spiritual quest in this conducive environment brings about self-confidence and self-reliance. Narsa becomes the Master's shepherd. Eventually he starts tending the sheep of other villagers as well. Narsa easily fits into the discipline and the routine of the Ashram while making a meaningful contribution in substantial manner. As a shepherd, the spiritual and pastoral environment (a self-contained world with which he totally identifies), impacts upon Narsa's personality and his herd seems to grow magically as a result. The echoes of Satyakama myth are apparent.

Narsa enjoys riding the sheep. While doing so, he believes he is Lord Shiva or Lord Rama astride a celestial mount. Thus, he is totally merged with the archetypes of these deities. He does not pretend to be Lord Rama or Lord Shiva. During the experience, he *is* Lord Rama or Lord Shiva. Thus, Narsa is treading the path of psychological wholeness or individuation in Jungian terms.

Narsa's divine experiences are given no credence by his aunt or foster mother. A unique and terrible encounter with a huge snake that he beats to death upsets Narsa, internally causing fear. Nature's nemesis is felt. The experience of Narsa is analogous to that of Wordsworth in *The Prelude*, Book I when a huge rock appears after he unties a boast from its moorings. In both cases, symbolic punishment is meted out by Mother Nature in all her majesty. Wordsworth writes:

> Fair seed time had my soul, and I grew up,
>
> Fostered alike by beauty and by fear.[3]

Narsa's protector is the Master's brother who shields him (Narsa) from the frequent and merciless beatings of his foster mother. Narsingh Srivastava compares the Master's brother to a 'saviour': "It was master's own brother whose character has been presented as that of an affectionate and generous man, who became his saviour by bringing him to his brother's ashram."[4] Narsa is a sincere and honest child. Moreover, the Master's brother's protection makes Narsa fearless, an essential attribute of a true quester. The brother is somewhat like a Campbellian teacher or sage who facilitates the growth of the seeker on his quest journey. Regarding the importance of such a protective figure, Campbell says: "For those who have not refused the call, the first encounter of the hero-journey is with a protective figure (often a little old crone or old man) who provides the adventurer with amulets against the dragon forces he is about to pass."[5]

As Narsa matures, more responsibilities fall on his young shoulders, including looking after the ten-month old child whom he entertains by telling various stories. In the course of time, Narsa's growth results in psycho-spiritual strength, courage, assertion, and self-respect. This is subtly alluded to by Rao:

> Narsa is now a big person. He can reach the Master's waist. He now wears long jackets and big slippers, and even a cap such as the sahibs wear. 'It protects the eyes;' the Master said. Besides he now knows how to read. He can read what is written on the top of tea-boxes, and trains, and once he had even tried to read the paper that the postman brings to the Master every day. Rangappa, the sullen student of the Master, gives lessons to Narsa and the other ashram boys. They sit every evening at lighting time in the verandah of the central building, and there they learn alphabets and words. (*CBS*: 110–11)

Eventually, Narsa begins to learn the Master's teachings like a Bhakta. "Mother, Mother" and "Matarama Vande Mataram" particularly appeal to his psychic self although he is yet unable to comprehend abstractions in the manner of one spiritually evolved. Regarding this paradox Bhattacharya observes:

> The world of Narsa's experience was a small one, and he was not much capable of abstraction. He sang the song *Vande Mataram*. He knew that it was about the Mother—Mother who was good, Mother who was kind, Mother who grew rice; but he wanted to know who this Mother was. He had lost his own mother too early to remember, and the only mother he knew was the wife of the Master. His auntie was also a kind of substitute mother, and there was the four-armed goddess whose picture hung by the temple door. But the conception of motherland was too complex for him.[6]

Under the Master's influence, Narsa comes to learn that "Mother" signifies motherland, i.e., India imprisoned by the red men. The master refers to Gandhi, his socio-political philosophy and the fact of his imprisonment. To Narsa Gandhi becomes a metaphor of Mother India.

After the understanding of the red men vis-à-vis Mother India dawns upon Narsa, his thoughts turn to violence out of sheer vengeance. He and Rami, Shankaranna's daughter, therefore, pelt a train with stones. As a result of this violence, the sensitive Narsa falls ill and is thus made to understand Gandhi's dictum of non-violence. Once this is clear, his sin is atoned for, and he is overtaken by the softest sleep signifying purification brought about by the catharsis of anguish. Hatred flies out of his heart. Transformation has taken deep roots and is eventually completed through Rami, his "wife Rami" (*CBS*: 117), the archetype of Narsa's anima in Jungian sense.

Narsa's individuation process in Jungian terms has an accidental beginning. As noted, he is orphaned at a very early age and is subsequently adopted by a so-called aunt. Narsa's quest, in fact, begins upon contact with the Master and his spiritually like-minded brother. Physical, psychological and spiritual growth results through diverse experiences in the favourable atmosphere of the Ashrama. Occupation and responsibility follow quite naturally. The Master, an archetype of the wise old man, proves an able guide in Narsa's journey towards individuation i.e., wholeness of being, or psychological totality of the self. At first, Narsa experiences the whole gamut of emotions coprising anger, violence, love, hate, but later, all conjoin to form a rapid flux which results in his contact with the inner world mainly through archetypal encounters. Even though fragmented and shadowy, the collective unconscious does make an appearance. The deeper and darker depths of the personal unconscious are revealed as they are; transformation is the by-product and individuation is gradually realized that eventually results in "psychic totality." This is virtually the "self," "[...] a centre neither of which coincides with the ego but includes it, just as a larger circle encloses a smaller one."[7]

The ninth story in *On the Ganga Ghat* is painted on an unusual canvas with its protagonist, Shivlal, a pure virgin pimp, and Nanna, a prostitute who turns out to be spiritually inclined. Shiv is drawn into the world of prostitution for the sake of an occupation, yet remains undefiled by its depravity. Shiv meets an evil and foul-tongued Sadhu who imparts a *mantra* to him. As such, Shiv accepts the Sadhu as the guru. After a great deal of travel Shiv and the Sadhu reach the holy city of Benares. Shiv's meeting with the Sadhu can be likened to a "mythic summons" *à la* Campbellian thought. Although apparently the relationship, viewed from outside, is debauched, it has deep psychological connotations as it is basically the severing of the connection with the habitual self. Thus begins Shiv's quest although he is unaware of it. It is somewhat like Erik Erikson's "quest for identity" or "for a place in society."[8] This improbable web woven by the author signifies the exterior physical passage one must traverse to connect with interiority and realize one's inner being.

Upon reaching Benares, the abode of Lord Shiva, Shivlal is drawn into the ostensibly dark world of prostitution and becomes a pimp, albeit an unusual one. Shiv flourishes as a pimp and comes into contact with his anima in the form of a "fat," Punjabi prostitute, Nanna who perceives a divine aura in Shiv and decides to work for him saying, "You stay here and take all the money. You are the Lord, I am the slave" (*OGG*: 107).

Shiv becomes a busy man and remains engrossed in his work; he forgets his tortured past; he meets all sorts of people and learns the ways of society, covert and overt. This notwithstanding, Shiv remains unsullied spiritually and maintains purity through reciting the esoteric *mantra* freeing him from the mire of desire. He is sincere and honest in his work, and may as well have been an ordinary shopkeeper. The apparent schism in a worldly sense is most evident when Shiv is shown to be a *bhakta* who sings hymns from *Kalbhairav Stotra* and *Chandi Stotra*. This makes him view women non-sexually: "It made every woman seem so like a mother [...]" (*OGG*: 108).

Shiv is like the pure lotus in a bed of mud, i.e., a Yogi in this tainted world. A parallel to the famous mystic saint Ramakrishna comes to mind as that great mystic viewed every woman as "Mother," an emanation of the "Cosmic Mother Goddess." Shiv's relationship with Nanna, his anima, his spiritual counterpart, is to be viewed in this light. Shiv's rich relationship with Nanna, his archetype, pure as it is, energizes him and prevents him from falling into the trap in which the woman serves as a "temptress."[9] Nanna, like Shiv, is also a quester for enlightenment. The fact that she views prostitution as "dharma" elevates her, eventually enabling her to attain *moksha,* i.e., liberation from worldly desire. Her "dharma" is a vital, regulating force.

Nanna once happens to overhear Shiv reciting the esoteric '*mantra*' and asks him to give it to her. Shiv, however, advises her to take it from his guru, the foul-tongued Sadhu. Nanna goes to the Sadhu, and after some initial difficulties, is imparted the secret *mantra* (a psycho-spiritual tool). Thus begins her journey on the road to enlightenment. Shiv's total cutting the umbilical cord of *maya* is of a dramatic nature brought about by the realization that the money he has saved, is a form of identification with the ego, i.e., the world of darkness and ignorance. This realization forces him to discard the money quite literally (with deep symbolic implications) on Divali night. As such, he frees himself from the shackles of the personal that otherwise remains cluttered with intricate shadow complexes. Now the Campbellian initiation is complete—an initiation which is magically transformative. The futility of desire is made apparent. The Campbellian journey beginning with the call for adventure (through contact with the "foul-tongued" Sadhu), the formal initiation by the Sadhu, realization of anima (Nanna) along with honestly performing his duties, and lastly the return (forsaking the gold) completes the cycle. In terms of Indian thought the quester, Shiv, achieves dissolution of the ego and is completely "established in the self."[10]

The most celebrated story of Raja Rao, "The True Story of Kanakapala—Protector of Gold" is a beautiful sketch of a learned brahman, Vision Rangappa, who emerges and evolves as a quester par excellence in search of the vision of Kashi Vishweshwara (Lord Shiva). Hosakere Rangappa as he is originally known is orphaned at the age of eighteen. Spirituality is ingrained in his being and he is loved for his innocence and simplicity by the people. He performs the duties of a Pandit (prayer, fast, etc.), and manages thus to eke out a living. But he is overpowered by a "mythic call" to undertake a pilgrimage to Kashi. Before undertaking the journey, he has it in his mind to eventually return to his village and take a chaste wife. His plans are accidentally foiled by fate when an epidemic spreads through the village. Since Rangappa is a pontifical Brahmin, he manages to gather a considerable sum of money to accomplish his proposed journey. After seeking the blessings of the village gods and the villagers, he begins his pilgrimage.

On the way, after meditation and sleep, he "sees" Kashi Vishweshwara (Lord Shiva) and his divine consort (Parvathi) in a dream. It is revealed that the pilgrimage is complete; the Divine Couple are touched by his bhakti (devotion). They bless him and assure that his family will always be under the auspices of their protection. The Holy Couple asks him to construct a temple on the top of the hill where they will sprout through the earth. Rangappa working at breakneck speed with the villagers manages to erect the temple and becomes Vision Rangappa.

The next day after ablutions, "purified and exalted," Rangappa has a vision of a Shiv-linga. For twenty one days he continuously meditates beside this "Udbhavamurti," "a stone rising out of the ground, carved with the images of the gods" (*P&R*: 4). A young shepherd spreads the news, and people come to hear of his (Vision Rangappa's) revelation. Vision Rangappa purifies the Divine Abode with hymns from the *Atharva-veda*. The villagers, overjoyed, rename their village Subehalli as 'Kashipura.' Vision Rangappa, now purified and enlightened, a Jungian wise old man and Campbellian quester who has successfully completed all three stages of the hero's journey, marries the third daughter of Pandit Shivrammayya and settles down in the village. He is there to facilitate others in their personal and divine seeking. This formal return is also necessary in Rao's world, steeped as it is, in tradition. In the Campbellian sense, however, the return occurs when the overjoyed villagers revel in his spirituality.

The "nuclear unit of monomyth"[11] flows effortlessly throughout the modern monomyth of Vision Rangappa. The story carries deep psychological overtones in which the break with the habitual self comes quite early. The social mask of Jung's persona is dispensed with quite early. The *antahkarana* or inner being is the visible quest right from the very beginning. It is largely of a conscious nature. The vision of the gods is like connecting with Campbell's "Queen Goddess of the world"[12] whose Indian counterpart is the cosmic Mother Kali. Encounter with the archetype of Shiva and Parvathi, the Divine Couple, is not mysterious and debilitating as Rangappa is already on the path to enlightenment with the beacon burning bright. He is well prepared because he has evolved gradually and the quest has always been firmly fixed in his mind. In the end, he is a saviour, a holy man, a successful Campbellian hero, or a Jungian wise old man. This particular story can be said to be spiritually the richest as it encapsulates all three strains—Campbellian, Jungian and the Vedantic.

Muthradas, a Vedantic quester, is portrayed in the fourth story of *On the Ganga Ghat*. Muthradas, pursued by a tragedy, sells his camels and leaves Vrindavan for Benares in the hope of obtaining "final release and union with Shiva."[13] Coming from a well-reputed Kanakamal family of traders, Muthradas, the eldest, is married to Lakshmi. Unfortunately, the couple remains childless due to a curse of Kanakamal's wife, Anusuyaben, who pronounced it for her husband's infidelity, i.e., "betrayal with a concubine" (*OGG*: 45). The curse will last for seven generations. Due to this, Muthradas adopts a son namely Moti Chand who is absolutely spoilt in the beginning, but later grows up into a responsible person and becomes a model husband too. But the curse is still effective, and he dies childless, followed by his mother, Lakshmi's death in a tragic accident. Traumatized, full of anguish, and unable to cope, Muthradas abandons his family and settles down in Benares. There Muthradas soaks himself in *Yoga* (physically as well as spiritually), through ecstatic discourses of *Tulsi Ramayana* by Pandit Uday Shankar. He immerses himself in *sattva* while studying the school of Vedanta. He is a *bhakta* who initially fails to comprehend Vedanta as he is not intellectually proficient in the lore.

Three years later, he is formally initiated by Guru Shankaranand his fixity of purpose and worship. He begins to comprehend the subtleties of Vedanta to a certain extent at this stage. Spiritual adventures of a sort flit through/upon his consciousness, resulting ultimately in the partial dissolution of the ego as per Indian philosophy or what Campbell calls "cutting off the inner dragon."[14] Thus, his patience, persistence and perseverance help him on the path to a higher spiritual consciousness. Working out his traumatic anguish, the life he has left behind, in the form of devotion (*bhakti*) to the Lord, can be likened to catharsis (the first stage of Jungian individuation process). As his personality is re-formed, nay, built anew, he comes in deeper touch with the 'self,' leading to elucidation (the second stage of individuation). Thus, he is in a slightly better position to somewhat comprehend the Vedantic state of dream and sleep, as it begins to crystallize and gradually unravel. But the "dragon" has not been totally cut off. The ego is still his focal point. Sankara's explanation—"seeing, hearing, thinking and knowing are always experienced by people in dream, moreover, as they are essentially the Self. If is directly known [...]"—is lost on him (*OGG*: 45). Lack of comprehension does not, however, discourage him as he attempts to imbibe understanding through repeated chanting of the *Updesh Sahasriyam*:

> There is no vision in me as I am without the organ of seeing. How can there by hearing for me who have no auditive organ? Devoid of the organ of speech. I have no action of speaking in me. How can there be thinking in me who have no mind? (*OGG*: 45)

At this point, spiritual progression is retarded and Muthradas dies without realizing the essential oneness of dream and sleep, aspects of Pure Consciousness. The story, however, is open-ended and leaves the reader with the hope somewhat suggestively, that Muthradas will succeed in the next incarnation when he resumes the quest for enlightenment.

Muthradas is a quester who has fallen by the roadside and is unable to complete the path to enlightenment. Seen in the light of Campbellian "monomyth"/quest-cycle, in Muthradas' case separation does occur, but initiation is incomplete. Jungian wholeness proves to be elusive. This may possibly be due to the fact that tragedy thrust the quest upon him and he began to tread this path full of shards by means of an entirely *bhakti*-type mode, in the manner of a man of blind faith, which cannot be negated as a vehicle to achieve the supreme state of consciousness. But, undoubtedly, it has pitfalls. Questers in the Ramakrishna mode, in the sense of absorption in the idol (i.e., the concrete manifestation of the subtle, invisible and the nameless), are few and far between. Nevertheless, the story of Muthradas is one of extreme tenderness and leaves the reader elated, as hope shines through at the end of the story.

Moti Khan, the protagonist of "Campanions," is disinterested in enlightenment, and satisfied in the world of desire (*maya*). He is forced by circumstances in the form of a guru reincarnated as a snake, to pursue the spiritual quest to literally find God. The serpent was Pandit Srinath Sastri in its previous birth and was cursed by Goddess Lakshamma to be born as a serpent in the next life because of his greed for gold. He was also granted the boon of liberation from the cycle of 'birth-death-rebirth' but only after having lived the life of a serpent. Eventually he becomes a vehicle for Moti Khan's salvation as a serpent.

Moti Khan, the reluctant quester, compelled as he is to undertake the spiritual quest, treads the narrow path of salvation at the behest of the serpent guru. Once on this road, he begins to see sense in the spiritual quest as opposed to the carnal one. He picks up the quest stage from his previous life and continuously meditates for twenty nine days before Sheikh Chisti's tomb at Fatehpur Sikri. Chisti awakens and blesses him. Enlightenment along with liberation from the torturing serpent is the result. Marriage with Maulvi Mahammad Khan's daughter follows. Upon the death of the couple and the serpent, all are buried together and are worshipped by community at large. Thus the trinity becomes a source of inspiration for other worshippers and questers.

On the surface the quest of Moti Khan and his snake companion seems to be simplistic. But it has deeper resonances. Moti Khan has completed his quest cycle in Campbellian mode. The snake, who actually is Pandit Srinath Sastri, is also liberated from the cycle of death and rebirth. Interestingly enough, the quest is imposed from without, both in Moti Khan's as well as in the serpent's case. The reluctant soldiers, however, do tread the path as ordered. The return is technically achieved as Moti Khan "became the guardian of Sheikh Chisti's tomb. The serpent lived with him [...]" (*P&R*: 34). Jungian individuation or psychological wholeness is also achieved. Moti Khan's catharsis is visible from his annoyance, irritation and desperation with the tyrannical dictates of the serpent. Gradually, with the passage of time, Moti Khan succumbs to the conditions laid down by the serpent and commences his quest journey; it is symbolic of his elucidation. The stages of education and transformation are encapsulated in Moti Khan's enlightenment which dawns upon him at Sheikh Chisti's comb. In a nutshell, Moti Khan attains the wholeness of being. In Campbellian terms, the return is achieved. The bestowing of the boons on society is technically achieved after his death as the common men's wishes are granted if they visit the *dargah*.

In the third story of Madhobha, the paranormal and the physical reality intermesh. Madhobha, a wrestler of low intelligence and soaked in physicality, is enticed by a disembodied spirit named Mohini. Madhobha, a devotee of Hanuman, is a quester circumscribed by tradition, who nevertheless attempts to scale great heights in seeking connection with the spirit, Mohini, whom he considers Ganga-born. The occultic connection is evident when Madhobha expresses his love for Mohini: "I have a rendezvous with a lovely spirit—I see her only on moonlit nights. And she is so beautiful. All the beauties of this earth seem as nothing" (*OGG*: 28). Madhobha further asserts the reality of Mohini, insofar as she is not of the world of the dead. His object of love does not appear in most of the tale, although the presence is felt by Madhobha who imagines to have a relationship with her.

Mohini is invisible throughout. Although the Hanuman Bhakta hears her sing, he cannot interpret the song. But the sound itself effects pure religio-spiritual experience in Madho. Mohini on her part finds purity in this *brahmachari* (celibate) and looks upon him as a perfect medium to realize Lord Rama. Mohini herself becomes the vehicle for the ignorant quester's salvation, ignorant in the sense that he is of the ritualistic prayer mould. But he has horse sense and is "shrewd," "grave," "playful" and "kindly." Strong and well-built, he is a salesman, always engrossed in his work; but pensively reflects on Mother Ganga and makes confession to her when he is free.

Madho is an orphan. As a great wrestler, he comes in contact with Sadanand, a Zamindar's Brahmin cook, and accepts him as his guru whom he eventually defeats in a wrestling match after two years, at the age of sixteen. His celibacy, the source of his strength, fortifies him enough to resist women in general. His guru continually admires him:

> 'There's strength in your limbs—and Bhakta Hanuman gives it to you—because there's virility in your loins. As long as like Hanuman you're a brahmachari, you will be a splendid wrestler—that is if the Lord willeth. Rama—Rama, He Raghupathi. May He protect you.' (*OGG*: 36)

Wrestling is the axis of Madho's life. But he is not prejudiced against women. His generosity is evident when he lends a large sum of money to his friend, Shankar as his wife is pregnant and the money is direly needed.

Madho is saintly and extremely generous. He sub-consciously desires to build a temple in honour of Lord Shiva in his native village. Madho's quest is undoubtedly naive and conventional. This is intersected by the yearning, the seeking, for ethereal Mohini, his anima, with whom he has established a psychic relationship of the state of the beyond due entirely to his *bhakti* (devotion) and its unalloyed purity. These are the traits which Mohini loves and respects. Carnal desire comes nowhere into play. The relationship is rather non-sensual in which Mohini's presence remains unbidden, but the divine quest, is felt. The story rises like a spiritual psalm. The princess (Mohini) is won in terms of the quest journey, but the conquest is mutual, and entirely spiritual in form. Madho is like an illiterate bumbling shaman whose wealth lies in the heart due to his devotion to Lord Hanuman. Mohini is the vehicle for his spiritual progression and transmutation. Individuation in the Jungian sense comes into play, although it is not highlighted but merely suggested.

In the tenth story, Ranchoddoss' daughter Sudha is portrayed as a celibate. She is devoted to the Lord wholeheartedly in the present life, whereas in her past life she was completely devoted to her husband. She realizes the futility of existence in which God is the only salvation. Sudha, a Vedantic quester, is in search of the Absolute and "hates" the idea of marriage. She has a vision that "[...] a Sadhu would come to initiate her and she would then become a true devotee of the Lord" (*OGG*: 115). Accordingly, Sunderanand comes and they undertake a journey to the Himalayas. Her family accepts this decision with equanimity. Sudha's transformation into an enlightened state is an outcome of an unwavering lifelong endeavour.

Ranchoddoss, Sudha's father, is inspired and thereby drawn to spirituality. The innate quest manifests itself in him in his repeated reading of and meditation upon the *Vishnu Purana* and *Bhagvatham*. Consequently, he gains deep spiritual insight which transcends the revolution of time.

Sudha returns to Benares, enlightened through variegated spiritual experiences, and contributes to society by public readings of the *Vashishta Ramayana*. Sudha has achieved complete dissolution of the ego. Waking, dream and sleep states, analogues of consciousness, subconsciousness and unconsciousness, are realized by her as a holistic play on cognition. The essence is one of pure Vedanta, or, in Jungian terms, wholeness of being of course with respect to Indian philosophy, while Jung falls a bit short of total spiritual metamorphosis. Campbell's hero-quester's stages of separation, initiation and return are quite clearly evident and thus need not be unduly explicated. In a nutshell, it is a monomyth.

Originally written in Kannada, "A client" is the story of a fallen quester, Ramu who is entrapped by an old, "crude and malicious" (*CBS*: 126) professional marriage broker who panders to the baser instincts of man. This broker is an embodiment of the Jungian trickster archetype and the personification of the negative side of the archetype of the wise old man.

Ramu, a simple and sensitive lad of the village Hariharpura, lands up in Bangalore with a view to furthering his education. Knowledge is his quest as well as his family's expectation. But Ramu's path crosses the broker, Nanjundayya's, a "queer old man," "a haunting old man." Ramu, a simpleton, unversed in the ways of the world, happens to pass Nanjundayya, the master of persona. But Ramu feels no overpowering attraction and is content to continue on his way. He is, however, accosted by Nanjundayya, selling himself to all by smiling. Rao describes Nanjundayya satirically: "He wore a gold-laced turban and a loose longcoat in the old fashion. He was bare-footed, and his dhoti, also gold-laced, was creamy white; and by contrast his wrinkled dust-covered feet seemed bluish green like cow-dung" (*CBS*: 120). The gaudily-dressed broker weaves his web through the practised art of flattery, apparent familiarity and affection.

Nanjundayya's quest is of a very base nature as it is purely material. This perfect conversationalist lures Ramu to the Udipi Coffee House and brings up "marriage," a magic word for Ramu. Ramu is distracted and rapidly begins to ruminate on the material advantages and disadvantages of marriage. Rao remarkably portrays Ramu's thoughts thus:

> To marry an uneducated girl, and be happy all one's life, then. ... To marry for money! Well, it would help one for a moment. But afterwards. ... To have one's life ruined because of a few rupees! Oh, no! How horrible. ... But then, how long to live like this ... cooking ... washing ... sweeping ... counting each pie as though it contained the germ of eternal happiness. Impossible. A good marriage is profitable for the moment. ... A room overlooking a spacious garden. ... A smiling wife bringing in hot coffee ... . The languor. ... The mother-in-law's supplication. ... A veritable small divinity ... . Books on the shelf, beautiful green, blue golden books. An electric light at the bedside. ... No smell of kerosene oil ... . Work till midnight... . Exams... . 'How have you done, Ramu?' 'Not bad" (In his heart: 'Excellent!'). Results ... . Ramu first! The eager, envious flattering looks of the class-fellows ... . And all Hariharpur shouting his glory. (*CBS*: 19–30)

As such, the fish has begun to nibble the bait.

Subsequently Ramu succeeds in repressing his desire to marry and firmly declares that he will not do so. Nanjundayya makes a tactical retreat and pretends to have accepted Ramu's decision. The broker respected by Ramu as a venerable old man adopts gentle persuasion to gain his end. Deceived, Ramu ponders: "After all, perhaps the old man is right. Old men are always so full of ripe wisdom … . Why not marry? Sofas … Hot coffee… ." (*CBS*: 135). A deceptive barrage of allurements follow which weaken Ramu's resolve.

The broker, on the pretext of accompanying Ramu home, misleads him to Vishweshwarayya's (Nanjundayya's classfellow and retired Director General of Police) house. Vishweshwarayya, ostensibly deferential, enquires about Ramu's education and its progress. Ramu feels uneasy but he is nevertheless caught in the broker's web although he does not understand the method as such. Ramu, "bewildered," "confused" and "lost," is offered happiness in the guise of a beautiful girl who enters the room:

> Suddenly the door opened, and a charming girl of eleven or twelve, dressed in a gorgeous Dharmawar sari of blue and gold, entered with a silver plate full of fruits and cakes and glasses of coffee, and placing it on the table by Ramu, went and sat between her father and Nanjundayya, her hands upon her knees, shyly, awkwardly. There was a crammed silence. (*CBS*: 140)

Nanjundayya, successful in his plot, bursts into laughter.

Thus, we can see that Ramu, the protagonist-quester, falls by the wayside in his quest for an education. He falls a prey to the designs of the broker, a negative personification of the Jungian wise old man. Though Ramu's quest is by no means deeply spiritual, yet it is intrinsically connected with the unfoldment and consequent flowering of the personality. Nanjundayya can be likened to "dreaded concoctor of poisons"[15] who leads the seeker to hell which is a symbol of degeneration and darkness, by riding roughshod over his psyche.

II
Categorizing Rao's Protagonist-Questers

After taking an in-depth critical view of Rao's protagonist-questers, and also analysing their quest stages in Campbellian and Jungian light, we may now categorize them on the basis of their accomplishments, thereby effectively highlighting their similarities and dissimilarities. First, there are questers who have completed their quest-cycle, e.g., Sudha, Moti Khan and Vision Rangappa; secondly, there are those who have just commenced their quest-journey, and also those who have reached the final phase such as Narsiga and Shivlal; and lastly are those who have fallen by the wayside on their quest journey, e.g., Ramu and Muthradas.

Now to specifically deal with the similarities and dissimilarities of the different questers. Sudha, Vision Rangappa and Moti Khan successfully complete the quest-cycle and spiritually uplift, educate, and enlighten the community, as a successful return envisages. Sudha's return, however, is different from that of Vision Rangappa and Moti Khan insofar as she becomes a religio-spiritual teacher. She can easily be placed in the group of those questers whose search for God began in their previous life. This is where Sudha and Moti Khan converge. Moti Khan, intensely carnal, is compelled to seek God as he was a *bhakta* in his previous life. Sudha's journey is rather smooth as she enjoys the support of her family on the path to enlightenment/psychological wholeness. Vision Rangappa is also encouraged and helped by his community. Vision Rangappa, unlike Sudha and Moti Khan, is much more literal as he has an intense, innate urge to undertake a pilgrimage to Kashi, his "mythic summons" coming directly from *antahkarana*. Moti Khan is acted upon from without but completes the quest due to his *karma* marked by devotion to the Lord.

Narsiga is of a totally different mould and his quest for spirituality is the most arduous as he has to contend with a hostile and unfavourable environment. But he overcomes this through his will alone by immersing himself in work which effects self-sufficiency. As a result, he grows psychologically and spiritually in a multifarious and multi-dimensional manner. All the examples listed so far are marked by contact with the Jungian archetype either of anima or animus—an essential aspect to attain wholeness of being or individuation. This is clearly evident in Vision Rangappa's, Moti Khan's and Narsa's union with their female counterparts bringing about an overall transformation in their personalities. Sudha, far more spiritually evolved, does not connect with the archetype of animus literally, but the fact is that she has already transcended this stage.

III
Child Questers

Child questers are a peculiar feature in Rao's fictional world. The child quester or "young hero"[16] is marked by a dynamic personality. According to Jung, "'child' means something evolving towards independence. Thus it cannot do without detaching itself from its origins: abandonment is therefore a necessary condition [...]."[17] This condition in a mythic sense can be seen in the case of the orphan, Narsa. Narsa responds to the given circumstances, howsoever painful, and attains a measure of independence and self-sufficiency. Moreover, he is pure, innocent, honest, sensitive and imaginative and thus, 'divine.' Life's bounty in all its beauty is not lost on him. Both the mundane and the divine are accepted by him. P.C. Bhattacharya appropriately observes:

> Narsa, on his part, was not quite a calm and a quiet boy. He played with the dogs, and pulled the tails of tethered cows. Once he even jumped on the back of his aunt and cried out "hoye-hoye" as though he were on a sheep. As he knew, like many other boys of his age, how to cry disproportionately loudly while receiving a beating.[18]

In "Akkayya," Kittu, the narrator, is yet another child-quester. He is sensitive, perceptive and imaginative and is intrigued by the fact of the widow Akkayya's shaven head. Kittu who loves Akkayya very much, innocently and persistently enquires about the riddle of widowhood. This "research into the mystery of widowhood"[19] comes out in the following conversation:

> 'Where are your children, Akkayya?' I [Kittu] asked, sheltering myself under her breasts.
>
> 'I have none,' she answered angrily.
>
> 'And I?' I managed to say.
>
> 'You .... You are Ranga's son, not mine.' She breathed hard.

'Why have you no children, Akkayya?' I asked again.

'Because, because I have no husband,' she answered indifferently.

'What is a husband, Akkayya?'

'Oh, shut up! And don't bother me with all your *Ramayna*. A husband is a husband, a man ... .'

'Am I a man, Akkayya?'

'I don't know!' she wailed. I was silent again. (*CBS*: 74)

On the whole Kittu is Rao's device to uncover certain repressed dimensions of Akkayya's personality. In addition, Rao's aim somewhat social, is to "clearly demonstrate the cruelty of Hindu marriage customs."[20] Narsingh Srivastava states that in "Akkayya," "Raja Rao employs a powerful narrative that evokes a child's reactions and responses to an old lady's love and affection as much as it unfolds the psychology of a neglected old widow."[21]

"India—A Fable," a modern-day parable, is the story of Pierrot, a five-year old French child. He is extremely imaginative and is fascinated by Arabia and its camels and the milieu as a whole. Pierrot's meeting with the narrator (a guru figure) in a park in Luxembourg, draws him gradually to India. The innocent child, full of wonder, is on an imaginative journey to Arabia with his camel 'Kiki.' As he sees his face reflected in the narrator's sherwani buttons, Pierrot is enraptured and spontaneously laughs and says, "Look, you have faces in your buttons. Ah, faces, faces [...]" (*P&R*: 105).

This meeting is fortuitous. The narrator hears of the child's fairy-tale world peopled with the camel 'Kiki,' Prince Rudolfe and Princess Katherine. Upon being told that the narrator's name was 'Raja,' meaning a 'Prince,' Pierrot identifies Raja with Prince Rudolfe, "The Prince of the oasis of Arabia" (*P&R*: 106). The narrator introduces the child to India and Pierrot's imagination takes a gigantic leap and his interest subtly shifts from Arabia to India. In place of prince and princess, the child learns of "[...] ladies with four arms and a golden crown on their heads and the water of Ganges, all sweet with perfumes, runs at their feet" (*P&R*: 108). Rao further describes the goddesses by saying that one is for the wedding of the night and she is "dark as bee." The other is meant for the wedding of the day and is "blond as butter." To further amplify their implications, Rao uses Vedantic symbolism and equates the former goddess with "dreaming" and the latter with "waking." Not only that, Rao gradually reveals various other peculiarities regarding India to Pierrot. For instance, the 'camel' of Pierrot's imagination is substituted by an 'elephant' and the oasis in the deserts of Arabia is replaced by the permanently flowing Ganges. Through such descriptions, the narrator makes Pierrot believé in India's infinite dimensions. Finally, Pierrot imagines that he is an Indian Prince, a Maharaja, a worshipper of the two goddesses and thereby gains insight and maturity.

The story is basically one of purity and innocence in the frame of the meeting of East and West. The narrator is a spiritual vehicle of the mature East in sharp contrast with the sensation-oriented and material West. It is not a story of confrontation but rather one of meandering harmony.

IV
Rao as a *Sadhak*-Quester

Here it would be pertinent to assess Rao as a quester. He has "always lived the life of a spiritual aspirant."[22] Raja Rao, an erudite philosopher and a self-proclaimed Advaita Vedantin, belongs to the rich tradition of Yajnavalkya, Shankara and Vidyaranya Swami. His family, as mentioned earlier, exercised a deep influence on him. Regarding this, Rao himself states:

> [...] when I was a boy four or five years of age, my grandfather a convinced Vedantin (from a family that can boast of having been Vedantins at least since the thirteenth century ...)—and my grandfather taught me *Amara*, that wonderful thesaurus which, like a grave and good Brahmin boy, I had to learn by heart [...].[23]

Considering this arduous and formative phase, Rao's sanskritized creations should not come as a surprise.

The eldest of ten children, Rao graduated from Nizam College Hyderabad and went to study French at the University of Montpellier as Professor Dickinson had advised. He became a writer to express his vision of life. He landed up in the halls of academia. This frenetic movement almost led to abandonment of writing till his guru, Sri Atmananda, stepped in.

Rao seems to have a double personality which is evident in his motive for going to France: "I wanted to become a monk in France [...]. But it took me a week to find out that it was not so; I became Indian immediately afterwards [...] I was so interested to spiritual matters. I wanted to become a Sanyasi. So I went to France."[24] But Rao, once there, discovered that he was in India. Disengaged, he began to clearly understand India's rich philosophical and cultural heritage. This led to a study of metaphysics for more than a decade. Thus we can see that Rao is a *sadhak* although he became one through circumambulation. His traditional background and life style may be construed as orthodox. But the fact is that he has imbibed the values of spiritual orthodoxy and assimilated them to the extent that they have become a part of his inner being. According to him, *dhyana*, *sadhana*, theoretical knowledge of truth must be combined with practical *Yoga* " [...] for a wholesome development of man's personality as well as the liberation of his self."[25]

Once when Raja Rao considered the idea of becoming a *sanyasi* formally, his guru advised him to continue writing as this was the *sadhana* best suited to him. Accordingly, he was convinced that it was through writing that he could attempt to make contact with the Ultimate Reality: "Writing is a prayer for me. I get pleasure (Ananda) [...]. I write just because I wish to write. It is a Sadhana for me."[26] Rao believed that he would continue to write even if he was alone in forest as literature was "Sadhana."[27]

The Indian epics, *Ramayana* and *Mahabharata*, exercised a profound spiritual influence on Rao which he acknowledged: "The book that has influenced me most is the *Ramayana*. What could be more glorious, more sacred, more fantastic, a book of books [...]."[28] Shakespeare, Dostoevski, Romain Rolland, Gandhi, Paul Valery, Andre Gide, Gorky, Yeats, Kafka,

Whitman, Coomaraswamy and Nietzsche have also impacted deeply upon Rao—the writer-cum-*sadhak* for whom writing had been a means of achieving enlightenment. In essence, it is part and goal of his quest.

Rao's stories maybe classified into three phases ranging from simple, social and domestic tales to complicated stories of the meeting of East and West. His first collection *The Cow of the Barricades* published in 1947 shows that Rao began as a socially committed writer. This was followed by stories in which Rao's preoccupation with various philosophical systems linked with metaphysics and East-West cross-cultural currents. These were published as *The Policeman and the Rose* in 1978. The later phase (i.e., late eighties and early nineties) was marked by an ostensible "return" to simplicity as evident in *On the Ganga Ghat* which was published in 1989. It presents various vignettes of Benares with the guru-disciple relationship and the resultant quest motif as its literary axis with Vedanta as its wheels. Rao's canvas remained in a state of continual evolution; stasis was absent through and through. With respect to Rao's first collection *The Cow of the Barricades and Other Stories* (1947), Narsimhaiah observes that

> [...] the collected stories have a rather more popular appeal because of the social preoccupations which Raja Rao shared with the writers of the thirties, though this writer being what he is, the religious impulse and the metaphysical imagination are unmistakable even in these.[29]

This *Kanthapura* phase, as it has been christened, flows with simple language, vibrant and vital, dealing with the concrete realities, harsh and crude, of rural life. The plots are basically traditional with respect to form and are, thus, unambiguous. Realism is unmistakable:

> Raja Rao has painted the village life in such a realistic and forceful manner that one cannot but marvel at his intimate knowledge of Indian life as well as his power of recreating that life within the limited compass of a short story and through the medium of a foreign language.[30]

We can therefore see that metaphysics, spirituality and Vedanta were largely absent up to this stage.

The mood, tone, and style undergo a dramatic shift in *The Policeman and the Rose* (1978). Heaviness is injected and the reader must patiently bear with the author if he is to perceive his meaning, ensconced as it is in metaphysical and Vedantic symbolism, all conveyed through philosophical erudition and obfuscating digressions. If the reader is patient, however, the poetic flavour of the stories surely shines forth. *The Serpent and the Rope* (1960), *The Cat and Shakespeare* (1965) and *The Chessmaster and His Moves* (1988) also belong to the same phase that baffles as well as bewilders if the reader lacks grounding in philosophy in general and Vedantic school of Indian philosophy in particular.

Quite amazingly, *On the Ganga Ghat* (1989) was brought out with a rare simplicity insofar as the style and language are concerned. However, unlike the early phase, here, the emphasis is more on the quest motif, i.e., the search for enlightenment. If during the earlier phase of his short fiction writing Rao remained socially committed, in the second and third phases, spirituality dominated his creative expression. For instance, through the modern parables in *On the Ganga Ghat*, Rao explicitly as well as implicitly works out the Vedantic quest for enlightenment, which, in a sense, is seeking linkages with the inner being. At the first glance the deceptive simplicity lulls the reader into believing that these stories belong to the *Kanthapura* phase but there is a marked difference. For instance, society has taken the back seat. The individual and his search for enlightenment have become primary. As such, Rao who began as a socially committed writer later assumed, the tone of an evolved Vedantist. Undoubtedly, the social and the domestic come into play but these are dwarfed by a profound sense of spirituality and metaphysics. The stories are mesmerizing and apparently contradictory. Benares as the locale hypnotizes the reader. Vijay Shankar states, "The contradictions and the brittle enchantments of Benares, its strange characters and their confused metaphysics come finally etched in this collection of short stories by one of India's greatest living authors [...]."[31] The stories are exquisitely sculpted, delightfully light and whimsical.

Rao's language as a story writer has a unique flavour as it is Indianised, yet not jarringly so. Indian metaphysics as well as

Rao's erudition have successfully transcreated English language as Rao uses it. He writes as if he had just simultaneously invented and discovered English while wearing Sanskrit spectacles.

Indian, 'Sanskritised' English remained a challenge, and a formidable one for that matter, to Rao, the *sadhuk*-writer. His expression is indeed unique. Irish writers like Yeats and Frank O'Connor were his inspiration as they moulded English according to their needs. Some critics may believe that Rao's knowledge of English is inadequate, but this is a rather prejudiced view as they fail to take into account Rao's background, experience and cross-cultural encounters along with their effortless fictional delineation. Rao is quite emphatic when he states:

> I will have to write my English, yet English after all—and how soon we forget this—is an Indo-Aryan tongue. Thus to stretch the English idiom to suit my needs seemed heroic enough for my urgentmost demands. The Irish, remember, had done it, not only with Yeats, but again with Frank O'Cornnor and Sean O'Faolain. Further, Joyce had broken in, as it were, from the side wings, giving us sound and symbol structures that seemed made for almost the unsayable. So why not Sanskritic (or if you will, Indian) English?[32]

Rao's conscious use of 'Sanskritised' or Indian English of an experimental mode, is extremely effective, capturing the true spirit of the Indian life, culture and thought along with the encounter of East and West. As such, through "[...] the medium of the English language the author seeks to communicate the Indian modes of feeling and expression."[33] Vasant A. Shahane remarks that Rao's English is not the King's English, but "[...] is indeed a transcreation of the native speech of the characters who inhabit [Rao's] fictional world and who breathe life into it."[34] In this way, Rao conveys the beauty of life and the quest in terms of Indian culture, tradition and thought in a lucid and remarkable manner.

Rao has broken new ground and is a contemporary Campbellian hero attempting to give India to the West in particular and the world at large in general. This is accomplished in *On the Ganga Ghat* through the mythic mode which rests on legend, based as it is, on the *Puranas* and of course the *Ramayana*, the *Mahabharata* and the *Vedas*. P.C. Bhattacharya rightly comments: "They [mythic legends] remain as appendages, and either evoke a particular mood, illustrate a particular point, or concretize a particular idea."[35] Rao's obsession with myth places him apart and far above other Indo-Anglian short story writers. Myth and metaphysics permeate and are conveyed through the use of philosophical symbolism replete with strains of Vedanta. This results in a unified vision.

Rao's description of the locale, the character and the manner in which conversation is struck up, show his skill and versatility in instilling life into the whole canvas. His words attain the proportions of psychic incantations as Rao uses them. For instance, observe Rao's description of Khandesh in the story of the same title:

> In Khandesh the earth is black. Black and grey as the buffalo, and twisted like an endless line of loamy pythons, wriggling and stretching beneath the awful beat of the sun. Between a python and a python is a crevice deep as hell's depths, and black and greedy and forbidding as demons' mouths. They seem to gape their mouths to gobble you ... to grapple you like crocodiles on a blazing day and drag you to the bottom of cavernous depths. *Baye* ... *Baye* ... *Baye* they seem to cry inaudibly, eager, rapacious, hungry. And they stream out breaths. The breaths are white and parched, curling and twisting and falling back like vermin. They search for a leg, a hand, an eye, a mouth, just to pull you into the abysm of the earth. Field on field is nothing but pythons and abysms—crocodiles waiting for their prey, vermin searching for a carcass. Then, suddenly, there is a yawning ravine in the endless immensity of the python-world [...]. (*CBS*: 146–47)

Another telling example follows in which Rao gives a poetic description of a whirlwind in Khandesh:

> All of a sudden a whirlwind rose over the fields. It seemed as though the earth vomited, spurting and flooding to the very skies. Round and swift it swept, brushed over the sands,

> swirled over the trees, and rushed into the air—and fell with a groaning, rasping cough. The stones on the railway lines glittered hot and bitter. Their glitter seemed the glitter of fangs. The clouds began to heap up. They roared. They grunted. And thunder shot against thunder. Then all of a sudden there was a commotion in the heavens, and lightning flew across the air, splitting a tree. The tree caught fire and burst into flame. The flame of sunshine danced with the flame of lightning [...]. And rain pelted against the earth. (*CBS*: 161)

Raja Rao was primarily a Vedantin and secondarily a creative writer, at least, that is what he would have us believe. This explains his preoccupation with the metaphysical as opposed to the mundane. His Vedantic sensibility left him unaffected by the contradictions of this world—good and evil, sacred and profane, etc. Life must be accepted in all its bewildering variety Akkayya's deteriorating physical condition in the last phase of her life is a case in point. It should by now be evident that Rao's quest cycle began with simplicity, evolved to complexity and returned once again to simplicity, though of a different sort. Rao's flow of words is like that of a river, the river of progression.

It will now be pertinent to briefly discuss the technical aspects of Sanskrit aesthetics which Rao seems to be steeped in. Sanskrit aesthetics has meanings of three kinds with respect to the word—*Abhidha* (denotation), *Lakshna* (connotation) and *Vyanjana* (resonance). This forms a pyramid with Vyanjana at the summit. *Shabda-Shakti* or loosely the power of words to impact upon the reader is the basis of Sanskrit aesthetics.

Abhidha signifies the primary level as the meaning is literal or denotative. *Lakshna* transcends surfacial meaning revealing implicit meanings. *Vyanjana* is at the peak and reveals abstruse and oblique concepts and/or states. *Vyanjana* is the vehicle to get to the truth of the matter, the pure meaning.

Rao's stylistic presentation of his stories is characterized by *Lakshana* and *Vyanjana,* as he psychologically and skilfully penetrates deep into, characterization and the overall intent. Meanings, both subtle and unique are drawn out in a poetically beatific manner by Rao. These meanings resound and reverberate in the reader's consciousness in such a way that the reader is imperceptibly made to think, feel and emote simultaneously. The perfect tool to comprehend this process is the capacity to assimilate which is known as *Sahridayata* (the highest degree of assimilation and also empathy). This is a process which both the reader and the writer need to undergo.

Rao's language, character portrayal, and delineation of social setting with a mythological and traditional backdrop present him as a *Sahridaya* with an in-depth understanding of his subject-matter. He seems to have realized the essence of Nada (sound). *Nada* has four levels—*Para, Pashyanti, Madhyama* and *Vaikhari*. *Para* is also called *sukshma* or subtle sound. This is analogous to *Anahat/Anhad Nada* (the unstruck sound) in Indian classical music.

The four levels of *Nada* explain Rao's creative process. For Rao, creativity is transcendence, because during the process of creation, the creator is merged with the Absolute. Personality and impersonality are conjoined. Rao actively believes in the importance of *Nada* as there is no clear line of demarcation traceable between four different levels; however, "a word," that is "the final word" may take on different roles thereby operating at different levels. In the lecture "The Critic and the Creator," Rao elaborates on the magic of a particular word:

> In difficult moments suddenly a word comes from somewhere as if by magic [*Para*], not something you thought of [...] that is the final word—yes, the final word. No writer comes by deliberation to the final word [...]. A word [...] gives the vibration of the object [*Pashyanti*]. The object is strongly felt [*Madhyama*] and it is the word that brings it out [*Vaikhari*]. So creation is the pure vibration of a human being in concentration [...]. Yes, this is the delight [...] of words.[36]

We can thus see that Rao, though a highly conscious writer, does not negate spontaneity in the sense of creativity. *Para* is marked by *spandan* or pure vibration, an offshoot of a 'word' that strikes and jolts as it is enormous in its potentiality.

The second level of *Pashyanti* brings about the ability to see inward through subtle transmutation of the 'word' to an apparently inanimate 'object.' This is an inextricable part of the writer's consciousness. *Madhyama* is the stage in which the object in question is strongly felt till it explodes into lettered expression bringing about inward communication. *Vaikhari* is the stage of outer expression. The initial *spandan* is analysed and digested to extract the writer's message. Rao, however, manages to merge the *Nada* and the *Vaikhari*, a rare and unique achievement.

These levels can also be interpreted in metaphysical terms. They are also called veils (*avaranas*) or folds, which a good writer uncovers during the creative process. Rao is of the view that the writer's objective is to realize the word as an eternal sound (*Anahad Nada*), a *mantra*, the most intensely "revealing form of poetic thought and expression."[37] Rao's article "The Writer and the Word," best sums up his view:

> Unless the author becomes an *upasaka* (devotee) and enjoys himself in himself which is *rasa* (aesthetic experience) the eternality of sound [...] will not manifest itself, and so you cannot communicate either [...] The word indeed is eternal. Man faces himself when he seeks the word. The word as pure sound is but a communication that comes from silence [...]. Unless the word becomes *mantra* no writer is a writer, and no reader, a reader.[38]

It should be unexceptionable to say that Rao's character-questers, his own life as a *sadhak*-cum-quester as well as a writer espousing Vedanta, and the various stages of its progression and evolution form a distinct quest-cycle, which is seemingly separate and compartmentalized, yet conjoined and unified at the core. It is all part of the Jungian and Campbellian journey of the hero/quester who responds to the "mythic summons" to search for the pot of gold at the end of the rainbow. Success and failure are but two sides of the same coin. The attempt is what matters. And no one can deny that Rao made the attempt and succeeded convincingly in churning out modern "monomyths" of universal appeal and relevance through his short stories.

Notes

1. Joseph Campbell, "Interview with Bill Moyers," Videocassette, Public Television Series, 1988.
2. See Joseph Campbell, *The Hero with a Thousand Faces*, Princeton: Princeton UP, 1949, pp. 37–38.
3. William Wordsworth, *The Prelude: A Parallel Text*, ed., J.C. Maxwell, Harmondsworth: Penguin, 1971, p. 50.
4. Narsingh Srivastava, *The Mind and Art of Raja Rao*, Bareilly: Prakash, 1980, p. 69.
5. Joseph Campbell, *The Hero with a Thousand Faces*, Princeton: Princeton UP, 1968, p. 69.
6. P.C. Bhattacharya, *Indo-Anglian Literature and the Works of Raja Rao*, Delhi: Atma Ram & Sons, 1983, p. 217.
7. C.G. Jung, *The Archetypes of the Collective Unconscious*, trans. R.F.C. Hull, Princeton: Princeton University Press, 1968, p. 142.
8. Robert A. Segal, *Joseph Campbell: An Introduction*, 1987; rpt. New York: Penguin, 1990, p. 34.
9. Campbell, p. 120.
10. Ibid., p. 243.
11. Ibid., p. 30.
12. Ibid., p. 109
13. Stella Kramrisch, *The Presence of Shiva*, Delhi: Oxford UP, 1981, p. 298.
14. Campbell, "Interview with Bill Moyers."
15. Jung, 1968, p. 227.
16. Ibid., p. 165.
17. Ibid., p.168.
18. Bhattacharya, p. 216.
19. Shyamala A. Narayan, *Raja Rao: Man and His Works*, New Delhi: Sterling, 1988, p. 12.
20. Ibid.
21. Srivastava, p. 124.
22. Ibid., p. 8.
23. Raja Rao, "Preface," *The Policeman and the Rose*, Delhi: Oxford University Press, 1978, p. xi.
24. M.K. Naik, *Raja Rao*, Bombay: Blackie & Son, 1982, p. 4.
25. Srivastava, p. 8.
26. "An Interview with Raja Rao" in Krishna Nandan Sinha (ed.), *Indian Writing in English*, New Delhi: Heritage, 1979, p. 20.

27. K.K. Sharma, ed., *Perspectives on Raja Rao*, Ghaziabad: Vimal, 1980, p. iii.
28. Raja Rao, "Books which Have Influenced Me," in M.K. Naik, ed., *Aspects of Indian Writing in English*, Delhi: Macmillan, 1979, p. 46.
29. C.D. Narasimhaiah, *Raja Rao*, New Delhi: Arnold-Heinemann, n.d., p. 2.
30. Srivastava, p. 120.
31. Vijay Shankar, "On the Ganga Ghat," book review, *Sunday Herald*, 29 October 1989, p. 5.
32. Raja Rao, "Preface," *The Policeman and the Rose*, p. xv.
33. "Publisher's Note," *The Cow of the Barricades*, p. vi.
34. Vasant A. Shahane, "Some Aspects of Indian English Writer's Creative Use of English," *The Literary Criterion*, 17, No. I (January-March, 1982), p. 77.
35. Bhattacharya, pp. 357–58.
36. Srivastava, p. 9.
37. Sri Aurobindo quoted in Srivastava, ibid., p. 11.
38. Naik, p. 11.

CHAPTER 4

Other Archetypes in the Quest Process

I
Archetype of Shiva

This chapter proposes to focus on Rao's mythological preoccupation with specific reference to various archetypes other than the guru viz., Shiva, Naga, Devi/Mother, Ganga, Cow, Hanuman, Rama and Krishna. These archetypes have a functional utility in the quest process, which forms the praxis of enlightenment. After working out the literal and mythological implications of these archetypes, their demythified connotations, if any, will be ferreted out in the light of Jungian perception and postulation of the archetypes of the collective unconscious and Campbellian thought.

For instance, Shiva, the Hindu god of destruction is the most worshipped form in Indian mythology. Shiva, in Jungian terms, is the archetype of the Self. He is the inner being, the inner guide to the discovery of the Self. He is Jung's wise old man as well. The self and the wise old man are not mutually exclusive. The perception of one necessarily points to the other. Quite often they are interlinked, and even merge with each other. The wise old man may actually be encountered as an exterior object, person, or facilitator of the search for self. The self is a symbol of wholeness or individuation. Shiva in his completeness, however, goes far beyond this. He is totality of being in a cosmic sense. His manifestation in the form of *Ardhanarishwar* (half-male and half-female form) implies the merger of the masculine and the feminine in the psyche, suggestive of the syzygy of Jung's anima and animus. In *Tantra,* this roughly corresponds to the biunity of Shiva-Shakti. The Chinese view these polarities as Yin and Yang. Jungian individuation or wholeness comes about only when both these aspects of the psyche are realized. With respect to corporeality, this is effected by the union of male and female. In this regard all cultures believe that one is incomplete without the other.

The movement and activity of the universe (Shiva being its agent) is dependent on Shakti (the Embodiment of Power) who imbues the world with motion. Shiva is part of it, yet transcends it. Mythologically, Shakti is the source that imparts life to Shiva without which He would be *shava* (corpse). Shakti is the Life Force (*Prangati).* A substantial body of mythology has grown around the archetype of Shiva especially in *Shiva Purana* and hymns in his praise or *Shiva Stotras*. Shiva is also the destroyer; He is *Rudra,* the god of destruction. He is, in this sense, an incarnation of terror and devastation. He is a demon-slayer and resides in the holy *shamshan* (crematorium). He inhabits the dark world of ghosts and phantoms, and is their leader. He is *Bhuteshwara,* the God of ghosts. As Death incarnate, He is *Kala* in the manifestation of Time itself, the Lord of death. He is the Head and Leader of the denizens of darkness, who waits for no man and dispenses justice impartially.

Shiva is also compassion and preservation. His compassionate nature and his role as the preserver of the balance between good and evil can be seen in the myth of the churning of the ocean. The ocean was churned by the *devas* (gods) and the *asuras* (demons) to extract *amrita,* (ambrosia) as well as *kalkuta* (poison). The poison threatened the existence of the whole cosmos. Shiva drank it to preserve the world. In another myth, the wrathful Ganga unleashed herself on the whole world threatening destruction. Shiva intervened by containing the river in his locks. Shiva is also the divine healer, redeemer who blesses devotees with inner strength. Thus, Rudra is paradoxically a destroyer and preserver at the same time, like Mother Kali.

Shiva as Rudra is in, on, and of the earth. Yet He is of the universe and beyond it simultaneously. He epitomizes consciousness. He is also the sage.

> In his terrifying aspect Siva is Rudra, the powerful in the sky, whose work begins on earth, the violent, who directs the ascent of the conscious being; his strength is pitted against ali evil, striking the sinner and the enemy. Tolerating neither imperfection nor hesitation, he is the most terrible of the gods [...]. But he is also the supreme healer. If he is opposed he destroys; if his aid is invoked he heals all wounds and cares for the sick and the suffering. The strength to struggle is his gift, as are also peace and final joy.[1]

Thus we can see that He is change, another name for renewal and regeneration. Destruction, entailing creation, and creation entailing destruction, are the essence of His being as the agent of change. B.C. Sinha observes:

> There is no doubt that he personifies destruction but indirectly it is reproduction. To destroy is therefore, to change or to reproduce. Here we see that the powers of Siva and Brahma have been confounded. Thus we can easily understand the deity of destruction to preside over generation.[2]

As consciousness itself, in human terms, Shiva stands for divine bliss. He is the calm and serene ascetic with the third eye meant to destroy the world of *Maya*. The third eye, a means of Supreme Vision, makes him *Trinetra.* An essential aspect of this vision is the form of Mahakala the One who transcends time. Stella Kramrisch associates this aspect of *Kala* with the dark side of Shiva as represented by *tamas* in Sankhya philosophy. She contends: "Kala is dark mode of Siva [...]. It is equivalent to *tamas*, the dark tendency of disintegration, of which Siva is the lord. As kala he swallows everything with the quality of darkness."[3]

As the dynamic mover of the universe, Shiva is Natraja or the King of Dance who engages in a frenzied dancing the very source of the world's motion and activity. In a spiritual sense, this is the method of a Yogi to attain enlightenment as it represents a selfless hankering for God. Sinha explains: "Like yoga, the dance induces trance, ecstasy, the experience of the divine, the realization of one's own secret nature, and, finally merges into the divine essence."[4] Shiva also dances on the cremation ground thereby maintaining a continuum of birth-death-rebirth or "the eternal flux and movement of the universe which this dance keeps ever in motion."[5] Stella Kramrisch sees in the *Tandav* (Cosmic dance) an activity which is five-fold:

> [...] Nataraja, the Lord of dancers, dancing, shows his five-fold activity, the expression of his divine totality. His dancing limbs convey by their movements and symbols, the five-fold action of creation, maintenance, dissolution, veiling-unveiling, and liberation.[6]

Thus we can see that Shiva represents life and death, motion and inertia, and is thereby the all-encompassing God. The dance is therefore the Eternal Cosmic Truth—the rhythm of the cosmos itself. Thus, Shiva is the Absolute. This archetype is illustrated by Donald and Johnson:

> Siva, in fact, is the personification of the Absolute, particularly in its dissolution of the universe. He combines two opposite things. He is an archetypal ascetic as well as an archetypal dancer. On the one hand he is a total tranquillity and on the other hand he is a Total Activity. These aspects are dual manifestations of an absolutely non-dual.[7]

Having discussed the archetype of Shiva in detail, we may now turn to the world of Rao's stories to see how this archetype is made to operate therein. The love-starved and bitter Akkayya invokes Shiva in His *Vishwa Roopa* (Cosmic Form) through a prayer. The suffering woman's faith in Shiva is benediction and grace. Before death, Akkayya remains bedridden for a long time. On the day of Shivratri, the presence of Shiva is manifested to her and she actually stands up with some assistance after forty eight days. Child-like exhilaration overwhelms her even though she collapses, "[Akkayya's] eyes still glowed with the ecstasy of a child and she lay in the bed smiling" (*CBS*: 85). She seems to have glimpsed the divine aura regaining beatific innocence.

"The True Story of Kanakapala, Protector of Gold" is a tale of Rangappa's pilgrimage to Kashi Vishweshwara and evokes the archetype of Shiva in the form of Lingam. While dreaming, Rangappa sees Kashi-Vishweshwara and His Consort, Parvathi. The divine couple desires that Rangappa must take care of and be in charge of the hill-top temple where they would "sprout" (*P&R*: 4). The vision is fulfilled: "On a rock at the very top, he saw the figure of Shiva as *linga* and Parvathi with her holy tress and crown, as though carved but yesternight, and yet how old and shapeful and serene" (*P&R*: 4). The Lingam is not a mere representation of fertility in the sense of the phallus; it rather implies the subtle body (*Linga Sharira*) of Shiva, which is equated one with the Absolute Reality. Rangappa obeys the divine command by meditating on the *Atharva-veda*. The dynamic nature of *Prakriti*, in the sense of regeneration, a symbol of the immortality of the soul, that is, "the imperishable Purusha,"[8] is thus stated.

Rao subscribes to the view that Shiva can be realized only through the grace of Parvathi. He writes echoing the hymn by Shankaracharya:

> O filled with essence and ever in plenitude,
> Beloved to life of Shankara [*Shiva*] himself,
> O Parvathi, give me alms. (*OGG*: 13)

This is owing to the fact that Parvathi being Shiva's anima, a necessary step for self-actualization or, in Yogic terms, connection with the Ultimate Reality embodied by Shiva. Campbell echoes this Hindu viewpoint when he states that the hero's path in quest journey is made through the encounter with the Cosmic Goddess. A psychological comprehension of this fact is found in *World Mythology*:

> Man must first rise to the plane of unity by pure untroubled meditation. It is only after this experience has been taken as far as possible that one can return without danger to the plane of multiplicity, for then in everything that comes into view one can see the divine scheme of things in its perfect and total harmony [...].[9]

Duality in non-duality is thus visible on the psychological as well as spiritual planes. Tagore refers to this as "motionless centre of movement"[10] or even as Eliot speaks of the "still centre" of the dance. Perception in its essence must be grasped in the sense of being as being, to be one in this state. This is what Rao means by "hearing is just hearing" (*OGG*: 14). "Nobody hearing" begins with the dissolution of the ego-ridden self.

Moti Ram, the illiterate taxi driver is devoted to Shiva whom he has realized through Parvathi. His *bhakti* reveals the nuances of *Nada* (Eternal sound) and he succeeds in ego-dissolution that culminates in salvation. His prayer is in the active *bhakti* mode, and takes the form of beating a drum. He states with a sense of clarity that "[…] to beat drum that Shiva's silence become sound could only be the gift of Mother Parvathi" (*OGG*: 18). The apparent contradiction of activity in inactivity and vice versa is a part of Shiva's *Vishwa Roopa* and is known to Moti Khan: "To a drummer night is like a drum. One hears the beats. You know that's why Lord Shiva has the drum in his hand" (*OGG*: 18). Upon elaboration, the extinction of the ego on the part of this ordinary taxi driver is also visible: "He alone beats the drum true who knows he is never there" (*OGG*: 18).

The story of Bholanath explores multifaceted Shiva archetype. In this story the characters' names for the most part are directly derived from Shiva. The protagonist, Bhola brings to mind the innocent Shiva in the myth of Bhasamasura. Bhola's guru is named Vishwanath; the name is reminiscent of Shiva presiding over the world. Vishwanath is likened to Bhola's personal Shiva. Bhola says; "The Great Vishwanath [Shiva] high up there looks after every one in the world, and this Vishwanath [his guru] here looks after me" (*OGG*: 83).

The locale of the stories in *On the Ganga Ghat* is Benares, the place where Shiva atoned for his sin of decapitating Brahma, and was thus redeemed. The setting unifies the book as a whole. Divinity in all forms—man, bird and animal—is the texture of the literary fabric and brings Shiva to mind as Pashupatinath, Lord of the animal kingdom. Stella Kramrisch explains the myth of Shiva's redemption from the sin of beheading Brahma: "At Kapalmocana, Siva was freed from his sin of having cut off the head of Brahma. The site [i.e., Varanasi] for ever remains the most holy abode of Lord Siva on earth. It was called 'Avimukta,' the region never forsaken by the Great God."[11] This incident is at the origin of the belief that immersion of the human ashes at Benares in the Ganga brings about *Mukti* (Salvation). Moreover, death in Benares means "death known and faced, transformed and transcended."[12] Benares is redemption and is beyond causality suggestive of Shiva as both cause and effect, yet neither: "In Benares there seems no reason for a cause, thus the result is no effect. No act breeds an act" (*OGG*: 10). In *On the Ganga Ghat*, Shiva as Natraja of the crematorium, the Eternal truth, is the goal to be realized by the foul-tongued Sadhu in Benares, the city of the Kalabhairav, a place of destruction and creation simultaneously. Benares as Kalabhairav is described by the Sadhu thus: "The city of Kala Bhairav is no place, for everything is destroyed there as it arises. So I go where there is instant destruction; therefore all is. Where Shivji danced on the crematorium is where the world is real. Time and space are burnt to ashes. To live, you must dance" (*OGG*: 104–05). Bholanath's Shivahood is foreshadowed in his practice recital of the *Shiva Stotra, Chandi Stotra* and *Brihat Stotra Ranakar*. He prays naturally while working:

> Worship Vishwanath, the Lord of Benares,
>
> Whose locks seem delightful with wavelets of the Ganga,
>
> He who is ever adorned on his left with Mother Gauri,
>
> (He again) beloved of Narayana,
>
> And the conqueror of the Bodiless God (Kama). (*OGG*: 78–79)

Rani Rasomani, seventy six, with "no teeth" and "whitey dim" eyes (*OGG*: 91) is an ardent devotee of Lord Shiva. The atmosphere of her household is conducive for prayer and devotion as her husband, Raja Pratap Chandra Majumdar of Bankipura, is a Brahmo-Samajite. The house is, therefore, filled "with the songs of enlightenment" (*OGG*: 88). Upon her husband's death, Rasomani moves to the holy city of Benares for good where she gives birth to Himavathi (daughter of the snows). Rani Rasomani seems to have transcended the world of Maya and is non-attached to her daughter.

Rani Rasomani immerses herself into Shiva completely even forgetting her own name. The limits of her physical body are not restrictive when it comes to having *darshan* of Shiva. "Lost" and "imperious," she exudes divine grace and elegance. She has realized the limits of "thoughts" (*OGG*: 91). For her Shiva is a reality per se, and the sight of him induces a state of religio-spiritual frenzy. Rao's description is enlightening:

> She sits as if the thought was but one, and one only—a thought is a thought, so there is no thought. When she thought of Lord Shiva he was present to her, with the serpent garland, the tiger skin, the Ganges crown, his third eye filled with compassion. For her Shiva was real. More real she would say than this hand, and she will beat her exquisite hands against the marble of the temple floor to prove Shiva was Shiva. (*OGG*: 91–92)

Words like "wise," "kind," "foolish" or "ignorant" fall short of interpreting her being. As a rose is a rose, "she was she" (*OGG*: 92). This gives us an idea of her enlightenment, a state in which the flame of her ego is completely extinguished.

Rao's stories in *On the Ganga Ghat* in particular, abound in the Shiva archetype—obvious, concrete and subtle. Ritualistic worship is the fuel to light the fire of the Self, the "I", "attributeless, and so unborn and deathless ..." (*OGG*: 130). Regular and faithful chanting of the *mantra* "Shivoham" with total focusing of being connects one with Pure Consciousness—Shiva incarnate. Regarding the immanence of Shiva, Rao writes in *The Serpent and the Rope* (again a hymn by Shankaracharya).

> Not hearing nor tasting nor smelling nor seeing
> But Form of Consciousness and Bliss;
> Shiva I am, I am Shiva.
> I am beyond imagination, form of the formless,
> ... ...
>
> Form of Consciousness and Bliss
> Shiva I am, I am Shiva.[13]

Rao's conception and propagation of the Shiva archetype blends well with the Mother Ganga archetype. The latter is symbolic of the inner Jnana Ganga which is none other than Pure

Consciousness, that is Shiva. The mythic Shiva takes on the psychological aspect, mundane and spiritual, and is simultaneously a symbol of the Self as well as a symbol of the journey to connect with, and merge in the Self in the Whitmanesque sense of the term.[14] For ordinary humanity, however, Kashi (Benares) is portrayed as the abode of the "I", the Self which is cosmic in proportions, and is in fact, Shiva incarnate. Benares is used as a dramatic magnet to move the reader to reflect upon the Self. This is in consonance with the spirit of Hindu religion and mythology. The belief of leaving one's mortal remains at the cremation ground of Manikarnika ghat "induced the believers in Hinduism to come to this place, which guarantees salvation [...]."[15]

This holy magnet is ensconced in Rao's psyche. The literal aspect is however transcended and the reader is transported to a world of subtle spirituality in which the mundane is not denied though it takes on a different dimension altogether.

II
Naga Archetype

The Nagas (serpents), descendants of the sage Kashyap and his wife, Kadru, are a highly vital and significant archetype of Hindu mythology. The Nagas are important vehicles and agents of the destruction of evil. This is immediately grasped in the form of Shiva whose body is bedecked with Nagas. Shesha Naga forms the bed of Lord Vishnu—the Preserver of the universe. Fabulous as well as powerful, the Nagas are denizens of the underworld (*Patala/Patalaloka*) with Takshaka as their king. Some are demoniac; some divine. They possess the power of assuming any form—human, half-human, reptilian, that of insects, etc., Vogel observes:

> The Nagas may occasionally assume human form, but they do not belong to the human world. Theirs is Nagaloka wherever that mysterious realm of snakes may be located. They are decidedly unhuman (*a-manusha*), and in Buddhist writings they are frankly classed among animals.[16]

The Naga as a symbol of virtue and divinity forms an important dimension of Hinduism. They are "the object of a fervent cult."[17]

The *Vedas* and the *Puranas* imparted sense of majesty to the Nagas, the most important archetype being the serpent kings Sheshnaga, Vasuki, and Takshak. Takshak is an evil trickster. Shesha, as Ananta is like the titan Atlas who bore the weight of the sky on his shoulders, though modern representations show him as the bearer of the earth like the serpent King. Shesha represents the eternality of Vishnu by forming his Cosmic bed at the dawn of creation. He is the symbol of eternity when he holds his own tail in mouth. The Atlas-Ananta connection is a Campbellian monomyth in its psychology and dimension. The office of Ananta-Atlas is eternal. Vasuki, the ruler of Nagaloka (serpent world) is second in hierarchy to Shesha. He allowed his body to be used as the rope during the churning of the ocean by the gods and the demons, and symbolizes the cosmic balance of good and evil, divine and demoniac. As Shiva's girdle, he helps the Lord to kill demons and "is supposed to be slung round that god's neck."[18] In his role as the Preserver of cosmic balance he is eternality. Takshaka, "poisonous, fierce and relentless,"[19] embodies trickery, deceit and deception in the mode of evil. Raja Rao's serpent-characters-cum-symbols are a manifestation of virtue and goodness espousing truth, honesty and sincerity. In "The True story of Kanakapala," the Naga Kanakapla as a destroyer of ills is obviously based on the mythic Shesha, the slayer of the demons. The story flows from the lips of Old Venkamma, Plantation Subbayya's sick mother, and is of the Puranic mode. Rangappa's vision of Shiva and Parvathi is followed by the appearance of Kanakapala, the protector of gold. A symbol of divine virtues, the serpent takes on the role of the guardian of the temple whose main duty becomes guarding Rangappa's gold from the avaricious British. With reference to this role of a serpent, Vogel contends:

> The possession of treasures, magic gems, and spell is, of course, a characteristic which the Nagas share with other classes of divine and semi-divine beings [...].
>
> In Buddhist tradition the serpent-demons are also represented as guardians of holy objects.[20]

This esoteric engagement duty and its dimension are given concrete form by Rao in the characterization of Kanakapala.

Insofar as human failings and virtues are concerned, "The tale is intended to tell how greed for money works in human hearts and turns them into devils, and how a particular family feud presents the universal truth of conflict between good and evil, selflessness and greed."[21]

The first part mainly concerns Rangappa and merely introduces Kanakapala. In the second part, Kanakapala assumes a pivotal role in the feud among Rangappa's descendants. One of them, Seetharmu, a "good-like boy," is learned, obedient, respectful and virtuous. Rangappa's pot of gold is the bone of contention between Seetharamu and his greedy, wicked elder brothers, Surappa and Ranganna along with the widow-sister, Sata, "clever as a jackal," and a "malignant minx" (*P&R*: 7).

The serpent zealously guards the gold as his duty dictates. The villains make an unsuccessful attempt to murder Seetharamu. Sata too fails in her attempt to kill him. Infuriated, Kanakapala now takes on the added role of Seetharamu's body-guard. They share a special affinity:

> [...] Kanakapala [was], furious for the first time, and [was], lying near Seetharamu's bed, to guard him from further harm. How he lay there, quiet and awake, eyes shining like jewels, and old, old skin dandruff-covered and parched, shrivelled like the cast off skin of a plantain. Somehow Kanakapala had a special love for Seetharamu. When he was born, they say Kanakapala had slowly slipped into the room, and stealing into the cradle, had spread his hood over the child, and disappeared with the swiftness of lightning. (*P&R*: 7)

Seetharamu and Kanakapala embody righteousness and truth as opposed to Surappa, Ranganna and Sata who are veritable personifications of evil. But even the divine snake does not attack the villains, "for being of the temple it can never sting a Vision-House man" (*P&R*: 8). He fails to realize that this is the age of Kaliuga, full of evil, which can be destroyed only through divine violence.

Seetharamu is ruthlessly beaten by his brothers over the issue of division of the property. No one in the village can take up his cause. He suffers in his simplicity, innocence and truthfulness till Kanakapala appears:

> It was Kanakapala, who, strange to say, suddenly appeared and, slipping between the two aggressors and Seetharamu, tried to separate them. But when they continued he roped himself round the foot of Surappa who staggered and fell. Then Kanakapala frightened Ranganna with his spread hood, and Ranganna ran out breathlessly [...]. (*P&R*: 9)

After some time, Seetharamu's corpse is discovered. Kanakapala is tricked out of the sanctum and all crevices are closed up. Kanakapala has apparently failed to protect Seetharamu and the gold. He takes his tail in his mouth and commits suicide:

> Furious he ran to the roof, and slipped into the eaves, but every chink and hole had been closed with cloth and coconut rind. He rushed back to the kitchen again but there was no one. He ran to the byre, spitting venom at every breath [...] and there was no one. Then, frantic, helpless, repentant, he rushed out of the door and scampered up the hill. Entering the temple, he went round and round the god and goddess, once, twice, thrice, and curling himself at the foot of the Divine Couple, swallowed his tail, and died. (*P&R*: 11)

But his presence reaches into life even from the dark portals of death. The brothers cannot find the gold and they are cursed to be childless and part of this self-negating cycle for seven incarnations: "[...] never till seven times are they dead and seven times are they reborn can they wear out their sacrilegious act" (*P&R*: 11). The evil is punished as justice demands. Kanakapala's death evokes the image of Kundalini, the unwinding of the serpent coil. In this state, *maya* [22] is transcended and one connects with Consciousness Pure, that is, divinity incarnate.

Through this story Rao perhaps emphasizes the importance of roots, that is, the unconscious. Elsewhere Rao advises: "Go back to your roots."[23] The serpent is a vehicle to rediscover and thereby imbibe and assimilate one's roots—the gateway of the unconscious. It may be stated here that for Rao the collective unconscious is not restricted to time past, and transcends the narrow and superficial division of time. Hence, it is as much of time past as of time present and time future. This is in consonance with the traditional Hindu view of *Kala* (Time) as an eternal continuum. The story thus is undoubtedly a modern "monomyth," yet culture specific.

"Companions" is the tale of an enlightened serpent who forces Moti Khan, a sensualist to tread the path of enlightenment. The serpent, reincarnation of Pandit Srinath Sastri, is condemned to take this form for the sin of asking for "a bagful of gold and liberation from the cycle of birth and death" (*P&R*: 29) by Goddess Lakshamma. Moti Khan and the serpent-sage fulfil a mutual need in each other. Moti Khan is the vehicle of the serpent's complete enlightenment and vice versa. Goddess Lakshamma explicitly stated this when Sastri demanded the gold. Gold and wisdom, in the worldly sense are ephemeral: "Gold and wisdom go in life like soap, and oil" (*P&R*: 29). Moti Khan initially views the serpent as "Satan" whose "race [...] caused the fall of Adam," and a "wretch" (*P&R*: 30). The serpent stalks him relentlessly and eventually succeeds in imposing his will on the reluctant Moti Khan. As time progresses, Moti Khan begins to evolve and realizes the fulfilling nature of the spiritual journey. This type of role of the serpents is explicitly referred to in *World Mythology*:

> The serpents, usually called Nagas and Naginis, have a triple mission on the terrestrial plane: in the first place, they forbid access to spiritual truths to those who are not worthy of them; in the second place, they confer them upon those who deserve them, and, finally, they strive to prevent these truths from going beyond the material plane.[24]

The serpent in "Companions" seems to have undertaken the second mission, that is, of conferring spiritual enlightenment on Moti Khan.

Women become inconsequential to Moti Khan, and his mind is fixed on the Lord. Carnality is sublimated. He hankers "to find God" (*P&R*: 32). This is of course initially from without but eventually the summons emanates from within. He steeps himself in Sheikh Chisti and is rewarded by God-discerning vision. Regarding the serpent he realizes: "Faithful shall he be, true companion of the God-seeker" (*P&R*: 34). He gets married and the serpent remains his companion, his guide. After the death of Moti Khan, the serpent also dies and is buried beside him (Moti Khan), symbolizing union in death as each facilitated the other on the road to enlightenment.

Regarding the significance of Rao's serpent stories, K.R. Rao observes:

> The two serpent stories for instance, belong to the oral tradition where the narrative meanders freely beyond the constrictions of time and space. The constant shuttling back and forth in time imparts to the stories a larger perspective. Raja Rao's unfaltering sense of situation and the ability to visualize and evoke the scene, enables him to use effectively the expressionistic techniques [...]. It is a world of 'dream and fantasy communicated through convincing images and the evocation of atmosphere.'[25]

The quote highlights the power and beauty of the two serpent stories. The use of the Naga archetype brings out "the Freudian superego and sometimes as some omniscient inner force—the *antaryami* or the inner conscience, observing and checking most vigilantly every carnal impulse that rises in Moti Khan [...]."[26] This in turn is evocative of the state of *kundalini*. Thus the two serpent stories, "Companions" and "Kanakpala" successfully embody the Naga archetype as a modern 'monomyth' based on tradition. Insofar as both transcend the dimensions time, they are complementary and fit well in the mould of Rao's praxis of enlightenment.

III
Devi/Mother Archetype

Jung regards the Devi/Mother archetype as a symbol as well as 'whole' in itself. Mother is a symbolic personification of qualities like protection, care, sympathy, fertility and fruitfulness. The archetype has immense potential for absorption: Jung uses the image of a "container" or receptacle to signify it. It is both empty and full simultaneously. It is therefore one of duality as elucidated in Hindu thought having both a positive charge and a negative charge, and as such, may be said to be Anima and

Animus or Yin and Yang. Viewed at a tangible level, it is both positive and negative at the same time, but this is not a contradiction; it is rather the two sides of the same coin. With reference to the tangibly positive aspect, Jung states:

> The qualities associated with it [Mother archetype] are maternal solitude and sympathy; the magic authority of the female; the wisdom and spiritual exaltation that transcend reason; any helpful instinct or impulse; all that is benign, all that cherishes and sustains, that fosters growth and fertility.[27]

Regarding a holistic interpretation, Jung clarifies: "Just as all archetypes have a positive, favourable, bright side that points upwards, so also they have one that points downwards, partly negative and unfavourable [...]."[28] Jung equates the negative side of the Mother archetype with the darker aspects of the psyche which deceive, cheat, seduce and poison. On the negative side the mother archetype may connote anything secret, hidden, dark; the abyss, the world of the dead, anything that devours, seduces, and poisons, that is terrifying and inescapable like fate.[29] This is analogous to Jung's archetype of the wise old man in its negative aspect, a bringer of poison, one who misleads to damnation and degeneration (not only psychic and physical but psychological and spiritual as well). Destruction and chaos, generally concomitant effects of each other, are its forms. The Devi is both terrible and benign. Kali embodies this form and manifestation and is indeed the Cosmic Force, dual in all aspects, of destruction and regeneration. Jung finds the best evidence of the emanation of the "paradoxical Kali," simultaneously terrible and loving in the concept of "Prakriti" (Primordial Nature) along with its three "gunas" (attributes) of *sattva* (goodness), *rajas* (passion) and *tamas* (darkness). In this vein he contends: "These are three essential aspects of the mother: her cherishing and nourishing goodness, her orgiastic emotionality, and her Stygian depths."[30]

Indian mythology and religion consider duality and non-duality as not contrary to each other, but as modes of appearance. And yet they retain the possibility of distinction. This is what the Devi is. Durga, Lakshmi, Parvathi and Saraswati, and of course Kali, are but her various manifestations. The world, according to Hindu thought, is both full and empty, separate and conjoined, in which everything exists, and also does not exist. I propose an attempt an elucidation of the positive and negative aspects of Kali at the tangibly perceivable, mundane level.

Duality is the Devi's typical nature and psychology. For example, Durga personifies ferocity projecting menace in expression, action and form. As Shiva's spouse, on the other hand Parvathi, is an epitome of beauty and tenderness projecting a state of being benign. Regarding the totality of the Devi in her various manifestations or roles Veronica Ions observes:

> For each of these roles she [the Devi] has a different name (Sati, Parvati, Durga, Kali), and they may roughly be divided into mild characters and fierce [...] this duality may also be traced back to pre-Aryan goddess, who was both bringer of fertility and exacter of living sacrifice.[31]

Kali, specifically, is the terrible goddess of *Kala* (Time) who takes birth when the world is replete with evil to restore balance. In psychological terms, she personifies the sublime and the grotesque, supreme love and abhorrence, destruction and nourishment, or the Mother who is tenderness herself. Commenting upon the idol of Mother Kali at Dakshineshwar, Campbell reveals:

> She [Kali] was Cosmic Power, the totality of the universe, the harmonization of all the pairs of opposites, combining wonderfully the terror of absolute destruction with an impersonal yet motherly reassurance. As change, the river of time, the fluidity of life, the goddess at once creates, preserves and destroys. Her name is Kali, the Black One [...].[32]

As such, Campbell brings the duality-cum-non-duality into focus: Kali signifies the totality of being, the totality of essence. In view of the "paradoxical" aspect of Kali, one may realize that creation is destruction; destruction is creation—one of the paramount and enveloping ideas of Hindu mythology with Shiva representing the animus of this universal truth. Kali also destroys and creates; creates and destroys simultaneously. She is terror and destruction, a divinity capable of demoniacal behaviour, yet one worthy of adoration as well as an epitome of love. With respect to her power to destroy and create, recreate, or regenerate, Campbell holds that this "represents the totality of what can be known."[33] He goes on to refer to an experience of Paramshansa Ramakrishna from *The Gospel of Sri Ramakrishna*, in which the mystic had a vision of a beautiful lady emerging from the Ganga, giving birth to a child, tenderly nourishing it and suddenly crushing and devouring it after assuming a terrible form, and finally, submerging and disappearing back into the Ganga. This is in all probability the best example, and once understood, the best explanation of the totality of Mother Kali, that is, the archetype as a whole.

The essential oneness of creation and destruction, and vice versa, illustrates the state of birth and death followed by rebirth and death, *ad infinitum*. This nutshell of duality and non-duality, the process of creation and destruction, the process of destruction and creation because one has to create to destroy; and destroy in order to create, has been beautifully pictured with respect to birth and death in particular, almost like a psalm by Walt Whitman:

> The smallest sprout shows there is really no death,
>
> And if ever there was it led forward life, and does
> not wait at the end to arrest it
>
> And ceased the moment life appear'd.
>
> All goes onward and outward, nothing collapses,
>
> And to die is different from what anyone supposed and
> luckier.[34]

The Devi mythology, is often associated with Mahashakti (Great Energy), the Goddess of the Cosmic Power with three major manifestations—Mahasaraswati, Mahalakshmi and Mahakali—the Animus of each being Brahma, the Creator, Vishnu, the Preserver and Shiva or Mahesh, the Destroyer respectively. The Animus is far more than literal. It is the corresponding charge of the polarities of the male manifestations. The fact that the various forms of the Devi are consorts of the Gods of the Trinity is evidence of totality through polarity, the form revealed being understood at any level from the most basic to the most esoteric and abstruse, i.e., physical, psychological, psychic, spiritual, etc.

Aurobindo regards Mahashakti as "original power, supreme Nature, holding in herself infinite existence and creating the wonders of the cosmos."[35] In *The Synthesis of Yoga*, Aurobindo discusses all the manifestations of the Devi including the most powerful one as Maheshwari:

> [...] Maheshwari, goddess of the supreme knowledge [...] brings to us her vision for all kinds and wideness of truth, her rectitude of spiritual will, the calm and passion of her supramental largeness, her felicity of illumination [...] Mahakali, goddess of the supreme knowledge [...] brings to us her vision for all kinds and widenesses of truth, her rectitude of spiritual force and severest austerity of Tapas and swiftness to the battle and the victory and the laughter, the attahasa, that makes light of defeat and death and the powers of the ignorance [...] Mahalakshmi the goddess of the supreme love and delight, and her gifts are the spirit's grace and the charm and beauty of the Ananda and protection and every divine and human blessing [...] Mahasarswati [is] the goddess of divine skill, and of the works of the Spirit [...] and the utilities of divine knowledge and the self-application of the spirit to life and the happiness of its harmonies.[36]

This quote, viewed at the surface level, seems to be devoid, of the aspect of duality in non-duality and vice versa, which is the Jungian "container" or receptacle of consciousness. However, what is intended here is to show the majesty of the Devi incarnations to firmly establish the premise of duality in non-duality and vice versa which is visible if one carefully reads between the lines.

Maheshwari in particular, is a symbol of virtues like serenity, comprehensive knowledge, wisdom, compassion, matchless grace and supramental vision. She is omniscience and omnipotence. Mahakali, the Goddess of *Kala* or Time, represents, however, unusual pace, energy, passion, will power, resistance and, of course, terror. Mahalakshmi is gentleness, beauty, harmony, bewitching charm, etc., and in essence is characterized by the benign. Mahasaraswati embodies wisdom, synchronized harmony, perfection (as an ideal) and meticulous attention to detail.

Som P. Ranchan, taking a cue from Sri Aurobindo, has focused on the different aspects of the Devi/Mother archetype in a psychological vein by analysing the nature, propensities and roles of the different manifestations such as Mahakali, Mahalakshmi and Mahasaraswati. Maheshwari of course has not been dealt with. Mother Durga is a representation of Mahashakti (Cosmic Power), a "Sovereign Power" who takes different forms (*Rupa*) to destroy demons which are symbols of evil attributes of the psyche of mankind. Ranchan's analysis is an attempt to effectively illustrate all levels in a psychological and demythified manner, encompassing the mundane as it is concrete. Thus a down to earth foundation is laid so that abstraction can be easily understood. Of the archetype of Mahakali, insofar as its duality of nature goes, Ranchan contends: "Mahakali comprises a male and female charge. The male charge, plurality of Mahakali is Rudra, god of destruction, dissolution in the service of change. The female charge is Saraswati, the goddess of knowledge, recollection."[37] The Goddess of Time is timeless and beyond our ken. The aspect of timelessness is evidenced by the fact that Mahakali was instrumental in slaying the demons, Madhu and Kaitabh, through Vishnu who killed them in mid-air, an atmosphere in which they were susceptible to death. Madhu and Kaitabh's fate at Vishnu's hands through the intervention of the Goddess, abiding both in time and timelessness, was inevitable and necessary as they personified the debased instincts of animalistic lust without recognizing and acknowledging the manifestation of immanent divinity of all creation. The successful quest at the lowest level, is one of harmony and goodness, the highest level being Jaspers' "being-in-itself," or Jung's utmost individuation, or Campbell's successful hero-journey, that is attainment of pure Vedantic Consciousness. Mahakali is a shaker of the whole universe. Force, valour, tremor and pace are her names. She is Divine commotion. This brings Vivekananda to mind, his poem, "Kali the Mothe"r in particular. He once said, "The whole of the ocean is present at the back of each wave."[38] This is the nature and the essence of the Mahakali-spirit marked by will, will and more will. Divine violence and bloodshed are Mahakali's metaphors and are part and parcel of the creative purpose in which destruction is inherent. She is the Goddess of Time who washes away and demolishes the established order. Ranchan states, "Mahakali demands that the old, the moribund, the regressive be swept aside."[39] This is Mahakali in her regenerative incarnation. Destruction is inevitable wherever Mahakali treads. Mahakali is change. In Jungian light, Ranchan observes, "Mahakali would be the terrible mother experienced by the world in the times of change, vicissitudes, by the individual caught between death-rebirth cycle."[40] At the psychic level, this means the destruction of dead faculties and potentialities with regeneration in its wake creating a fresh vision and renewed faculty of perception. Power, strength, vigour, vitality are the hallmarks of Mahakali to bring about creation, destruction, regeneration—in fact, change. Traditionally, Mahalakshmi is the goddess of harmony and beauty. With reference to the Mahalakshmi archetype, Ranchan states:

> She is in charge of the world of plurality, diversity and manifold differentiation [...]. The archetype of Mahalakshmi comprises two polarities. The male polarity is Brahma who created the second stage gods of archetypes such as the Vedic gods [...]. With his restless energy Brahma is constantly augmenting the forms, the archetypes. The Female polarity is Laxmi who in conjunction with Vishnu and other gods becomes the beautiful amazon fighter. She is the Eternal Virgin who will take energies from all the gods, do their work but belong to none.[41]

Grandiloquence and dogma are not a reflection of this archetype. Mahalakshmi is the bearer of the divine torch lighting the pathway of spirituality and aesthetics, and for the less evolved, ethics. Bewitching beauty and endearing charm are aspects of her manifestations which bestow boons of fortune and prosperity ranging from the physical (material) to the spiritual depending upon the level of the devotee and his/her method of worship. But duality is still present:

> In times of well-being, she is the *Lakshmi* of men,
> Granting (them) prosperity (*Vrdhi*) in (their) home(s);
> In times of privation, then she exists as *alaksmi*,
> for the sake of destruction.[42]

Mahalakshmi is in a continual turmoil and incessant battle with her animus as represented by the demon Mahishasura—a paragon of intellect, power and valour despite his bestiality apparent in his buffalo-form. The form of the buffalo signifies a state of low-evolution in spite of his mental and physical gifts. His power is egocentric and his vision, circumscribed. In slaying this demon, the Goddess as Chandika, overcomes, nay, destroys her own negative animus. She restores balance to the universe, the balance of the divine and the demoniac without which struggle is absent. The balance is essential for unfolding life's joys and sorrows, its successes and failures, its activity and inactivity, etc., all of which work in unison to bring about harmony—a state of polarities of the male and female charge. As a whole the Mahalakshmi manifestation "[...] demands cooperation, harmony, differentia, functional hierarchy of entities, qualities, flavours. She is against the animal ego seeking aggrandizement."[43] She is the vehicle to dissolve negative ego, the ego marked by haughtiness and despotism. Ranchan argues that she is psychologically Jung's Anima, "the Great Mother, Anima mundi, threatening and destructive for badly formed egos."[44]

The archetype of Mahasarswati is all encompassing, a symbol of comprehensive wisdom finely tuned to counterbalance perfection and meticulous attention to details. Ranchan views this as a process largely psychological in nature.

> She [Mahasaraswati] comprises two parts, one Vishnu, the other Parvati: Parvati in conjunction with Rudra dissolves the world of time, space causality that Mahakali brought forth, and that Mahalaxmi maintains. She takes the Sadhak into ecstasy, Samadhi, radical, total transformation—a transformation in which the veil is lifted from the face of the inscrutable.[45]

She is beyond spatio-temporality which she dissolves as Parvathi in conjunction with Rudra. Even Mahakali's creation of causality—an illusion in itself—is not spared, nor allowed to continue into existence, the existence which Mahalakshmi preserves. Spiritual encounters with her are soul-searing causing a complete metamorphosis in the seeker's search for being. Divine spirituality is her personality and form. Thus she destroys worldly desire gradually. The demons of *Maya* (illusion) and *Avidya* (ignorance) are crushed in her wake as she is the living embodiment of comprehensive wisdom.

To encapsulate all three forms, Ranchan's observations are pertinent. According to him, Mahakali resides in the domains of sages and *drashtas* (seers); Mahalakshmi is the inspiration of heroes; Mahasarswati is the spiritual beacon of the gurus. Ranchan goes on to observe that in order to establish a full and rich relationship with the Mother archetype, the *sadhak* must realize all four aspects of the Devi. The first requirement for this is devotion to the point of complete surrender; secondly, gnosticism which requires a cognitive approach with the power of instantaneous recognition; thirdly, the transformative which signifies a metamorphosis of profane consciousness to sacred consciousness; and lastly the dynamic, marked by activity and vigour.

The Mother archetype is pervasive in Rao's fiction. Rao's perspicacity along with its creative cultural mix lends a unique content and form to his characterization. The female triad of Javni, Akkayya and Nimka delicately dance in the reader's consciousness. Beti Bai, Padma, Rani Rasomani and Nanna are equally meaningful from the viewpoint of the present analysis.

"Javni," the story of an illiterate and innocent domestic servant at the Revenue Inspector, Ramappa's house, is one of extreme suffering and pain. Javni is "[...] past forty, a little wrinkled beneath the lips and with strange, rapturous eyes. Her hair was turning white, her breast were fallen and her bare broad forehead showed pain and widowhood" (*CBS*: 3). This description is somewhat subliminal suggesting that Javni was quite beautiful as a young girl. The fact that Javni does not collapse under the burden of suffering and pain is entirely due to her selfless worship of the Goddess Talakamma. She does not rave and rant at her suffering but heroically and cheerfully endures it. Javni is cow-like in her docility. She is faithful and takes pride in doing her duties. Javni has imbibed the archetype of the Mother as the Talkamma *bhaktin*. Her motherly love extends to and encompasses even animals like the "calf," her surrogate son.

Javni's tale is one of incessant and extreme woe and suffering. Married at the age of eighteen, she soon becomes a widow. Despite the intense shock, she survives and endures all this in the prevailing social milieu in which widowhood is castigated. Cruelly treated by her in-laws and subsequently by her brother, Bhim and his wife, she ends up as a domestic servant at a residence for the Revenue Inspector. Light enters her life upon contact with the benevolent Ramappa and his sister, Sita.

Though Javni has suffered great abuse, she bears ill-will to none. She loves her brother's son dearly for whose well-being she sacrifices a lamb to her Goddess every three years. Javni's innocence, simplicity, gentle nature and above all, her faith in Goddess Talkamma, save her from disintegration. At one point, however, she begins to crack and entertains thoughts of suicide: "I wept and sobbed and often wanted to go and fall into the river. But I know Goddess Talkamma would be angry with me, and I stopped each time I wanted to kill myself" (*CBS*: 15). Talakamma's presence thus dissuades her from the immoral and cowardly act.

Javni's endurance and her innate goodness border on the heroic. Her simplicity is the vital weapon in her spiritual arsenal to contend with life at all levels. Her simple faith in the Goddess is her anchor in life's turbulent ocean. The narrator's question as to what Goddess Talakamma has given Javni, incenses her as she proclaims:

> 'All! Everything! Should I live if that Goddess did not protect me? Would that child come to me if the Goddess did not help me? Would Mother be so good to me if the Goddess did not bless me? Why, Ramappa, everything is hers. O Great Goddess Talakamma, give everybody good health and long life and all the joys! Protect me, Mother!' (*CBS*: 18–19)

It is clear that "Her religion was not specifically of the *Vedas* or *Upnishads* or of *Gita*; nor was it as propounded and preached by such philosophers as Shankara and Ramanuja. Hers was that simple faith of a villager who worships with greatest devotion even a pebble smeared with red paint and placed under a peepal tree."[46]

At the end Ramappa and his sister, Sita, have to leave and Javni is tearful—spiritually pure in vision and imbibing Goddess Talakamma. In this reaction, she emotionally declares Ramappa and Sita to be Gods:

> 'Ramappa, how can I help but weep? Shall I ever see again a family of gods like yours? Mother was kind to me, kind like a veritable goddess. You were so, so good to me, and Master—.' Here she broke again into sobs. (*CBS*: 22)

Javni, the domestic maid, in her unlimited devotion has realized the essence of being through equanimity. This harmony borders upon the spiritual and is a direct result of centring her being in the Devi Talakamma. Her unswerving faith and complete surrender to the Goddess endow her with enormous inner strength and magnificent grace.

The presence of the Mahakali archetype is felt in Javni's will to sustain. This will is indefatigable and eternally courageous; it is a force that moves mountains. The Mahakali aspect of terror and destruction is, however, absent despite the ease with which she could have succumbed into a negative Mahakali, a torturer and tormenter, disseminating misery to all. Allusions to her "rapturous eyes" that shine brightly and to the divine *teja* on her face make her Mahalakshmi. Her beauty and grace, and her motherly devotion to her demoniacal brother's son show her purity and her *bhaktibhava* that transcend narrow prejudice and vindictiveness. These, too, are an illustration of Mahalakshmi sensibility. Her fixity of purpose, as witnessed in her selfless devotion to Talakamma, brings to mind Mahasaraswati. Love and tolerance are her methods to live life. Regarding the Mahakali aspect in Javni, P.C. Bhattacharya observes.

> Javni the maid servant belonged to a vanishing tribe, but Javni the woman is eternal. She was like the mother cow. The cow might be hungry; she might show her bones through her skin. But she also has an all enduring patience, and gives her

> nourishing milk to all who want it. She was like the mother earth. Man treads on her, man misuses her, and man even does violence to her in his brutality. But mother earth has no caste. She knows no caste. She does not complain. In her own silent way, she sustains and nourishes the millions of living beings that crawl, slide or walk on her.[47]

"Akkayya" is the tale of a child-widow, a bitter old woman, who dries up inside, harbouring hate to life and people in general. Akkayya, the protagonist, however, begins to paradoxically redeem herself upon contact with children. Akkayya, an unwanted parasite, denied love and shelter by her brothers and in-laws, is forced to take refuge in her sister's house. Her sister is kind. Akkayya somehow develops a bond with her Grandnephew, Kittu. This relationship is the high point in her life and is the pole star in her life which is in seminal form, the catalyst for positive transformation.

Kittu, the narrator of the tale, is intrigued by Akkayya's shaven head and lack of worthwhile attire. The absence of the vermillion mark on her forehead also brings questions to his mind. His curiosity brings to the fore that Akkayya was married off at the age of eight or nine to a very old minister who soon died and left her a child-widow.

Akkayya is caught in the social web which restricts her growth, both physical and psychological. Her shaven head, and sterile attire and bearing were forced upon her. The trauma, entirely from without, sapped her psyche creating bitterness and hate in its wake. Denied love and affection, she, quite understandably, exuded hate. However, as the story unfolds, we realize that this is not Akkayya's nascent and innate nature. Caught in the vortex of physical sufferings and psychological turmoil, in which sexual frustration and repression play a major role, Akkayya slips into the negative Mahakali mould in atragic mould.

Before becoming a widow, Akkayya was "brilliant" and "intelligent" as a child. Her knowledge of the scriptures was far beyond her years. It is suggested that knowledge meant purity to her. In this phase of her life, she can be said to have had a

Mahasaraswati sensibility. However this phase does not last long. The social ostracism that she has to face consequent upon her widowhood forces on her the personality of a negative Mahakali.

As a child-widow, a whirlwind of events assailed the unprepared innocent child in Akkayya. Circumscribed by society, she was forced to take the arduous role of the mistress of the house with all its backbreaking chores. Without protection her knowledge of the scriptures lost its guiding influence and was submerged into the dark recesses of her unconscious only to surface later on as totally sterile.

Buffeted by misfortune from place to place Akkayya was finally accommodated by her magnanimous sister. Her sister's house becomes the breeding ground of her motherly nature. She showers her grandnephew, Kittu, in particular and the rest of the household children in general, with love and affection:

> [...] when by some strange misfortune three of my aunts successively died, leaving three, eight and five children, she had always enough children to take care of, and she treated them all alike, kind when they were good and severe when they were mischievous. (*CBS*: 81)

Thus, the love-starved Akkayya has not totally thrown love and affection out of the door. Quite interestingly, she retains the capacity to give. At the age of sixty, Akkayya is struck by a terrible and chronic disease. A stench, like a 'manure pit,' emanates from her. The suffering magnifies her general inner frustration making her harsh and abusive to the point of being foul-tongued. Her disposition is compounded by senility. This is, however, punctuated by emotionally warm and spiritual states when she hears about her dear Kittu who is her "little darling." In fact, her face shines. She cries "Kittu ... Kittu ... My darling Kittu ... My son, my child, Kittu!" (*CBS*: 94).

Her death is better than her life. As a dying woman, hope dominates the canvas as she is surrounded by children, who signify purity. Her attitude at this stage is rather motherly in a spiritual sense, as it is non-attached. She is like a nourishing mother cow: "And when the children left her she forgot them as the cow forgets her young ones. But God always supplied her with orphan children, and as you will soon see it was these who stood around her as she breathed her last. That was her karma!" (*CBS*: 81). The story of Akkayya with all its pathos and sufferings has been aptly encapsulated by Bhattacharya:

> 'Akkayya' is the story of a childless child-widow. None loved her although she hungered for love. She could not find solace even in religion. Her pitiable life dragged on to the last destined moment until death came to her rescue, but not before she suffered disagreeable old age, sickness, stench and senility.[48]

This is a simple narration which, however, lacks the spirit of the evolution of Akkayya's being. The most important thing to realize is that Akkayya with multiple frustrations, including the sexual, is capable of experiencing regeneration and renewal and actually does so on life's shard-strewn road. No doubt, Akkayya is sex-starved. That notwithstanding, sex is not the focal point. More accurately, she is a love-starved wife, as well as a love-starved human being.

Initially, Akkayya begins her life as Mahasaraswati, a brilliant and intelligent child with some basic knowledge of the scriptures. When suffering rears its cruel head, in the form of widowhood, she is impregnated with a negative Mahakali consciousness. Abandoned by her peoples in-law, brothers and their families, at the age of eighteen, she finds refuge is her sister's house. Stuck as she is in the mire of hate, degradation and despair, she cannot rise above these and is still dominated by negative Mahakali consciousness. The ray of transformation is found in the child Kittu and extends to other children. The Mahalakshmi mould makes its appearance, but Mahakali still exists side by side. Ultimately, however, in death, Mahalakshmi prevails as she is enveloped in and interacts with purity in the form of children—a purity in her personality which was nipped in the bud by cruel fate. Vindictiveness leaves her at last.

Akkayya's story is one of withering and shrivelling up—a virtual death-in-life. Her personality is 'reduced' because of lack of social justice circumscribed by narrow prejudice and fossilized ideas and rituals which are life-negating. Society imposes a kind of nihilism upon Akkayya; it reduces her humanity. But the story is not just a cry for love and justice; it is also a tale of heroic proportions which illustrates the dynamic and illimitable power of love to heal and transform. It is a veritable parable of love which touches the divine and evokes the image of an oasis in the desert of hate. The protagonist is an unconscious *bhaktin* of love, i.e., Mahalakshmi. Kittu pays the ultimate tribute to her when the question of her funeral rites arises. As no male member takes the responsibility of performing Akkayya's obsequies, a Brahmin is recruited to do so. The ending is open with respect to whether the rites were actually performed. Kittu's description of this state of affairs is a veritable epitaph for the soul-scarred Akkayya:

> I think, between the three brothers of my grandmother, my father, and a cousin of ours, none of them wanted to take the responsibility of performing Akkayya's obsequies. At last one of her brothers called a Brahmin, and giving him a few rupees, asked him to perform the 'necessary' ceremonies. I do not know whether the Brahmin did it. Anyway, here I have written the story of Akkayya, maybe her only funeral ceremony. (*CBS*: 95–96)

There is a big difference between Akkayya's and Javni's temperament. It is a direct case of how each acts in and reacts to life. Javni projects serenity and equanimity in the face of suffering. Her simple faith sustains her. Akkayya, possibly because she has been dealt with a greater blow, and that too at a tender age, is virulently hateful, aggressive and fiery. Javni comes into contact with kindness in the form of Ramappa and his sister, Sita. She can relate to them affectionately (which is reciprocal) as a mature adult. But adulthood is forced upon Akkayya when she is ill-equipped to take on this role. Javni's worship of the Goddess Talakamma is a great comfort and a guiding factor in her sojourn on earth. Blind faith is her sustenance. With such a beacon, she does not falter on the path to 'Mahalakshmihood.' Akkayya, however, has no such anchor. The battering she receives renders even her knowledge of the scriptures as sterile, which cannot effect a life-affirming attitude and personality.

Bitterness is the vehicle for negative Mahakali to dominate her life. Javni is always submissive and surrenders to religion totally in the archetype of Goddess Talakamma. This is emotionally and spiritually elevating. Her worship provides roots and enhances the quality of her life. Akkayya, on the other hand, is steeped in alienation and isolation which impair and mutilate her psyche. Javni's simplicity makes it easier to navigate through the sea of sufferings. Akkayya is more complex. In addition, her personality is not nourished and enriched enough from within and without before the avalanche of injustice buries her. The basic difference between Javni and Akkayya is well rendered by K.R. Rao:

> While Javni ostensibly suffers from social ostracism, Akkayya falls a victim to the destructive insularity of the puritanical tradition. While Javni seeks to sublimate her tormenting sense of isolation by cultivating a native and innocent faith in her gods and goddesses, Akkayya antagonizes her gods by a tradition of religiosity which cannot offer her such a simple faith. Consequently, she cracks up from within and the rumblings of her inner disintegration are heard all around in the household. Her love turns into hate and she directs the hate with a subconscious fury towards the family which, in treating her like a parasite, becomes parasitical itself.[49]

Her "cracking up from within" signifies the negative Mahakalihood which dominates her till she dies. The story "Nimka" is set in Paris. It traces the evolution of the protagonist, Nimka, from suffering to wisdom. A cross-cultural tale of a beautiful Russian Caucasian girl who develops a fascination for India in general and the narrator in particular, explores the transformative power of good in relation to evil. Nimka swears by Tolstoy's dictum that "evil must be met with good" (*P&R*: 99). As a waitress in a restaurant, a frequent visiting place of students, Nimka comes in contact with the narrator who introduces her to Gandhi. Gandhi inspires her; his portrait adorns the wall of her room along with Tolstoy. She grasps Mahatma Gandhi's cosmic power, interpreting it in a global context: "Mahatma Gandhi [...] is not a man, he is not a saint, he is a country" (*P&R*: 103).

Nimka is an ethereal creature and the story unfolds delicately against a romantic background. There is an aura of romance to Nimka's idealistic view of life and the world at large. Thus she is drawn to figures like Tolstoy and Gandhi. The creative setting (Paris is considered to be a fertile city for creativity), Nimka's fact of being an expatriate, and her subsequent fascination with India beautifully intermesh to form a harmonious whole. Love plays an important part in Nimka's life and development. The narrator believes that Nimka may be in love with him, but he cannot respond as he is culturally "different." The cultural barrier in the narrator's mind is best illustrated in his own words:

> She could not imagine me and the necklace altogether—that necklace was made of pain, it stood there as a reminder of man's inner strength against outer odds—it meant struggle and passion and poverty—the bow of Rama is easier to break than to twist the screw of that Russian necklace, the hand that could twist it, needed a more masculine grasp, a more painful nobility, a graver happiness. The Indian is too simple in his depth—if there's no concierge and the cat, there's no goodness. Success is sin. Gandhi is poverty. The Maharaja is proof of truth. Truth is unnaked. Love is unsaid. So, Nimotchka fell in love with Michel. (*P&R*: 101)

The Indian is not the only one for whom Nimka is unapproachable. Most of the other students also think of her as wearing an other-worldly halo. Nimka also believes that the narrator and the land from which he comes is esoteric and therefore other-worldly. A stream of ethereal romance imagined but not achieved, runs through the story. She cannot marry the narrator as he is "too far, too distant and different" (*P&R*: 102). On the other hand, Michel kissed her once. This is "improper," and so he too is unattainable. The story of Nimka brings to mind fables of ladies and knights of yore.

Esoteric knowledge and aspirations, imbued with an aura of romance characterize Nimka and her vision of life which unfolds as a microcosm in a macrocosm. Essentially it is one of a girl with a pure heart whose pole star is wisdom in thought, word and deed. In this sense, she can be said to be an image in the Mahasaraswati mould.

Nimka marries Count Vergilian Karmaloff, a restaurant owner, twenty years her senior. The marriage is unsuccessful as the Count, a widower, is also a degenerate gambler. Hope is momentarily offered in the form of a new-born son who is named Boris. But gambling continues to hold more attraction for the Count, and Nimka and her son have to deal with despair, hunger and poverty. Eventually, the Count gambles away everything and deserts his family never to be seen again. Nimka is comforted, however, in mothering Boris. This gives her greater strength to endure. Boris becomes the focus of her life. However, at the age of seventeen, Boris belies Nimka's hopes by leaving home with the unfulfilled promise that he will come back to take her away to a better life. Nimka's suffering begins as an expatriate in France. She lives an ethereal life, although this 'etherealism' is in direct conflict with her sensual being. The opposite sex considers her to be a goddess. The narrator cannot cross cultural boundaries. The relationship with Michel is not consummated because of her ethereal nature. But Nimka bears it all like a true stoic. Her stoicism comes to the fore in her disastrous marriage with the Count and the subsequent desertion by her son, Boris. But Nimka endures. The crux of her endurance is her cross-cultural view in general, with respect to Gandhi in particular: "She believed that one day truth would reign in the world. She hoped Mahatma Gandhi might still save the world" (*P&R*: 103). Nimka's wisdom, ethereal and empirical, is cosmic in mode and universal in message. Miseries befall her one after another. But courage and fortitude continue to manifest themselves. She seems to have unconsciously imbibed the Hindu view of the real nature of sorrow and joy. They are transitory and complementary. Through her life she has grasped the knowledge of karma. To quote from the text:

> Her heart contained an intimacy of sorrow that was almost kin of joy. She was warm, of course, and spoke beautifully. Her French accent had that silvery touch of the Slavs that makes the language almost sing. Nimka asked nothing of life. She asked

nothing of me. When I said goodbye, she did not say when shall I see you again? She knew the life that has ended is eternal. (*P&R*: 103)

Nimka's life is that of a *karamyogi* in which formal worship plays no part. Nimka has no gods or goddesses, although Tolstoy and Gandhi are her heroes, her inspiration, her hope of life in the eventual evolution of the world. Wisdom in the abstract, transcending cultural boundaries is her spiritual vision. Her ethereal personality, untainted by misfortune is a source of strength and purity which acts as a purifier of her truth consciousness. Nimka is not worldly; the ethereal pushes the worldly far into the background. As a matter of fact, the worldly is inconsequential as she does not even realize its existence and thereby, certainly, not its importance. Wisdom of the divine mode, graceful and elegant, is what she is, and this is how she perceives the world. Poised perennially above the worldly, residing in the lighthouse of knowledge, she embodies Mahalakshmi consciousness. As a lady like that of medieval legends she is not in a stasis. As one steeped in the Mahasaraswati archetype, she evolves continuously under the burden of suffering and pain. Her divine wisdom is founded on love and goodness which never leave her. These widen her vision and perception of reality, human and divine. Her life is in a flux—incessant, ever striving for purity in the form of wisdom. Equanimity in the face of joy and sorrow is her most outstanding quality of which love, tolerance, goodness and a desire to comprehend are inseparable components.

The story with its cross-cultural setting, characters and influences, has an appeal which is universal. Nimka's nobility of birth, her expatriate status, the fact of carrying her Russian roots with her (Tolstoy being the most dramatic example), the Indian influence and connection and of course her ethereal nature provide a beautiful canvas to show individuation in the development of a psyche that is pure.

Beti Bai, Padma and Nanna are minor characters in Rao's fictional world. Beti Bai, a silent suffering wife, is mercilessly beaten by her husband Motilal, a "swine of a bania" (*CBS*: 23).

Beti Bai indulges in ritual worship of Mahalakshmi, praying for her son's return with a daughter-in-law. At one point, she is beaten far worse than usual. Her back bleeds as a result. She bears it all as befits a conventional Hindu wife. Her submissive nature is her constant strength in this morbid environment. She regards Mahalakshmi as omniscient and omnipotent, and her *bhakti* takes on certain qualities of the Goddess.

In the story of Shankar, his wife, Padma is presented as an incarnation of Lakshmi, the bearer of good fate and fortune. In fact, Padma means Lakshmi, and Rao characterizes her as such:

> However, since Padma came into the house, everything changed. Padma was Padma [Goddess Lakshmi] herself, a lotus born, and such a gentle, civilized, sweet-voiced girl for this "barbarian Benares brahmin," he [Shankar] would say to himself. Since the day she came the aspect of the house changed [...]. (*OGG*: 64)

Thus we can see that she causes a positive change in the household making "the whole house sing" (*OGG*: 67). Her power is not confined to the mundane. Shankar is mesmerized and frequently experiences trance-like states or "compounded silences" (*OGG*: 65). On the whole, one can see that she is of the Mahalakshmi sensibility.

Viewed in the light of Vedantic thought, Nanna is technically a sinner because she earns her livelihood through prostitution. But, as a matter of fact, she is a spiritually evolved being who is soaked in compassion and wisdom. She rises above the mire that is her abode. She has sublimated the carnal into the spiritual and thus in a non-attached manner, she views her profession as 'dharma.' The nature of her *sadhana* stems from truth consciousness. Three facets of Mahashakti—Mahakali, in her dynamism; Mahalakshmi, in her grace; and Mahasaraswati, in her wisdom of the ways of the world—shine forth in her life and actions.

Thus we find that the variegated aspects of Devi archetype (Mahakali, Mahalakshmi and Mahasaraswati) find expression in Rao's stories. Sometimes this archetype is expressed in totality whereas in the case of others, only one or two dominant aspects are highlighted. Javni, for instance, becomes the personification of Mahalakshmi archetype whereas Akkayya, represents the negative aspect of Mahakali archetype.

IV
Archetypes of Mother Ganga and Cow

Mother Ganga is a perennial and timeless archetype in Indian mythology representing purity and sanctity. Ganga is the most sacred river in India "whose waters are said to have the power of cleansing from all past, present, and future sins [and] is believed to be divine [...]."[50] In Hindu mythology, Ganga is the eldest daughter of Himalaya, her younger sister being Uma (Paravati), is Shiva's spouse.

The Ganga is celestial, of divine origin. The great sage, Bhagiratha, provided a spiritual instrument for mortals to taste divinity by bringing about the descent of Ganga from heaven to earth. Once this was accomplished, the ashes of his dead ancestors in particular, and humanity at large could experience and enjoy eternal heavenly bliss through the purification of the cremated ashes in holy Ganga waters. This feat, however, was almost impossible as Ganga became wrathful due to her reluctance to descend to earth, the world of mortals. Bhagiratha invoked Shiva to stem the mighty torrential wrath of Ganga who, unappeased, attempted to sweep away even Shiva, "the Great God [...] down to the nether regions."[51] The tide was stemmed by Shiva and released from the tangled coils of his matted locks to form the seven sacred streams. Thus, Bhagiratha's ancestors, including sixty thousand sons of the mythic king Sagar, were redeemed. Wilkins quotes from Griffiths' *Ramayana*:

> Soon as the flood their dust bedewed,
> Their spirits gained beatitude,
> And all in heavenly bodies dressed
> Rose to the skies' eternal rest.[52]

The Ganga through apotheosis is the symbol of ultimate purity as far as freedom from the continual cycle of birth, death and rebirth is concerned. The great sage Shankaracharya elucidated the origin, evolution and culmination of Ganga referring to her as the Lovely Goddess:

Descending from the king of Mounts [Himalaya]
Saving one and all that dip in her waters
Sporting in (the company of) the Sea
Removing the fear of rebirth once for all,
Imitating (in her course) the curved shape of the
Serpent Adisesha
Assuming the form of a fresh creeper
Sporting in the region of the Kasi
Excels Ganga: the Lovely Goddess.[53]

Thus we can see that Ganga is a purifier, protector and liberator. The myth of the descent of Ganga from the heavens is somewhat parallel to the dispersion of fire to mankind by Prometheus. But the Ganga myth embraces more cosmic proportions as it embodies purification of karma which is ever present and of a regenerative and liberating nature in a larger sense. This is evident in *On the Ganga Ghat* as "traditionally a celestial river comes down to earth in compassion for human suffering [...]. A bath in her is supposed not only to wash away our karma—the accretions of all our past lives—but also free us from rebirth for ever" (*OGG*: 128–29).

The river Ganga is a powerful archetypal motif in Raja Rao's fictional world. Rao, especially in *On the Ganga Ghat*, has woven a beautiful pattern around Ganga which "flows fierce and fresh" purifying all (*OGG*: 59). At yet another level, Ganga signifies progression; it flows perpetually, representing 'flow' or 'continual going.' Etymologically, the root for Ganga is *gam* which in Sanskrit means to go. Generally, a river has always been a source of inspiration for poets and creative writers. As such, the Ganga (more aptly Mother Ganga as it is much more than a mere flow of water for Indians—a venerable and divine Mother, a giver of life, a protector, a symbol of purity, vitality, etc.) has inspired a large number of creative artists and writers in India. As a result, an enormous body of literature has grown around this archetype. The archetype of Mother Ganga forms an important part of the mythic imagination of Indians. The Ganga myth has been considerably dealt within the great Indian epics and other scriptures such as the *Ramayana*, the *Mahabharata* and the *Puranas*.

The archetype of Mother Ganga forms the warp and woof of the world of Rao's stories in *On the Ganga Ghat*. Interestingly enough, the river Ganga with its different dimensions becomes the canvas on which life in its variegated form has been painted. In Rao's magnum opus, *The Serpent and the Rope* also, Mother Ganga is in a vibrant and perennial flow enrapturing the protagonist, Ramswamy. It is like consciousness itself, a parallel of Ramaswamy's quest for truth. Ramaswamy is the microcosm. Ganga is the macrocosm. For Rao, Ganga is Truth (the Absolute) and is always 'pure.' Ganga liberates one from the endless karmic cycle. Ganga represents humanity which nevertheless can aspire to Truth. Rao elaborates in *The Serpent and the Rope*:

> Truth is the Himalayas, the Ganges humanity. That is why we throw the ashes of the dead to her. She delivers them to the sea, and the sun heats the waters so that, becoming clouds, they return to the Himalayas. The cycle of death and birth goes on eternally like the snows and the rivers.[54]

In essence, Rao views the Ganga as a metaphysical truth under the apotheosis of mother goddess.

Rao's Ganga is psycho-spiritual and its flow is perennial. It is like the flow of thought emanating from the mind but the state of the mundane is not denied nor negated. At the mundane level, the water of the Ganga is just water. It can be perceived, heard, touched, felt, tasted, seen and smelt. At the spiritual level, however, Ganga is eternal truth and pure consciousness.

In the story of Bhedia, Jhaveri Bai (a cow) takes the reader for a dip in the Ganga. Jhaveri Bai tests the temperature of the water and gradually eases in immersing herself up to her neck. This act is symbolic of the cleaning of sins, or rather gradual spiritual evolution by merging oneself in the Ganga, the metaphor of consciousness. Unlike *On the Ganga Ghat*, in *The Serpent and the Rope* and *The Chessmaster and His Moves*, the evolution towards spirituality is more technical in nature. In these two novels, the symbolic connotations of Mother Ganga are more faithful to epic literature as the Ganga is primarily a symbol and cannot be experienced to the same extent by the senses as in *On the Ganga Ghat*. Ganga in its perceived existence or as a physical entity evolves rapidly to different states. C.N. Srinath observes: "It is fascinating to see how the fact becomes image, the image symbol and the symbol, myth. The Ganga is all these perhaps less of a fact. For, no river can be a fact and certainly not the Ganga."[55] There are no such exclusive compartmentalisations in *On the Ganga Ghat* as the mundane and the divine exist side by side.

Rao's Ganga serves all types of devotees whether their method is *Bhaktiyoga, Rajyoga* or *Jnanayoga*. The literal Hindu belief that a dip in the Ganga ensures entry into *Sawarga* (heaven) is also there in the foreground and the background. Rao remarks:

> Ultimately, when the time [the moment of death] comes, you ask your son, uncle or grandfather for the Ganga-*jal* as you begin to heave a heavy breath and you sputter yourself in, and now move into immortality. (*OGG*: 125)

The Sanctifying power of the Ganga is most strikingly present in the story of Bhim, the parrot-siddha, who in his previous incarnation as Rani Prabhavati, rejects palatial splendour and glory in favour of wishful death by drowning in the holy Ganga thinking that "a Ganges death were better than a palace rot" (*OGG*: 21). Due to this act, the Rani is reborn as the enlightened Bhim. For the Hanuman bhakta Madhobha who is an illiterate simpleton, the Ganga is a "real Mother." Innocently, he apologizes to the Mother for not observing the ritual:

> 'Gangaji,' says Madhobha, 'do be kind to me. You know I never pray—I just forget to pray. You know I have no time to come and bathe in you often. I sit under a tap, by the shop, and have a quick shower. But all water is Ganga water. Gangaji, you know my heart is all with you. I worship you, Mother, as a calf worships its cow." (*OGG*: 33)

The essential oneness of water, circular in being and origin, also finds place in *The Cat and Shakespeare*:

> 'Where does water come from?'
> 'From the tap?'

'And the water in the tap?'
'From the lake?'
'And the water in the lake?'
'From sky.'
'And the water in the sky?'
'From the ocean?'
'And the water in the ocean?'
'From the rivers.'
'And the river waters?'
'They make the lakes.'
'And the tap water?'
'Is river water.'
'And so?'
'Water comes from water,' she said.
'And the river flows.'
'And then?'
'The lakes give water to taps.'[56]

The same thought is reflected in *On the Ganga Ghat*:

> O, let water flow, Lord, that the earth turn not away from its fulcrum, whirl, earth, that the Ganga flow, round and around on herself, from earth to sky and from the heavens back to the Himalayas. The circle is the end of all beginnings as the Ganga is of water. (*OGG*: 124)

In the story of Shankar, the Ganga is viewed as a "giver of gifts" by the protagonist. Of a mathematical bent, Shankar equates 'zero' (*shunya*) with the Ganga. He likens Mathematics to the Himalayas as he believes an ascent is necessary to understand mathematics or reach the Himalayan peaks. It is a "mantra" for him (*OGG*: 73). This brings to mind the Buddhist concept of Shunyata. This is not a negative state but rather one of supreme bliss, the receptacle being the evolved soul. In the seventh story, the protagonist Bhola is lost in a perpetual trance on the banks of the Ganga. Bhola states:

> 'Man lives for happiness, as Vishwanathji [his guru] says. And if happiness is on the Ganga I say take it, eat it, be submerged in it, as you're with the Ganga. Sometimes when the red dawn breaks on the Ganga. I cannot bear the veiled white silence over

> the river—it brings tears to my eyes. I do not know why, but never for father or mother have I wept as I do for the Ganga—this Ganga is my father, this Ganga is my mother." (*OGG*: 83–84)

Thus, for Bhola, Mother Ganga represents the Absolute Truth, which can be realized after taking dips into the holy Ganges.

> You plunge and plunge again into the Ganga. And you are suddenly aware of a fragrance of holiness and the touch of a deep white truth. And when you spit that water out, how your belly gurgles in happiness. (*OGG*: 84)

In the last story, Rao depicts Ganga as the Mother of Compassion. The Ganga and its flow are likened to knowledge. When knowledge, as Ganga, as *Jnana Ganga*, flows, death is dissolved into truth. As Sri Shankara said: "She is nija bodh rupa, she is the form of consciousness pure" (*OGG*: 127). Rao sees the Ganga as an outer symbol of consciousness representing wisdom. Benares is the hub of the Ganga and is indeed a living human organism (*shariram*). It is the focal point of consciousness, the epicentre of connection with spirituality:

> My body, the holy site, in Benares,
> Spreading within me as knowledge, the Ganges,
> Mother of the three worlds.[57]

In *On the Ganga Ghat*, Ganga takes on human qualities like compassion of a magnanimous nature and temperament. She gives the bounty of "song to the songstress, limbs to the brave, paddlepush to the boat, and child to the wife" (*OGG*: 73). The progression of Ganga culminates in "I" or "Jnana Ganga" in the last story. The perennial flow seems to have come to a standstill. The Ganga has become the Self, the inner being. But something is missing and that is flux through which one identifies and comprehends illusion and reality, truth and untruth. An invocation follows to reassert the dynamic as opposed to the static—Mother Ganga, "flow on" (*OGG*: 127). This contention is echoed in Rao's Guru, Atmananda's epigraph—"Water does not flow"—which is a pointer for questers to tell the true nature of *maya* (illusion) from *moha* "a bewilderment, an inability to understand the totality of a situation, of a thing."[58]

Finally, Raja Rao ends up entreating and imploring Mother Ganga who signifies the inner "Jnana Ganga," "I" and the Self, to flow on:

> One cannot go to the Ganges. One cannot go to the "I." For if you dare have a deep look on the Ganges evenings, and see the Ganga unflowing, then you know there is no Ganga. Water is just water. So, O, Mother Ganga, please be gracious, and,—flow. (*OGG*: 127)

In this way, Rao goes beyond the mythological perspectives of the Ganga, the most completely personified of all the holy rivers in India.

Raja Rao has made a considerable use of animal symbolism in his stories. Animals such as cow, serpent, dog, camel, elephants and also birds, make a frequent entry into the world of his short fiction. The protagonist of "The Cow of the Barricades," for instance, is Gauri, the cow. She is a veritable goddess, heroic in her moves characterized by a strong inner drive and strength that magnify her role from that of an ordinary cow to a hero. Another cow-character appears in the story of Bhedia in *On the Ganga Ghat*, who is named Jhaveri Bai. She has a remarkable capacity to relate to Bhedia, the protagonist. Jhaveri Bai, like Gauri is graceful and elegant.

In Indian mythology, the cow is the most revered of all animals. By the vedic age, the cow had taken on the divinity of the Mother. The Aryans venerated the cow as "mother of the world." The cow was and still is a sacred symbol of worship. B.C. Sinha observes:

> The cow is of all animals the most sacred. Every part of its body is inhabited by some deity or other. Every hair on its body is inviolable. All its excreta are hallowed. Not a particle ought to be thrown as impure. On the contrary, the water it ejects ought to be preserved as the best of holy waters—a sin destroying liquid which sanctifies everything it touches, while nothing purifies like cow-dung.[59]

Mother cow, as a nourisher, imparts energy and purity. This role is evident in the myths of Nandini and Kamdhenu. Kamdhenu in her divine power is known as the provider of all sorts of food. Regarding this type of divinity of the cow, Hopkins states: "She has all the female beauties and 'the six flavours of ambrosia;' her milk rejuvenates for ten thousand years."[60] The psychological divinity of the cow, as the Mother archetype, is, of course, an evolution from the level of the physical. Regarding the cow as Mother, Jung makes a reference to the cow among other animals. He points out that "[…] there are many animals [associated with the mother archetype] such as the cow, here, and helpful animals in General."[61] The cow's majestic divinity is proclaimed by the *RigVeda*:

> Gauri, fashioning waters, has lived and measured out, she the one-footed, two-footed, four-footed, eight-footed, and also becoming nine-footed. She is the Thousand-Syllabled in the highest Heaven.
>
> —*RIGVEDA* (*P&R*: 36)

In *On the Ganga Ghat*, Rao venerates the cow as the first born of animals:

> 'God you made the elephant and the peacock, the bear and the porcupine—even the dog did you make and the hyena, creatures of the earth. But the cow, Lord, you made as your first child. …' (*OGG*: 59)

The most striking example of this reverence to the cow is found in "The Cow of the Barricades." Here Gauri, the cow, is presented at two levels—realistic and symbolic. At the realistic level Gauri is a cow in flesh and blood whereas at the symbolic level she stands for Mother India, Mother as a protector, a true disciple to the Mahatma, a freedom fighter, etc. It is to be noticed that the name of the cow in the *Rigveda* prayer is the same as in this story. Gauri is likened to "the symbolic grafting of the Kamdhenu motif"[62] by K.R. Rao.

Gauri is initially shown as one who worships the Master, her Guru. Her love is manifested in the form of affectionately nibbling the Master's hair. She has a human dimension. The

Master calls her his "baton-armed mother-in-law," a description which evokes the image of Durga. She is also referred to as a "great Mother's vehicle" (*CBS*: 175). Other disciples are at a loss to comprehend Gauri's relationship with the Master. Viewing her as a strange visitor, the merchants equate her with Goddess Lakashmi. She is drawn as a "fervent soul" who will take rebirth as a sage due to her "compassionate" and "true" sacrifice as an embodiment of Mother India symbolizing freedom in totality. Gauri's sacrifice transcends heroic dimensions merging the mundane and the divine. Her martyrdom establishes her as a Goddess—a great protector, redeemer, an agent for regeneration, an amalgam of Mother India and spirituality. The Mother India aspect is spotlighted by P.C. Bhattacharya thus:

> The cow is obviously a symbol. She is Mother India in bondage; she is the all sustaining and life-giving mother earth; she is the sacrificing spirit of Dadhichi; she is all that is meek but strong, silent in speech but thundering in action, that dies in compassion so that others may live in happiness. She is comprehended by only a few like the Mahatma and the Master, and they too cannot describe her adequately.[63]

Thus, through Gauri, Rao propagates passive resistance, the non-violence (*ahimsa*) of Mahatma Gandhi.

The story of Bhedia is about relating with the Mother cow, Jhaveri Bai. Bhedia is apparently a freak, an idiot. But unknown to most, he seems to be metaphysically inclined, though unconsciously. No one seems to understand and care for Bhedia. He is a social outcast who finds shelter with Jhaveri Bai, the all-absorbing Mother.

Jhaveri Bai is found inevitably at Dashashwamedha Ghat on the Ganga. Surprisingly, she never steals: "Unlike the other cows she does not go and steal. She stands in front of a shop as if to say: "Will you honour me? And the cow always got her mouthful of fruits or grains [...]" (*OGG*: 56). Perpetual contemplation of the Ganga, reminiscent of its flow, is her *ṣadhanạ* from which she seems to extract the truth. Her evolved state makes her a Brahmini cow. Everyone loves her due to her transparency: "She is what she is" (*OGG*: 56).

Jhaveri Bai is the veritable mother of Bhedia. She and Bhedia share a rich relationship because of each other's purity and innocence. Love is the basis of this relationship and is reflected in her behaviour: "She also loves licking Bhedia, when Bhedia stands before her. Sometimes for hours Bhedia and Jhaveri Bai have long conversations" (*OGG*: 56). *Karuna rasa*—tender emotion and compassion, one of nine rasas in Sanskrit aesthetics—is the form of her divine, maternal love which is heart-moving and heart-rending. Upon the disappearance of Bhedia's friends, Mohone and Kishan, Bhedia's attention is focused entirely on Jhaveri Bai, the Mother:

> 'Now, I only have you,' says Bhedia to Jhaveri Bai.
>
> You are the Mother, and you are the Father, you are the Prince and you the charioteer. Lick me Goddess for your saliva is as honey. In Benares all dust is musk, in Benares all tears are nectar, in Benares there are no slaves and no animals! For all creatures are free [...]. (*OGG*: 57)

Bhedia has thus formally deified her; her *Sthithaprajna* consciousness is brought to the fore. Jhaveri Bai faithfully observes rituals by immersing herself in the holy Ganga. All in all, her divinity is initially suggested, contemplated on and illustrated and finally established.

The treatment of the cow motif as an archetype extends to human female characters like Javni and Akkayya. Javni is cow-like in her meekness, docility and submissiveness. Akkayya's motherly attitude towards children is evocative of the cow. Thus, through these modern "monomyths," Rao has in fact redeified and divinised the cow as the Mother archetype. His cow-characters immediately bring the grand Kamdhenu to mind and highlight the protective and nourishing aspect of Mother Cow. After reading Rao's cow stories, the reader gets reabsorbed in Hindu mythology and Hindu scriptures. This is done in such a way that the worldly and the divine come to co-exist. The rungs of the spiritual ladder to enlightenment are concrete. The archetype is human. Once this state of being is established, one can relate to the archetype at the levels of the worldly (corporeal) as well as the spiritual (divine) separately as well as together.

V
Archetypes of Hanuman, Rama and Krishna

Mythologically, Hanuman, also known as the son of the God of Wind (*Pawansut*), is a faithful and sincere ally, and a true companion of Rama. He is also the chief of the army of monkeys (*Vanar Sena*) in Rama's war against demons (*Rakshasas*) led by the demon king, Ravana. Besides his faithfulness, Hanuman is also an epitome of courage, valour and enormous strength. Due to the virtues of self-surrender and devotion, Hanuman leaves an indelible impression upon the mind of all. According to Coomaraswamy and Sister Nivedita, such a surrender and obedience to the master are unheard of in world literature.

> It may be questioned whether there is in the whole of literature another apotheosis of loyalty and self-surrender like that of Hanumana. He is the Hindu ideal perfect servant, the servant who finds full realisation of manhood, of faithfulness, of his obedience; the subordinate whose glory is in his own inferiority [...]. Hanuman is captured and placed by the *Ramayana* amongst religious conceptions of the highest import.[64]

There exists a strong bond between Rama and his faithful servant, Hanuman. Because of his unswerving devotion and loyalty, Hanuman has been elevated to the status of a god. Hanuman is an able general with "lustre, courage, good name, efficiency, capability, humility, refinement, manly prowess, achievement, wisdom [...]."[65] One cannot think of Hanuman without thinking of Rama and vice versa. The bond is sure; the link inextricable. He is the god of strength like Hercules, although the monkey god has greater power and majesty. The Hanuman-Hercules connection is an evidence of the monomyth. Hanuman appeals to the rustic sensibility and imparts strength—physical, psychological and spiritual—to the seeker at any plane. In serving Rama, He is selfless and expects no reward.

The Hanuman archetype is dealt with most effectively in the story of Madhobha in *On the Ganga Ghat*. Madhobha, originally a weakling, becomes a tower of physical prowess due to the worship and grace of Hanuman. He reached holy Benares and "[...] found no difficulty in finding a job: he looked so strong, he could lift a mountain. And in Benares there aren't such hefty people any more" (*OGG*: 35). This is an obvious reference to his Hanuman-like strength. He serves his employer dutifully, loyally and faithfully. He regularly visits the temple, prays to Rama and undertakes religious fasts. His strength is not just physical, but also spiritual.

This Hanumana-bhakta, Madho comes in contact with an ethereal spirit, Mohini, a seeker of Rama. The rustic simpleton becomes a perfect medium for the spirit's (Mohini's) salvation, as he is pure of heart. This relationship is of benefit to both. Madho is benefited by being blessed with Rama's grace, Mohini by being Rama's vehicle. The invisible Mohini whom he can only hear, reveals a divine vision to Madho:

> One day when I sat at dusk on the parapet of a terrace, and there was absolute noiselessness, I heard a strange sound as if Sri Rama was going back to Ayodhya, such the pleasant splendid noise of horses and elephants. I looked down and it was you [Madho]. I followed you to the temple. I saw Ramji himself standing behind Hanuman to bless you. I have lived so long looking for some one who could take me to Ram [...]. We have to go through a man. And a man who has never touched a woman is our man. You are that—one can see from the curls of your eyebrows. We can smell it in the smells of your skin, at the pores of your hair [...] (*OGG*: 37)

This describes their mutually sustaining roles and their relationship as a whole. The carnal does not enter into Madho's mind: "What need of a woman more worthy than a Mohini?" (*OGG*: 37).

Madho's absorption in Mohini is symbolic of his immersion in Rama. Whenever he is engaged in conversation with her, he becomes oblivious of his surroundings. Once while talking to Mohini, his master disturbs Madho. He reacts violently and calls his master a "pig." Strangely enough, next morning when his master reminds him of his misdemeanour, he remembers nothing. He begs forgiveness calling himself a "heavy sleeper." This highlights his Hanuman-like attribute of loyalty. The story is open-ended as the reader is left with Madho's desire to see the spirit, Mohini.

The story of Madho is a miniature myth suggestive of the larger "monomyth." Echoes of Rama with Hanuman in the foreground, chime clearly. Madhobha assumes the proportion of Hanuman consciousness. Mohini assumes the proportions of Rama consciousness. Madho is the archetypal model servant. Mohini is suggestive of Ramahood. Just as in the *Sunderkanda* "A firmer and finer relationship between Ram and Hanuman is established,"[66] similarly a strong bond develops between Madho and Mohini. Both are questers in their own right.

Comparatively minor representations of the Rama archetype are found in other stories of Raja Rao. In "The Little Gram Shop," Beti Bai worships Lord Rama and prays for her son, Chhota's return home. Her devotion to the Lord is marked by optimism, will and unshakeable faith. As a giver of gifts and a bestower of boons, Rama occupies a central place in Rao's fiction. He is the provider of wealth, heir, home, and is the divine healer. In the story of Bhola, He is the "protector" and the "Fount of Compassion:"

> Who can protect you ever from your primal destiny, unless it be Sri Rama himself. Ravana had to be killed to attain liberation, so Ravana had to abduct Sita. Thus alone could Ravana's head be on Sri Rama's feet. And this was all the play of Sri Rama himself, he, Sri Rama, the very fount of compassion [...]. (*OGG*: 77)

Rao believes that Rama is the embodiment of Vishnu and is ever present physically on the earth to dispel illusion: "Sri Rama [is] none else than Sri Vishnu who took the human form for our redemption from Maya" (*OGG*: 80). Rao's vision of Rama is cosmic as he believes that "[...] everything on earth, the good and the bad, come to the one single end—touching the holy feet of Sri Rama" (*OGG*: 80). Thus Rama is immanent, and the source of all emanation. Purity, redemption and Moksha are there for one who strives to realize Lord Rama.

Another archetype which is briefly touched upon by Rao in his stories is that of Lord Krishna. Lord Krishna appears during *Kaliyuga* when evil must be ruthlessly destroyed. The epic hero is beyond time and activity but remains in the action mode so that the world does not come to an end. His activity is meant to be emulated. He is "the Supreme Lord, the unity that lies behind the manifold universe, the changeless truth behind all appearances, transcendent over all and immanent in all."[67]

He is thus the *Virata Swaroopa* (the cosmic form), the universe as well its receptacle. As the agent of destruction of evil, He is worldly in his cleverness, ruthlessness and politics. He is the embodiment of courage who inspires his devotees like Arjuna and dispels their misgivings.

In the story of Muthradas, Raja Rao evokes an image of Krishna as the dawn "auspicious" suggests the sound of His flute awakening His cattle (*OGG*: 40). Bhedia also sings to Jhaveri Bai, the cow, a song reflecting his recognition of the Mother archetype in the same manner that Krishna viewed Yashoda. The song is imbued with Krishna's pranks of innocence:

> When Kanhia went to steal
>
> And the mountains moved
>
> Yasodha came from the kitchen and cried:
>
> 'He, you mischief, you diamond'
>
> And hung him to her breast. (*OGG*: 57)

From the foregoing discussion, it becomes evident that Rao has effectively used archetypal motifs to serve the praxis of his vision of enlightenment, specifically in the mode of the quest process. Shiva is Time in all its aspects, worldly and spiritual, and is yet above it all. He represents duality and non-duality and yet transcends them: He is absolute truth, indivisible and one. The Devi, according to the myth, in the form of Durga, the perfect incarnation, incarnates in answer to the prayers of Brahma, Shiva and Vishnu. Thus she directly emanates from Reality. The Ganga is simultaneously a quest and a process both of which are mutually inclusive. She is the inner knowledge and "Jnana Ganga," through which one can realize the self. Kali, in her negative and positive roles, represents the Cosmic balance of good and evil. As good, she is the demon-slayer in her terrible form and ensures the uprooting of evil to the utmost degree.

Shiva is the Cosmic God from whom the universe emanates and is imparted motion. He is the complete Hindu Trinity in Himself: Creator, Preserver and Destroyer. The Nagas, both good and evil are residents of *Patalaloka*/underworld, reminiscent of the world of darkness. Rama and Hanuman are incarnations on the human plane to show humanity the way to God. Krishna appears only when evil dominates and must be ruthlessly destroyed. He is the prime mover in which is the locus of all creation, destruction and time. Mother cow is the concrete nourisher who has been deified due to her nurturing role. Mythologically she is the source of ambrosia (*amrita*) which psychologically implies 'spiritual food.' Rao has illustrated all these archetypes exquisitely through character, locale and backdrop. Consciousness is emphasized as the vehicle and goal of fruitful living. Only with this in mind according to Rao, can one evolve, connect with the Self, and evolve further to attain individuation. The Self is the source which, however, needs the presence and guiding hand of a guru to manifest itself. Rao has imaged well a world of concrete archetypes within the parameters of the quest process.

Notes

1. Pierre Grimal, ed., *World Mythology,* New York: Excalibur, 1981, p. 220.
2. B.C. Sinha, *Hinduism and Symbol Worship,* Delhi: Agam Kala Prakashan, 1983, p. 95.
3. Stella Kramrisch, *The Presence of Shiva,* Delhi: Oxford University Press, 1981, p. 277.
4. Sinha, p. 117.
5. Donald and Jean Johnson, *God and Gods in Hinduism,* Delhi: Arnold-Heinemann, 1972, p. 42.
6. Stella Kramrisch, p. 440.
7. Donald and Johnson, p. 119.
8. Stella Kramrisch, p. 167.
9. Pierre Grimal, ed., p. 221.
10. Ibid.
11. Stella Kramrisch, p. 298.

12. Diana L. Eck, *Benares: City of Light*, Princeton, N.J.: Princeton UP, 1982, p. 84.
13. Raja Rao, *The Serpent and the Rope*, 1960; rpt. Delhi: Orient Paperbacks, 1980, p. 114.
14. Whitman's concept of the Self has cosmic dimensions and is characterised by inherent divinity, infinitude and all-inclusiveness. It transcends the merger of "I" and "You" and is inclusive of the whole phenomena comprising earth, air, water, etc. There is no recoil from the mundane, carnal and trivial as these are viewed as the stepping stones to realise the sacred, sublime and divine. See Roshan Lal Sharma, "Whitman's Concept of the Self," *Walt Whitman: A Critical Evaluation*, Delhi: Vrinda, 2000, pp. 17–24. Also see "Song of Myself," Walt Whitman, *Leaves of Grass*, eds., Sculley Bradley and Harold W. Blodgett, New Delhi: Prentice Hall of India, 1986.
15. Bidyanath Saraswati, *Myth and Reality of a Classical Cultural Tradition*, Shimla: Indian Institute of Advanced Study, 1975, p. 57:
16. J.PH. Vogel, *Indian Serpent Lore*, Varanasi: Indological Book House, 1972, p. 3.
17. Pierre Grimal, ed., p. 238.
18. Vogel, p. 202.
19. Ibid., p. 203.
20. Ibid., pp. 22–23.
21. Narsingh Srivastava, *The Mind and Art of Raja Rao*, Bareilly: Prakash, 1980, p. 126.
22. *Maya* in the present context is not just the veil of illusion, it signifies much more than that. For instance, Brane has viewed *maya* in terms of an "inexplicable mystery," as a "power of self-becoming," as "duality of consciousness and matter," as "primal matter," as "concealment" and as "one-sided dependence." See Donald A. Brane, *Maya in Radhakrishnan's Thought: Six Meanings Other than Illusion*, Delhi: Motilal Banarasidass, 1984, pp. 101–129.
23. Asha Kaushik, "Meeting Raja Rao," *The Literary Criterion*, XVIII, No. 3 (July-September 1983), 35.
24. Pierre Grimal, ed., p. 238.
25. K.R. Rao, *The Fiction of Raja Rao*, Aurangabad: Parimal, 1980, p. 26.
26. Srivastava, p. 134.
27. C.G. Jung, *The Archetype and the Collective Unconscious*, trans. R.F.C. Hull, Princeton: Princeton University Press, 1968, p. 82.
28. Ibid., p. 226.
29. Ibid., p. 82.
30. Ibid.

31. Veronica Ions, *Indian Mythology*, London: Paul Hamlyn, 1973, p. 91.
32. Joseph Campbell, *The Hero with a Thousand Faces*, Princeton: Princeton University Press, 1968, p. 115.
33. Ibid., p. 116.
34. Walt Whitman, *Leaves of Grass*, New Delhi: Prentice Hall of India, 1986, pp. 34–35.
35. Sri Aurobindo, *The Synthesis of Yoga*, Pondicherry: Sri Aurobindo Ashram, 1976, p. 731.
36. Ibid., p. 752.
37. Som P. Ranchan, *Durga Saptashati: A Transcreation*, Sahibabad: Holy Faith, 1986, p. 4.
38. Quoted from *Flashes from Vivekananda*, Madras: Sri Ramakrishna Math, n.d., p. 8.
39. Ranchan, p. 5.
40. Ibid.
41. Ibid.
42. Thomas B. Coburn, *Devi Mahatmya*, Delhi: Motilal Banarsidass, 1988, p. 157.
43. Ranchan, p. 5.
44. Ibid.
45. Ibid., p. 57.
46. P.C. Bhattacharya, *Indo-Anglian Literature and the Works of Raja Rao*, Delhi: Atma Ram & Sons, 1983, p. 202.
47. Ibid., pp. 205–06.
48. Ibid., p. 206.
49. K.R. Rao, p. 34.
50. W.J. Wilkins, *Hindu Mythology, Vedic and Puranic*, Varanasi: Indological, 1972, p. 460.
51. Sister Nivedita and Anand K. Coomaraswamy, *Hindus and Buddhists*, London: Mystic Press, 1987, p. 321.
52. Wilkins, p. 467.
53. C.N. Srinath, *The Literary Landscape: Essays on Indian Fiction & Poetry in English*, Delhi: Mittal, 1986, p. 97.
54. Rao, *The Serpent and the Rope*, p. 35.
55. Srinath, p. 86.
56. Raja Rao, *The Cat and Shakespeare*, 1971; rpt. New Delhi: Orient Paperbacks, 1992, p. 46.
57. Rao, *The Serpent and the Rope*, p. 216.

58. K.D. Prithipaul, *Moha: A Study in the Metaphysics of Error in Brahminical Tradition,* Madras: Southern Publications, 1988, p. 11.
59. Monier Williams quoted in Sinha, *Hinduism and Symbol Worship,* p. 13.
60. E. Washburn Hopkins, *Epic Mythology,* Varanasi: Indological, 1968, p. 17.
61. Jung, p. 81.
62. K.R. Rao, p. 37.
63. Bhattachbarya, p. 230.
64. Sister Nivedita and Coomaraswamy, p. 22.
65. V. Sitaramiah, *Valmiki Ramayana,* New Delhi: Sahitya Akademi, 1982, p. 93.
66. Ibid., p. 89.
67. S. Radhakrishnan, *The Bhagvadgita,* New Delhi: Blackie & Son, 1982, p. 30.

Conclusion

To conclude, it can be averred that the theme of enlightenment pervades the world of Raja Rao's stories. He has employed certain archetypal and other motifs having unmistakable religious and mythological connotations to convey this theme. The functional utility of these motifs lies in the fact that these are made to operate within the praxis of enlightenment.

The guru-disciple relationship is ingrained in the Indian psyche and serves as a pivot on the path to enlightenment. The veneer of modern Indian consciousness may seem devoid of guru-disciple relationship; however, a perennial current of this relationship still obtains at the subliminal level. In fact, the guru-disciple relationship is a pervasive reality of Indian life. Moreover, the fundamental belief of Hindu spiritual thought is that every soul/*jiva* (living creature), consciously or unconsciously, is moving on its way to salvation. To further elucidate this point, one may recall the Hindu belief in the theory of the transmigration of souls, the endless cycle of 'birth-death-rebirth,' and the eternal wheel of *karma*. The guru-disciple relationship as it prevails in India is germane to the quest process. Raja Rao has been a prominent Indian English writer who dealt with the guru-disciple motif at length, and all the characters in his stories may be placed in two categories: (a) seekers or disciples (b) wise old men or gurus. The primary focus of this study has been to show how the disciples' psycho-spiritual growth is brought about by this relationship.

For Rao, the guru-disciple relationship in its traditional mode is a soul-making process. Upon closer psychological scrutiny, it unfolds entirely new facets that corroborate its existence and relevance in the disciple's quest for enlightenment. An objective assessment of the conventional mode of guru-disciple relationship and its concomitant factors—initiation, life in *ashrama,* discipline, *brahmacharya* (celibacy), etc.,—reveal that this relationship aims at the holistic growth of the disciple.

The guru-disciple relationship, the quest process, and enlightenment are interlinked and intersect one another. Seen in terms of a process, the relationship helps the disciple break free of his conditioned persona and become self-dependent by outgrowing the strong bondages of infantile 'dependencies.' Nitin Trasi's apprehension seems appropriate when he comments that "Forgetting the basic purpose of having a guru, he [the disciple] may merely get used to relying upon him for psychological support for the material problems of life."[1] After abandoning this narrow, snug and secure arena of his complexes which, psychologically speaking, form his personal unconscious, the disciple jumps out and moves freely to experience the world at large.

Keeping in mind the Jungain archetype of the wise old man, it has been shown that Rao's delineation of the guru archetype is holistic in the sense that he brings about negative as well as positive aspects of his being. Rao remains true to the spirit of the Indian tradition and thought in as much as he portrays the positive side of the wise old man (that is as a 'bringer of enlightenment'). However, "A Client" presents a vivid and convincing portrayal of the negative side of the guru archetype in which he serves as a 'bringer of poison' causing the downfall of the disciple. Raja Rao seems to be very fond of his guru characters. He introduces them variously in his stories. For instance, Rao introduces traditional gurus who are well-versed in the scriptures and are self-actualized and enlightened. Such gurus are there in Sankaranandji, Vishwanathji and Sadananda in *On the Ganga Ghat*. The Master-characters in "The Cow of the Barricades" and in "Narsiga" may be viewed as model Gandhian gurus. A variation is provided in the very first story in *On the Ganga Ghat* where Rao presents a 'demythified' guru, Moti Ram, a taxi driver who is living entirely in an egoless state of being. He is a *Shiva-bhakta* (devotee of Shiva) and has unconsciously imbibed Shiva sensibility which he reveals through disjointed expressions. For Rao, merely the presence of the guru is effective and transformative one. This is evident in "The Policeman and the Rose" where the Retired Police Commissioner, a guru figure, does not make a physical appearance in the story, but remains entirely in the backdrop. His presence is charismatic and metamorphoses the profane consciousness of the disciple/seeker (I-narrator) to the sacred one. Likewise in Rao's magnum opus, *The Serpent and the Rope*, the guru does not appear physically, though his illuminating presence is felt in the background all through the novel.

Another interesting feature of the dynamics of guru-disciple relationship is the subtle and subliminal manifestation of the abstract characteristics of the guru in the praxis of enlightenment characterized by formal/informal schema of quest. For instance, effective 'instruction' emanates from the guru. He is the one who instructs and thereby bestows upon his disciples the recognition of reality and the realization of truth. Moreover, the guru is not the one who falsifies his instruction and teachings; he rather lives by them and thus exemplifies his teachings. As an 'influence' the guru not only influences one or two of his disciples, but his influence extends and benefits humanity at large.

The quest motif is pervasive in diverse literatures of the world. The present century is marked by chaos, turmoil, erosion of values and wreckage of traditional institutions. In such an age of terror and awe, the very existence of a person is endangered. Since time immemorial, 'quest for identity' has remained the primary consideration of an individual. Writers like Hemingway, J.D. Salinger, Hermann Hesse, Joyce and Faulkner (to name only a few) have chiefly employed the quest motif in their works. Raja Rao's use of the quest motif emanates from and is steeped in Indian culture, thought, mythology and folklore. However, Rao's employment of the quest motif in the book has been viewed in the light of Campbellian and Jungian standpoints vis-à-vis the quest process. In fact, Rao's delineation of quest motif which has a traditional, cultural matrix encompasses both Jungian and Campbellian frameworks. Nevertheless, due to Campbell's non-empiricist stance, as compared to empiricist Jung, Rao seems to be nearer to the former in that he is a myth-maker and creates his own 'monomyths.'

Rao's creative sensibility is steeped in Vedanta and as such, the *leitmotiv* of Vedantic quest remains predominant in his shorter fiction. For instance, *On the Ganga Ghat* is an emphatic predication of the Vedantic quest. In addition to it, the strains of Sufic and Tantric quest also come to the fore. In "Companions," for instance, Rao has fused Sufic and Vedantic quests. In the same story, the snake (Pandit Srinath Sastri) acquires the dimensions of Tantric *Kundalini* even though at a symbolic level.

Like gurus, we may also categorize various questers in Rao's stories. Some of the questers like Sudha, Vision Rangappa and Moti Khan have attained enlightenment by completing their quest cycle *à la* Campbell by successfully returning to serve the community, or society at large. Other questers like Narsiga and Shivlal have reached the middle of their quest journeys. Questers like Muthradas and Ramu have been placed in the category of fallen questers. Muthradas' quest journey is interrupted by the blow of death whereas Ramu is trapped by a trickster namely Nanjudayya. Questers like Ranchaddoss Sunderdoss and Nanna have been categorized as beginners in their quest journeys. As stated, Campbellian return on the part of the hero has a practical utility as it is directly linked with the welfare of the society. However, it may be noted that in Rao's world of shorter fiction, the Campbellian return is not at all necessary. What matters most is the right initiative, technically called initiation.

Like Rao, his characters are also theistic questers. He seems to have consciously employed quest for enlightenment as a tool to knit together the whole world of his stories. The quest for truth or the attainment of Vedantic Pure Consciousness emerges as the major theme in his novels such as *The serpent and the Rope, The Cat and Shakespeare* and *The Chessmaster and His Moves* as well. Rao deals with the Vedantic quest in the stories such as "The Policeman and the Rose," "India—A Fable," and almost all the stories in *On the Ganga Ghat*. His spectrum of quest includes questers like Vision Rangappa who may be classified as conscious seekers, whereas the likes of Narsiga are unconscious ones. Even the reluctant questers like Moti Khan—who drags his feet and initially resists the influence of the guru, make their entry into the fictional universe of Rao's stories. Lastly, there are questers who are forced by circumstances to tread the path to spirituality, such as Bholanath and Muthradas in *On the Ganga Ghat*.

As a *sadhak*-writer, Rao has remarkably observed, perceived, imbibed, assimilated and transcreated the truth of human experience, and has also explored various levels of human consciousness. Rao's introduction of realistic, social and metaphysical strains within the framework of the Vedantic vision highlights his disposition as a creative writer. Rao's conscious or unconscious, apparent or subtle expression of the enlightenment theme is not a matter of chance for him. He is, in fact, a Vedantin for whom the search for truth is the final ideal. As a quester-writer, Rao's subtle perception, perspicacious expression, his rare insights into the minds of his characters, his "impersonality" *à la* Eliot and his sense of "objectivity" are the hallmarks of his stories. Moreover, on Rao's part too, there has been an ample evidence of "the deepening of consciousness,"[2] which always stood him in good stead thereby enabling him to enjoy the "bliss of deep meditation"—a state that is synonymous with enlightenment. His fundamental questioning in regard to the simple mysteries in small and insignificant happenings of our day to day life make one pause and ponder about his spiritually evolved status:

> Life is so mysterious. Why should you, coolie with a number—87, 54 or 49—stitched on your shirt, alone carry our luggage? Why not one whose number is 55, 31 or 48? What connection of stars linking one with the other, Jupiter with Mercury or Saturn squaring the moon, have created this situation that Bhaiya

> Ram, Bhagat Ram or Durga Das, coolies of Mughal Sarai, carry our luggage and never will we see them again? How could this be? And the monkeys that were disturbed by our hagglings, the bats that were irritated and the two curs—yes, those two curs, Paul and I will never meet again. Only the Ganges flows, Mother Ganges carrying our memories away. Who could, Lord, who could carry the memory of the millions and millions that have been born since the beginnings began and where have all the dog-and-the-pilgrim-contacts gone? (*OGG:* 13)

As regards distinction between the wise old man and the hero, it may be said that the former holds much superior a place since he is the beacon of enlightenment for the latter. The main point of difference is that the hero may attain wise-old-manhood whereas the wise old man may not necessarily have heroic dimensions. This is evident in the story of Ranchoddoss in which Sudha's husband's guru (in her previous birth) is succeeded by his (guru's) own disciple. Likewise, the hero may also become a wise old man after returning to society and contributing substantially in the spiritual upliftment of other questers or common people. The wise old man, on the other hand, has an enormous amount of experiential wisdom to his credit. In Jungian terms he is a individuated psychological being.

The Campbellian hero represents the Western man who is markedly different from his Eastern (especially Indian) counterpart represented by different questers in Rao's stories. The Western quest, in fact, is a "quest for identity" *à la* Erik Erikson, which implies that one must be convinced of one's being, existence and identity in the society: "[...] the quest for identity is a quest for a place in society, a place expressed most concretely in a career."[3] Not much credence is given to the spirituality in the formal sense of the term as the primary focus is on materiality. Contrarily, the Eastern quest begins from the point where the Western quest ends. This means that material prosperity is not rated higher than psycho-spiritual growth. Here the focus is more on the inner, psychic life. As such, the Western quester would prefer a 'richer' and a 'fuller' life as compared to his Eastern counterpart who would prefer to have an instantaneous recognition of the futile, illusory world of materiality and would prefer the exploration of the psyche, self and the inner being (*antaratma*). The adventurous life that a Western quester leads stands in sharp contrast with that of an Indian spiritual seeker who does not have to perform too many adventures on the physical plane. He is lost in complete abstinence and finally becomes non-attached to the outside world even though remaining aware of and wakeful to what happens in his immediate surroundings. After realizing the futility of this *mayavic samsara* (illusory world) and subsequently attaining enlightenment, the Indian seeker acquires the dimensions of a guru. Whereas an Eastern quester moves from the physical or materialistic plane to the inner world, the Western quester is concerned more about his proper placement in society. He rates individual uniqueness very high. An Indian quester, on the other hand, believes in utter dissolution of his ego-ridden self.

In the quest process as delineated in Rao's stories, archetypes other than the guru namely Shiva, Devi, Ganga, Hanuman, etc., play a significant role as they signify the 'roots' of his questers. Rao is steeped in the belief that a quester's connection with them is a necessity. Just as in Jungian individuation process, the quester, after overcoming the complexes of the personal unconscious, encounters various archetypes to attain psychological wholeness. Similarly, in Rao's quest process too, the questers, until they realize the total essence of any one, or two, or all the archetypes, cannot undertake the quest journey successfully. Rao himself has all through his life been emphasizing the connection with one's roots. His preoccupation and in-depth relationship with India (i.e., his roots) is evident in *The Serpent and the Rope*:

> It was India I wanted to see, the India of my inner being [...] India for me became no land—not these trees, this sun, this earth; not those ladle hands and skeletal legs of bourgeois and coolie; not even the new pride of the uninformed Indian official [...] but something other, more centred, widespread, humble; as thought the gods had peopled the land with themselves [...]. The India of Brahma and Prajapathi; of Varuna, Mithra and Aryaman; of Indra, of Krishna, Shiva and Parvathi; of Rama,

> Harishchandra and Yagnyavalkya; this India was a continuity I felt, not in time but in space [...]. It is perhaps in this sense that India is outside history.[4]

Furthermore, in an interview with Parthasarathi, Rao confesses that "By force of circumstances, purely accidental and sentimental, I have lived abroad. My roots are in this country (India). [...] I lived abroad but I am chained to my country."[5] As such, Rao has an intense awareness of his roots i.e., India with her rich cultural and spiritual heritage. Rao's fascination with the above archetypes is evident from their recurrent use in his fictional world. It is as though everything that a man thinks, speaks, does, imagines and actualizes has its seed in one archetype or the other. Nothing, for Rao, can exist beyond them, or devoid of them. They are the signifiers of the Invisible behind the visible and the Changeless behind the changing.

It is difficult to agree with the commentators who maintain that Rao's introduction of various archetypes in his stories is factitious, contrived or artificial. The fact of the matter, however, is that Rao has infused new life into the traditional myths by retelling or renewing them. In this process of the rejuvenation of the traditional myths, Rao becomes inevitably obscure. But to be difficult may not necessarily be irrelevant, or even factitious. Indeed, the presence of different archetypes in Rao's writings corroborate the fact that he has assimilated the essence and imbibed the true spirit of these archetypes.

Narsiga's most significant encounter is with the archetype of Mother Nature. Not only that, he also comes in contact with archetypes such as Shiva and Rama though at an imaginary level. Vision Rangappa also completes his quest journey after meeting Shiva and his divine consort, Parvathi. This contact marks the culmination of Vision Rangappa's pilgrimage (quest) to Kashi Vishweshwara. Similarly, Moti Khan meets Sheikh Chisti after a rigorous penance and comprehends the essence of existence. This encounter with various archetypes is analogous to "the encounter with the Goddess" in Campbellian quest cycle. Rao's effective and convincing use of various archetypal motifs in the quest process, which signifies the praxis part of enlightenment, gives us a glimpse of Rao's grassroots assimilation of these all.

For instance, Shiva is not an abstract entity, though he has been portrayed as the One who is Timeless or beyond time (Mahakala); One who is transcendence personified; One who governs the whole of the cosmos; One who is the Lord of destruction. Rao presents an entirely demythified view of Shiva as he is also reflected through the simpletons such as Moti Ram, the taxi driver, Bholanath, Shankar, etc. Likewise, the Devi (Mother) archetype on the one hand represents the Eternal Feminine *à la* Toni Woolfe; on the other, she is Shakti, the archetypal force behind the universe.

Mahakali, the Goddess of divine violence is a counterpart of Toni Woolfe's Amazon. She is powerful and merciless when involved in destruction. Mahalakshmi is enchantingly beautiful with harmony of the male and female charge and represents eros. She is similar to Toni Woolfe's Hetera (companion) who has a dynamic and sensual relationship with the Animus. Mahasaraswati, the embodiment of perfection to the point of the divine, is in psychological terms, the integrator of consciousness, regenerating and renewing life, and is indeed Toni Woolfe's Mother. The archetype of Mother Ganga becomes more convincing when it takes on the symbolic connotation of "Jnana Ganga" or the stream of inner knowledge. The archetype of Mother Cow stands for all that is compassionate and true. Similarly, the Naga archetype is symbolic of Tantric *Kundalini* which in its awakened form brings about the transformation of the disciple. Hanumana archetype stands for all that is bold, strong, virile and valorous.

Each of Rao's stories may be taken as a lively sketch of a particular facet of Indian life. Raja Rao's faith in and assimilation of certain values, governing superstitions, his undaunted and unshakeable belief in Indian gods, goddesses, India'a cultural, philosophical and spiritual richness, vibrant mythology, remarkable folklore, legends and overall Indian consciousness—all have been beautifully woven by him in the holistic fabric of the aesthetically rich and invigorating world of his stories. Naturally, the Vedantic strain predominates. Moreover, the theories of *Karma* and *Dharma* find a subtle expression in Rao's stories. In the Hindu theory of *Karma*, it is held that every happening in the life of an individual is either pre-destined, or a consequence of one's actions in the past. *Dharma* signifies a regulating force in life. It has certain ethical connotations as well; it signifies a moral force that controls, directs, governs and guides human behaviour and actions. The psyche of Rao's characters seems to be steeped in both the above-mentioned theories. Besides, his characters believe in the theory of the transmigration of soul as well. As such, they seem to have a realization of the fact that the life they are living is merely a stage in the cosmic evolutionary cycle of 'birth-death-rebirth' with sole destination of enlightenment in the sense of *mukti* (salvation).

Finally it is the *sthithaprajna* sensibility, as defined in Chapter 2 of the *Gita,* which is the *modus operandi* behind the creation of the world of Raja Rao's shorter fiction. *Sthithaprajna* does not imply indifference or non-attachment as it has often been taken to mean. A *sthithaprajna* has a higher capacity to feel pain, anguish, joy/delight. Rao's *sthithaprajana* sensibility comes to the fore when he describes the deeply felt anguish of Akkayya. While describing Akkayya who is suffering from a terrible and incurable disease, Rao does not show any sign of repulsion. On the contrary, he seems to have felt deeply Akkayya's anguish and helplessness. As a *sthithaprajna,* Rao does not show any sign of hypalgesia. He is susceptible to life in all its forms, howsoever ugly or repulsive. Rao equates sorrow with *mahadukkha.*[6] He views it in terms of the philosophy of Being and Becoming. According to him, the Being is the Absolute, the Changeless. He views sorrow in the light of the process of Becoming, which signifies flux of life. The Being remains absolutely unaffected by the changes that occur in the phenomenal world. Rao's delineation of the characters of Bhedia, Bhim, Jhaveri Bai, Rani Rasomani, Kanakapala, Nanna, etc., corroborates his *sthithaprajna* sensibility. Rao, an embodiment of *sthithaprajna* sensibility as he is, shows greater empathy towards the sufferings of his characters. However, at no point does he sentimentalize their plight; rather, a sense of equanimity prevails in Rao's response to/portrayal of his characters as a creative artist.

Thus a serene poise or equanimity permeates the world of Rao's shorter fiction. It is further intensified by a strange kind of sufficiency on the part of his characters representing Indians and their typical attitude of taking things as they come in a seemingly 'passive' mode unlike the Westerners who are facing the 'identity crisis' due to hyperactivity. Rao's characters, by and large, are not atheist existentialists; they have a theistic bent of mind and have faith in God and supernatural powers. This faith is their 'dharma' and it regulates their lives.

Notes

1. See Nitin Trasi, *The Science of Enlightenment,* New Delhi: D.K. Printworld, 1999, p. 130.
2. See D.P. Chattopadhyaya, *Religion, Philosophy and Science: A Sketch of a Global View,* Shimla: Indian Institute of Advanced Study, 2006, p. 46.
3. Robert A. Seagal, *Joseph Campbell: An Introduction,* New York: Mentor, 1990, p. 34.
4. Raja Rao, *The Serpent and the Rope,* 1960; rpt. New Delhi: Orient Paperbacks, 1968, pp. 246–47.
5. P.C. Bhattacharya, *Indo-Anglian Literature and the Works of Raja Rao,* Delhi: Atma Ram & Sons, 1983, p. 195.
6. In *Daughter of the Mountain,* which will be published this year, and is the second of *The Chessmaster* trilogy, Rao shows his profound understanding of "sorrow." At *Samvad* India, Makarand Paranjape quotes the first paragraph of Rao's unpublished manuscript:

   "Behind all sorrow is the Mahadukkha, the great sorrow of the sorrow that will be. What is can never become. Between is and is [is] the stolen space where becoming vaunts its existence. But in truth, even the in-between is, thus becoming never was nor will ever be. Sorrow, the becoming, surfing, and eddying over the vastitude of our oceanic reality. Fools suffer for they take the wave to be the ocean. Water never becomes anything, but remains ever water. The waves—I was crossing the Japan sea—spill high on the rocks of Ninimuttu, from where Buddhist monks sailed over to Nippon, but the waves go back, again and again, having made aeons of effort to become land—they always reach back to the ocean. La mer, la mer, toujours recommence. In the ocean fishes eat fishes, coloured, many-limbed and

many-headed, eaten by monsters ever heavier and long but with one single head, and finally man comes with his boats, nets and electronics and drags them out of their home, to eat them for his own being: becoming eats back becoming to be. Thus samsara ends in nirvana. And the cycle rolls on."

See Rangel-Ribeiro, Victor. "Raja Rao (1908-2006)" 12 July 2006. <kitabkhana.blogspot.com/2006/07/raja-rao-1908-2006.html>

Bibliography

(a) Primary Sources (Short Fiction)

Rao, Raja. *The Cow of the Barricades and Other Stories*. Madras: Oxford University Press, Champak Library, 1947.

——. *The Policeman and the Rose*. Delhi: Oxford University Press, Three Crowns Books, 1978.

——. *On the Ganga Ghat*. New Delhi: Vision Books, 1989. New Delhi: Orient Paperbacks, 1993.

(b) Secondary Sources

Fiction

Rao, Raja. *Kanthapura*. 1930; rpt. London: Allen and Unwin, 1938. Bombay: Oxford University Press, Champak Library, 1947. New York: New Directions, 1963. Madras: Oxford University Press, 1963. New Delhi: Orient Paperbacks, 1971.

——. *The Serpent and the Rope*. 1960; rpt. New Delhi: Orient Paperbacks, 1980. London: John Murray, 1960. New York: Pantheon Books, 1963. New Delhi. Hind Pocket Books, 1968. Westport, CT: Greenwood, 1976. Delhi: Oxford University Press, Educational edition, 1978. New York: Overlook, 1986.

——. *The Cat and Shakespeare*. 1971; rpt. New Delhi: Orient Paperbacks, 1992. New York: Macmillan, 1965.

——. *Comrade Kirillov*. New Delhi: Vision Books, Orient Paperbacks, 1976.

——. *The Chessmaster and His Moves*. New Delhi: Vision Books, 1988.

——. *Daughter of the Mountain.* To be published.

——. *A Myrobalan in the Palm of Your Hand.* To be published.

Non-Fiction

Rao, Raja. *The Meaning of India.* New Delhi: Vision Books, 1996.

——. *The Great India Way: A Life of Mahatma Gandhi.* New Delhi: Vision Books, 1998.

Books Edited by Rao

Rao, Raja and Iqbal Singh , Eds. *Changing India: An Anthology.* London: Allen and Unwin, 1939.

——. *Whither India?* Bombay: Padma Publications, 1948.

Rao, Raja. *Soviet Russia: Some Random Sketches and Impressions by Jawaharlal Nehru.* Bombay: Chetana, 1949.

Rao's Contributions to Books

Rao, Raja. "Recollections of E.M. Forster" in K. Natwar Singh, Ed. *E.M. Forster: A Tribute with Selections from His Writings on India.* New York: Harcourt, Brace and World, 1964, pp. 15–32.

——. "The Meaning of India" in P. Lal, Ed. *The First Writers Workshop Literary Reader.* Calcutta: Writers Workshop, 1972.

——. "The Caste of English" in C.D. Narasimhaiah, Ed. *Awakened Conscience: Studies in Commonwealth Literature.* Delhi: Sterling, 1978, pp. 420–22.

——. "The Cave and the Conch" in Maggie Butcher, Ed. *The Eye of the Beholder: Indian Writing in English.* London: Commonwealth Institute, 1983, pp. 44–45.

Rao's Fictional Contributions to Periodicals

Rao, Raja. "Javni." *Asia.* New York (November 1933).

——. "Akkayya." *Cahiers du Sud.* Paris (December 1933), (French version).

——. "A Client." *Mercure de France.* Paris (August 1934), pp. 31–48. (French version).

——. "In Khandesh." *The Adelphi.* London (November 1934).

——. "The True Story of Kanakapala, Protector of Gold." *Asia.* New York (September 1935).

——. "The Little Gram Shop." *Vendredi.* Paris (1937), (French version).

——. "The Cow of the Barricades." *Asia.* New York (August 1938).

——. "Companions." Broadcast from the Lucknow Station of All India Radio in 1941 or 1942. [Publishers' Note to *The Cow of the Barricades and Other Stories*].

——. " Narsiga." *Horizon*. Bombay (1944).

——. "India: A Story." *Encounter* 1.2. London (November 1953), pp. 59–63.

——. "The Cat." *Chelsea Review*. New York (Summer 1959).

——. "Nimka." *The Illustrated Weekly of India*. Bombay (19 May 1963), pp. 16–17.

——. "The Policeman and the Rose." *The Illustrated Weekly of India*. Bombay (6 October 1963), pp. 36–39.

——. "Creatures of Benares (1)." *World Literature Today* 62.4. Norman, OK (Autumn 1988), pp. 540–43.

——. "Creatures of Benares (2)." *World Literature Today* 62.4. Norman, OK (Autumn 1988), pp. 543–46.

Rao's Non-Fictional Contributions to Periodicals

Rao, Raja. "Pilgrimage to Europe." *Jaya Karnataka* 10.1. Dharwar, India (1931), pp. 27–22 (in Kannada).

——. "Europe and Ourselves." *Jaya Karnataka* 10.3. Dharwar, India (1931), pp. 204–07, (In Kannada).

——. "Romain Rolland, the Great Sage." *Jaya Karnataka* 11.1. Dharwar, India (1933), pp. 46–51, (In Kannada).

——. " Pandit Taranath." *Asia*. New York (January 1935), pp. 10–15.

——. "The Premier of Sakuntala." *Asia*. New York (June 1943), pp. 365–68.

——. "Jupiter and Mars." *Pacific Spectator* 8 (1954), pp. 369–73.

——. "Varanasi." *The Illustrated Weekly of India*. Bombay (3 September 1961), pp. 12–15.

——. "Trivandrum." *The Illustrated Weekly of India*. Bombay (25 February 1962), pp. 12–16.

——. "Meaning of India." *The Illustrated Weekly of India*. Bombay (25 February 1962).

——. "Fables for the Feeble." *The Illustrated Weekly of India*. Bombay (December 1962), pp. 46–47.

——. "Books Which Have Influenced Me." *The Illustrated Weekly of India*. Bombay (10 February 1963), p. 45.

——. "Diwali Comes to Ramu" *The Illustrated Weekly of India*. Bombay (17 November 1963), pp. 15–19.

——. "Andre Malraux among the Gods of India." *United Asia* 16.2. Bombay (March–April 1964), pp. 122–28.

——. "Jawaharlal Nehru: Recollections and Reflections: A Symposium." *The Illustrated Weekly of India*. Bombay (15 November 1964), pp. 64–67.

——. "The Gandhian Way: Replies to a Questionnaire on Gandhi." *The Illustrated Weekly of India.* Bombay (14 February 1965), p. 39.

——. "The Writer and the Word." *Literary Criterion* 7.1. Mysore (Winter 1965) pp. 229–31. Rpt. in *Critical Essays on Indian Writing in English.* Ed. M.K. Naik et al., Dharwar: Karnatak University, 1968. Rpt. in *World Literature Today* 62.4, Norman, OK (Autumn 1988) pp. 538–39.

——. "Irish Interlude." *The Saturday Review.* New York (25 June 1966), p. 21.

——. "The Moon Light in Lucknow." *The Illustrated Weekly of India.* Bombay (5 November 1966), pp. 15–19, (12 November 1966), pp. 20–23.

——. "The Climate of Indian Literature Today." *The Literary Criterion* 10.3. Mysore (Winter 1972), pp. 1–7.

——. "Autobiography: Entering the Literary World." *The Journal of Commonwealth Literature* 13.3. London (April 1979), pp. 28–32. rpt. In *World Literature Today* 62.4. Norman, OK (Autumn 1988), pp. 536–38.

——. "The Word." *Colonial Consciousness in Commonwealth Literature.* Ed. G.S. Amur and S.K. Desai, Bombay: Somaiya Publications, 1984.

——. "The Ultimate Word." *Temenos.* (London) 9 (1988).

Rao's Contribution in Verse

Rao, Raja. "Expiation of a Heretic." *Jaya Karnataka* 10.10. Dharwar, India (1932) pp. 718–19. (in Kannada).

Interviews with Rao

A.S.R. "Meeting with Raja Rao Recalled." First Instalment. *Illustrated Weekly of India,* (25 September 1966) p. 13.

Balu, Shakuntala. "Meeting Raja Rao." *Economic Times,* (25 January 1987) p. 3.

Bhattacharji, Shobhana. "Interview with Raja Rao." *The Book Review,* New Delhi (September–October 1982), pp. 63–67.

Brierre, Annie. "An Interview with Raja Rao." *Illustrated Weekly of India* (10 March 1963), p. 26.

Gokhale, Ashok. "Indians who made it." Cover story in the special issue on "Indians in America: Crisis of Identity." *India Today,* New Delhi: July 16–31, 1980, p. 42.

Gondal, Yotesh. "Raja Rao: Obscure but Rhythmic Writer" *New Delhi,* New Delhi and Calcutta, Vol. 3, Issue 7, August 18–31, 1980, pp. 60–64.

Jussawala, Feroza. "Raja Rao." *Interviews with Writers of the Post-Colonial World.* Eds. Feroza Jussawala and Reed Way Dasenbrock, Jakson: University Press of Mississippi, 1992, pp. 140–55.

Kamath, M.V. "The Brahmin and the Rabbi," *The Illustrated Weekly of India,* August 24, 1980, p. 47.

Kaushik, Asha. "Meeting Raja Rao." *Literature Criterion* XVIII (3), 1983. p. 33.

Kohli, Suresh. "Ambivalence and Individuality." *Indian and Foreign Review.* 6(17), (15 June 1969), p. 11.

——. "Raja Rao: The Man and His Mask." *Times Weekly,* (13 September 1970), p. 4.

Jitendra, Arya. "Face to Face." *Times Weekly,* (16 August 1972), p. 8.

——. "Interview with Raja Rao." *Illustrated Weekly of India,* (5 January 1964), p. 44.

Mathur, O.P. "Excerpts from an Interview with Raja Rao." *Indian Political Novel and Other Essays.* Allahabad: Kitab Mahal, 1995, pp. 191–98.

Niranjan, Shiva. "An Interview with Raja Rao." in K.N. Sinha (Ed.), *Indian Writing in English,* New Delhi: Heritage, 1979, p. 19.

O'Brien, A.P. "Meeting Raja Rao." *Prajna.* Golden Jubilee Number, Benaras (1966), pp. 16–17.

Paniker, Ayappa. "A Conversation with Raja Rao on The Cat and Shakespeare." *Chandrabhaga,* 2, 1979, p. 14.

Paranjape, Makarand. "Art of the Matter: Raja Rao's The Meaning of India: The Collection of Essays." *Indian Review of Books* 6.2. (16 November–15 December 1976), pp. 6–8.

Paris, Arthur and Radhakrishnan Radhika. "Award-winning Raja Rao Likened to Joyce, Proust." *India Abroad,* (27 May 1988), pp. B4–B5.

Parthasarathy, R. "'The Future World is Being Made in America:' An Interview with Raja Rao." *Span,* New Delhi, (September 1977), pp. 29–30.

Ranchan, Som P. "A Meeting with Raja Rao" I, II, III, IV, *Thought,* Delhi, July 13, 20, 27, August 3, 1968.

Rangra, Ranvir. "Beyond the Body and Mind: An Interview with Raja Rao." *Interview with Indian Writers,* New Delhi: B.R. Publishing Corporation, 1992.

——. "I Write to Myself: An Interview." *India Literature,* (July–August 1988), pp. 113–23.

Reddy, P. Bayapa. "A Conversation with Raja Rao." *Studies in Indian Writing in English.* Ed. P. Bayapa Reddy, New Delhi: Prestige Books, 1990, pp. 88–92.

Shankardass, Rama. "Face to Face," *Weekend Review,* 2(28), 15, June 1968, p. 16.

Shekar, Ratna Rao. "Seventy Years of Solitude." *Society,* (August 1985), pp. 30–33.

Subramanian, K. "Meeting Raja Rao." *Kakatiya Journal of English Studies* 3.1. (1978) pp. 70A–70C.

Vasu, S.V. "Raja Rao: Face to Face." *The Illustrated Weekly of India*, Bombay (5 January 1964), pp. 44–45.

Wohl, Elizabeth. "Raja Rao on America." *Span*, New Delhi, (January 1973), pp. 35–37.

Books on Rao

Bhattacharya, P.C. *Indo-Anglian Literature and the Works of Raja Rao*. Delhi: Atma Ram & Sons, 1983.

Celly, Anu. *Women in Raja Rao's novel: A Feminist Reading of the Serpent and the Rope*. Jaipur: Printwell, 1995.

Dayal, P. *Raja Rao: A Study of His Novels*. New Delhi: Atlantic, 1991.

Dey, Esha. *The Novels of Raja Rao: The Theme of Quest*. New Delhi: Prestige, 1992.

Hardgrave, Robert L. *Word as Mantra, The Art of Raja Rao*. Ed. Robert L. Hardgrave. New Delhi: Katha Publications in association with University of Texas, Austin, 1998.

Mittapali, Rajeshwar and Pier Paolo Piciucco. Eds. *The Fiction of Raja Rao: Critical Studies*. New Delhi: Atlantic, 2001.

Naik, M.K. *Raja Rao*. Bombay: Blackie & Son, 1982.

Nanda, Nivedita. *Raja Rao and the Religious Traditions: Study of the Serpent and the Rope*. New Delhi: Anmol Publications, 1992.

Narasimhaiah, C.D. *Raja Rao*. New Delhi: Arnold-Heinemann, 1973.

Narayan, Shyamala A. *Raja Rao: Man and His Works*. New Delhi: Sterling, 1988.

Niranjan, Shiva. *Raja Rao: Novelist as Sadhaka*. Ghaziabad: Vimal, 1985.

Niven, Alastair. *Truth Within Fiction: A Study of Raja Rao's* The Serpent and the Rope. Calcutta: Writers Workshop, 1987.

Paranjape, Makarand. Ed. *The Best of Raja Rao*. New Delhi: Katha, 1998; rpt. 2000.

Raja Rao: 1988 Neustadt Laureate. Special issue of World Literature Today 62.4. (Autumn, 1988).

Ramachandra, Ragini. *Raja Rao: An Anthology of Recent Criticism*. Delhi: Pencraft International, 2000.

Rao, K.R. *The Fiction of Raja Rao*. Aurangabad: Parimal, 1980.

Rao, Sudhakar. A. *Socio-Cultural Aspects of Life in the Selected Novels of Raja Rao*. New Delhi: Atlantic Publishers, 1999.

Sethi, Rumina. *Myths of the Nation: National Identity and Literary Representation*. Oxford: Clarendon Press, 1999.

Sharma, I.D. *The Semantic Universe of Raja Rao: Mind and Art of Raja Rao as a Story Teller*. Delhi: Indian Publishers' and Distributors, 2006.

Sharma, Jai Prakash. *Raja Rao: A Visionary of Indo-Anglian Fiction*. Ed. J.P. Sharma. Meerut: Shalabh Book House, 1980.

Sharma, K.K. Ed. *Perspectives on Raja Rao*. Ghaziabad: Vimal, 1980.

Sharrad, Paul. *Raja Rao and Cultural Tradition*. New Delhi: Sterling, 1987.

Singh, Parminder. *A Semiotic Analysis of Raja Rao's the Serpent and the Rope*. New Delhi: Bahri Publications, 1991.

Singh, R.S. *Raja Rao's Kanthapura: An Analysis*. Delhi: Doaba House, 1973.

Srivastava, Narsingh. *The Mind and Art of Raja Rao*. Bareilly: Prakash, 1980.

Tripathi, J.P. *Raja Rao: The Fictionist*. Delhi: B.R. Publishing, 2003.

(c) Critical and Other Sources

Books

Aesop's Fables. New York: Magnum, 1968.

Agnihotri, G.N. *Indian Life and Problems in the Novels of Mulk Raj Anand, Raja Rao and R.K. Narayan*. Meerut: Shalabh, 1984.

Albright, Evelyn May. *The Short Story: Its Principles and Structure*. New York: Macmillan, 1931.

Ali, Syed Mashkoor. *Indian Writing in English: A Critical Response*. New Delhi: Creative Books, 2001.

Allen, Walter. *The Short Story in English*. Oxford: Clarendon, 1981.

Alphonso-Karkala, J.A. and L. Eds. *A Bibliography of Indo-English Literature*. Bombay: Nirmala Sadanand, 1974.

Anand, Mulk Raj. *Gauri*. Originally published as *The Old Woman and the Cow* (1960), New Delhi: Mayfair, 1981.

Angiras, Ramakant Sharma. *Trilogy of Tantra*. Karnal: Natraj, 1989.

Arnold, Sir Edwin, trans. *The Light of Asia and Indian Song of Songs (Gita Govinda)*, Bombay: Jaico, 1949.

Aurobindo, Sri. *Letters on Yoga*, Vols. I, II, III. Pondicherry: Sri Aurobindo Ashram, 1979.

——.*The Future Poetry and Letters on Poetry, Literature and Art*. Pondicherry: Sri Aurobindo Ashram, 1972.

——. *The Synthesis of Yoga*. Pondicherry: Sri Aurobindo Ashram, 1976.

——. *Essays Devine and Human*. Pondicherry: Sri Aurobindo Ashrama, 1994.

Avalon, Arthur (John Woodroffe), Ed. *Principles of Tantra*. Madras: Ganesh, 1960, Delhi: Shivalik Prakashan, 2002.

Ayyar, C.V. Narayana. *Origin and Early History of Saivism in South India*. Madras: University of Madras, 1974.

Bande, Usha. *Mothers and Mother-Figures in Indo-English Literature.* Jalandhar: ABS Publications, 1994.

Bach, Richard David. *Jonathan Livingston Seagull.* New York: Macmillan Publishing, 1970.

——.1977; rpt. *Illusions: The Adventures of a Reluctant Messiah.* New York: Dell/Eleanor, 1989.

——. *One.* New York: Dell/Reissure, 1989.

——. *Stranger to the Ground.* New York: Dell, 1990.

——. 1994; rpt. *Running from Safety: An Adventure of the Spirit.* New York: Delta, 1995.

Badal, R.K. *Indo-Anglian Literature: An Outline.* Bareilly: Prakash, 1975.

Bahadur, K.P. *The Wisdom of Sankhya.* New Delhi: Sterling, 1978.

Balarama Gupta, G.S. *Essays on Indian Writing in English.* Gulbarga: J.I.W.E. Publications, 1975.

Bates, H.E. *The Modern Short Story: A Critical Survey.* London: Michael Joseph, 1972.

——. *The Modern Short Story: A Critical Survey.* London: Macmillan and Co. Ltd., 1941.

Bäumer, Bettina and John R. Dupuche, eds. *Void and Fullness in the Buddhist, Hindu and Christian Traditions: Sunya—Purna—Pleroma.* New Delhi: D.K. Printworld (P) Ltd., 2005.

Bernard, Theos. 1989; rpt. *Hindu Philosophy.* Mumbai: Jaico, 1998.

Besant, Anne and Dass Bhagvan. 1905. rpt. *The Bhagavad Gita.* Madras: The Theosophical Publishing House, 1979.

Bharati, Agehananda. *The Tantric Tradition.* London: Rider, 1969.

——. *The Light at the Centre: Context and Pretext of Modern Mysticism.* New Delhi: Vikas, 1977.

Bhatnagar, R.S. *Dimensions of Classical Sufi Thought.* Delhi: MLBD, 1984.

Bhattacharya, Bhabani. *Music for Mohini.* New York: Crown, 1952.

——. *Shadow from Ladakh.* London: W.H. Allen, 1966.

——. *Steel Hawk and Other Stories.* Delhi: Hind Pocket, 1968.

Black, E.L. and Parry J.P., Ed. *Aspects of the Short Story.* London: John Murray, 1959.

Borev, Yuri. *Aesthetics.* Moscow: Progress, 1985.

Brane, Donald A. *Maya in Radhakrishnan's Thought: Six Meanings other than Illusion.* Delhi: MLBD, 1984.

Brent, Peter. *Godmen of India.* London: Allen Lane, 1972.

Britannica Ready Reference Encyclopedia. New Delhi: Encyclopedia Britannica (India) Pvt. Ltd., 2005.

Brome, V. *Jung: Man and Myth.* London: Paladin Books, 1980.

Brunton, Paul. *The Wisdom of the Overself.* London: Rider, 1969.

Bucke, Richard Maurice. *Cosmic Consciousness*. New York: Penguin, 1991.

Burtt, E. *In Search of Philosophical Understanding*. Indianapolis: Hacket, 1967.

Campbell, Joseph. *The Hero with a Thousand Faces*. Princeton: Princeton UP, 1968.

——. *The Power of Myth*. With Bill Moyers. Ed. Betty Sue Flowers. New York: Doubleday, 1968.

——.1959; rpt. *The Masks of God: Primitive Mythology*, Vol. I. 1970, New York: Penguin Books, 1976.

——. 1962; rpt. *The Masks of God: Oriental Mythology*, Vol. II. 1970, New York: Penguin Books, 1976.

——. 1964; rpt. *The Masks of God: Occidental Mythology*, Vol. III. 1970, New York: Penguin Books, 1976.

——. 1968; rpt. *The Masks of God: Creative Mythology*, Vol. IV. 1970, New York: Penguin Books, 1976.

——. 1971; rpt. Ed. *The Portable Jung*, tr. R.F.C. Hull. New York: Viking, New York: Penguin, 1976.

Canby, Henry Seidal and Deshiell Alfred. *A Study of the Short Story*. New York: Henry Holt, 1935.

Chetananand, Swami. 1997, rpt. *God Lived with Them*. Kolkata: Advaita Ashrama, 2001.

Chattopadhyaya, D.P. *Religion, Philosophy and Science: A Sketch of Global View*. Shimla: IIAS, 2006.

——. *Indian Philosophy: A Popular Introduction*. New Delhi: People's 1986.

Chaudhuri, Haridas. *The Essence of Spiritual Philosophy*. Ed. Dionne Somers. New Delhi: Indus, 1990.

Chaudhury, Nirad C. *Hinduism*. New Delhi: B.I., 1979.

Clarke, J.J. *Jung and Eastern Thought: A Dialogue with the Orient*. London and New York: Routledge, 1994.

Coburn, Thomas B. *Durga Mahatmya*. Delhi: Motilal Banarasidass, 1988.

Codd, Clara M. 1958; rpt. *The Technique of Spiritual Life*. Madras: The Theosophical Publishing House, 1985.

Coelho, Paulo. *The Alchemist*. Trans. Alan R. Clarke. New Delhi: Harper Collins, 1998.

Coomaraswamy, A.K. *Buddha and the Gospel of Buddhism*. New York: Harper and Row, 1964.

Coukoulis, Peter P. *Guru, Psychotherapist and Self*. California: De Vorss, 1976.

Cuddon, J.A. 1976; rpt. *Dictionary of Literary Terms and Literary Theory*. London: Penguin, 1991.

Dasgupta, Surendranath. 1927; rpt. *Hindu Mysticism.* Delhi: MLBD, 1996.

——. *A History of Indian Philosophy,* Vol. I. 1922; rpt. London: Cambridge UP, 1963; Vol. II, 1932; rpt. 1965; Vol. III, 1940; rpt. 1961; Vol. IV, 1949; rpt. 1961; Vol. V, 1955; rpt. 1962.

Deutsch, Eliot. *Advaita Vedanta: A Philosophical Reconstruction.* Honolulu: East-West Centre, 1969.

Dhalla, Kamal H. *A Bibliography of the Indo-English Short Story. Journal of Indian Writing in English,* VII, 1, January 1979.

Dhawan, R.K. Ed. *Commonwealth Fiction,* Vol. 3. New Delhi: Classical, 1988.

——. *Modern Indo-English Fiction.* New Delhi: Bahri, 1982.

Donald and Jean Johnson. *God and Gods in Hinduism.* Delhi: Arnold-Heinemann, 1972.

Dumoulin, H. *Zen Enlightenment: Origins and Meanings.* Tokyo: Weatherill, 1979.

Durant, Will. 1926; rpt. *The Story of Philosophy: The Lives and Opinions of the Greater Philosophers.* New York: Washington Square Press, 1961.

Dutt, Indu, trans. 1969; rpt. *A Tagore Testament.* Bombay: Jaico, 1992.

Dutt, Toru. *Ancient Ballads and Legends of Hindustan.* Allahabad, Kitabistan, 1941, pp. 90–100.

Dwivedi, A.N. Ed. *Studies in Contemporary Indian Fiction in English.* Allahabad: Kitab Mahal, 1987.

——. *Studies in Contemporary Indian-English Short Story.* Delhi: B.R. Publishing Corporation, 1991.

Eck, Diana L. 1993; rpt. *Encountering God: A Spiritual Journey from Bozeman to Banaras.* New Delhi: Penguin, 1995.

——. *Banaras: City of Light.* New Jersey: Princeton UP, 1982.

Eliot, T.S. *Selected Poems.* London: Faber & Faber, 1954.

Erikson, Erik. *Dimensions of a New Identity.* New Delhi: Life and Life, 1975.

——. *Identity: Youth and Crisis.* New York: W.W. Norton, 1968.

Evans, Richard I. *Dialogue with C.G. Jung.* New York: Praeger, 1981.

Falconer, A.E.I. *Sufi Literature and the Journey to Immortality.* Delhi: MLBD, 1991.

Forster, E.M. *Aspects of the Novel.* (1927) Harmondsworth: Penguin, 1962, 1968.

——. *A Passage to India.* (1924) Harmondsworth: Penguin, 1961.

——. *The Hill of Devi.* Harmondsworth: Penguin, 1983.

Frazer, J.G. *The Golden Bough.* London: Macmillan, 1957; rpt. 1970.

Freud, Sigmund. *The Complete Introductory Lectures on Psychoanalysis* (tr. J. Strachey), London: Allen and Unwin, 1971.

——. *The Interpretation of Dreams.* 2nd Ed., trans. James Strachey. London: The Hogarth Press, 1953.

Fromm, Erich. *The Art of Being.* New York: Crossroad/Continuum, 1992.

——. *The Art of Loving.* New York: Harper & Row, 1956.

Frost, Gavin and Yvonne. *Tantric yoga: The Real Path to Raising Kundalini Power.* Delhi: MLBD, 1996.

Gambhirananda, Swami, trans. 1957; rpt. *Eight Upnisads,* Vol. 1. Calcutta: Advaita Ashrama, 1995, Vol. 2. 1996.

Gandhi, M.K. 1927, rpt. *An Autobiography* or *The Story of My Experiments with Truth.* Ahmedabad: Navjivan Publishing House, 1990.

Geertz, Clifford. *The Interpretation of Cultures.* New York: Basic Books, 1973.

Gibran, Kahlil. *The Prophet.* New Delhi: UBSPD, 1998.

——. *The Wisdom of Kahlil Gibran.* New Delhi: UBSPD, 1993.

——. *The Broken Wings.* Trans. Anthony R. Ferris. New Delhi: Srishti Publishers and Distributers, 1998.

——.1992; rpt. *Khalil Gibran Reader.* Mumbai: Jaico, 1997.

Goddard, Dwight. 1938; rpt. *A Buddhist Bible.* Delhi: Book Faith, 1999.

Golomb, Jacob et al., Eds. *Nietzsche and Depth Psychology.* Albany: State University of New York Press. 1999.

Govinda, Lama Anagarika. 1960; rpt. *Foundations of Tibetan Mysticism.* B.I. Publications, 1994.

Goyandka, Jaydayal trans. 1984; rpt. *Srimad Bhagvadgita.* Gorakhpur: Gita Press, n.d.

Grimal, Pierrie, Ed. *World Mythology.* New York: Excalibur, 1981.

Grover, Sanjay. *Nine Days to Nirvana.* New Delhi: Life Positive, 2000.

Guerin, Wilfred L. et al., *A Handbook of Critical Approaches to Literature.* New York: Harper & Row, 1966.

Gupta, Mahendranath. 1944; rpt. *The Gospel of Sri Ramakrisna.* Vol. 1 and 2. Trans. Swami Nikhilananda. Madras: Sri Ramakrishna Math, 1985.

Harrex, S.C. *The Modern Indian Novel.* Calcutta: Writers Workshop, 1971.

Harshananda, Swami. *A Dictionary of Advaita Vedanta.* Bangalore: Ramakrishna Math, 1995.

Hayman, Ronald. *A Life of Jung.* Soho Square: Bloomsbury, 2002.

Hesse, Hermann. 1954; rpt. *Siddhartha.* London: Picador, 1991.

——. 1972; rpt. *The Journey to the East.* Frogmore, St. Albans: Panther, 1976.

Hiriyanna, M. *Essentials of Indian Philosophy*. 1949; rpt. London: Allen, 1978.

——. *Outlines of Indian Philosophy*. 1932; rpt. London: Allen, 1973.

Hopkins, E. Washburn. *Epic Mythology*. Varanasi: Indological, 1968.

Hume, Robert Ernest. *The Thirteen Principal Upnishads, translated from the Sanskrit*. OU Press, 1931.

Indich, William M. *Consciousness in Advaita Vedanta*. Delhi: MLBD, 1980.

Ions, Veronica. *Indian Mythology*. London: Paul Hemlyn, 1973.

Iyenger, K.R. Srinivasa. *Indian Writing in English*. Bombay: Asia, 1979.

Jain, S.K. *A Select Bibliography of the Indian Short Stories and Historical Fiction in English, Indian Literature*, XII, 2, 1969.

Jha, Akhileshwar. *The Imprisoned Mind*. New Delhi: Ambika, 1980.

Jha, Rama. *Gandhian Thought and Indo-Anglian Novelists*. Delhi: Chanakya, 1983.

Joyce, James. *Finnegans Wake*. New York: Viking Press Inc., 1939.

Jung, C.G. *Modern Man in Search of a Soul*. 1933; rpt. London: Routledge & Kegan Paul, 1976.

——. *Psychology and Religion*. New Heaven: Yale UP, 1964.

——. *The Psychology of the Transference*. 1969; rpt. London: Ark Paperbacks, 1983.

——. *The Archetypes and the Collective Unconscious*. 2nd ed., Trans. R.F.C. Hull. Princeton: Princeton UP, 1968.

——. *Symbols of Transformation*. 2nd ed., Trans. R.F.C. Hull. Collected Works, Vol. 5. New York and London, 1967.

——. *Psychological Types or The Psychology of Individuation*. Trans. H. Godwin Baynes. London: Kegan Paul, Trench, Trubner & Co. Ltd., 1946.

——. *The Collected Works*, Vol. 4. *Freud and Psycho-analysis*. Trans. R.F.C. Hull. London: Routledge & Kegan Paul, 1961; Vol. 7, *Two Essays on Analytical Psychology*, 1953, 1st ed., 1966, Revised ed.; Vol. 8, *The Structure and Dynamics of the Psyche*, 1960, 1st Ed., 1969, 2nd ed.; Vol. 9, *Civilization in Transition*, 1964; Vol. 11, *Psychology of Religion: West and East*, 1958; Vol.12, *Psychology and Alchemy*, 1953, 1st ed., 1968, 2nd ed.; Vol. 13, *Alchemical Studies*, 1967, Vol. 15, *The Sprit in Man, Art and Literature*, 1966; Vol. 17, *The Development of Personality*, 1954, 1st Ed., 1964, 2nd rpt.

——.*Jung on Active Imagination*. London: Routledge, 1997.

——. *The Psychology of Kundilini Yoga*, ed., Sonu Shamdasani. London: Routledge, 1996.

Kafka, Franz. *Metamorphosis and Other Stories*. trans. Willa and Edwin Muir, Penguin, 1968, p. 19.

Kapur, Subodh, ed. *Encyclopaedia of Indian Heritage* in 90 Volumes. New Delhi: Cosmo Publications, 2002. Volumes 19–23, *The Vedanta Philosophy*; 24–27, *Upnishadic Philosophy*; 49, *Shakti*; 50, *Bhagvad Gita*; 51, *Sri Krishna*; 52–53, *Six Systems of Indian Philosophy*; 54–55, *Yoga Philosophy*; 62–63, *Indian Mysticism*; 64, *Hindu Mythology*; 70–71, *Saiva Philosophy*; 73, *Sakta Philosophy*; 77–79, *Tantra Philosophy*; 87, *Symbolism and Hindu* Worship; 88, *Meditation, Yoga and Sadhana*; 90, *Panchtantra and Hitopadesh.*

Karnani, Chetan. *Eminent Indian English Writers: An Assesment.* Jaipur: Rawat Publications, 2001.

Kesarkodi, Ian and Watson. *Studies in Hindu Wisdom.* New Delhi: Hind, 1981.

Khan, Hazrat Inayat. *The Sufi Message,* Vol. X. Delhi: Motilal Banarasidass, 1990; Vol. I, *The Way of Illumination,* 1988; Vol. IV, *Mental Purification and Healing,* 1989; Vol. V, *Spiritual Liberty,* 1989; Vol. VIII, *Sufi Teachings,* 1990; Vol. XI, *Philosophy, Psychology, Mysticism,* 1990; Vol. XII, *The Divinity of the Human Soul,* 1990.

Khosla, K. *The Sufism of Rumi.* Dorset: Element Books, 1987.

King, Bruce. *The Commonwealth Novel since 1960.* London: The Macmillan Press Ltd., 1991.

Kishore, B.R. *Rigveda; Yajurveda; Samveda; Atharvveda.* New Delhi: Diamond, 1998.

Klein, F.A. *The Religion of Islam.* New Delhi: Kitab Bhawan, 1977.

Kramrisch, Stella. *The Presence of Siva.* Delhi: Oxford UP, 1981.

Krishna, Gopi. *Higher Consciousness: The Evolutionary Thrust of Kundalini.* New York: D.B. Taraporevala Sons & Co. Pvt. Ltd., 1974.

Krishnamurti, J. and Bohm David. 1985; rpt. *The Ending of Time.* Madras: Krishnamurti Foundation India, 1996.

Krishnamurti, J. *The First and Last Freedom.* London: Victor Gollanez, 1969.

Kulshreshtha, Saroj. *The Concept of Salvation in Vedanta.* New Delhi: Ashish, 1986.

Kumar Shiva. K. Ed. *Modern Indian Short Stories.* Delhi: Oxford UP, 1983.

Lemon, Lee T. *A Glossary for the Study of English.* Delhi: Oxford UP, 1974.

Lokeswarananda, Swami. *Aspects of Vedanta.* Calcutta: The Ramakrishna Mission Institute of Culture, n.d.

Lott, Eric. *Vedantic Approaches to God.* London: Macmillan, 1980.

Lutyens, Mary. *The Second Penguin Krishnamurti Reader.* London: Penguin, 1970.

Macfie, J.M. 1993; rpt. *Myths and Legends of India.* Calcutta: Rupa, 1996.

Machwe, Prabhakar. *Hinduism: Its Contribution to Science and Civilisation.* New Delhi: Vikas, 1979.

Madan, T.N. Ed. *Way of Life: King, Householder, Renouncer*. New Delhi: Vikas, 1982.

Maharshi, Ramana. *The Spiritual Teaching of Ramana Maharshi*. Shambala: Boulder & Co., 1972.

Maitra, S.K. 1941; rpt. *An Introduction to the Philosophy of Sri Aurobindo*. Pondicherry: Sri Aurobindo Ashrama, 1993.

Mangalwadi, Vishal. *The World of Gurus*. New Delhi: Vikas, 1977.

Markandaya, Kamala. *Possession*. Bombay: Jaico, 1967.

Martin, Raymond, ed. 1997; rpt. *Krishnamurti: Reflections on the Self*. New Delhi: Bluejay Books, 2000.

McCutchion, David. *Indian Writing in English*. Calcutta: Writers' Workshop, 1969.

McGuire, William and Hull, R.F.C. Eds. *C.G. Jung Speaking: Interviews and Encounters*. London: Thames and Hudson, 1978.

Mehta, Kamal. *The Twentieth Century Indian Short Story in English*. New Delhi: Creative Books, 2004.

Mehta, P.P. *Indo-Anglian Fiction: An Assessment*. Bareilly: Prakash, 1979.

Mehta, Rohit. 1973; rpt. *J. Krishnamurti and the Nameless Experience*. Delhi: MLBD, 1999.

——.1966; rpt. *From Mind to Supermind: A Commentary on the Bhagvad Gita*. Delhi: MLBD, 1997.

——. and Shridevi Mehta. 1990; rpt. *J. Krishnamurti and Sant Kabir: A Study in Depth*. Delhi: MLBD, 1993.

Melwani, M.D. *Themes in Indo-Anglian Literature*, 2nd ed. Bareilly: P.B.D., 1977.

Merson, A.J. *Modern Short Stories*, an edited work. Bombay: Macmillan India Ltd., 1981.

Mookerjee, Ajit and Khanna Madhu. *The Tantric Way: Art, Science, Ritual*. Delhi: Vikas, 1977.

Moore, Charles, A. Ed. *The Indian Mind: Essentials of Indian Philosophy and Culture*. Honolulu: East-West Center Press, 1967.

Mukherjee, Meenakshi. *Twice Born Fiction*. New Delhi: Arnold-Heinemann, 1971.

——. *Realism and Reality: The Novel and Society in India*. Delhi: Oxford UP, 1985.

Murti, Sachidananda. *Revelation and Reason in Advaita Vedanta*. Delhi: Motilal Banarsidas, 1959, rpt. 1974.

Naik, M.K. *A History of Indian English Literature*. New Delhi: Sahitya Akademi, 1982.

——. Ed. *Aspects of Indian Writing in English*. Delhi: Macmillan, 1979.

——. and A. Narayan Shyamala. *Indian English Literature 1980–2000: A Critical Survey*. Delhi: Pencraft International, 2004.

Narasimhaiah, C.D. *The Swan and the Eagle*. Shimla: IIAS, 1969.

Narayan, R.K. *An Astrologer's Day and Other Stories*. London: Eyre & Spottiswoode, 1947.

——. *The Guide*. Mysore: Indian Thought, 1963.

——. *Swami and Friends*. London: Hamish Hamilton, 1935.

——. *Waiting for the Mahatma*. East Lansing: Michigan State UP, 1955.

Narayan, Shyamala A. "Voyage as Motif in Indian English Fiction." *New Perspectives in Indian Literature in English: Essays in Honour of Professor M.K. Naik*. Ed. Yaravintelimath, C.R., Balarama Gupta G.S., Venugopal C.V. and Singh Amritjit. New Delhi: Sterling, 1995, pp. 127–36.

Neale, Donald Walsch. *Conversations with God: An Uncommon Dialogue*. Charlottesville: Hodder & Stoughton, 1998.

Nikhilananda, Swami. *Hinduism: Its Meaning for the Liberation of the Spirit*. Madras: Sri Ramakrishna Math, 1968.

——. Trans. *The Gospel of Sri Ramakrishna*. New York, 1942.

O'Neil, L. Thomas. *Maya in Sankara: Measuring the Immeasurable*. Delhi: MLBD, 1980.

Organ, Troy. *The Self in Indian Philosophy*. The Hague: Mouton, 1964.

Pallan, Rajesh K. *Myths and Symbols in Raja Rao and R.K. Narayan*. Jalandhar: ABS Publications, 1994.

Pande, G.C. *Neuroscience, Consciousness and Philosophy*. Shimla: IIAS, 2001.

Parameswaram, Uma. *A Study of Representative Indo-English Novelists*. New Delhi: Vikas, 1976.

Patel, S.R. *The Human Quest*. Bombay: Shri S.R. Patel Foundation, 1989.

Pathak, R.S. "The Indo-English Novelist's Quest for Identity." *Explorations in Modern Indo-English Fiction*. Ed. R.K. Dhawan. New Delhi: Bahri Publications, 1982, pp. 1–15.

Prabhavananda, Swami. 1960; rpt. *The Spiritual Heritage of India*. Madras: Sri Ramakrishna Math, 1978.

Prabhupada, Swami. 1972; rpt. *Bhagvad-Gita As It Is* (Complete Ed.). Los Angeles: The Bhaktivedanta Book Trust, 1981, Mumbai, 1986.

Prasad, V.V.N. Rajendra. *Five Indian Novelists: B. Rajan, Raja Rao, R.K. Narayan, Arun Joshi, Anita Desai*. New York: Stosius Inc./Advent Books Division, 1997.

Prithipaul, K.D. *Moha: A Study in the Metaphysics of Error in Brahminical Tradition*. Madras: Southern, 1988.

Purani, A.B. 1958; rpt. *The Life of Sri Aurobindo*. Pondicherry: Sri Aurobindo Ashram, 1995.

Radhakrishnan, S. *Indian Philosophy*. Vols. I and II. London: Allen, 1941.

——. *The Bhagvadgita*. New Delhi: Blackie & Son, 1976.

——. *The Hindu View of Life*. London: Macmillan, 1927.

——. Trans. *The Principal Upanisadas*. London: Allen & Unwin, 1953.

——. *Eastern Religions and Western Thought*. Delhi: OUP, 1939.

——.1994; rpt. *The Principal Upnishads*. New Delhi: Harper Collins Publishers India, 1998.

——. and Raju, P.P. Eds. *The Concept of Man: A Study in Comparative Philosophy*. New Delhi: Indus, 1995.

Rama, Swami. 1978; rpt. *Living with Himalayan Masters*. Honesdale, Pennsylvania: The Himalayan Institute Press, 1999.

Ranchan, Som P. *An Anatomy of Indian Psyche*. Delhi: Ajanta, 1987.

——. *Durga Saptashati: A Transcreation*. Sahibabad: Holy Faith, 1986.

——. *Revisioning Gita*. Delhi: Konark, 1991.

Reid, Ian. *The Short Story*. London. Methuen, 1977.

Rizvi, Saiyid Athar Abbas. *A History of Sufism in India*, Vol. II. New Delhi: Munshiram Manoharlal, 1983.

Rolland, Romain. *The Life of Ramkrishna*. Trans. (from French) E.F. Malcolm-Smith, Calcutta: Advaita Ashrama, 1986.

Ryder, Arthur W., trans. *Panchtantra*. New Delhi: Jaico, n.d.

Sachdeva, I.P. *Yoga and Depth Psychology*. Delhi: MLBD, 1978.

Saletore, R.N., ed. *Encyclopaedia of Indian Culture*. New Delhi: Sterling, 1985.

Sankara. *Atmabodhah (Self-Knowledge)*. Swami Nikhilananda, trans. Madras: Sri Ramakrishna Math, 1967.

Santhanam, K. Ed. *An Anthology of Indian Literature*. Bombay: Bharatiya Vidya Bhawan, 1969.

Saraswati, Bidyanath. *Myth and Reality of a Classical Cultural Tradition*. Shimla: IIAS, 1975.

Sayings of Sri Ramakrishna: An Exhaustive Collection. Madras: Sri Ramakrishna Math, n.d.

Segal, Robert A. *Joseph Campbell: An Introduction*. New York: Penguin, 1990.

Shah, Idries. *Thinkers of the East*. London: Penguin, 1971.

Sharma, Deba Brat Sen. *The Philosophy of Sadhana*. Karnal: Natraj, 1983.

Sharma, Roshan Lal. *Walt Whitman: A Critical Evaluation*. Delhi: Vrinda Publications (P) Ltd., 2000.

Sharma, Ved, ed. *A Profile in Creativity: Poet, Professor, Person: A Festschrift on Som P. Ranchan*. Delhi: Konark, 1992.

Shastri, Ramnarayandutt. *Shreedurgasaptashati*. Gorakhpur: Gita Press, n.d.

Shaw, Valerie. *The Short Story: A Critical Introduction*. London: Longman, 1983.

Shirwadkar, Meena. *Image of Woman in Indo-Anglian Novel*. New Delhi: Sterling, 1979.

Siddhantashastri, Rabindra Kumar. *Saivism through Ages*. New Delhi: Munshiram Manoharlal, 1975.

Singh, Karan. *Hinduism*. New Delhi: Criterion, 1987.

Singh, R.S. *Indian Novel in English: A Critical Study*. New Delhi: Arnold-Heinemann, 1977.

Sinha, B.R. *Hinduism and Symbol Worship*. Delhi: Agam Kala, 1983.

Sinha, K.N. Ed. *Indian Writing in English*. New Delhi: Heritage, 1979.

Sister Nivedita and Coomaraswamy, Anand K. *Hindus and Buddhists*. London: The Mystic Press, 1987.

Sitaramiah, V. *Valmiki Ramayan*. New Delhi: Sahitya Akademi, 1982.

Sivaramkrishna, M. *Radiant Eternity*. New Delhi: Sterling, 1996.

Speeches and Writings of Swami Vivekananda, Vol. I. Jaipur: Printwell, 1988.

Srinath, C.N. *The Literary Landscape: Essays on Indian Fiction and Poetry in English*. Delhi: Mittal, 1986.

Stevens, A. *Archetype: A Natural History of the Self*. London: Routledge, 1982.

Stevens, A. *On Jung*. London: Routledge, 1990.

Stoddart, William. *Sufism: The Mystical Doctrines and Methods of Islam*. Wellingborough, Northamptonshire: Thorsons Publishers Ltd., 1976.

Storr, Anthony. *Jung*. London: Fontana/Collins, 1973.

Tacey, David J. *Remaking Men: Jung, Spirituality and Social Change*. London and New York: Routledge, 1977.

Tagore, Rabindranath. *Gitanjali*. London: Macmillan, 1913.

——. *Hungry Stones and Other Stories*. Calcutta: Macmillan, 1916.

Taimni, I.K. 1965; rpt. *An Introduction to Hindu Symbolism*. Chennai: The Theosophical Publishing House, 1997.

Tandon, P.N. *Consciousness: Clinical and Beyond*. Shimla: IIAS, 2001.

Tattwananda, Swami. 1956; rpt. *Upnishadic Stories and Their Significance*. Ed. V.A. Thyagarajan. Calcutta: The Author, 1973.

The Complete Works of Swami Vivekananda. Vol. I-VIII. 1951; rpt. Calcutta: Advaita Ashrama, 1992.

The Holy Bible. Authorised (King James) Version. The Gideons International, 1978.

Trasi, Nitin. *The Science of Enlightenment: Enlightenment, Liberation and God: A Scientific Explanation*. New Delhi: D.K. Printworld (P) Ltd., 1999.

Trimingham, J. Spencer. *The Sufi Orders in Islam*. London: Oxford UP, 1971.

Underhill, Evelyn. *The Essentials of Mysticism and Other Essays*. Oxford: Oneworld, 1995.

Upadhyaya, Baldeva. *Bhartiya Darsana*. Varanasi: Ghaukhambha Orientalia, 1984.

——. *Sanskrit Sahitya ka Itihaas*. Varanasi: Sharada Niketan, 1990.

Venkateshwaran, Shyamla. *Indian Fiction in English: A Bibliography*. Mysore: Mysore University, 1970.

Venugopal, C.V. *The Indian Short Story in English: A Survey*. Bareilly: Prakash Book Depot, 1975.

Vijayan, O.V. *The Infinity of Grace*. New Delhi: Penguin, 1996.

Vivekananda, Swami. *Vedanta: Voice of Freedom*. Kolkata: Advaita Ashrama, 1987; rpt. 2002.

Vogel, J. PH. *Indian Serpent Lore*. Varanasi: Indological, 1972.

Voriskova, M. *Gypsy Folk Lore*. London: Paul Hamlyn, 1967.

Walsh, William. *Indian Literature in English*. London: Longman Group, 1990.

Warrier, A.G. Krishna. *The Concept of Mukti in Advaita Vedanta*. Madras: University of Madras, 1961.

——. *God in Advaita*. Shimla: IIAS, 1977.

Watt, William Montgomery. 1967; rpt. *Companion to the Quran*. Oxford: Oneworld, 1994.

Welbon, G. *The Buddhist Nirvana and Its Western Interpreters*. Chicago: University of Chicago Press, 1968.

Whitman, Walt. *Leaves of Grass*. New Delhi: Prentice Hall of India, 1986.

Whitmont, Edward C. 1969; rpt. *The Symbolic Quest*. Princeton, N.J.: Princeton UP, 1978.

Wilkins, W.J. *Hindu Mythology, Vedic and Puranic*. Varanasi: Indological, 1972.

Williams, John Alden, ed. *Islam*. New York: Washington Square, 1963.

Williams, Monier. *Indian Wisdom or Examples of the Religions, Philosophical and Ethical Doctrines of the Hindus*. New Delhi: Rupa, 2001.

Wood, Clement. *Dreams: Their Meaning and Practical Application*. New York: Greenberg, 1931.

Woodroffe, John. *The Word as Power*. Madras: Ganesh, 1957.

——. *The Serpent Power*. New York: Dover, 1974.

——. *Sakti and Sakta*. Madras: Ganesh, 1969.

Wordsworth, William. *The Prelude: A Parallel Text*. Ed. J.C. Maxwell. Harmondsworth: Penguin, 1971.

Yadugiri, M.A. "Content Structure in Three Indian Short Stories." *Explorations in Modern Indo-English Fiction*. Ed. R.K. Dhawan. New Delhi: Bahri Publications, 1982. pp. 71–79.

Yatiswarananda, Swami. 1959; rpt. *Adventures in Religious Life*. Madras: Sri Ramkrishna Math, n.d.

Yeats, W.B. *Autobiographies*. London: Macmillan 1961.

Yogananda, Paramhansa. *Autobiography of Yogi*. New York: The Philosophical Library, 1946.

Yogi, Raushan Nath. *Hinduism and Its Dynamism*. New Delhi: Rakesh, 1987.

Young-Eisendrath, Polly and Terence Dawson, Eds. *The Cambridge Companion to Jung*. Cambridge: Cambridge UP, 1997.

Zakaria, Rafiq. *Muhammad and the Quran*. New Delhi: Penguin, 1991.

Zimmer, Heinrich. *Myths and Symbols in Indian Art and Civilization*. Ed. Joseph Campbell. Princeton, New Jersey: Princeton UP, 1946; rpt. 1972.

——. *Philosophies of India*. Ed. Joseph Campbell. New York: Pantheon Books, 1951.

Articles, Reviews and Interviews Journals

Ali Ahmed. "Illusion and Reality: The Art and Philosophy of Raja Rao." *The Journal of Commonwealth Literature*. 1968, No. 5, pp. 16–28.

Alterno, Letizia. "The Mystic Cat: Reality and Maya in The Cat and Shakespeare." *Kakatia Journal of English Studies* (KJES).Vol. 22, December 2002.

Anjaneyulu, D. "The Art of Raja Rao." *Thought* (9 May 1964), pp. 12–14. Rpt. in *Triveni* 66.3. (1997), pp. 58–62.

Anon. "India's Search for Self-Expression." *Times Literary Supplement*, August 10, 1962.

Arora, V.K. "The Use of Myths in Raja Rao's Kanthapura." *Glimpses of Indo-English Fiction*. Vol. 3. Ed. O.P. Saxena New Delhi: Jainons Publications, 1985, pp. 80–94.

Chaddah, R.P. "The Mahatma in Modern Indo-English Fiction." *The Indian P.E.N.*, XLII, Vol. 11–12.

Chari, V.K. "Rama's Tragic Quest: A Reading of The Serpent and the Rope in the Light of Rasa Theory." *Littcrit* 36–37, 19. 1–2 (June, December 1993), pp. 5–20.

Chaturvedi, S.P. "Raja Rao as a Short-Story Writer." *Perspectives on Raja Rao*. Ed. K.K. Sharma. Ghaziabad: Vimal Prakashan, 1980, pp. 109–119.

Das, Gopal. "Souls in Search of Salvation." Rev. of *On the Ganga Ghat*, by Raja Rao. *Indian Book Chronicle* 15.10. (October 1990), pp. 4–5.

Dey, Esha. "On the Ganga Ghat and Other Stories." *The Novels of Raja Rao: The Theme of Quest*. New Delhi: Prestige, 1992, Postscript II, pp. 246–55.

Dhalla, Kamal H. "The Indo-English Short Story: Background and Beginnings." *Indian Scholar*. 1 and 2, July 1979.

Duggal, K.S. "Vignettes of Varanasi," A Review of *On the Ganga Ghat* by Raja Rao. *Indian Express*. December 17, 1989, p. 4.

Gemill, Janet Powers. "Raja Rao: Three Tales of Independence." ["Narsiga," "In Khandesh," and "The Cow of the Barricades"]. *World Literature Written in English* 15.1 (1976), pp. 135–41.

——. "Raja Rao's *The Cow of the Barricades*: *Two Stories*." ["Javni," and "A Client"]. *Journal of South Asian Literature* 13.1–4 (1977–78), pp. 23–30.

——. "Elements of the Folktale in Raja Rao's *The Cow of the Barricades*." *World Literature Written in English* 20.1. (Spring, 1981), pp. 149–61.

Gorlier, Claudio. "Magic and Reality in R.K. Narayan's Man's Eater of Malgudi and Raja Rao's *On the Ganga Ghat*: A Skeleton Key to a Parallel Reading." *Quest* 13.2. (December 1999) pp. 17–23.

Harrex, S.C. "Raja Rao: Companion of Pilgrimage." *Studies in Australian and Indian Literature*. Ed. C.D. Narasimhaiah. New Delhi: Indian Council for Cultural Relations, 1971, pp. 257–73.

Harrex, S.C. "Typology and Modes: Raja Rao's Experiments in Short Story." *World Literature Today* 62.4. (Autumn 1988) pp. 591–95.

Hema, M.S. "Care of the Self: Raja Rao's *The Chessmaster and His Moves* and *On the Ganga Ghat*." Ed. Viney Kirpal. *The Postmodern Indian English Novel: Interrogating the 1980s and 1990s*. Bombay: Allied Publishers, 1996.

Iyenger, K.R. "Literature as Sadhana." *Aryan Path,* Vol. 40, No. 6–7, June–July 1969.

——. "Contemporary Indian Short Story." *Indian Literature*. New Delhi: Sahitya Akademy, September, 1970.

Kalinnikova, Elena J. "Ancient Indian Philosophy and Raja Rao's Works." *Perspectives on Raja Rao*. Ed. K.K. Sharma, Ghaziabad: Vimal Prakashan, 1980, pp. 23–31.

Kaushik, Asha. "Meet Raja Rao." *The Hindu*. April 18, 1978, p. 8.

——. "Meeting Raja Rao." *The Literary Criterion*. 18, No. 3 (July–September 1983), pp. 33–38.

Kisly, Lorraine. "Living Myths: A Conversation with Joseph Campbell." *Parabola,* 1 (Spring 1976), pp. 70–81.

Krishnama, B.G.R. A Review of *The Policeman and the Rose* by Raja Rao. *The Hindu*. 8 August 1978, p. 5.

Kumar, Shiv K. "In Search of Excellence: A Tribute to Raja Rao on Receiving Neustadt International Prize." *Hindustan Times* (4 December 1988), p. 13.

Kumar, Sudhir. "India is Not a 'Desh': It is a 'Darshan." A Review of the *Meaning of India* by Raja Rao. *Indian Book Chronicle 22.11*. (November 1997), pp. 8–10.

McCutchion, David. "The Novel as Sastra." (1961) in Meenakshi Mukherjee, Ed., *Considerations*. New Delhi: Allied, 1977.

Mehta, Rajesh. "Raja Rao's *On the Ganga Ghat:* Benares Redefined" in Kamal Mehta, Ed., *The Twentieth Century Indian Short Story in English*. New Delhi: Creative Books, 2004. pp. 97–104.

Moyers, Bill. "The Power of Myth: An Interview with Joseph Campbell." *New Age Journal*, 5 (July/August 1988), pp. 56–60, 80–83.

Mukherjee, Meenakshi. "Raja Rao's Shorter Fiction." *Indian Literature*. Vol. X, No. 366–76.

Naik, M.K. "The Achievement of Raja Rao." *The Banasthali Patrika*, Rajasthan, No. 12, January 1969.

——. "The Chessmaster and His Moves." A Review of *The Chessmaster and His Moves* by Raja Rao. *Indian Literature* 32.2. (1989), pp. 173–78.

——. "Not Quite Pandit Jagannath." A Review of *On the Ganga Ghat* by Raja Rao. *Indian Literature* 33.2. (March–April 1990), pp. 151–55.

Narasimhaiah, C.D. "Indian Writing in English: An Introduction." *The Journal of Commonwealth Literature*. 5, No. 1 (July 1968), pp. 42–48.

——. "Raja Rao's *The Serpent and the Rope*." *The Illustrate Weekly of India*. September 1, 1963.

Narasimhan, Raji. A Review of *The Policeman and the Rose* by Raja Rao. *Hindustan Times*. 11 June 1978.

Niranjan, Shiva. "An Interview with Raja Rao." *Indian Writings in English*. K. N. Sinha, Ed., New Delhi: Heritage, 1979, pp. 19–28.

——. "Myth as a Creative Mode: A Study of Mythical Parallels in Raja Rao's Novels." *Commonwealth Quarterly* 4(14, 1980).

——. "*On the Ganga Ghat*." A Review of *On the Ganga Ghat* by Raja Rao. *Indian Literature* 33.2. (1990), pp. 151–55.

Parameswaran, Uma. "Shakti in Raja Rao's Novels." *ACLALA Bulletin*. 1972, No. 9, pp. 4–27.

——. "Siva and Shakti in Raja Rao's Novels." *World Literature Today* 62.4. (Autumn 1988), pp. 574–77.

Paranjape, Makarand. "In Search of Truth." Rev. of *The Meaning of India*, by Raja Rao. *Indian Reviews of Books* 6.2. 16 November–15 December 1996, pp. 8–10.

Parthasarathy, R. "An Interview with Raja Rao." *Span*. September 1977, pp. 29–30.

Raizada, Harish C. "Literature as Sadhana: The Progress of Raja Rao from *Kanthapura* to *The Serpent and the Rope*." *Indo–English Literature:*

A Collection of Critical Essays. Ed. K.K. Sharma. Ghaziabad: Vimal Prakashan, 1977, pp. 157–75.

Ramachandra, Ragini. "On the Ganga Ghat: An Assessment." Ed. *Raja Rao: An Anthology of Recent Criticism*. Delhi: Pencraft International, 2000, pp. 186–90.

Ramaswamy, S. "The Sanskrit Charge in Raja Rao: The Word and the Sabda Tattva." *Comparative Perspectives on Indian Literature*. Ed. A. Ramakrishna Rao. New Delhi: Prestige Books, 1992, pp. 103–12.

Ranchan, Som P. "A Meeting with Raja Rao." *Thought*. 1968, 20, No. 28, 14–16; No. 29, 14–16; No. 30, 14–16; No. 31, 14–16.

——. "Ramaswamy's Dilemma: An Analytical Interpretation of *The Serpent and the Rope*." *Language Forum* 7–14 (1981–82): 101–09. Rpt. in *Explorations in Modern Indo-English Fiction*. Ed. R.K. Dhawan. New Delhi: Bahri Publications, 1982, pp. 101–09.

——. "The Serpent and the Rope: India Made Real." *Illustrated Weekly of India*. 13 March 1966. pp. 45–47. 3 April 1966. pp. 33–35. 10 April 1966. pp. 33–35.

Rao, Raja. "Books which have Influenced Me." *The Illustrated Weekly of India*. February 10, 1963, p. 45.

——. "Entering the Literary Worlds." *The Journal of Commonwealth Literature*. 3, No. 3 April 1979, pp. 28–34.

——. "The Writer and the Word." *The Literary Criterion*. 7, No. 1, 1965.

——. "Varanasi: Cities of India." *The Illustrated Weekly of India*. September 3, 1961, pp. 12–15.

——. "Why I Chose English." *The Indian Express*. August 8, 1977, p. 5.

Razdan, B.M. and Ranchan Som P. "The Serpent and the Rope: India Made Real." *The Illustrated Weekly of India*. March 13, 1966; April 3, 1966, and April 10, 1966.

Review of *On the Ganga Ghat* by Raja Rao. *Times of India*. 10 Dec. 1989, p. 3.

Shahane, V.A. "Some Aspects of the Indian Writer's Creative Use of English." *The Literary Criterion*. 17, No. 1 (January-March 1982), pp. 75–78.

Shankar, Vijay. "On the Ganga Ghat." *Sunday Herald*. October 1989, p. 5.

Shaphered, R. "Symbolism in *The Cat and Shakespeare*." *World Literature Written in English, Commonwealth General Journal*, xiv, 1975.

Sharma, P.P. "Quest for Wholeness: A Central Preoccupation of Raja Rao's Fiction." *Perspectives on Raja Rao*. Ed. K.K. Sharma. Ghaziabad: Vimal Prakashan, 1980, pp. 32–43.

Sharma, Roshan Lal. "The Enlightenment Theme: A Study of the Motifs in Raja Rao's *On the Ganga Ghat*." *Revaluations*. Vol. 1, No. 1, Winter 1995, pp. 43–54.

——."Raja Rao's Portrayal of the Ganga in *On the Ganga Ghat." New Horizons: A Research Journal.* Vol. III, January 2006, pp. 1–10.

——."A Note on the Quest Motif in Raja Rao's Story 'Narsiga.'" *Research Digest: A Quarterly Research Journal of Higher Education.* Vol. 1, No. 1, July–September 2006, pp. 16–18.

——."Sufic Interpretations of Walt Whitman's 'Song of Myself.'" *Studies in Humanities and Social Sciences (SHSS), Journal of Inter-University Centre,* Indian Institute of Advanced Study, Shimla, Vol. XII, No. 2, Winter 2005, pp. 61–74.

Soni, N.C. Review of *The Policeman and the Rose,* by Raja Rao. *Journal of Indian Writing in English* 7.2. (July 1979) pp. 110–11.

Thorpe, Michael. "Indian Novel and Story in English." Review of *The Policeman and the Rose,* by Rao. *Literary Half-Yearly* 19.2 (July, 1978) pp. 161–62.

Unnikrishnan, K., "Guru - Disciple: A Paradigm for Indianness in Raja Rao's Fiction." *Makers of Indian English Literature.* Ed. C.D. Narasimhaiah. New Delhi: Pencraft International, 2000, pp. 141–48.

Venugopal Rao, C.V. "Raja Rao.". *The Indian Short Story in English: A Survey."* Ed. C.V. Venugopal. Bareilly: Prakash Book Depot, n.d., pp. 60–74.

——. "Raja Rao: A Short Story Writer – A Study." *Journal of the Karnatak University (Humanities).* 14 (1970), pp. 159–70.

Vyaghreswarudu, B. "The Growth of Mind and Art of Raja Rao: His Short Stories." Eds. Rajeshwar, Mittapali and Pier Paolo. *The Fiction of Raja Rao: Critical Studies.* New Delhi: Atlantic, 2001.

Wasi, Jehanara. "Metaphysical Quest." *Economic Times.* 16 November 1986, p. 41.

Websites

Aikant, Satish. "Raja Rao." *The Literary Encyclopedia.* 23 January 2004. <http:www.litencyc.com/php/speople.php?rec=tru&UID=5032>

Alterno, Letizia. "Tribute to Raja Rao." A Raja Rao Site. <rajarao.free.fr>

——. Official website on Raja Rao. <www.rajarao.com>

——. "Raja Rao." *The Guardian.* 17 July 2006. <books.guardian.co.uk/obituaries/story/0,,1822076,00.html>

Center for Asian Studies, University of Texas. <http://inic.utexas.edu/asnic/cas/>

Chaddha, R.P. "About Chessmaster's Moves." *The Tribune.* 14 April 2002. <www.tribuneindia.com/2002/20020414/spectrum/book6.htm>

Neustadt International Prize for Literature to Rao. <www.ou.edu/worldlit/neustadt/>

Parthasarathi, R. "Editing Raja Rao." *The Hindu*. 30 July 2006. <www.hindu.com/mag/2006/07/30/stories/2006073000170400.htm>

Raine, Kathleen. "India Beyond Sorrow." Review of *The Meaning of India*. <http://resurgence.gn.apc.org/articles/raine.htm>

"Raja Rao: Sacred Wordsmith." *Life Positive*. July 1999. <www.lifepositive.com/mind/arts/poetry-fiction/rajarao.asp>

"Raja Rao." Biographical Sketch. <www.kirjasto.sci.fi/rao.htm>

"Raja Rao." Wikipedia. <en.wikipedia.org/wiki/Raja_Rao>

Rangel-Ribeiro, Victor. "Raja Rao (1908–2006)." 12 July 2006. <kitabkhana.blogspot.com/2006/07/raja-rao-1908-2006.html>

Rao, Raja. Bibliographical Information. <www.rajarao. com/project.html>

——. "Scholar, Philosopher, Literary Artist." 8 July 2006. <www.rajarao.com/home.html>

Singh, Amardeep Singh. "Raja Rao (RIP) and Czeslaw Milosz." 10 July 2006. <www.lehigh.edu/~amsp/2006/07/raja-rao-rip-and-czeslaw-milosz.html>

"The Raja Rao Publication Project." Sponsored by Linguistics Research Center, University of Texas. <www.utexas.edu/cola/depts/lrc/>

Index